MW01104846

IMMORTAL

DAVID A KERSTEN

To my good friend Terry

Copyright©2015 David A. Kersten

All rights reserved. No part of this publication may be reproduced, distributed, or transmitted in any form or by any means, including photocopying, recording, or other electronic or mechanical methods, without the prior written permission of the publisher, except in the case of brief quotations embodied in critical reviews and certain other noncommercial uses permitted by copyright law.

This is a work of fiction. Names, characters, businesses, places, events and incidents are either the products of the author's imagination or used in a fictitious manner. Any resemblance to actual persons, living or dead, or actual events is purely coincidental.

ISBN 1519545371
ISBN-13 978-1519545374

Dedicated to my biggest fans, David Jr., Angela, and Shayna. Love you guys.

CONTENTS

Prologue

Nobody should have to bury their own child. It was all Phil could think about as he looked across the two caskets toward his longtime friend.

A snowflake settled on the shiny lacquered surface of the smaller casket. Black umbrellas quietly opened without disturbing the eulogy being delivered. He didn't bother to bring an umbrella. It wasn't that he hadn't expected snow, quite the contrary. Rain or snow seemed normal at a funeral, almost a requirement for the ritual of mourning to be complete. Weddings should be sunny and warm; funerals should be overcast and cold. When it was the other way around, things didn't seem right.

A stray snowflake landed on his cheek, adding to the moisture already there. He was the only man here not swallowing his tears. Even Jack, a man burying both his wife and his child, seemed to be holding back. *Maybe he doesn't have any left to give*, he thought, feeling a fresh wave of sorrow through his heart.

The turnout was larger than Phil expected. Jack Taggart lived for two things: his family and his job. If he wasn't hard at work he was usually at home with Jenny and their daughter. It didn't leave much room for friends. As far as Phil knew, aside from showing up once in a while for his weekly poker game, Jack's only other socializing involved dinners with him and Barb. He hadn't expected to see more than Jenn's mother, Mabel, her farmhands, and perhaps a few neighborhood women Jenn socialized with during the day. Yet the graveside ceremony was crowded. Jack had that effect on people. Every person he interacted with in his life seemed to gain some sense of loyalty to the man. Phil was no different. He would follow Jack to the ends of the earth if he was asked.

He looked out across the sea of black dressed mourners. One face stood out. General Romeijn's full military dress and large array of shiny adornments weren't what caught Phil's eye. His very presence here felt disrespectful. Surely the man wasn't using such a solemn occasion to meet for business. He resolved to avoid the man today; whatever he was here to talk about could wait until tomorrow.

When the second casket finished its final descent the crowd slowly dispersed. Phil stuck around, quietly waiting for the funeral attendees to leave. He knew most of them, but there would be time to mingle at the reception. He purposefully didn't make eye contact with the General as the man left. Jack stood at the smaller grave, staring at the casket down in the hole. Not wanting to rush him, Phil walked over and put a hand on his friend's shoulder. "Jack, take all the time you need, I'll be in the car with Barb." Jack nodded but never looked up.

~~~~

There wasn't enough room for all the food, let alone the guests who occupied nearly every inch of the living room and kitchen. Unaffected by the pallor of grief in the house, a few children weaved their way through the adults, bored and looking for something to keep them occupied.

The condensed moisture on the windows sparkled with sunlight, spraying golden rays through the haze of tobacco smoke. Making its first appearance of the day, the sun managed to draw some of the guests out into the yard, relieving the congestion in the house. Phil made his way through the rooms, making small talk with each group of people, even shaking a few hands and thanking them for coming. He spotted Mabel, sitting alone in the living room, an empty folding chair nearby. He grabbed it, pulling it over next to her so he could sit. "Mabel, can I get you anything?"

She looked up at him, a fake smile on her heavily lined. She wasn't very old, he recalled, barely in her fifties. After burying her daughter and grand-daughter, however, she could have passed for eighty. "No thank you, Phil. This is a wonderful reception. I can't thank you and your wife enough for the help. It's been a difficult week."

"Come on, Mabel, you did most of the work, we barely got the opportunity to help." The compliment brought another fake smile. "If there's anything I can do for you, please, don't hesitate to ask." He started to rise, not expecting a response.

"Actually, Phil, there's one thing." He sat back down, giving her his full attention. "Take care of Jack. He's really hurting and doesn't want me around to remind him of Jenn and Ally. He may try to act strong, but this could destroy him, and it wouldn't be fair if that happened. He's a good man."

Phil swallowed a few times, holding back the tears that welled to the surface. Clearing his throat, he said, "I promise you, Mabel, I'll be there for him. Don't you worry, though; he'll come around and realize he needs people like you in his life." This time the smile reached her eyes.

When they'd arrived at the house, Jack went straight upstairs to his room without a word, ignoring his guests. He had yet to make an appearance. Phil noticed a couple heading for the door and decided it was time to get Jack down here to at least acknowledge some of the fine people who had come to pay their respects.

Heading toward the stairs, he saw the General and his entourage and tried to pass unnoticed. Despite his efforts, the General spotted him and called out, "Phil, can I have a word with you?"

He let out a sigh. "Can it wait until Monday? I was just heading up to convince Jack to come down here before all his guests left."

The General put his arm around Phil's shoulders, guiding him toward the front door. "This will just take a moment."

The air was brisk but not too bad for early January. He pulled his wool jacket close and watched his breath turn to fog as he said, "What can I do for you, Ed?" Although Phil wasn't military, he also wasn't a close enough friend to call the General by his first name.

Narrowing his eyes at the slight, the General said, "Before you jump to any conclusions, let me say I did show up here out of respect for Jack, not to do business. I still need a quick word." Looking across the street to an empty park, he said, "Walk with me." It wasn't a request, and he didn't wait to see if Phil would follow.

As the sole owner of his contracting firm, Phil was his own boss. Unfortunately, most of his business came from the military, and that meant he couldn't just blow off the General. Even so, he nearly turned back to the reception, regardless of the consequences.

"How do you think Jack's holding up?"

Rolling his eyes and following, he responded, "Well, his wife and child died less than a week ago, how do you think he is?"

Unfazed by the sarcasm, the General said, "I can't imagine how difficult that would be to go through. I have three children of my own, and even now that they're grown up, I can't imagine losing one of them."

"Jack's a strong person, he'll get through it. If you're worried about how this will affect the job, don't be. He already offered to be at work tomorrow, but even with him taking a few weeks off to grieve we'll meet our timeline."

Finally the General stopped, the look of irritation on his face suggested he was no longer going to ignore Phil's insolent tone. "Do you know why I told you to hire Jack when he retired?"

Phil shrugged, "He had a lot of experience cutting through the red tape while in the Army. I figured you saw this and knew he would be a good fit as my main foreman."

"His experience was a good fit, but that wasn't why I pushed him on you. Did he ever tell you about how he became an officer?"

"Yeah, something about covering up for an idiot colonel who eventually returned the favor by nominating him for OCS. Why?"

"That idiot colonel is my son." *Whoops.* Phil looked off in the distance, not wanting to make eye contact at the moment. "Don't worry, I know he isn't the brightest boy, but every father wants to see his children succeed. When Jack covered for my son and kept a potentially career ending mistake off the records, I was the one who pulled the strings to get him into Officer Candidate School. See, that was my way of thanking him for his discretion. However, I never got the opportunity to thank him for saving my son's life that day. For that I'm eternally grateful and have the utmost respect for the man." He paused, allowing his words to sink in. "Despite your dislike for me Phil, at least give me the benefit of the doubt for why I'm here."

Phil felt a pang of guilt. "My apologies, General." However, he wasn't about to let the man off the hook that easily. "So why am I standing in the middle of a park and not tending to my grieving friend?"

"I needed to have a discrete word with you, away from certain ears. When I spotted you inside it dawned on me that we wouldn't have a better opportunity."

Despite his annoyance, this piqued Phil's interest. "Go on."

"There's another project, and I want your crew on it. In fact, I want you to head up the whole project."

"We just started the one here."

"I understand, this will take some time to plan and the sooner we start planning the better."

"And what makes this different from any other job?"

"Well, aside from me and a couple other Generals, the military won't be aware of this one. We need to keep it that way."

This came as a surprise. *What other interests could the General serve?* "Who's funding it then?"

The General laughed. "The military."

"I'm confused, Ed. What are you saying?"

"I'm saying we're putting together a very large project, funded with money Congress earmarked for defense, but without anyone's knowledge."

Several alarms went off in his head. The last thing he wanted was to get involved with anything illegal. "You're going to need to be a little less cryptic here, General."

"I can't offer a whole lot at this time, but I can tell you this much: the project is coming from the NSA, and despite not even the President knowing of its existence, it's perfectly legal."

The wind picked up, cutting through the heavy wool jacket. He shivered and said, "Before we start talking specifics, I'll need a little more reassurance before we get started."

"I understand, don't worry about that part now. We need to establish a way to discuss this outside regular channels. I'm pretty sure my office isn't being watched, but I don't want to take any chances. I can almost guarantee Army Intelligence watches you closely, and I wouldn't be at all surprised to find that other agencies were keeping an eye on you and maybe even tapping your phones."

None of this surprised Phil. When a civilian is privy to as many secrets as he is, someone is going to be making sure he isn't talking to the Russians. It didn't bother him all that much, they paid him very well and he didn't have anything to hide from his government. "What do you suggest?"

The General smiled. "I hear you like a good card game. How about Las Vegas?"

Phil chuckled. "I can make that work. Barb loves playing the slots. When do we go?"

"I think next month would be good. I'll have all the initial information ready to go. This is going to be huge, Phil. It'll make the project here look like you're playing in the sand at the beach. The money will be good too, the kind of money you can pass on to your grandkids."

Part 1

Chapter 1

It looked like an old military aircraft hangar; something built in the 60's. A large concrete quonset hut spanning at least two hundred feet in width and several hundred feet in depth, it stood hidden in the forest, high in the mountains and isolated from civilizations both old and new. With a roof blanketed in grass and brush, it was just another part of the landscape when seen from above, a small clearing in the forest surrounded by tall pine and cedar guardians. In fact, the only hint of the presence of a man made structure at all was the barely noticeable symmetricity when flying directly above it. If Wendy hadn't had Bartholomew to point it out, she would have easily missed it.

Being in the middle of nowhere had ensured its escape from the looting and plundering just about every other standing building had endured over the centuries. None of the old maps showed even the smallest of towns in the area for at least a dozen miles. "Bart, how did you find this?" she asked.

"My clan passed through this area when I was young," the giant man rumbled. "For a couple months we made camp just a few miles from here. I came across it while exploring, but it held little interest to me back then. I never even told my clanmates about it. In fact, until you started asking about pre-war buildings that were still standing, I didn't even remember it. Now that I see it again, it brings back a lot of childhood memories."

Wendy looked up at the giant man and smiled. "I hope they're good ones." Bartholomew just smiled back; a look that might have terrified her if she didn't know the man so well. His leathery hairless skin and sheer size certainly gave him the appearance of a hideous monster, but she preferred to think of him simply as a man.

Technically he was still human, albeit a genetically engineered sub-species that most people referred to as 'Mutes.' A giant, even by the standards of his own race, he was truly an anomaly. By nature, Mutes had a far lower intelligence than the average human, but even by human standards Bart would be considered a genius. It wasn't his size or his intellect that set him apart from others of his kind however, it was his compassion. The giant man was one of the kindest people she knew, and there was no doubt he would do anything for her, even though they had only known each other for barely two months.

They located the door after careful examination of the area. Bart told her to step back and then effortlessly tore out roots and brush thicker than Wendy's arms. In moments the area was clear and a heavy rusted door sat before them, practically begging to be opened. Bart reared back a fist the size of a bowling ball and smashed it into the middle of the door knocking huge chunks of rust and dirt from around the doorframe. The sound of his blow echoed outward in the forest startling a flock of birds several hundred yards away.

She winced at the noise. Between the nuclear fallout and the unnatural biological weapons released on the world centuries ago, many horrifying creatures had mutated and evolved on this planet. Some were quite dangerous and it was always best to keep a low profile. Bart seemed unconcerned, which added a small measure of comfort.

He pulled a pry bar from his pack. The six foot long bar weighed close to sixty pounds and was nearly two inches thick. Usually it took two men to pry open a door of this nature but Bart took the bar in one hand and jammed it in the gap near where the doorknob used to be. Again with a seemingly effortless maneuver, he popped the door open. The sound the door made when the heavy steel bolt snapped free of the jamb was loud enough to reverberate through the woods, once more causing her to wince. Tossing the bar aside, he gripped the edge of the door and wrenched it open, hinges squealing and moaning in protest. As fine dust settled around the opening, Bart stepped back and acted as if he had done nothing special.

The opening was dark, a void that made Wendy both anxious and nervous. This was the part she loved the most: the unknown of an unexplored building. The void beckoned her to enter. Unslinging her rifle, she flicked on the powerful flashlight. Bart waited for her to make the next move. She suppressed a smile. The doorway was normal sized, meaning it was a tight fit for a man of his size. It was ironic: one of the largest and most fierce predators on the planet was terribly afraid of small, dark, tight places. "Inside it should be big and open, I'll go first," she said reassuringly.

"Please be careful, Little Red." She patted him on the arm and then steadied her nerves. As excited as she was to explore, the building could be the home to any number of critters, and even the most harmless were fiercely protective of their home. Most were far from harmless.

The flash on the end of her rifle illuminated the dust hanging in the air around the entry. There wasn't much to see just past the door. The floor had a layer of dust and fine dirt at least a few inches thick. For several years the thin gap in the door would allow dust to enter, at least until the rust sealed it up. As she moved into the building she noticed the temperature drop about ten degrees. The air was stale and unmoving with just a hint of old iron, motor oil, and a familiar scent – Cosmoline. This was a good sign.

The door behind her slammed shut with the brief scream of rusty hinges. Startled, Wendy spun around. A muffled roar barely penetrated the thick concrete walls. Adrenaline shot through her system and she threw herself against the door with reckless abandon. It barely moved. Another roar and the howl of something feral could be heard, louder this time. Stepping back, she slammed her meager weight against the door again, this time pushing it open several inches.

Through the gap she saw movement; something large crossed her limited field of vision and it wasn't Bart. Wedging the rifle through the gap, she pushed with all her strength, trying to force the door open. Briefly the idea that her guardian had shut the door for her protection flicked in her mind but she quickly dismissed it. Her only thought was to get out there and help her friend.

The door finally opened with another wrenching scream. She squeezed through the opening and nearly tripped on a carcass, large and bloodied and laying squarely in her path. Vaulting the carcass, she quickly assessed the scene. To her left, Bart was squared off with three more large creatures. They looked like wolves, only twice the size. Next to the giant man they still looked big. Bart spotted her and shouted, "Red! No!"

He didn't look at her, but rather above her. Instinct took over and she dropped to the ground, rolling over just in time to see another beast pounce from above. She rolled two more times to avoid becoming a soft landing and then somersaulted into a crouch, all maneuvers she had learned so many years ago in the gym. Of course, that training was to protect her from a man with sexual intentions, not a three hundred pound predator. The beast landed harder than it probably expected, took a tumble, and quickly recovered.

It wasn't quick enough. Wendy brought the assault rifle to bear and squeezed the trigger. It burped loudly, throwing out a dozen lethal rounds. The animal spun around with the impact and thrashed as it died. She didn't move the gun away from the target until it came to rest, one leg still twitching but otherwise clearly dead.

Bart's battle roar diverted her attention back to his fight. His arms spread out as he charged the three beasts in front of him. A chill went down her back at the sight of her gentle giant charging into these menacing beasts. She raised the rifle, prepared to help however she could. The giant dove for the middle beast, but caught the two on either side in his grip as he crashed into the third. Wendy heard a faint yelp along with a sickening crackle of multiple bones. With an agility that should not have been possible for a man this big, he rolled through the dive and slammed the two beasts in his grip together and then threw them to the ground as if they were merely pillows. With another wet crunch they lay still.

Jumping to his feet and roaring again, the big man looked for his next target. If the pack had more hunters, however, they'd already fled.

Running toward her, he said, "Little Red, are you okay?"

Still jacked up on adrenaline, she retorted, "I'm fine! Why the hell did you slam the door like that?"

This brought him up short, a look of confusion on his face. "Well, to protect you, of course. If one of those beasts had jumped through that door before I could kill it…"

"I could have handled it!" she interrupted. "You scared the crap out of me, all you had to do was warn me and I would have been out here to help."

Sheepishly he looked at the ground and kicked at an imaginary rock, obviously hurt by her sharp retort. The adrenaline left her body and with it her anger. Suddenly she felt really bad. He was just trying to protect her, and clearly he had the situation under control. She chastised herself for snapping at him then apologized out loud. "I'm sorry, Bart, I know you were just trying to protect me. I guess I'm just not used to that sort of thing. Thank You."

Bart looked up and smiled. "My pleasure, Little Red. Are you injured? I saw that tumble and your condition…"

"My what?" she interrupted again.

"You know, being with child and all. A tumble like that could be bad for a newly forming baby."

"How do you know I'm pregnant?"

Bart looked at her with confusion on his face. "This morning after breakfast you were throwing up. And you have a certain glow about you that you didn't have a few weeks ago. It doesn't take a doctor to spot a woman with child."

This shut her up. She wasn't quite ready to accept that she was going to have a baby. She was only a month along and so far all she noticed was the morning sickness. "I'm fine, Bart, my… condition… is still new. Thank you for asking though."

She turned back to the door. "Unless you think there are more of those beasts around, we need to get back to exploring. Can you open that door up a little more?"

He walked over and forced the rusty door the rest of the way open. "If it's okay with you I'm going to clean these carcasses up while you explore. Those furs will keep me nice and warm this next winter. Would you like me to make some stew for lunch?"

The thought of food, particularly from animals that moments ago were trying to kill them, made her nauseous. "Uh, no thanks, I'm not very hungry."

She turned to go back into the building. "If you see any sign of danger inside, just call out and I will be there," Bart said. After a moment, he added, "Not that you need my help defending yourself, of course."

~~~~

The building had a distinctly military feel. Thick reinforced concrete structures were abnormal outside the military, particularly in a place as isolated as this one. It would have made more sense to be a simple sheet metal building, something lightweight enough to haul in with 4x4 trucks or even helicopters. The building had no windows either, another sign it was not an ordinary warehouse or hangar. Given that the land around the building could easily be cleared and turned into a functional airstrip, Wendy had half expected to see some military aircraft in here.

It was disappointing to see simple excavation equipment. Backhoes, front loaders, and rock trucks, all well used and packed into the building in a manner that suggested they were being stored for the long term and not just put away for the weekend. The door she used to gain entrance had been in the rear of the building. Back here, the equipment was all pushed together, packed so tight you would practically have to climb over it to get toward the front of the building. Thankfully they had left a narrow corridor on the left side so the offices there could still be accessed.

She made her way toward the front of the building, skipping the offices for now. Rubbing her shoulder, she suddenly felt exactly how foolish it had been to throw her body against that door. Nothing felt broken but she wouldn't be sleeping on that side tonight.

As she walked, she took a mental inventory. Her mind churned, trying to put the pieces together. *Why so much excavation equipment up here in the mountains? Was this a mine of some kind? If so, why no major roads leading out?* Even after centuries, most major roads could still be spotted from the air. The way the ground had been packed, trees and plants grew slower in the soil and you could see the pattern from the air. It wasn't just the maps that showed no roads coming up here – there was no sign of anything from the air either. That doesn't mean there wasn't a road up here at one point, just that if there had been, it hadn't been used enough to leave a lasting scar.

From the standpoint of scrap, this was a lot of steel, and that was good. The smell of Cosmoline suggested some of the equipment might even be preserved well enough to get running. It certainly looked intact. Worst case scenario, a few men could be sent here to tear into this equipment and haul back tons of steel to be recast into building materials. This find was a major score even if nothing else came of the mysterious nature.

The closer she got to the front of the building, the more the equipment varied. Now she was seeing machines reminiscent of tunnel boring equipment. There were even several concrete trucks and what appeared to be concrete pumps. She had spent a few hours scouting the area from the air and never saw anything the even remotely resembled a structure. *What the hell were they building? And where the hell did it go?*

Finally she reached the end of the equipment. The area opened up for at least a hundred feet before the building stopped at what appeared to be a large hangar style door spanning well over fifty feet in width. Like the smaller door she entered through, dirt had piled up along the bottom where dust had been able to get past the seam between the door and the ground. Over time it had sealed itself up, much like the back door. The corners of the building held some old spider webs, but as tightly sealed as the building was, they hadn't lasted long without anything to feed on. There was no sign of moisture infiltration at all, which combined with the cool dry air up here in the mountains meant it was very possible some of these machines could be brought back to life.

Along the far wall were workbenches. Tools and parts hung on the walls, obviously all used for maintaining the vast array of heavy equipment. *Another treasure trove.* Already this was by far the most valuable discovery she'd ever made. Aside from the Freezer, it might be the most valuable New Hope has ever had.

Wendy scanned the shelves and workbench. She spotted tools she had used while in the military, stuff used to work on aircraft. Combined with the large door, it confirmed that at one time they had stored and worked on aircraft of some kind here. But it didn't answer any of the myriad of questions running through her head. Turning her attention to the offices, she hoped maybe she could solve the mystery.

Chapter 2

Wendy was digging through the drawers when Jack walked in. He looked around at the piles of clothes and blankets in disarray around the room and with a grin and a chuckle he asked, "What the heck are you doing?"

She didn't even pause, "I'm looking for your diary," as if that would explain it all.

He went to the nightstand and opened the drawer all the way. The old diary was there, in a sealed bag to prevent further decay. He carefully pulled it out and set it on the bed. "Now, can you tell me what this is all about?"

It took a moment for Wendy to climb to her feet, her slightly swollen belly preventing a graceful movement. "Wipe that grin off your face, mister. You try standing up with a bowling ball protruding from your belly."

Still waiting for an explanation, he began to gather the clothes on the floor, folding them and putting them back in the drawers where they belonged. In the last few months this sort of activity hadn't really been abnormal for her, but it bothered her far more than it seemed to bother him.

She picked up the diary and headed to the living room without a word. When he followed her into the room, she said, "Dammit, I just need to check something. I'll tell you when or if I find it."

He just shrugged and went to the kitchen. "Would you like a glass of water, hon?"

She smiled, despite her annoyance, frustration, excitement, and need to pee. "Sure, just put it on the coffee table." She was turning the pages, looking for a name. Over and over she ran into the name, but she needed more and was sure it was in here somewhere. Near the end, she found a list. He'd written the full names of all the people who had helped him in life. Near the top of the list was the pay dirt she was looking for.

"Bingo! I knew it!" She sat back, feeling vindicated and excited.

He brought the glass in and set it down. "Well, what was it you so desperately needed my diary for?"

She was so excited she had to put her thoughts together before starting. He waited patiently. "Okay, so I was up on Medical talking to Teague, trying to get him to find me another pilot. I'm sick of fixing these damned flyers all the time, and want to bring back a couple pilots that can walk and chew gum at the same time without breaking something."

He shrugged and said, "Jerry hasn't been doing too bad lately…" Her glare stopped him cold. She waited to see if he would interrupt her again. He just smiled and said, "Sorry, go on." She had to admit, he was far more patient than she was. If he'd been doing this to her she would've tackled him by now and started beating the answers out of him.

"Well, he's been busy lately and finally got irritated enough to just give me access to the files."

When the Freezer had first been discovered, they downloaded the computer files and used them to pick out their next candidate. Those files mostly consisted of scans or pictures of the original documents from each 'occupant's' military and medical records, not a real database that could be searched easily. Converting those images into a format more useable was a massive project, and New Hope just didn't have the resources to waste on something like that. Unfortunately, it meant if you wanted to find someone with a particular set of skills, it could take many hours of sifting through the thousands of records. Only about a third of the five thousand original occupants had been viable candidates for recovery. To bring those people back with memories intact, they only needed the candidate's head, so around fifteen hundred frozen heads resided in the custom built cold room in the bowels of New Hope. When you found the record of someone you were interested in bringing back, you looked in New Hope's computer to see if they were available.

"I sat down and started going through them, looking for someone suitable to fit my needs. I came across a file that was locked, and asked Teague about it. He didn't know, so I took it to Marcus to see if he could work some of his magic."

Jack interrupted again, "Marcus is still here? I thought he left yesterday?"

She sighed at the interruption. "This was a couple days ago. Now, can you please stop interrupting me?" Jack put his hands up but didn't say anything more. "Anyway, Marcus was able to break the encryption and get me access to the file. When I started reading it I was confused. This guy wasn't military. He seemed to be some kind of contractor but even that was unclear. Then I came across the name. It looked familiar but at first I couldn't place it. I felt like I'd seen it when exploring the Warehouse, so I headed back there to check it out."

"Wait, you mean the site up in Oregon in the mountains? Where you found all the heavy equipment a few months ago?"

Her eyes lit up, "Yeah! You know how we never figured out the purpose of that building? Well, it wasn't for a lack of trying. I spent several days digging through those offices and poking around the area looking for a clue but never found anything of interest." She paused to take a sip of water. "But when I came across that name in the files, the image in my mind was of the Warehouse. I just couldn't remember what the connection was. I guess maybe all these hormones in my body are screwing up my memory or something."

"Are you saying you found the connection? It would sure be nice to bring back someone who could shed some light on that place. You know, I have some theories about it, but maybe I just think that way because…"

Frustration erupted and she waved her hands in his face, interrupting him. "Hey, do you want to know the rest of the story or not?" Without waiting for him to nod, she said, "Yes, I found a connection, but it gets better!

On the flight back I couldn't shake the nagging feeling that I had still seen that name somewhere else before. I kept mulling it over, but it was like trying to remember something that's just dancing on the edge of your memory but you just can't seem grab it. Then this morning I had breakfast in the kitchen on the medical level and I started reminiscing about the first time we met, and suddenly everything snapped into place! That's why I rushed back here to find the diary. I was right; I'd seen the name in your book."

Now she was the one rambling, and it seemed to be getting on his nerves. He made a motion for her to continue.

"Subject number 2395 is one Phil Norland, born 1915, died 2006." She waited for his reaction.

To her disappointment, he didn't seem to react at all. All this build up and now he just sat there in stunned silence, as if he hadn't even heard her.

"Hello! Did you hear me? The file was for Phil Norland, your old boss!"

Finally she got the reaction she had hoped for. "Are you saying Phil was there all along? And that we have him in our cold rooms?"

"He was in the files, and we have his tube number. All we have to do is get him out of cold storage and get him in a tank. The next one will be open in just three days!"

Without warning he stood up and pulled her to her feet, wrapping her in an embrace that was both wonderful and a little too tight, given her condition. "Thank you, Wendy; you don't know how important this is!"

She wriggled loose and with a proud smile said, "There's a little more." She picked up her datapad and pointed to an entry.

He took the pad and read it. "It says he went private in 1969. No mention of any projects after that. The Warehouse is clearly a military project, but you said you found his name up there?"

"Look at the last entry again. He kept his military security clearance until *after* the project was completed. Why would he have clearance to military secrets if he was no longer doing projects for the military?"

He nodded, "That's a good question. But if the job in Oregon was military in nature, why would it be omitted from his top secret file?"

"Jack, we searched that area for days. Whatever he was working on had to be huge. Considering it was your old boss, don't you think maybe he was working underground? Maybe there's another facility like Montana around there, or better, maybe something more like this one."

Jack shrugged, "Or maybe whatever he built was destroyed in the war. Phil's company built a lot of buildings long before I went to work for him on his military stuff. Even if this is nothing, Phil could be a great asset to New Hope. Plus I would really enjoy getting to see my old friend again." He grabbed his own datapad and called down to Teague. When the man answered, he said excitedly, "Teague, I want the highest priority put on recovering Phil."

"Who?"

"Subject 2395, it's an old friend of mine, Find him, and do everything you can to ensure he doesn't lose any memory." This last part wasn't really necessary; Teague always put forth his best effort to ensure his patients were handled with the utmost care.

"No problem, Jack, I will get right on it. Oh, and tell Wendy I am sorry I was so short with her the other day." He clicked off.

Jack sat down heavily and leaned back in the couch, looking more relieved than he had in weeks. The weight of his new job worried her. Actually, the stress she was adding to his life with her mood swings and other peculiarities associated with pregnancy were what concerned her more. He didn't let it show, and in truth had acted with more patience, love, and understanding toward her than she had thought possible. But she knew how stressed out he was, and lately she hadn't even been able to feign any kind of intimate mood, let alone participate in any intimate activities.

She'd been trying to come up with a way to make it up to him, and discovering this information couldn't have come at a better time. Despite his loving nature and his seeming complete dedication to her, they weren't married, and there were a lot of women still around who wouldn't hesitate to jump into bed with him if given even the slightest chance. Deep down she trusted him implicitly, but remembering that trust when your moods changed on a minute by minute basis was not always easy.

She cuddled up to him, resting her head on his chest. His heartbeat was strong, probably because of the rush of adrenaline starting to ease up after such great news. Knowing she'd made his day, and maybe even his week gave her a peace of mind she too hadn't felt in a while. Furthermore, she felt valuable to him again, and for whatever reason that stirred up something else. "Jack," she said seductively, running her hand down his leg, "I have one more surprise for you."

Chapter 3

Tara entered the room, hesitated at the door, and finally approa
She was a bit too insecure for his tastes, but over time he was sure she wou...
come around. Two short weeks ago she woke up for the first time in over
three centuries, so he expected a period of adjustment. Working for a man
who had been more or less alive for the past two centuries probably played a
role in her inability to feel confident in her job. At least that was the
impression he got from most of the Reborn he had worked with over the past
four years. "Sir?"

"Tara, how many times do I have to tell you, you can call me Teague or
Doc if you would like, we don't practice that much formality these days." He
reflected on that statement with irony and even some remorse, but only a
little. In his early years, before the cities fell, he might have lost his position if
he had taken the liberty of calling his mentor by his first name. Times change
though, and after more than a century of struggling to just survive, formality
seemed to be overrated.

She shifted uncomfortably before finally saying, "Um, I can't find it."

He finally turned to her with a sigh. "Find what?" He had sent her on a
number of errands earlier, and it was not unusual for her to return empty
handed. Her lack of confidence sometimes made it a chore to figure out which
of her tasks she was unable to perform.

"The head. I mean the subject. 2395?"

He stopped what he was working on and gave her his full attention.
"You forgot how to identify it, or you just can't locate it?"

"I can't locate it. It isn't there. 2393 is there, 2399 is there, and
according to our records 2395 should be right between them. There's an
empty spot though, like it was there before."

Normally he would've just chalked it up to her tendency to give up too
fast when trying to locate something for him, but they had gone over the
procedures for recovering a subject three times. As meek and insecure as she
appeared, she was no idiot. "Did you check with Gregory?"

Gregory had been one of three men assigned to guard the cold rooms.
Although New Hope was far from an insecure facility, the subjects in the cold
room were not just priceless in value but critical to the very survival of
humanity. Nobody, especially Jack Taggart, was going to leave that kind of
wealth unguarded. "Yes, he said you and I were the only two who had
removed any of the subjects since we got them here."

"Well, someone is lying, especially if it was once there. We have only
removed fourteen subjects, and none of them were anywhere near that
location. That room was packed full, I saw to it myself." He was beginning to
become concerned. Having made a decision to investigate further, he headed
out of the room without another word. Tara followed.

~~~~

Jack sat in his office, feeling pretty good about his day. Despite the workload in front of him, he felt lighter than he had in weeks. Wendy's discovery was great news, but he had to admit to himself that he was more elated from the intimacy that had followed. He hadn't really realized how much he had been missing that kind of attention.

This had been a difficult few months. Once the chaos of assuming leadership had died down, the real work began. The community pretty much ran itself without needing anyone to micromanage, but there were dozens of monumental decisions to be made. Each one could end up being the deciding factor between extinction and survival of the human species. These decisions took research, and that meant countless hours studying recent history, speaking with the former council members, and even trying to establish relations with other communities.

Unfortunately, he seldom had time to work on any real problems because he was inundated with requests from those who had cast their vote for him. Every time he turned around someone was asking him for a favor, pitching some new idea, or just wanting to be heard. Some of it was important and pertained to the big decisions he knew had to be made soon, but much of it was petty and shortsighted. He expected it, at least to a certain extent, but the time drain meant he couldn't seem to make enough progress on the important items.

The result was having almost no free time for a personal life. On the rare occasions he and Wendy had a chance to eat a meal together their conversations revolved mostly around the baby. Even in bed they didn't get the luxury of falling asleep in each other's arms. The pregnancy made her restless and uncomfortable, and for the past couple months her tossing and turning prevented those coveted moments of human contact.

Although sex was not the reason he was with Wendy, he had to admit that his young body's virility had made their increasingly rare love life more of a challenge than he had expected. In his mind and heart he was satisfied with his relationship, and the excitement of having another child made keeping his desires in check mostly a non-issue. Nevertheless, long stretches without sex or even a little non-sexual intimacy seemed to make dealing with his job even more stressful.

It certainly didn't help that every woman in New Hope who wasn't already pregnant flirted with him openly, often suggesting outright that they could take over for Wendy while she was pregnant. He realized it was just the culture of the native population, but it still bothered him. It was tough enough not to think about other women now and then, even more so when those other women seemed to sense it and didn't respect his commitment to Wendy.

In fact, it was his lack of understanding of the culture that made this job truly stressful. If all he had to deal with was a full schedule and a little sexual tension, his life would actually feel pretty normal. Learning to relate to the people he was trying to lead was his struggle.

The native population was something of a mystery to him, and until he understood everything about it, he didn't feel like he could make a major decision that would affect their future.

The Reborn were easier to understand, after all many of them were not born all that much later than he was, and they all served the same country. But all of them, including those who grew up in the 50's and 60's, had experienced decades of change after he was already dead. No amount of history could help him to understand the impact of the changes in culture they had lived through.

The irony of ending up the elected leader of a group of people he was so disconnected from was not lost on him. The burden it brought motivated him to study history harder and to take the time to talk to anyone who had something to say. He needed to learn his people before he could expect to guide them.

Fully intending to take advantage of his relaxed state by diving into more historical research, he reached across the desk for his datapad. Just as he settled in, the door chimed. Tempted to ignore it, he sighed and tapped the icon on the datapad to open the door.

Expecting another stranger asking for a moment of his time, he was pleasantly surprised to see Teague walk through the door. Lately they hadn't been face to face much at all, and usually when they did meet up it was in the evening. Unfortunately, the look on his face told Jack this wouldn't be a social visit.

Teague took a seat across the desk without pausing for pleasantries or permission. Despite appearing to want to get right down to whatever business brought him here, he didn't speak right away.

"Am I going to have to guess why I get the pleasure of your company this afternoon, Teague?"

"Sorry, Jack, I feel a little out of sorts just interrupting your afternoon. I have a lot on my mind. How are things going here? Is this a good time?"

Jack smiled and leaned back in his chair. "Lately there isn't such thing as a 'good time.' Seems like I'm spending half my day just trying to remember what I was doing before I got interrupted the last time."

The ironic humor was lost on Teague. "You need to get a council together and start offloading some of the responsibility on others. There has been more going on in the past four months than we dealt with in the past century and you are trying to take it all on by yourself."

This was not an unusual conversation lately. In fact, just about every conversation with Teague had been focused on the idea of forming a cabinet or council to handle the day to day issues and free up Jack to get back to what he was best at: making things happen. He knew damn well Teague was right, but he was not particularly interested in rehashing a subject that had been beaten to death. "Teague, I've told you I'm working on it. Coming up with a government structure from scratch isn't all that simple. Besides, everyone I trust is needed elsewhere at the moment."

Teague actually scoffed at this. "You have to get over this thing with Theodore. You can't judge all of New Hope by the misguided actions of one man."

"Seven men, so far, and who knows how many more?"

Teague waved a hand dismissively. "Most of those men are pawns. Everyone chooses sides at some point; they were just misguided in their choice. Besides, they didn't understand the impact of what they were doing. This has been their home for far longer than any of the Reborn and they didn't like how things were changing. Their loyalty is to New Hope, and now that you are elected leader, to you as well."

"See, this is the problem Teague. New Hope is filled with two very different types of people and that's always going to lead to prejudice and bigotry. The natives voted for me because I acted when the council was hesitating and I got lucky and scored a big win for New Hope. The Reborn voted for me because they want to keep the ideals and freedoms they grew up with. Yet the natives are afraid of the kind of change those ideals will bring. If Theodore hadn't revealed his treasonous plans, he would have easily been able to divide this community by playing on those fears and the election would have been a lot closer. I'm stuck in a corner right now and any way I act I'm going to end up upsetting one group of people."

"This is why you need to get a council together. Staff it with an equal number of Reborn and natives and allow them to work out the details for you."

"But if I don't know whether I can trust them, how am I going to avoid another act of treason? You understand the value of what we have in our cold storage rooms, Teague. Wealth like that can bring anyone power, and power can lead to corruption."

Teague paled. With a sigh he said, "Honestly Jack, I was never a leader, so I don't have a good answer for you. Perhaps setting an example with Theodore and Red will show people you won't tolerate any kind of activities that put the people of New Hope at risk. Or perhaps you need to work harder at winning over the native population so nobody will have a reason to rebel." This wasn't helping, and Teague seemed to sense it and change the subject. "Speaking of Theodore, what are you thinking of doing with him?"

It was Jack's turn to pale. Theodore's fate had been weighing heavily on his mind, and he didn't have much longer to decide. The trial was less than two weeks away and he had already postponed it several times. "I don't know. The man was responsible for the loss of three of New Hope's people and put a lot more at risk. He was planning to sell out all of us for more power."

They sat in silence for a moment. "It's a shame really. Theodore was a valuable member of the council and played a key role in New Hope even being here. We wouldn't have half of the resources we have if he hadn't been so good at working with the other communities."

18

"You don't need to remind me, Teague. My job would be a lot easier right now if I had Theodore as an asset. I'm struggling enough with trying to come up with what is best for our own native population, trying to understand and work with the other communities is way out of my expertise."

"Well, I can't help you there, I have never even been to any of the other communities, let alone negotiated with any of them. Wendy and a couple other salvagers are the only ones who have even traded with them in recent years. At least you have met some of the other community leaders."

"Yeah, but that's going slowly. They don't trust me, and I haven't even been to any of the other communities either. We always meet halfway. If I can't see where and how they live, how can I even begin to understand them or figure out how to work with them?"

"Sounds like you need help." They made eye contact and both men chuckled.

"So is this why you came down here Doc, to bust my balls about politics?"

His expression turned grim once again. "Actually, no. And this isn't going to help you with your trust issues either. We have a problem with your request to get subject 2395 in the tank."

Jack's heart sank. "Freezer burn?" Despite careful selection, some of the corpses recovered from the Freezer were beyond Teague's ability to bring back. It would be a real shame if they couldn't bring back Phil. The man would be perfect for a council member, someone Jack could trust implicitly.

"Actually, I can't answer that. We can't locate the remains."

Confusion. "Wait. Are you saying we didn't get him? Or is he just misplaced?"

"I'm saying that we got him, and he was here, but he is now missing."

"How? I mean, that room is under constant guard. How do you know he was here at all? Wait, just take it from the beginning and tell me everything you know."

Chapter 4

Chuck eased the flyer into the flight bay and set it down gently. "Damn it's good to have you back Emmet. It just wasn't the same running patrols with Wayne. He's a good guy and all, but not much for conversation. All he talks about is the big ambush in Idaho."

Emmet waved him off as if casually shooing a fly away. "Hell Chuck, I'm just glad to be alive." With a laugh he continued, "I have to admit though, I wish I hadn't missed all the fun. The stories I've heard make the last few years sound pretty boring."

"Excitement like that isn't always what it's cracked up to be. I mean, sure, it makes for some great stories, but frankly I'll take the monotony of an uneventful patrol over catching a few bullets any day of the week. Besides, I spent most of that week flying search missions looking for Wendy and her crew, and the most action I saw after our little encounter at the Freezer was on a computer screen."

Emmet's eyebrows danced as he chuckled at this. Chuck always got a kick out of how expressive the man's face was, and those eyebrows took on a life of their own when he got into telling a story. "I hear what yer sayin' brother, but don't act like you weren't a big part of the most interesting thing to happen to New Hope in over a century."

It was Chuck's turn to wave him off. "I was a glorified limo driver for the real stars. Well, that and a human shield. You should've seen Jack in action, though. Not even a week after getting out of the tank and he was out there kickin' ass like he's been doing it for years. I have to be honest, after you went down and I took a bullet, I thought we were done for sure. Then he doesn't just save our asses, he somehow rallies the whole community to get off their butts and do something about securing the Freezer before we lost the whole thing."

"Damn, brother, I never seen you talk like this before. You sure you ain't got a man crush on this dude?"

Chuck blushed. It was true, he wasn't one to tell stories, and he sure as hell wasn't one to gush about anyone like this, at least not someone who wasn't female. He punched Emmet in the arm, "Fuck you. I'm just saying, the guy impressed even me, and you know how hard it is for me to be impressed by anyone."

Emmet just laughed then fell silent as they waited for the motors to wind down. Emmet's expression turned somber. "You know, Jack came to meet me the day I got out of the tank and woke up for the first time. Teague rewound my memories so I didn't know who he was, but we chatted for a bit and I gotta say, I like him. He told me all about that day and how I saved everyone. I don't know about that, really, if anything I probably just reacted to the threat and recklessly lost my life."

Chuck shook his head, "Regardless of why you did it, your actions did save our asses. I certainly owe you, and Jack feels the same way. You should feel proud for what you did."

"See, that's the thing. I'm not sure I know how I should feel right now. I mean, I'm happy I'm here again, but the truth is, the guy who saved your ass is dead. I might seem to be the same fun loving guy who tells great stories, but I have a ways to go before I can come to terms with who I really am."

"Is that why you took so long to get back out here with me? I figured you'd be back to work a couple days after you got out of the tank."

"Honestly, yeah, I wasn't sure how I would feel getting back to the life I remember. This body has never been outside of New Hope. I wasn't sure at first that it would be what I wanted. I think I was burned out before all this happened, and hell, for all I know that might have been what influenced me to do what I did."

They sat there in silent reflection. Finally, Chuck smiled and said, "Fun loving guy? And who the hell ever told you that your stories are great?" Both men laughed. "I asked Teague to try to give you a better sense of humor and try to make you a little better looking, but it seems he only gave you a bigger ego."

"Oh come on Chuck, you know he can't really do that. Can he?" The way he said that made Chuck laugh again.

"Same old Emmet, far as I'm concerned" he said, shaking his head.

As they got out of the flyer, Jack approached. Emmet looked at Chuck and said under his breath, "Here's your boyfriend now." Chuck punched him again. Emmet laughed and rubbing his arm said, "Heya Boss, how's Wendy doing?"

"Full of hormones and mean as a snake most days. Otherwise she's doing great Emmet, how are you? Feel good to get outside again?"

"Shit howdy it does. Don't get me wrong, the past couple months has been a real kick being freshly reborn again, but I needed to get out of here for a bit. The local women are fun but it gets exhausting after a while! Even Jade paid me a visit, which was a little weird considering how things ended between us. At least for me it was weird. I'll never understand the locals, Boss, they just don't see things the way we do."

"You don't need to tell me that, Emmet." He smiled and shook his head as if the very subject had been on his mind. Turning to Chuck, he said, "Got a minute?"

"Considering you came all the way down here to greet me, I suppose I can make a few minutes for you." He turned to Emmet, "Same time tomorrow?" With a simple nod and a slap on Jack's shoulder, Emmet headed to the rail car.

Chuck assumed Jack wanted to talk in private, so they headed over to a table at the far corner of the flight bay. There were only a few people in the massive cavern and none of them were nearly close enough to overhear, even if they weren't busy. They sat down. "What's up Jack?"

"We've got a problem."

"Shit," Chuck laughed, "we've got lots of problems." Both men smiled.

"Someone managed to steal a head from the cold storage rooms. And it happens to be one that could turn out to be pretty important."

"How the hell did that happen? Aren't Gregory and his men watching that room around the clock? And what the hell would anyone *here* want with a head?"

"I don't know, but it's troublesome to speculate. I was hoping you might have some insight into how someone could have pulled this off."

All traces of humor were gone. "Do you think it's still here in New Hope, or are you asking how someone could get it out of here undetected?"

"Honestly, I don't have a clue. If it's here, I'd sure like to know how they're keeping it cold without turning the room into a furnace."

The only small containers they had to keep the heads cold enough for long periods used Peltier cooling, which was an electronic means of piping heat from one place to another. One side of the cooler stayed cold, the other side hot, and the energy it took to keep the head super cooled meant the outside of the container would kick off enough heat to turn one of the apartments in New Hope into an oven.

"Have you asked Marcus to see if he can use the computer system to locate a room that's above normal temperature?"

"Actually, Marcus is gone for a while, and he isn't reachable. I have Teague looking into it though."

"Gone? Don't tell me he's back working on his pet computer project."

"Yeah, and as long as he's there, we can't reach him."

"At least the guy could have waited until you got everything under control here."

"What, you don't think I have things under control here?"

Chuck realized he might have insulted Jack with that comment and quickly backpedaled. "Oh, no, I'm just saying, you have a lot to do and Marcus could at least help you out with it until you get settled in..."

Jack was laughing, "I'm just yanking your chain, Chuck. You're right; it would've been nice if he could've stuck around a little longer. It's my own fault, really. I practically kicked him out of here. I figured the man waited two centuries to get back to his project and he's completely entitled to do whatever he wants. He did a good job of preparing me and I guess I wanted to get started on some ideas without him hovering. Anything I fail at now is my own fault, not Marcus'."

"Given any more thought to getting a cabinet together so you can ease up and take care of the more important things, like Wendy?" In the past few weeks, Chuck had spent more time with Wendy than Jack had, and while she hadn't outright told him she was a little resentful of their lack of time together, he could see it in her eyes and hear it in their conversations. The look on Jack's face right now told him he was feeling it too.

"I'm starting to think I can't put it off much longer. How would you like to be head of security?"

"Hell no! I'm happy with what I'm doing now, Jack, and besides, from what you're saying, whoever takes on the responsibility of security is going to have a shit storm dropped on their head." Jack laughed, despite how serious Chuck was. "I'm serious Jack, you have a real mess on your hands."

"Sorry, I'm not laughing at the situation, just that I figured you would say no. I wouldn't have bothered to ask if I didn't need someone I could trust, and you are one of the few. It's a serious offer though."

"I appreciate it, Jack, I really do. I'm a grunt, and I belong out in the field doing what needs to be done. The last thing I want is to have to deal with politics."

"I hear you there. It's about the last thing I ever wanted too. I'm good at cutting through red tape, not creating it." Both men chuckled at this. They both spent their former lives in the military, Army specifically, and if there's one thing a career military man understands, it's the red tape.

"So who do you think I should pick for the job? Not sure who I can trust and this latest situation proves that there is still at least one person here who isn't on our side."

Chuck pondered this for a moment before answering, "If I were in your shoes, I'd talk Caleb into resuming his former role. I know you don't really trust any of the old council, but the man kept this community secure for two centuries. I have a hard time believing he would sell it out to Cali or anyone else just for a little bit of luxury or power. If not Caleb, Chin seems to know his way around our system, and there's no question you can trust him." Chuck knew Chin fairly well and knew the man would die before letting anything bad happen to New Hope.

Jack just nodded, not looking too convinced. "I'll keep that in mind. Back to the reason I came down here. If someone were to make off with a head, could they have gotten away without anyone noticing? Far as we can tell, everyone is accounted for here. They would have had to leave and get back without being detected by anyone."

Again, Chuck thought about this for a moment before answering. "Smuggling something out of here would be a piece of cake. Quite a bit of traffic comes and goes each day. First there are the regular patrols. That's three to four shifts of guys like me scouting about a thousand square miles of land surrounding New Hope looking for anything out of the ordinary or just being ready to intercept anything our sensors pick up. Then you have scavengers coming and going all day long, sometimes one or two crews, sometimes more. Sometimes traders go out, and they carry all kinds of cargo that nobody really checks. Hell, even your own diplomatic missions could have been the vessel for getting something out of here."

"Wait, are you saying it's possible that someone who went with me to meet with another community could have been the thief? How's that possible?"

"That's exactly what I'm saying. Anything is possible because we all trust each other and don't pay that much attention to what others are doing. You remember the containers we used to bring the heads back in? Those were basically a cooler with some liquid nitrogen in them. Only good for a few hours, but they didn't give off any heat and were easy to conceal in a storage compartment or with other cargo. Someone could have stashed it in the hold a half hour before you got down here, then when you were busy talking politics, grabbed it and handed it off to someone from another community."

"Dammit! I can see we have a long way to go with security. Are you positive you don't want the job? Hell, Chuck, I'll get you a cushy apartment down on my level and give you anything you want. I really need a guy like you watching my back!"

Chuck just shook his head. "Sorry Jack. You know I've got your back. But trust me, if the shit hits the fan here, you want me in the field where I know what I'm doing and can be an effective tool for you, not sitting in a cushy office pushing paper around and staring at video feeds."

Jack's shoulders drooped a little, as if more weight was added to them. "Okay, I understand. Look, I still want you to help me out here. Get me a list of everyone who could possibly have gotten out of here since we closed up the Freezer. And I want your opinion on whether or not they can be trusted."

"It'll be a long list and I can't promise it'll be complete, but I can have it to you later tonight. Just let me know if there's anything else you need. And take a few hours off to pay attention to Wendy; she's too much of a stone cold bitch when she isn't getting enough love from you."

Jack laughed at this. Chuck knew just about any other man would have ended up on the floor for saying something like that about Wendy. "Thanks Chuck, I'll tell Wendy you said hi. See you later." He got up and headed to the rail car.

Chuck leaned back in his seat and reflected on the conversation. He had complete faith that Jack would make the right decisions, but the man was certainly having a rough time. Theodore had done more damage than he probably realized. He'd created distrust in New Hope, and it wasn't just Jack who was feeling it. This news of a theft of their most valued resources was just one more reason not to trust anyone. It wasn't that Chuck had ever really believed the council members valued the individual lives of the citizens of New Hope. In fact he knew sooner or later they'd be willing to sacrifice a few of their citizens if it meant benefiting the community as a whole. But in his mind everyone here, including those with a different idea of morality or freedom, were patriots, loyal to New Hope and incapable of selling out the rest of the community for personal gain. Theodore's actions destroyed that perception, and now everyone was potentially untrustworthy.

Chapter 5

Theodore was restless. Then again, lately he was restless all the time and he wasn't sure exactly why. He knew for certain it wasn't because he was isolated from other people – he had internally isolated himself since he was a teenager and he usually thrived on isolation. He had plenty of things to think about, so the time spent here alone shouldn't affect him.

Perhaps it was his inability to collect information and actively plan his next step. If he could get out of this room, talk to people he knew were loyal to him, at the least he could set something in motion that might get him out of incarceration. His ambitious plans to gain leadership of all communities were lost, he recognized that. However, he wasn't about to give up on at least regaining his status with New Hope, if not in actual power, at least in reputation.

Besides, given enough time, he was confident he could regain control of New Hope. After all he was one of the founding fathers, and nobody was better suited to lead than those who created the community. He had plenty of time. After two centuries, he no longer feared death. His current body was barely forty years old, and it would be another half century before he was ready for renewal. As far as he was concerned, he was immortal, destined to live forever. However, immortality wouldn't be worth anything if he didn't have the respect he deserved. It would be pure hell if he had to spend it in a cell.

He didn't fear a trial, and in fact was wondering why he still hadn't been called in front of the council. There was no way the new 'leader' of New Hope would execute him, of that he was confident. Jack Taggart believed in the sanctity of life, and that would work to Theodore's favor. Furthermore, Theodore knew too much, things that could put the future of New Hope in jeopardy. Even if Jack was impetuous enough to try to banish him, surely his former council mates wouldn't allow it. No, he would most likely end up sentenced to some menial tasks, perhaps some more time alone in a cell like this one, and in the end he would be set free to become a productive member of the community again. That was how things were done back in Jack's era, and it was as worthless then as it would be now. Of course, Jack won't see it that way; his ideals would continue to blind him as they had since the day he woke up in Teague's recovery room.

In the long run, what Jack felt was right wouldn't matter much anyway. There was little question he was merely a puppet. After two centuries of living with Marcus, one thing Theodore knew for certain was the man would never willingly give up his power. Marcus had an angle here, and while he wasn't quite sure what it was exactly, he knew it existed.

Theodore would deal with his punishment, bide his time, and wait for opportunities. When the time was right, he would start quietly building support. He figured within a decade, maybe two, he could regain his status and perhaps even dispose of this thorn in his side named Jack. Marcus would be a more difficult opponent, but he was confident he could overcome his former superior.

This confidence led him to believe his anxiety had to be caused by his inability to set things in motion. Plus, four months of sitting in this room with only his jailors to feed him the occasional bit of news meant he didn't know the true extent of the damage Marcus' puppet had already caused. *Who knows what kind of mess Jack is making out there? Imagine if he had opened up trade with the other communities.* A sudden and massive wave of anxiety forced him to stand and pace again.

Through the anxiety a revelation made its way to his brain. He connected his restlessness with the train of thought that seemed to trigger it and the world seemed to stop completely. *Oh Shit.*

Realizing where his anxiety was coming from, he sat down and closed his eyes, frantically running the scenarios through his head. *This is bad.* His intentions all along had been to usurp control from Marcus, and while his ambitions had perhaps grown too large to manage, he never intended for the community he had built end up in ruins. He wanted to be the rightful leader, not the bringer of destruction. Part of his plan involved some misinformation regarding other communities. With his incarceration, he was unable to influence any negotiations between New Hope and other communities, and that could lead to some devastating blunders.

He needed to act, but there was only one way to do that right now, and it would only make his situation worse, so it wasn't an option, at least not yet anyway. They needed to come to him, and sooner or later they would. When they did, he needed to be prepared. With effort he calmed the anxiety and focused on forming a plan.

~~~~

Jack found Tiny in the kitchen on the medical level. He didn't recall ever seeing the big man taking his meals anywhere else. Everything on this level was concrete or steel, so when Tiny spoke his deep voice reverberated in the room, almost startling Jack despite expecting it. "Hey, Mad Dawg, what brings you down here?"

Jack could never figure out if Tiny was using his old nickname mockingly or if he really just liked using it. All of the Reborn were military in their former life, mostly Army and mostly enlisted men. They all had nicknames, usually given by their drill instructor within the first week of basic training. Heck, there were men Jack only knew by their nicknames. Despite this, Tiny was the only person in New Hope that regularly referred to him by 'Mad Dawg'. "I was just thinking the same thing about you, Tiny. How's life treating you?"

The truth was, Jack was kind of hoping to run into the big man, he had some ideas kicking around in his head and wanted to talk about them. He grabbed a bowl of the slimy gelatin that made up most of the food supply in New Hope, filled a cup with water, and took a seat at the table facing Tiny.

"I can't complain, and even if I could, nobody would listen." They both chuckled. "Actually things are pretty good. I'm not missing going out on patrol all the time, and I kind of like managing the jail. It can be boring at times, but it gives me more time to socialize." Jack had put him in charge of handling their prisoners, now that their holding cells were full.

"Good to hear. I might have a little more work for you, something that might be right up your alley." The food tasted like spaghetti today, one of the flavors he particularly liked. If it weren't too early in the day still, he might even grab a bottle of what passed for beer here.

Tiny set his own bowl aside and waited for Jack to continue.

"What do you think about the five men in lockup?"

"Red's guys? They're a bunch of prejudicial assholes. That and they abandoned fellow soldiers during a battle."

"Do you think they abandoned them willingly or do you think Red coerced them into leaving?"

Tiny mulled it over before answering, "Well, I haven't noticed them bragging to each other or anything like that, so I don't think they're proud of what they did. As far as motive though, I'm no psychologist but I suppose I have a little insight." He paused to see if Jack wanted to hear his thoughts. Jack motioned for him to continue. "These guys are basically this generation's version of racists. Back in our time... uh, I mean, back in *my* time, most of the racism I ran into was fueled by ignorance. There were always the racists who'd been raised to hate, but more often people just disliked what they didn't understand or saw as different. Regardless of why you hate, when there is conflict or division, you will stand next to those you think are the same as you and make an enemy of those who are different."

"So you think they saw us as different and followed Red's lead because one of their own kind was acting that way?"

Tiny shrugged. "I'm not sure, but if four white guys were beating up a black guy, I'm probably going to side with the black guy, even if I have nothing else in common with him. Hell, even if he deserves the beating."

"But nobody was beating these guys up, if anything, they were the instigators here."

"Are you sure about that? Have you questioned them to find out their motives?"

Tiny had a good point. "No but I suppose it's time. Let's have a talk with them, one on one, and see what they have to say for themselves."

"Sounds good, when do you want to do it?"

"Now works for me." Tiny seemed to hesitate. "What, do you have something else to do?"

Tiny looked past Jack and smiled. "Hey, baby."

Jack turned around to see Teague's new assistant walking into the kitchen. He couldn't remember her name. As soon as she spotted Jack, she stopped, looking somewhat like a deer caught in a car's headlights. She looked from Jack to Tiny, and back again, then appeared to be poised to turn tail and leave. "Jack, you've met Tara haven't you?"

"Yes, I believe I have. Teague's assistant, right?"

Tara still stood there, looking unsure of herself. "Yeah. Nice to meet you again, Jack. I... uh... I can go if you two are busy."

Jack looked back at Tiny, and saw an expression on the big man's face he hadn't seen before. *Good for him*, he thought. "No, actually I was just leaving. Tiny, I'll meet you in your office in about an hour. Have a nice lunch."

~~~~

An hour later, Jack knocked on the door to Tiny's office. He could have just pressed the button and gone in, after all his status as leader gave him full access to every room in the underground facility. He also could have called ahead with his datapad just before arriving and had the door open when he arrived but the truth is he seldom thought about using the technology. Perhaps he simply preferred knocking on the door.

The door opened and the big man smiled from his desk. "Thanks for giving me a chance to hang out with Tara on her lunch break, Jack. Teague keeps her pretty busy so we don't get much time to just sit and chat."

Jack waved him off. "Hell, Tiny, all you had to do was tell me you were meeting someone, this could have waited. It's not as if the men in that cell are going anywhere. I just figured you hung out on that level because it's quiet."

"Usually that's exactly why I go there for lunch. I like the solitude. Plus I get to meet the new guys once in a while, which is kind of refreshing. I just happened to be there when Tara was first brought out of the tank. We ended up chatting for a while and hit it off. Life's been quite a bit better since we met."

"I bet. I'm glad to hear it, Tiny. You'll have to bring her over for dinner some night. I'll let Wendy know and she can plan something."

Tiny looked a little uncomfortable. "I appreciate that, Jack, but let's hold off on that for a bit. If you haven't noticed, Tara's a bit... well... she's kind of shy and she gets nervous when she's around anyone new. That's one of the reasons I meet her on the medical level every day."

"Well, consider it an open invitation, whenever you feel comfortable bringing her around. Now, let's get one of these men in here to have a little talk."

Tiny seemed relieved to change the subject. He pressed a button on his desk and said, "Ron, bring Clayton in here please." The door opened a moment later and the guard escorted a tired and haggard looking man, arms bound behind him with cuffs. Tiny looked at Jack questioningly.

Jack picked up on it and said, "Go ahead and uncuff him." The guard took off the cuffs then with a nod from Tiny, left the room. "Please, have a seat."

The man sat down. Jack didn't hesitate to dive right in. "Clayton is it?" The man nodded. "How're you doing, Clayton?"

"How do ya think I'm doin? I'm tired and I'm sick of being locked up."

Tiny piped up with his deep voice, "Well, maybe you should have thought about that before you went and abandoned a bunch of your fellow soldiers during a dangerous mission."

The man's shoulders slumped. "Yeah, well, I didn' say I don' deserve to be here. I know I fucked up. We all did. None of us shoulda listened to Red. So what's gonna happen to us now? You gonna kick us outta New Hope? Or are ya just gonna put a bullet in our heads?"

Tiny didn't relent, "If it was my choice, I would've shot you for treason. The only reason you're still alive is because Jack here is a much nicer guy than I am, and for some reason he wanted to see what you had to say for yourself!"

If Clayton could have made himself smaller, he would have. "I ain' proud of what I done, but I done it all the same." He looked up at Tiny, then at Jack. "You Reborn don't have the first clue how much you fucked up our lives. I ain' sayin' it's an excuse or nothing, but ever since you all came along, we ain't really belonged here no more."

Jack was interested in hearing where this was going. "What exactly does that mean?"

"You realize me an' the other men are all unable to father a child, right? Well, that didn't leave us with much value here. I mean, Marcus was willing to take us in and all, which was great, but we still had to figger out a way to pull our weight around here. So we took to patrollin' the area, makin' sure there wasn't no threats getting close to New Hope, and drivin off any Mutes that looked as they might be trouble for us. We put our lives on the line every day, and it got us enough respect to have a decent life. We couldn't give the women no kids, but they still liked us just the same and let us share their beds. It was a hell of a lot better than life outside on our own. Then we found the Freezer an' everythin' changed. Suddenly there was a bunch more men here, men who could give the women babies, and men who knew how to fight, how to defend, and wasn't afraid to go out and face the dangers outside. Hell, you was all even educated properly and had stories of how things were back before the cleansing started. You think the women still wanted us in their beds after that? Hell no. You took everythin' we had an' didn' even give us the common courtesy of sayin' thanks for providin' such a great place for you to live. Far as Marcus and Teague and all the 'foundin fathers' was concerned, you were the saviors of humanity. Well whoopdee fuckin doo, if it wasn't for us you'd still be a bunch of corpsicles stuck in hole, just waitin' for the power to go out so you can rot like the rest of the dead from your time.

"I woulda given my life to make sure the people here was safe and sound every day, and now nobody but Red gives a shit about what happens to me. So yeah, if you think I deserve a bullet to the head for what I done, then quit fuckin' around and jus' do it already."

Jack was stunned, both at the defiant outburst as well as what he had to say. All these weeks of trying to figure out what makes the native population tick and in thirty seconds this man gave him insight he never would have gotten from reading or even from talking to people like Teague or Chin. Ever since he woke up in this place, he'd been told how the Reborn were going to be the saviors of mankind. He never stopped to consider what kind of effect this would have on those people who had been struggling since the day they were born. Perhaps if he had understood this before, he would've known not to mix locals and Reborn on a mission that critical.

However, as much as he appreciated the insight, he wasn't about to let up on this man. He wanted answers. "So, if I'm understanding you right, you figured you could get a few of the Reborn killed, stop any chances of New Hope continuing to bring back more Reborn, and regain your status here?"

Clayton shook his head, "No, not exactly. I mean, I didn' care much if a couple Reborn got cut off from us and got chased outta there by them Mutes, but I didn't think they'd get killed or nothin'. Shit, they was all armed to the teeth and armored up, and there wasn't but a few dozen Mutes left. I jus' wanted them gone from New Hope. Besides, Red told us how if we failed that mission, Cali would get the Freezer an' Red would end up runnin' New Hope. With him in charge, we knew we'd get some nice jobs here and our women would let us bed with them again. I told you, I'd give my life to protect New Hope, I ain' no murderer. If I'd thought our pullin' outta there was gonna get someone killed, I wouldn'ta done it."

Jack leaned back in his chair, taking in all of what the man had said. This was what he was after. His new understanding of the underlying tensions didn't forgive what Clayton and the others did, but it made it a heck of a lot easier to decide what to do with them. "If I give you another chance to be a part of New Hope, how can I trust you?"

Tiny broke in, "Jack, I think that would be a mistake. These men are traitors to this community. We can't let them just walk away from this like nothing happened."

The look he shot Tiny shut him up quickly. There was a silence while he waited for Clayton to say something.

"All I can do is give you my word, which don' mean shit right now. I can assure ya though, if you give me a chance, I won' let ya down, sah. You don' know what it's like livin outside on yo own. Mutes ain' even the worst things out there. I maybe didn' like living with the Reborn, but it shore beats bein' dead or fightin' for yo life ever' day."

A shiver went down Jack's spine. He hadn't given a whole lot of thought to what other dangers might exist outside the security of New Hope, but he figured there was good reason Marcus was so adamant about their next home being underground again. The mutes were obviously a violent menace, but it seemed to Jack they would soon have the numbers to make that threat manageable. The way Clayton talked about living outside, it seemed Jack had a lot more learning to do.

~~~~

After Clayton had been returned to his cell, Jack turned to Tiny, ready for an argument. Even expecting it, the big man's deep voice startled him. "Dammit, Jack, you know we can't let these men just go free! They got a man killed and they need to pay for that! And don't think for a second you can trust any of them. He put on a fine act there, but I still don't trust him, not one damn bit!"

"Are you done yet, Gunny?" The tone of Jack's voice cooled the big man instantly.

"Sorry, Sir. I just think you're making a big mistake."

He softened his tone, but only a little. "First off, they didn't exactly get a man killed. Kenny is dead because he didn't listen to orders and got himself killed. Second, they were acting under orders from their superior officer. Now, that doesn't excuse them, but given the situation we are in now, I don't think killing five men is going to solve anything. Sending them packing isn't going to help us either. I came to you wanting to know if these men could be rehabilitated, and I got my answer. I believe they can. But it isn't going to be easy on them."

Tiny obviously wasn't happy, but he would get over it. He was a Marine, after all. "So what are you thinking we should do?"

"Well, remember I said I have something that would be right up your alley? I want you to train them. I want them broken down and built back up the way the Marines would have done it. I want these men to be loyal and ready to take orders without so much as hesitating. And I think you're the man to do it."

This was obviously unexpected. Jack couldn't tell if Tiny was ready to laugh or to punch him. Maybe both. They stared at each other for at least a minute, maybe longer. Tiny was the first to blink. "Shit, Jack, why didn't you tell me this before we brought him in?" He nodded and said, "Okay, this might actually work. Of course, this is going to be one hell of a workload for me. I might enjoy running these guys into the ground though. I suppose a ten week crash course in discipline will be enough to break these guys and build them back up."

"Make it twenty weeks, and don't be nice to them. Work them hard, and break them down hard. If one of them comes apart, we'll deal with him some other way. Make it clear to them from the start that they have a choice, they can either tough out your training or they can find a home elsewhere. I'm giving you full control over this, so if you think any of them are resisting your discipline, you have my authority to send them packing. You aren't the one being punished here, so find another Reborn with experience as a drill sergeant and share the workload. If you need any help, just let me know. I don't want to find out you're neglecting your new honey because you're spending all your time making these men's lives hell."

Tiny smiled. "Thanks, Jack. This *is* gonna be fun."

Chapter 6

After a few more hours of work, Jack took Chuck's advice and called it an early night. He spent the evening catching up with Wendy. They made an agreement not to talk about the baby, so most of the conversation either focused on the politics he was struggling with or the work she had been doing.

As her belly grew, the amount of maintenance work she was able to do had diminished, so most of her time had been spent flying the salvage teams around. There was something she really enjoyed about rummaging through the ruins and discovering items they could use. While a lot of what they found was brought back to New Hope to be recycled into something useful, it was the oddball items she found that she most enjoyed. Some of it she traded with other communities for luxuries like farm fresh foods and booze. The really great finds were saved for decorating their home.

Since moving in to the spacious family apartment reserved for Jack's new role as leader, she had taken the time to decorate it with all sorts of interesting finds. Some of it was fine art – a statue, piece of pottery, or even the occasional painting that was in good enough shape to reframe and hang on a wall. The rest could be considered junk by many: various knickknacks from her time – a weathered license plate, a souvenir cup from Disney World, a baseball and a bat, or even an old cassette player.

Jack enjoyed the old items, but none of them meant more to him than his prize possession – a scale model of a 1965 Ford Mustang she presented to him a month ago as a gift. She had found it under a workbench in the Warehouse. It had survived the years in nearly perfect condition thanks to being in a sealed display case. There was only one other material possession he valued more, and that was his diary. Now that she had tied his old boss to the Warehouse, the model took on even more meaning. Phil always envied his Mustang; perhaps the model had belonged to him.

Jack wasn't sure if she enjoyed salvaging as much as she enjoyed spending time with Bartholomew, the giant Mute genius she had befriended in the aftermath of the big battle in Idaho. Bart had become an invaluable resource for New Hope. His knowledge of the area surrounding his home had yielded several new citizens for the community; two of the men they found were even fertile. While this wasn't as big of a boon since the discovery of the Freezer, men like that were still incredibly rare, and every little bit helped diversify the DNA pool.

The discovery of more people wasn't even the most valuable contribution Bart had made to New Hope though. The gentle giant was a wizard with electronics. Wendy had been bringing him whatever electronics, computer, and communications equipment she could convince Jack to part with, and Bart managed to piece together an incredibly powerful communication system. It not only allowed him communication with New Hope but also allowed him to listen in on some kinds of communication between other communities. On top of this, he had figured out how to tap into a satellite that previously was assumed to be controlled by Cali. If New Hope had access to that kind of intelligence four months ago, a lot of deaths might have been avoided.

Along with the electronics, an incredible wealth of technological information was made available to him and it took his natural expertise with electronics to an entirely new level. In fact, Marcus had even been by to visit him and discuss some technology that Jack could only imagine was fairly complex.

It was unfortunate they couldn't bring Bart to New Hope. Even if Jack could convince the big man to come live with them, which Wendy assured him would never happen, it just wouldn't work out. His size wasn't even the real issue there, although the facility they lived in was never built to accommodate someone that large. The real problem was simply that he was a Mute. He preferred the term "Evolved", but regular humans had grown to fear the Mutes, primarily because most of them were quite savage fighters who would stop at nothing to loot and pillage any human civilization they came across. Most of the soldiers of New Hope had learned to shoot any Mute on sight and ask questions later. The irony was that his intelligence and demeanor made some of the men in New Hope look like savages in comparison.

He and Bart had become fast friends, partly because of his relationship with Wendy, of whom Bart was very fond. The giant had a great personality once you got past his menacing size, and Jack had little reservation about Wendy spending so much time with him.

After getting caught up on what she'd been doing for the past several weeks, the conversation turned to Jack They spent nearly an hour talking about the options for forming a cabinet or council of some kind, or at the least assigning various responsibilities of the community to specific people. Wendy always took the time to listen to him talk about the issues he was dealing with, and although she admitted she was far from being a politician, she always seemed to have some good advice for him.

When Jack first took over as leader, he figured he could run the community like he did a jobsite. After all, everyone here except the newly Reborn knew their job and needed little supervision. The community was not all that large, and he had managed work crews and military units numbering far more people. He disbanded the old council and decided to take on all the responsibilities himself.

The problem with his strategy was simple: he had always been 'middle management' and never the head boss. In the Army, there was always someone who ranked higher, and politics played little role in his relatively low rank of Captain. After retiring from his military career, he was second in command to Phil, and while he had full control of his men, the projects, budget, and timeframe were all dictated by Phil, or whoever Phil answered to.

In this job, he had to make the decisions that everyone else had made for him in previous jobs. There was nobody to answer to, and nobody even offering him guidance. Of course, that wasn't entirely true, he had to answer to the people, and everyone seemed to have an opinion on how things should be run. Despite being in power for several months, today's decision with the men in lockup had realistically been the first major decision he had made. There were a lot more decisions of that caliber that would have to be made soon too, and he had been putting them off for too long.

There was no longer any question of whether he should set up some 'middle managers' to help run New Hope and free his time up to work on those major decisions. It was now only a question of who he would pick and how much power he would give them. Discussing it with Wendy was nice; there wasn't the pressure he usually felt when talking with others about it, even those he considered as friends like Teague and Chuck.

In fact, the entire evening was nice. Even though she didn't have many answers, talking to Wendy about his difficult decisions seemed to ease the burden of his responsibility.

Unfortunately, the romantic mood she had been in earlier in the day was gone, probably due to the news that her discovery of Phil's remains had not only turned out to be a false hope but also revealed more treachery from within. She seemed really disappointed, even though it had nothing to do with her. For the first time in weeks they went to bed at the same time. Jack was content to just get to hold her. He fell asleep with her in his arms.

~~~~

The next morning, they sat down for a quick breakfast and talked about their plans for the day. Wendy said, "I'm going to go spend the day with Bart. He intercepted some chatter between Cali and one of their scavenging teams and thinks he has the location of an old recycling facility they've been picking over. It's supposed to be a veritable gold mine of resources. We're going to go check it out."

"Please be careful, we still haven't heard from Cali at all and we have no idea what they've been up to. If they catch you raiding one of their salvage areas things might get ugly."

"Don't worry, honey, Bart is going with us this time, and nobody's going to mess with us while he's around."

That was a relief. "Okay, but remember, Bart isn't bulletproof. Please, at least wear an under suit. Just in case."

She frowned. "Those things aren't very comfortable when you have a belly like mine."

He smiled at this. "You're barely beginning to show." He wasn't making fun of her; she was only about four months along, and while she had a well-defined baby bump, it was going to get much, much bigger in the coming months.

"Barely?? I feel like I am carrying around a damn watermelon. And have you seen my ass recently? It's going to take me months to get my figure back."

She looked like she was about to cry, and he felt bad because he was just trying to make her feel better.

He slid closer to her and put his arm around her. "I *have* seen your ass recently, and it's still as fantastic as the day I met you. And don't get me started on your breasts. In my book you're sexier than ever."

She started to smile, but then frowned. "You have no idea how sore these damn things are! And you're just saying I'm sexy because you're horny, and you're horny because I'm never in the mood at the right time. I don't even know why you're still with me."

Just like that, she was crying. He wasn't sure what else to say to comfort her so he tried shifting the subject. "Don't worry about me, Wendy, I'm not going anywhere. At least not with another woman. I'm actually heading toward Nebraska to meet with Andrew today."

She sniffled but leaned into him a little more, taking the bait. "Wisner Camp? Who's taking you? And why don't you ever ask me to fly you on some of these meetings? Are you worried my fat ass will be too heavy to get the flyer off the ground?"

He couldn't help but laugh, "Your ass isn't fat, and I know you'd be an exceptional pilot. I don't take you because you're too good looking, and a hot pregnant woman might be too tempting of a target for them. No way am I going to put you at risk like that." He was only half kidding. A pregnant woman was a valuable person, and one who was on her first pregnancy with a man who had no other kids running around yet was worth her weight in gold to any community. In fact, there wasn't a community in the world outside of New Hope who could claim they have both a woman and a man with DNA that is completely unique to the current gene pool, let alone one who hasn't given birth to her first child yet, a child who will also have DNA that is of no relation to any other living person on the planet. It was no exaggeration to say that Wendy was priceless right now. And from what he had seen of New Hope's own local women, beauty like hers was pretty rare too. It wasn't that he believed any community would start a fight over her, but he was trying to build relationships, and waving a prize like her in their faces would not help.

She rolled her eyes at the comment, probably completely unaware of what kind of value she had to the rest of the world. "Whatever, if you don't want me to go, I get it, but I still worry about you."

"Shouldn't be any reason to worry, Wisner Camp is friendly. Plus, folks outside of New Hope might not know exactly what we got from Montana, but they know it has to do with fertility. Nobody is willing to jeopardize potential trades by pulling anything stupid. Besides, we'll be meeting in Colorado, about halfway again. I'll have Anton and a few of his handpicked men with me. We'll be careful. It isn't like I'll be sitting in the middle of their town unprotected."

"They don't really have a town. The leadership and most of their fertile men live in some old missile silo they converted into makeshift living quarters and the rest of the citizens live above ground, fairly spread out from one another, in fortified ranches."

She said it off hand but it came as a bit of a surprise to him. The truth was, Jack didn't really know how most of the other communities lived. Every bit of information he read regarding anything outside of New Hope was vague and without any kind of detail. As far as he could tell, Theodore had been the only person here who had visited other communities personally, and given the current circumstances it wasn't like Jack could just start asking the man questions about it. He'd never thought to ask the scavengers, he just assumed the trading they did always took place the same way his meeting today would happen - in a neutral location far away from where they live. "Really? You've been to these silos?"

"Not personally, but the people I trade with talk about it once in a while."

This was good information. "What about other communities, do you get access to where they live?"

She shrugged, "I've been to the main town of Deering, but I couldn't tell you much about it other than how it looks like an old military compound. There's a pretty solid wall built around the residential homes, but otherwise it's mostly old Quonset huts. From what I've seen, traders at most places usually set up a camp outside of town, sometimes at a farm or ranch. Did you know we're the only community that doesn't have a farm or ranch?"

Again, this was information he really didn't know. "Don't all communities have the same slime machines we have?"

"Nope, we're the only one. That unit was put in before the cities fell. Have you ever seen how big that machine is? Thankfully I don't have to fix it that often, I really don't need to be reminded what the food is made of. I suppose it's a good thing we have it though, not like you can grow much in a desert."

This was true. It worried him that he hadn't really thought about it much. Just one more important detail he'd been overlooking. If that machine broke down it could cause some pretty major problems for New Hope. It reminded him of how many vulnerabilities this community had, particularly with someone living here who was not completely loyal. "Hey, who normally tells you what needs fixing around here?"

"Usually Nick. Sometimes Teague."

"Teague? You mean when he needs the medical equipment worked on?"

"No, he typically fixes and maintains his own equipment. The guy is super anal about it and from what I can tell he built most of it to begin with."

"So why would he be telling you about other things that need fixing?"

"He would get it from the council. Any time they made a decision, Teague was the delivery man. Poor guy, as much as he did for this place he never got much respect in the council."

Jack nodded in agreement. "Yeah, when I officially make him head of medical I will make sure he is equal in authority to all the other members."

"You're so sweet. But why are you asking about maintenance?"

"I'm just still thinking about who to put in charge of that stuff."

"Hmph."

"Hmph? What does hmph mean?"

"I don't know, I guess it just means hmph."

He waited, knowing she had something on her mind. Perhaps sensing he was waiting for her to say something, she finally spilled it. "Didn't we spend enough time talking about this last night? If you don't think Scott is the right man for maintenance, then put Nick in charge. Why do you keep second guessing yourself?"

"Good question. I guess I'm not all that good at this leadership thing." At that moment, he really felt like he was in over his head. Give him a job to do and he will do it and probably better than anyone else. Leave him to figure out what jobs needed to get done and apparently he would miss some details. Lately he felt like he was stalled out, unable to act because each time he figured out what he needed to do, he found out he needed to do something else first.

She pulled away from him and put a scolding look on her face. "Hogwash, Jack. You know you can do this job just as good as everything else you have done."

"Hogwash? I haven't heard that term since..." He missed Mabel. Times like this when he felt overwhelmed, she was really good at reminding him that he wasn't a quitter.

"Since?"

"Oh, never mind. Who was the old man I put in charge of scavenging for the operation at the Freezer?"

"George?"

"Yeah, he does a lot of trading, doesn't he?"

"Yeah, he's the one who took me out the first few times, showed me where each community sets up trading posts, and even introduced me to some of the men he'd been trading with for years. He knows more about trading with the communities than anyone here."

"Does he know any of the community leaders?"

She shrugged again, looked down at what was left of her cold breakfast and pushed the bowl away with a grimace. "I dunno, Jack. I suppose you could ask him. He's a nice enough guy, always friendly, so he probably does. He sure knows the outside world as good as anyone could. Do you really think my ass still looks good?"

Jack sighed. She was obviously bored or irritated with this conversation.

"You know, if you'd rather talk politics, then why don't you just... go do what you have to do!"

"Sorry, baby, I just can't help but think about this stuff. There's so much to do and what I really want right now is just to crawl into bed and hold you for the rest of the day."

She leaned back into him, one hand on his chest. "So let's go do that. My plans can wait."

He was instantly aroused. His tablet beeped. He glanced at it, noting the time. "Dammit! If I don't get going I'm not going to make it to that meeting on time. I really need to go."

She snuggled in closer, put a pout on her face and said, "Hmmm. Are you sure? You don't have ten or fifteen minutes you could spare?"

This was torture! The tablet beeped again. He sighed and extracted himself from her embrace. If only she had been in this kind of mood twenty minutes ago, but twenty minutes ago she was crying. "I wish, more than you can imagine."

Now it was her turn to sigh. "Okay, but when you get home tonight, I don't care what kind of mood I'm in, you are going to use every bit of romance you can muster to get me in the mood. You hear me?"

He smiled seductively as he stood up then leaned in to kiss her. "You can bet on it, baby, be safe out there today. I gotta run. See you tonight!"

Chapter 7

The last person Caleb expected to show up at his new apartment was Jack. "Hello, Jack, to what do I owe the honor of your visit today?"

"Hello, Caleb, I apologize for not calling ahead, I have a lot on my mind, as you can imagine, and I figured it would be faster just to pop in on you for a few minutes. I hope you have the time." Caleb knew he wasn't really asking. At least he was being polite and somewhat formal. The lack of formality in New Hope was one of its few failings.

"Of course Jack, for you I would always make time. Come in." He led Jack into his living room.

"How's the new apartment working out? Do you miss the old one?" Jack had offered to allow all the former council members to remain in the more luxurious quarters reserved for the leadership, but Caleb had declined.

"It is working out just fine, thank you. My last place was always much more room than I needed. I never did find the time to settle down with a woman, and since I can't have kids there is little reason to occupy such a large apartment."

Jack winced a little at the comment, reminding Caleb of how sensitive the man was about issues like infertility. "Relax, Jack, I have been at ease with my fertility for nearly a century and a half, you certainly don't have to worry about making a faux pas on the subject." If it put the man at ease, Caleb didn't notice. "Can I get you something to drink?"

"No, thank you, this won't take too long." The men sat down. "I feel like I need to clear the air between us before getting into what I came here to discuss."

Shaking his head, Caleb interrupted, "Please, you did what you had to do. Marcus was right all along, even if we didn't see it. The discovery of the Freezer catalyzed a change that the old council could neither avoid nor control. Just shifting the balance of power to someone new wasn't enough; we needed to wipe the slate clean in order to bring about the change in leadership that will be required to take humanity out of the risk of extinction and into a new era."

"Still, perhaps I was a bit hasty in dissolving the council so quickly. I admit, after Theodore's treason I simply didn't know who to trust."

Nodding, Caleb said, "I am glad you acknowledge that your act was perhaps a bit premature, it speaks highly of your character. I have to admit myself that I wasn't sure how I would feel after being displaced so... abruptly. After all, my entire life has been spent doing my job, and at the moment I am jobless. That is quite a transition for one to make, particularly when one has been alive for nearly two centuries." Perhaps there was a little animosity.

"Speaking of that, how have you been handling your transition? When I retired from the Army I thought I would have a hard time myself, but I had the fortune to jump right into a career that was even more engaging than my former one."

"Honestly, Jack, I thought I would be going crazy. The odd thing is, this has been incredibly liberating. As a child I spent all my waking hours either in school or studying. As an adult during the reign of the Enclaves of Science, my job was my life. Even if I had known as a young adult that I was infertile, I wouldn't have pursued a family of my own. My parents had some prominence in Saber Cusp, and I was expected to carry that on. When the cities fell, things didn't get easier. I can imagine you've been a bit overwhelmed in your new job. It took four of us to run New Hope, and much like the EoS, our jobs here consumed our entire lives."

"Four? You mean five, don't you?"

Teague. It took effort to keep from showing his disgust at the idea that Teague was an equal to the rest of the council. It was true the man had quite literally saved their lives, but in the years following, he had shown himself to be incredibly indecisive and unable to make the hard decisions. Caleb had to be careful here, he knew Jack was fond of the man and would be offended if Caleb dismissed him so easily. "True, there were five of us, but Teague was always busy doing what he does best. His job was too important to waste his time dealing with the minutia of leadership."

Jack merely nodded at this. "So you were saying?"

"Yes, I guess what I am getting at is how the majority of my life has been spent working, and that job has always been chosen for me. Being relieved of my responsibilities has opened up new possibilities I never imagined. I could literally do anything with my life and the choice is completely mine. I have never experienced a feeling quite like it."

"I'm truly happy to hear that, I had feared that you wouldn't fare well in the transition. If I might be so bold as to ask what sorts of endeavors you are now pursuing?"

This time he couldn't hide his reaction, which most likely looked like one of embarrassment. The truth is he had not yet settled on anything, and while he had unlimited paths in front of him and no fear about choosing one, he had not yet decided what he wanted to do, "Well, I have some ideas, but I have yet to actually get started with any of them. I was thinking... well... I might... I mean... What I could be doing..."

Jack cut him off there, "Sorry, I wasn't trying to put you on the spot, I was just curious." Caleb, still flustered, waved him off as if to say he hadn't done that, even though that was exactly what he had done. "Look, here's the deal. I find myself in a situation where I need to start trusting someone or I will fail as leader of New Hope. You never gave me reason to distrust you."

Caleb seldom had reason to lie to anyone. He had nothing to hide, especially from the ruling class. "Jack, I don't know how I can assure you, but my loyalty to this community far outweighs any ambitions I have felt in my life. I will always tell you like it is, regardless of whether you want to hear it."

"I believe that, Caleb, or I wouldn't be here."

"When you showed up at my door I was quite sure you were here to ask for advice. Now I am less certain."

Leaning back in his seat as if nervous, Jack took a breath. "Okay, here's the situation. Red and Theodore aren't the only traitors in New Hope. There's at least one more person here who is acting against us, or at the least putting their own personal interests ahead of the community. I could spend the next several weeks, or even months, doing what I can to find who this person is, but frankly I don't have the time. In my haste to start fresh, I eliminated some of my greatest assets, particularly an expert in the field of internal security. Now I find myself wanting someone who can take on that role, and I believe you are the most qualified."

For the second time in this conversation, Caleb was left speechless. His vision of the unlimited paths before him began to dim. "I… Are you asking me to resume my role as councilman?"

"No, actually, I'm asking you to resume your role as head of security, but it won't be quite the job you used to have. Your exclusive authority will end with the ability to enforce the laws. Officially your title will simply be Head of Security.

"You will be one member of several in my 'Executive Advisor Board'. Individually you will each have limited authority, but as a group you will have the power to act on my behalf for most tasks. If for some reason the capacity to do my job as leader is compromised, there will be a succession of leadership, but until that can be defined the EAB will be able to act with complete authority. Furthermore, I'm not asking for a lifetime of service. I'm no king and I am not royalty, and neither are you or any member of the board. At some point, someone else will be elected leader and that person will have to put together their own Executive Advisor Board. In fact, at this time I am only asking for a commitment of one year. After you serve your year, if you decide it isn't for you, you're free to pursue whatever your heart desires."

This was intriguing. He had never considered the idea of a job that had an expiration date, but suddenly those paths before him began to reappear. It would allow him time to consider what he would do with his newfound freedom without the boredom he had been feeling over the past several months. "Well, I am not sure what to say. How soon do you need an answer?"

"Immediately, actually. I realize this is as abrupt as my dissolving of the council, but as you know, I'm a busy man. Among other things, I have to leave to visit with Andrew from Camp Wisner soon, and before I leave I want someone working on things here."

"And if I decline? Who will you choose?"

"Honestly, I'm not completely sure, I have others in mind, but everyone I have chosen is better suited to do other things."

Unsure of what to say, the silence stretched on. Finally Jack made to stand up. "Okay, I accept. I will take the job."

Settling back into the chair, Jack smiled and said, "Excellent, I am very happy to hear that. Now, I'm short on time here but we have a few things to discuss and there will be a few items I want you to take care of while I am gone."

~~~~

With his step just a little lighter, Jack headed to the flight bay. After his pitch to Caleb, he had similar visits with Thomas and Scott, all equally successful. His new Executive Advisor Board was far from complete, but this was a great start.

Thomas was an easy choice for overseeing all patrol and salvaging operations. Before Jack had been brought back, Thomas was Marcus' first attempt to find a suitable successor. However, the way Marcus had put it, the man showed promise right up until he realized his ability to make decisions off the battlefield was somewhat impaired. It seemed that if there wasn't an immediate threat, he overthought things. That didn't mean he wasn't good at what he did, and he had proven his worth to Jack in the months since he led the infiltration into Saber Cusp.

Thomas' official title would be Head of Defense, even though New Hope had no formal military force. The only job he had been assigned so far had been to get with Chuck and continue to investigate who could have left New Hope with Phil's remains.

Scott was not such an easy choice. As an engineer, he was very well suited to be Head of Maintenance, but he was a fairly young Reborn. This morning's realization of how vulnerable this community really was had given him second thoughts. Perhaps someone who was far more familiar with all the critical systems in New Hope would be better suited for this position. Ultimately though, it was Scott's military background that weighed the decision in his favor. Any internal threat to New Hope could in fact devastate the community. Just a few days without a critical system like the food machines or water purifiers would force a major disruption in everyone's lives. If an attack like that were coordinated from the inside with something outside, another community, like Cali, could easily force their surrender. Jack wanted someone who could keep this aspect in mind as well as actually understand the systems. Scott was better suited, so he became the first choice. He eagerly accepted the position.

He didn't get a chance to visit Teague, but he already knew his friend would join. Caleb was instructed to contact him on Jack's behalf. This afternoon the four men would meet to start discussing other items that need addressing. Tonight Jack would have a brief meeting to hear what they had to say. For the next several weeks, there was going to be some late nights spent planning and working out details, but in the long run this would take a massive load off of Jack's shoulders and put into place a government that would be far more effective and structured than anything New Hope had in the past.

He was kicking himself a little. If he'd done this a couple months ago when he should have, he wouldn't be running late right now and he would have had the luxury of spending more time with Wendy this morning. Despite the way he had to rush out of there this morning, the idea of coming home tonight put a smile on his face. That Advisory Board meeting tonight would be very brief indeed.

~~~~

"Are we still on for today?" Anton had already stowed his gear, checked to make sure all his men were ready to go, and even helped Jerry with the pre-flight check.

"Yeah, Jack is just running behind. Again. How are things going on the home front?" Chin was sitting at the now permanent command center in the flight bay. Six large displays were mounted above the desk, all but one was on. Some showed feeds from the aircraft Jerry was preparing, the rest had various feeds of data, including a satellite feed that, at the moment, was dark. He leaned back in the chair, the displays behind him.

"Hell, I can't complain. Christine is preggers again. Kids are doing great, and my son is turning out to be a chip off the old block."

"I assume congratulations are in order?" He was, of course, referring to whether Anton was the father.

"Absolutely, and I owe that to our new leader. Christine had already been talking about getting pregnant with someone else, per the Council's recommendation. Now that Jack has changed the rules, I don't have to worry so much about having to share my wife with other men."

Chin shrugged. "Honestly I've never understood why it bothers you guys so much. It isn't like sex means anything. Asking your wife to only have sex with you is like asking her to only use your bathroom. Why would you make all the effort to hold back your body's natural urge to screw?"

Anton just shook his head. The locals were a strange bunch of people, his wife included. He supposed if he'd been raised to believe sex was as normal as talking about the weather he might feel different. It was one thing when there were only a few people here who could father a child, but that had changed. Soon there would be over a hundred virile men in New Hope, and there was no need to dictate who had to procreate with whom to keep the gene pool clean. "I have a great sex life, Chin. I love my wife and it makes sex much better. Why would I need to have a physical interaction with another woman when I can have both a physical and emotional interaction with Christine? You probably wouldn't understand I guess."

"Hey, I've been in love before, and I know how much better sex is with someone you love. That doesn't mean she's always in the mood when you are though, and face it, when she's pregnant, there are going to be long stretches where you aren't allowed to even touch her. Why force yourself to avoid other women, particularly when she doesn't care one single bit if you partake of some pleasure once in a while?"

Sadly, Chin was right about one thing: none of the locals saw a point to monogamy. Christine would probably be happy if he ended up in the sack with someone else, particularly during times when she wasn't in the mood. "Because it matters to me. I don't want her sleeping with anyone else, and I wouldn't feel right doing what I wouldn't want her to do."

Chin laughed, "HA! See, you didn't say you didn't have a desire to be with other women, just that you don't want to be a hypocrite. You are just holding yourself back because of your own insecurities. Christine loves you, man. There isn't a swinging dick in New Hope that will get her to leave you or feel for anyone but you. That's the real difference between the locals and the Reborn, monogamy means something different to us. Sex means too much to you. It's what's in here that matters." He pounded his chest. "You want to know why I wouldn't want to fall in love with a Reborn woman?"

"No, but I know you're about to enlighten me."

"Because even if she loved me, the first time she felt attraction for another man, she would suppress those feelings. You know what happens when you want something you can't have? You obsess over it. You want it more. The last thing I would want is to be intimate with the woman I love and have her thinking about some other guy. If she feels attraction toward him, let her have her way with him, and she'll quickly forget all about him because of her feelings for me. Of course, the problem there is all you Reborn fall in love with everyone you have sex with."

"Why the hell are we talking about this, Chin?" He was a little irritated with the conversation. He had similar discussions with his wife in the past, and he didn't want to relive them with Chin. Admittedly it was interesting to hear it from a native born man's point of view, but even that was a little awkward. He hadn't engaged in an in depth conversation about sex with another guy since he was a horny teenager. It was time to change the subject.

Chin just laughed, "What else are we going to do? I'm just sitting here waiting for Jack to show up so we can get this show on the road. Besides, you're the one who brought it up."

"The hell I did! You asked about my family and I answered."

"Well, maybe I like making you uncomfortable." He laughed some more.

"You know, you can be a real asshole."

"Yeah, I know." They both laughed. Chin wasn't exactly what Anton would call a close friend, but he still considered him a friend. They had worked together for a few years now, although Chin seldom went out on patrols any more. Ever since the violent fight that left him with the vicious scar across his jaw, he didn't seem to have a problem staying here and keeping an eye on patrols and scavengers.

"You're full of shit too. I was with plenty of the local women before I met Christine, and I don't feel a thing for them."

"Oh yeah? Who?"

"Let's see, there was Annabelle. She was fun. And then there was, um, let's see…" he paused for dramatic effect, "Oh yeah, Cat. Wow that woman is aggressive."

"Aww, you didn't just go there!" Chin spun his chair around as if he had work to do and was done with this conversation. He didn't stop talking though. "That's frickin gross, man, why would you say something like that?"

Laughing hard, Anton replied, "Yeah, that Cat is a real firecracker. Tons of experience. She taught me some things."

"And you are one sick bastard, Tony, you know that? You can't talk about my grandmother that way. Ewww." He visibly shivered. "You better not have messed around with her." He still didn't turn back around, but he was shaking his head.

"What's wrong, Chin, you can dish it out but you can't take it?"

"Oh, I can take it, but that's going too far."

He patted the man on the shoulder, "Come on, Frances, I'm just messing with you." There were two things that Chin had a hard time with: His grandmother, who through the miracle of cloning was nearly twenty years younger than him and practically a sexual predator these days, and being called 'Frances', which his grandmother usually did when there were enough people around.

Chin spun around and stood up, stepping right up to Anton. "It's Frank, dammit!" Anton actually thought for a second he might have gone too far, but after a tense moment, Chin visibly suppressed a smile and sat back down. "Don't make me start telling you stories about Christine."

Anton frowned, but before he could say anything, the rail car pulled up. Jack stepped out and headed toward them. "Sorry I'm late boys, are we ready to go?"

Chin stood up to greet Jack. Anton reflexively stood at attention, not quite as relaxed around their leader as Chin. "Yes, sir! Everyone's saddled up and ready to ride."

"Well what are we all standing around for then?"

Anton turned toward the aircraft, signaling his men to get loaded up. Jack looked at Chin and said, "Wendy get to Idaho okay?"

"Yup, she's been checking in regularly. No worries there, she had to take a medium transport and I've been watching the radar on board. There's no activity anywhere near that area, and there's certainly nothing Bart can't handle."

"Who went with her?"

"Just Robert. The other salvagers are with George up at the Warehouse. None of them are very comfortable around Bart so they all opted out."

"Robert? You mean Bobby Dee?" Bobby Dee was the nickname of one of the Reborn. He had been a career enlisted man in his former life, but fancied himself a disc jockey and rap music artist. From what Anton had heard of his 'mad skills', it was clear why he had never quit his day job.

Chin chuckled, "The one and only. I guess he overheard Wendy talking about heading to an old electronics recycling plant and he wanted to go along, hoping to find some old audio equipment, whatever the hell good that would do."

"Well, at least she'll have Bart with her." Jack patted the man on the shoulder, "Thanks, Chin." He turned and headed toward the waiting aircraft.

Anton followed and as they walked away, Chin said, "Keep your mind on your job you sick bastard." He laughed as he sat back down.

"What was that all about?" Jack asked.

"Oh, we were just yanking each other's chains. He was giving me crap about not sleeping around with the local women so I told him I had been with a few, Cat included."

"Oh, damn! I bet he didn't like that," Jack laughed, "Did you really…?"

"Hell no!" Anton interrupted, "That woman is way too aggressive for me. She tried a few times but I was always preoccupied when she showed up. Frustrated the hell out of her." Both men laughed.

"Listen," Jack said in a more serious tone, "take one more look at the cargo bay, make sure there isn't anything extra hidden in there."

It was a very peculiar request and prompted Anton to question it. "Why would anything extra be stashed there?"

"Just take a look, please. I'm sure there won't be anything out of place, but I have reason to believe there has been in the past."

This was concerning. If someone was taking something out of New Hope that wasn't supposed to come out, it might mean there was another traitor in their midst. "Should I be concerned, sir?"

"Please, Anton, call me Jack. Look, don't worry too much about it; just be on your toes. If you see anything out of the ordinary, let me know, discretely."

"Sir, I mean Jack, if you suspect something might happen on this trip, maybe we should cancel. Or at the least, get you set up with some armor." It was Anton's job to make sure Jack was safe and secure, and if there was a risk here he didn't want to take any chances.

"Honestly, I don't think there's anything to worry about, at least not on this trip. I've got my under suit on, just in case." He lifted his shirt to reveal the bulletproof satin like black material normally worn under combat armor. "I'm certainly not worried about Andrew or anyone from Camp Wisner causing any trouble. At this point I'm more worried about our own men."

"Well, you don't have to worry, Jack, the men I picked are all solid and loyal, I can promise you that much."

"If I doubted that, Anton, I wouldn't have picked you. Let's mount up." Jack started climbing into the back seat of the aircraft.

"Jack." Jack turned back to him. "My friends call me Tony." Jack smiled, nodded, and climbed in. Anton took a few minutes to look over the cargo hold before climbing in himself. Nothing looked out of the ordinary, but until they got back home he would be on alert, watching for anything unusual.

Chapter 8

The information Bart had intercepted panned out. They were in salvage heaven. The best part about this place was it was relatively intact. Most of the massive concrete building was still standing and it had protected the contents inside from the elements. Man-made objects could survive longer than expected, as long as they were kept out of the sun and out of the rain. The other factor in survivability was keeping the critters out. Animals were extremely adept at turning just about anything into a home, which usually destroyed the object beyond value in the process.

This old recycling facility appeared to have been a working business right up until the war reached this part of the country. Out back there was a massive pile of steel scrap, covered in rust and dirt. Wendy knew from experience that there would only be a couple feet of rust and dirt protecting the metal underneath from the elements. If New Hope could get their new excavator out here with a small crew, they could uncover hundreds of tons of steel that could be turned into building materials for their new home.

The steel by itself was invaluable, but that wasn't even the tip of the iceberg. Dozens of bins were scattered throughout the yard, each full of aluminum or copper. If Cali wasn't already rich with minerals that yielded copper, steel, and aluminum, they would have cleaned this yard out the day they found it. Another great score for New Hope, as long as they can get it all without Cali finding out.

Inside the building was a gold mine of electronics. Massive bins filled with circuit boards, hard disk drives, metal electronics cases, glass, and copper wire waiting to be stripped of its insulator. In an adjoining warehouse, thousands of used computers and other electronics waited to be stripped down for recycling.

Oddly, the place had not been picked over very much. There were obvious signs of recent activity here, but Cali must have just discovered this place or it would be picked pretty clean by now. So far, Wendy had found several electric motors that looked ready to run, a few hundred pounds of copper wire, and six small bins filled with hard disk drives.

Old hard drives are a great find for salvagers. New Hope has two technicians who are wizards at extracting data from old disk drives, even after several hundred years. Usually the data is junk, but every so often some really good information is found. Many computers from just before the war were used to access the internet, and aside from pornography, the most popular internet sites were news and 'wiki' sites, filled with information that could be used to piece together a more accurate history. All that information got cached on these drives and if they could pull it off, they could add it to their already extensive database of information.

Bobby dug through the computers in the warehouse, not being very careful, as if it really mattered much. He pushed several machines out of the way to see if anything he was after was buried under them. Some of the stacks were well over fifteen feet tall. "Bobby, be careful, those are stacked like a game of Jenga, if you move the wrong one you're going to knock something loose and end up with a concussion." She shook her head. At least he was enthusiastic. All the way here he'd been going on about finding some old tube amplifiers or mixing boards. The last thing anyone in New Hope needed was Bobby Dee trying to start a rave. *Who has time for a rave after an apocalypse?* She let him dig though; there was no harm in it, as long as he didn't hurt himself.

"Don't worry, sugar, Bobby Dee's in the house, and nothin's gonna stop him from finding what he's after."

Who referred to themselves in the third person? "Well, then knock yourself out, just not literally."

Dragging one of the crates of wire toward the door, she heard a crash and a shout. *Shit, that didn't take long.* Turning back to see if he was hurt and needed help, a roar and a screech sent a chill up her spine. She had never heard that sound before but there was no question it meant extreme danger. Grabbing her side arm, she rushed back into the second warehouse.

On his back, scrambling backward like a crab, Bobby was frantically trying to get away from the nightmare that had made this pile of electronics its den. If it weren't for the fierce looking creature less than thirty feet from him and poised to attack, she might have found his action amusing.

Unlike the beasts they encountered at the Warehouse, she was familiar with this one, if only from stories. The salvagers called them Hellcats. Ten to twelve feet long, they looked like a mountain lion with no hair and scaly leather-like skin. Reportedly they had razor sharp claws over eight inches long, and some even claimed their saliva contained a paralyzing poison, although nobody could confirm it. Only a few have been seen and none had ever been taken down. Wendy instinctively knew the only way to survive was to get out of there as fast as they could.

She took aim and fired rapidly. At just under forty yards, few of her shots missed their mark, but if the bullets penetrated the cat's thick leather skin, it sure didn't seem to notice. Her intent was to drive the creature back just long enough to allow Bobby to get to his feet and get out of the warehouse. Unfortunately, all she managed to do was shift the cat's attention from Bobby to her. Cursing, she ejected the spent magazine and drove home a new one, then fired off three quick shots before turning to run.

The cat flinched as one round grazed its face, opening a gash under its left eye. With a terrifying cry, the massive cat sprung toward her, easily covering over thirty feet in one stride. Fear propelled Wendy toward the entrance to the warehouse, pushing her body harder than it was ever meant to be pushed.

Not three strides later, the doorway darkened. With no ability or intention to stop, she reacted by diving low, instinctively curling into a ball to protect her baby. Bart charged through the opening and hurdled over her as she slid past. She hit the wall next to the door before coming to a stop.

Ignoring the pain, she looked up at Bart's hulking form standing defiantly between her and the charging Hellcat. He roared in challenge, but the cat didn't so much as hesitate. Taking one last stride, it leapt to attack. Bart dove into the air to intercept.

The two titans met in midair and came crashing down on a pile of old computers. Stunned by the display of raw animal power, Wendy watched helplessly. Bart caught the massive cat around the neck, swinging his body around to try to gain the feline's back and avoid the giant claws that would most likely shred even a Mute's tough skin. The cat shrieked and thrashed, muscles rippling across its long sleek body as it tried to bring its ferocious weapons to bear. A sharp crack elicited a howl of agony as the cat's tail lashed Bart's back like a whip. Apparently the cat's claws and teeth weren't its only weapons. The giant man released one of his arms and reared back for a mighty blow. The hammer of a fist drove into the cat's head, eliciting a scream that almost sounded human. However, loosening his grip came with a price. The cat managed to twist around, getting one massive hind leg between them. Bart merely grunted as the claws raked his thigh. Blood splattered across the floor in front of Wendy.

The two forms parted as the cat broke free. Bart rolled to his feet in a graceful move that seemed to defy physics. The cat leapt away, tumbled once, and shakily regained its feet before turning back toward the giant Mute. Obviously injured, it emitted a low growl and slowly backed away.

A deafening roar erupted to the right of the animal. From behind a pile of electronics, Wendy saw a six foot blue flame reaching toward the giant cat. It took just under two seconds for Bobby to empty the two hundred round magazine of his M74 assault rifle into the flank of the Hellcat. The animal went down, thrashing in its death throes.

Wendy jumped to her feet and ran toward Bart, who had sunk to one knee. "Are you okay?"

Breathing hard from the exertion of the fight, he held up a hand and waved her off. "I'm fine, Little Red, I just need to catch my breath." She immediately saw the two foot gash running across his back. The beast's tail had been like a razor, splitting his shirt open and digging deep into his flesh. Blood pooled under him, running off his leg like a river.

"Lie down on your stomach and let me patch this up before you bleed to death." He didn't hesitate, looking increasingly weary.

She grabbed her pack and threw it open, contents spilling out on the floor. It took her a moment to locate the first aid kit. She wasn't sure any of this would work with his biology, but if she didn't do something, he would surely bleed out. First, she applied most of the tube of coagulant to Bart's shredded thigh. She winced as she did this, even though he didn't. The gashes were at least an inch deep, enough to cause a regular man to bleed out in minutes. The tree trunk sized thighs made even the canyon sized gashes look fairly minor. The amount of blood pouring from them, however, didn't look minor at all. Once the coagulant was in, she cringed as she dug in and smeared it around. This did make the giant squirm a little, but he still didn't utter a sound.

By the time she started applying the medicine that would accelerate the healing the bleeding had slowed to a trickle. This was a relief as it was a good sign the medicine would also work. Once that was applied, she wrapped the leg with a bandage. Then she turned her attention to the gash in his back. There wasn't enough bandage to cover a wound this long, so after applying the coagulant and medicine, she grabbed the bottle of super glue and started gluing the gash closed.

"There we go, how are you doing?"

"It stings a little and I feel a little tired but I'll be fine. Where's your funny little friend?"

She glanced around but didn't see him. "Bobby! Where are you, are you okay?"

She heard a muffled, "Help! I'm buried!"

She got to her feet and moved toward the pile she had seen the gunfire erupt from. Keeping her eyes on the Hellcat's body, she skirted the pile of electronics. It was clear the animal was very dead. Bobby's aim had started low; the first few rounds appeared to have glanced off the beast's strong hide. As the gun climbed, the flechettes in the bullets had started penetrating, and once that happened, the rounds exploding inside the cat's torso had devastated its internal organs. If that weren't enough, onslaught had continued until it had ripped the spine apart, the two ends were now clearly sticking out from the open crevasse on the side of the massive creature. "Over here!"

Wendy pulled her eyes away from the dead cat and looked to her right. All she could see was a pair of legs sticking out of a pile of old electronics. She cursed and began systematically moving the various bits of technology, being careful not to cause another avalanche. Once uncovered enough, she quickly checked him for injuries. His armor, particularly the helmet, had protected him from the falling debris. "How the hell did you end up under this pile?"

He looked around at the pile of junk he'd been half buried under, as if he wasn't sure. "I pulled the trigger all the way."

She almost laughed. "Yeah, you sure did."

"I didn't expect it to kick so hard! I guess I stumbled backwards into this pile and next thing I knew everything went dark. Did I hit that... thing?"

"Oh, you hit it all right. You practically cut it in two!"

Still clearly dazed, she began to worry about a concussion. When he barked, "HA!" she jumped.

"What!?" she nearly yelled, concerned something was really wrong.

He pushed a few more computers out of the way and sat up. Reaching over, he reverently extracted a black metal box from the pile. "Holy shit, it's a Marantz!"

Shaking her head and rolling her eyes, all she could say was, "Oh, Jesus."

A dangerous sounding growl echoed from deeper in the warehouse. Perhaps the Hellcat was protecting a family. It seemed she'd found the reason this place was left practically untouched. It was time to leave.

~~~~

The trip took around two hours. Jack would have been content to use the time to think about his new Executive Advisor Board, but Anton, sitting next to him, asked, "So, what sorts of things do you talk about in these meetings?"

Jack studied the man, wondering if he could possibly be involved in the theft of the head. He decided he trusted the man. "Trading, mostly, but I'm hoping to start working out a new alliance in this meeting."

"Is there an old alliance?"

"Not really. But there were talks a while back, before any of us were Reborn. I want to finish what was started."

"Sounds reasonable. But why did the old talks stop?"

"We discovered the Freezer."

"Did they find out about it and get mad at us or something?"

"No, actually we just didn't want them to find out."

Anton nodded. "Sure, but how would they find out if all we were doing is talking?"

"The whole reason for the talk of alliance had to do with figuring out a better way to keep the population from becoming too inbred. See, no single community has enough virile men to keep growing the population. The common practice was to share the men. Bring a man who isn't related to anyone in your community in to get a few women pregnant. That way the next generation has more combinations of people who can get together who aren't siblings or cousins. It was done as a trade, usually a man for a man, and after the contract was completed the men went back home."

"Oh, so if they did a trade, the guy visiting might catch wind of what was going on in Montana?"

"Exactly. Plus with all this new DNA, New Hope didn't really need to trade men any more. There was no gain for us and the risks were too high. So we stopped trading."

"And then there goes the trust, right?"

"You got it. So the talks got suspended. It's a shame too, the way I understand it they were right on the verge of making a deal that would bring several smaller communities under one roof. New Hope was the best choice – we had the room and it was a safe and secure place to live."

"So what happened after we stopped trading?"

"Well, we still needed the resources we could trade for, especially with Cali, who wasn't a part of the planned merger. So we started trading fertilized eggs for resources."

"Seems like that would work just as good as sending a man to get some of their women pregnant."

"Not exactly. See, the natives are all carriers of the virus that causes infertility. The Reborn aren't, we were conceived from uninfected fathers and hence never became carriers ourselves. We were immunized before the virus ever infected us. Our children, as long as they are immunized before birth, are the same. A native born father who is virile still passes the virus to the child. Whatever gene he possesses that prevented his own infertility will get passed to about one in twenty of his children. The rest will be unable to father children. Since the other communities don't know about the reborn, they will always assume a fertilized egg only has about a fifty percent chance of being male, and a five percent chance of being a virile male."

"But a fertilized egg we send them would produce a fertile male every time right?"

"Well, half the time. It could still turn into a female."

"So when we trade a virile man, he has sex with more women and makes more babies, whereas one egg is like having sex with one woman, getting her pregnant, and leaving."

"Exactly. A trade would usually last several months. The man would impregnate several women, and a few weeks into pregnancy they could determine if the child was going to be virile or not."

"And if not?" Anton asked as if he didn't want the answer.

Grimly, Jack replied, "They would terminate the pregnancy and start over."

"Holy shit. You know, I never asked about this stuff. I just figured the few men New Hope who could father children before we came along had only been allowed to get so many women pregnant, not that they aborted most of the babies he made. Why not just have them?"

"Well, it didn't make any sense to have a ton of people who couldn't reproduce. Resources are already scarce, and a man who can't father children is just a mouth to feed, protect, and house. At least that's the way they look at it. It makes sense I guess."

"I suppose it does. Still, I just can't imagine living in a world like that. I have a hard enough time figuring out the women here as it is."

"Well, you're living in it now. Hopefully we can change things. That's what I'm trying to do with meetings like this one today."

"So, are you still talking about forming one large community?"

"Well, they probably think that's where this is headed, but the game has changed. We now have the variety of DNA available to fix this inbreeding problem and allow every community to expand at a more natural rate."

Anton looked confused. "Does this mean we're going to start spreading the reborn among different communities?"

"Not exactly. The reborn are valuable. New Hope is going to grow fast in the coming years and we will need to be able to leverage this wealth for the resources we will need to expand our community."

"So you *are* talking about trades then."

"Not yet. This is a delicate time. Nobody outside of New Hope knows exactly what we found in Montana. If we let on that we have what could effectively solve the biggest problem every community has had for the last hundred and fifty years, we would be putting ourselves at great risk. They might take it upon themselves to try to seize what we have. The last thing we need is a power struggle right now. Power struggles lead to war. I'm trying to prevent that from happening while still allowing what we have to springboard the human race out of extinction."

"Wow, I didn't realize these meetings were so important."

"Neither do the other communities, but they'll soon find out. Before that happens, I want to have something in place to control the situation."

"And what would control this? Once they know what we have they are going to want it, and I can see how this could become very dangerous. We don't exactly have an army to help defend New Hope."

"My idea is to form a central government, a council that will keep each community working together and not against each other. Each community would have equal representation in this council, so nobody would have reason to wage war with anyone else to take what they have."

Anton didn't say anything for a while, seeming to take in just how important this could be. If Jack could pull this off, it would be as historically important as the formation of the United States over five centuries ago.

Finally, he said, "What if they don't want a central government telling them what to do?"

"Well, hopefully they will see how this can help them. The last thing I want to do is let them die off, and frankly without the resources we have, there's a very good chance of that. I suppose we could go another couple decades and when they see our population explode, they wouldn't have much choice but to join. Of course, at that point, existing members of the new government will be hesitant to allow communities who don't have much to offer our new nation an equal representation. My job will not just be to figure out how to form this new government, but to convince everyone it will be in their best interests without outright telling them we have thousands of virile men available."

"Holy shit."

"What?"

"I just realized how complicated your job is, Jack. I wouldn't want to be in your shoes."

Jack laughed, "Yeah, I wasn't exactly aware of what I was getting into myself."

~~~~

Per Anton's request, Jerry circled the clearing twice, scanning for heat signatures that would reveal dangers. Seeing nothing out of the ordinary, he gently put the aircraft down at the edge of the clearing. The man was getting better and fewer people joked with him about nearly landing in a tree once.

Jack examined the area as they came down. To one side of the clearing was another flyer, nearly identical to the one they flew. Each community had at least one aircraft, and all aircraft came from the same production lines in the old EoS cities. Like most items left over from that time, they were incredibly valuable as new production was impossible, at least in the foreseeable future. It would be a long time before mankind had the resources to start building technology like this again.

Andrew, dressed similar to Jack in what passed for formal attire these days, sat idly on a folding chair near the center of the clearing. Two of his men were leaning against the aircraft a few dozen feet away, appearing to be telling jokes to each other. The pilot of the craft was in the cockpit, and he looked asleep. Jack cursed himself for being late. It was bad form, even if it was somewhat unavoidable.

Before the propellers had begun to slow, Jack threw the door open and hopped out, garnering a curse from Anton who likewise jumped out his own door. Jack didn't wait for his entourage to follow as he quickly made his way toward the center of the clearing.

"My sincere apologies, Andrew, I hope you haven't been here long."

"It is quite all right, Jack. The weather today is beautiful, and I would be lying if I said I was not enjoying a little time sitting here alone in such a beautiful place with no interruptions." The man wasn't kidding. The clearing was located not too far from where Grand Junction, Colorado had once been, right in the heart of the Rocky Mountains. It was late Summer and even up at this elevation it was around eighty degrees outside. A cool breeze tickled them just enough to keep the air fresh with the scent of the surrounding pine tree.

"Mind if I pull up a chair and enjoy it with you for a bit?" He glanced at Anton who immediately turned back toward the flyer to grab a chair.

"Not in the least."

"So how are things in Camp Wisner?"

"Oh, we can't complain. Our harvests should be good this year and we haven't had a single attack from Mutes since last winter."

"Is that usually a problem?"

Andrew considered that for a moment before answering, "Sometimes. There has only been one group that was big enough to persist in trying to take us down. It was about fifty years back. They laid siege to our community for three weeks before we were able to kill them off. We lost four men and one woman in that fight, and one of those men was a seeder."

"Seeder? As in he wasn't sterile?"

Andrew smiled, "What do you call your seeders?"

"Virile, I suppose. I've also heard the term breeder."

"You are a strange man, Jack. Much different than any other man I have met. Where did they find you?"

"Montana." It wasn't a lie.

The answer seemed to satisfy Andrew, at least for the time being. "Well, where I'm from, we call them seeders. Men who can't father a child are called 'empties.'"

"So, if it isn't too forward to ask, how many seeders do you have left?"

The look he got from Andrew told him the question was indeed a little too forward. "Not enough. Of course, if we had enough, we wouldn't be talking about joining together with other communities. We have some resources though, good farmland that yields food, soy, and livestock. And we have a quarry and can provide limestone or gravel. Problem is we have tapped out the gene pool from the other small communities. All except for Cali. Heard they lost some flyers a while back and haven't been talking with anyone much lately. Can't say I miss dealing with those sonsabitches, but it poses a bit of a problem for us."

For the same reasons Jack wasn't ready to share the details of what was found in Montana, he also wasn't planning to share what really happened with Cali.

"Is that what you would like to talk about? Another trade?"

Until now, Andrew had been fairly casual in his conversation and was leaning back in his seat, seeming to care more about the sunshine than the conversation. He sat up now, signifying it was time to talk business. "Certainly. However, what I really want to do is discuss how you are able to bring us fertilized eggs that never yield empties."

The rumor, which Jack had reinforced over the past several weeks, was that New Hope had figured out how to fertilize an egg and then determine at that point whether the child born from that egg would be missing the genes necessary to procreate.

"What if I told you I would share all our secrets, just as soon as we can form an alliance."

"I would say I was expecting this conversation sooner or later. It is true my community is struggling, although if we can make it past the next two decades we might have enough Seeders to keep going, provided we get a few more fertilized eggs from New Hope. However, there are a lot of rumors regarding your community over the past several years, and I am hesitant to join any community that has been so secretive. I knew Marcus well back before the cities fell. We shared the same viewpoints concerning the direction humanity was heading, even before the churches declared war on each other. With him out of the picture, I don't feel like I have enough reassurance right now to place the fate of my community in New Hope's hands, even if they have made key strides in screening for infertility."

"I understand your hesitation, but I'm not asking you to join my community. Quite the contrary. In fact what I'm proposing would be forming a separate government made up of representatives from each of the communities who join. Together we can set laws that every man would be required to follow, while still allowing each community to govern itself as it sees fit. Any community pledging allegiance to this government would be able to share in the wealth and knowledge of all the communities under its rule, including our secrets regarding sterility."

Andrew opened his mouth then closed it. At a loss for words, it was several moments before he finally said, "So you're telling me you only want to form a union of independent communities, not push us into joining New Hope under *your* rule?" His tone was somewhat accusing, and this confused Jack.

"I'm not sure where you got the idea that I want to rule over anyone other than my own community. I believe we all follow roughly the same ideals and my goal is to make sure we are coming together as a nation with those ideals."

Andrew's eyes narrowed. "Say I believe you, what makes you think joining together as a nation will help me and the other communities overcome our population problems?"

"I can assure you that once we have come together under one set of ideals, and I'm satisfied we are all working toward the same goal, we will flourish as a nation, faster than you can possibly imagine."

If Andrew appeared confused before, he was positively stunned now. "Are you saying you have some kind of cure?"

Jack was preparing to answer when the man's attention seemed to shift to the tree line behind Jack. Then he turned to his men and started signaling in a manner that suggested urgency. Jack's internal alarms went off, signifying something wasn't right here. He glanced at Anton, seeing the man was already on alert, scanning their surroundings and ready for whatever was about to happen. Turning back to Andrew he said, "What's wrong, Andrew?"

Andrew turned back to him, a look of confusion and frustration on his face. "I didn't know, dammit!" He turned back toward his men, now frantically making gestures. Jack had no idea what the gestures and signals meant, but he wasn't about to wait to find out.

He managed to ask, "What the Hell is that supposed to mean?" before all hell broke loose.

In all directions, men burst forth from behind trees, all fully armed and armored. Anton's men had already approached Jack's position and now they sprang into action, forming a tight circle with Jack in the middle. Jack pulled the sidearm from Anton's holster as he stood up then assumed a defensive crouch and took aim at one of men closing in on them. "Stand down or we will open fire!" Anton shouted. The men didn't slow down.

Jack shouted, "What the hell are you doing, Andrew! There's no need for this, tell your men to stand down!"

Glancing toward the aircraft on the opposite side, he spotted Andrew's two guards. They weren't facing Jack and his men, however. In fact they appeared to be pointing their weapons at the men closing in on them. Andrew was running toward them, still gesturing.

Anton shouted again for the men to stand down. "Take one more step and we *will* open fire!" Glancing over his shoulder, Jack counted twenty men plus Andrew's two guards. They numbered five if you counted Jack, who was horribly unprepared for a fight like this. "We're sitting ducks here!" Anton obviously saw this but there was no direction to run. Suddenly their flyer came to life, the electric motors screaming as they were fed full throttle. It would take a few moments for the aircraft to gain the thrust it would need to take off, but the action kicked up a lot of dust and pine needles and gave them an opportunity to run. They only needed a direction to go.

Anton started toward the tree line, Jack and the rest of the men following as if sharing one mind. There was no way they could get into the flyer before being cut to pieces or overwhelmed, but making a break for the trees meant they might be able to punch a hole through the circle of men closing in on them and gain some form of cover so they could defend themselves. If they could reach cover and the aircraft got off the ground to provide protection, they had a chance to survive this ambush.

It might have worked too, if not for several concussion grenades exploding all around them. Anton and his men were equipped with special ear plugs that allowed them to hear perfectly but not suffer damage from small arms fire. They weren't nearly enough to stop the concussive effects of the grenades, however. Jack had no protection at all and was hit with the full effect. His world erupted in pain from every sense and he didn't even feel his stunned body slam into the ground.

Chaos. All he could hear was silence; all he could see was nothingness. Jack was a veteran of combat though, and despite the loss of his senses, he wasn't about to give up.

Hands grasped his arms, pulling him up. He fought it off, feeling fists connect with armored plates. An elbow hit something soft and the grip on his right arm loosened.

The silence erupted into loud ringing; muffled shouts distant in the background. Shapes coalesced all around him, unidentifiable. He used whoever had a hold of him on the left to leverage his body closer to vertical, managing to get one leg under his body. Springing up while pivoting toward his left, he slammed his body into the second person, completely shaking the one he had connected with moments ago. The shouting got louder and he swung blindly at whoever was trying to restrain him. The punch, if it could be called that, missed, only catching enough of a helmet to break at least one finger.

He got his second leg under him. With only one assailant holding him and his vision clear enough to see his outline through the haze, he attacked, driving his full weight into the man. His elbow leading the blow, he connected solidly with the helmet, rattling the man enough that his grip loosened. He pivoted and brought a knee up, catching the man in the hip and sending him off balance. He was free and did his best to take in the chaos around him without pausing. The flyer was to his right, closer than the tree line. It seemed his best hope for cover, so he turned toward it and put all his strength into closing the distance.

The ground rushed up and hit him hard enough to break a rib. Someone had caught his feet just as he went to sprint and took him down hard. As he turned over to fight the new assailant off, two more men moved in from the sides and got hold of his arms. This fight was over.

Anton and his men were struggling, but even if they could break free of their captors, three more men were standing there waiting to put a bullet in them. The men holding Jack lifted him off the ground. Someone kicked the backs of his legs, bringing him to his knees. His shoulders popped painfully as the men roughly pulled his arms behind his back and restrained him at the wrist with some sort of hand cuff. Breathing was difficult with his obviously broken ribs and he was starting to see stars. Adrenaline was probably the only thing keeping him conscious.

"I suppose you are wondering what is going on?"

Jack turned toward the voice, but couldn't locate who was talking. "I have a pretty good idea, and I'm telling you now you're making a huge mistake."

The man laughed. "Jack, you have no idea what kind of world this is, but trust me, you will learn. Load them up!"

The two men hauled him to his feet and directed him toward his own flyer. This is when he saw Jerry's body on the ground next to the aircraft, most of his head gone. Without thinking about consequences, he lashed out at the men, driving his shoulder into the one on the right and then kicking out at the one on the left. A shot rang out and pain exploded in his left leg. Fueled by rage and adrenaline, he brushed off the pain and sprinted toward the trees. Another shot, this time the pain exploded on his already broken and bruised right side. He stumbled and went down. Before he could get back on his feet, the two men caught up and began to pummel him into submission. It was nearly impossible to defend himself from the onslaught with his hands tied behind his back, and pain exploded with each blow.

"Enough!" The words rang out and the men instantly stopped. Struggling to stay conscious, Jack felt the men haul him to his knees again. He didn't have the energy to stand. The same voice that stopped the assault said, "Time to teach him a lesson." His world went black.

Part 2

Chapter 9

Matthew yawned, rubbing his eyes in an attempt to focus on the small screen in his hand. Counting food stores and supplies was almost as exciting as watching your hair grow. He entered the last counts and sent the results to the main computer. Without checking the final analysis, he knew levels were approaching critical. After a lifetime of inventories, you got a pretty good feel for how much was enough.

Flipping the light switch off as he left the store room, he buzzed Tobias. It took a moment, but finally the old farmer answered, "Yeah?"

"Hey, Tobe, I just finished the inventory."

"And?" The old man was never much for words.

"Well, I haven't looked at the final results yet, but I think it's as you suspected. If you want, I can call you back in a few minutes when I get to my office to give you the exact figures. It doesn't look pretty though."

A short pause, then, "I want to know exactly where we stand." He clicked off without another word, none was necessary.

The elevator reached level fourteen and he stepped off into an empty hallway. Rounding the corner at the end of the hall, he collided with Angela, sending whatever was in her arms flying in all directions. "Oh jeez, I'm sorry." He bent down and picked up her things. "I didn't think anyone was working today, so I wasn't... well, you know." He held the items out and she took them with both hands, lightly brushing his as he let go.

Smiling, she said, "No problem Matthew, I wasn't paying attention either. Speaking of work, what are you doing down here on the day of rest?"

He liked Angela. A lot. The idea of being dishonest with her knotted his stomach, but sometimes leaders had to keep things from the people in order to keep the peace. If word got out the Head of Supplies was doing inventory on Restday, people would wonder why. That could lead to problems. "Oh, just going over my speech for next week. You?"

She shrugged, "I was bored, not much going on this Restday, so I thought I'd come down and clean my office."

For the millionth time in his life, he saw an opening to ask her on a date. They grew up together, studied together during learning, and socialized with the same people, but she had never so much as hinted at taking their friendship to the next level. As a teenager he lacked the courage to try. Before he found his courage, she started working on his level, and dating someone from your level was usually avoided. As department head, it was actually illegal. He always had to be careful with his feelings; he didn't want to send the wrong message. "I can't imagine someone like you would be bored on your day off. I thought you were into the Net?"

The Net was one of the few sources of entertainment in the city. A virtual world where only your imagination limited what you could accomplish. It was an escape, really, a place where you could pretend you were outside, with a sun and a sky and birds chirping in the trees. Your avatar, the representation of your body, could become anything you wished – a bird, a shark, a horse, or something fantastical like an angel or a dragon. Within the Net was a series of games and adventures you could dive into, wasting away all the hours of your life if given the chance. It was more popular with the kids, who tended to have more time to get involved than the adults, but well over half the population of Sanct was involved at some level.

"I felt like I was spending too much of my free time hooked up, so I quit. Now I find myself with nothing much to do." She somehow managed to look distracted and embarrassed at the same time.

"You know, if you found yourself a boyfriend, you might have something to do with your time off. Someone as beautiful as you shouldn't be working on Restday." The words just fell out of his mouth unchecked. He immediately cursed himself.

"Is that an offer, Matthew?" As lifelong friends there wasn't much she could say that would tie up his tongue, but that certainly did it.

"Um..." This got awkward in a hurry. He frantically thought of a way to extract himself from this situation without making it worse. Unfortunately, she seemed to be enjoying the awkwardness and continued to look at him mischievously. He needed to shut this down without hurting her feelings. He decided to take the honest approach. "If we didn't work on the same level, I would have asked you on a date a long time ago, Angela."

He wasn't sure what reaction he expected, maybe a smile or some embarrassment, but he certainly didn't expect to see her get angry. "Did Carter put you up to this? This sounds like something you two would pull. You really shouldn't mess with a woman's head like this, Matt!" She turned and stomped off toward the elevator.

Stunned by her outburst, he watched her walk away, nearly reaching the elevator before he came to his senses. "Wait! Angela! I'm sorry!" He ran toward her, not sure what to say. "I was just being honest." He just kept talking, hoping it would get her to stop. "Why would Carter have me tell you how I feel?"

She turned back to him unexpectedly, nearly causing another collision. Sobbing, she said, "Matt, I wasn't spending my Restday cleaning my office. I was trying to decide what to do with my life. I feel like I don't have any sense of direction, like my whole life is scripted for me. I'm almost thirty years old and I haven't even found someone to spend my life with!" He hadn't seen her cry since they were fifteen, and he felt bad that he was the instigator. "Here I am, trying to decide if I should change careers, probably the biggest decision of my life, and on a day when nobody should be around, you show up out of the darkness and tell me you would have asked me out if we didn't work together? If this is a joke…"

"No! I wouldn't joke about something like this. I didn't know you were going through such a difficulty in your life." He realized how close he was to her and took a breath to steady his nerves. "Look, I meant what I said, but by no means was I trying to influence you in any way! I... I don't want to give you the impression I'm not interested, even though a man in my position can hardly start dating someone on his own level." It sounded so analytical, so cold, but that was probably why he headed up the Supplies division. His personality was well suited to counting beans.

She stopped sobbing and he reached up and wiped a tear from her cheek. "Are you really planning to change careers? What would you go into?" It was an attempt to change the subject. Her tears made him uncomfortable.

She composed herself and looked him in the eye. "Systems. I'm thinking about moving to systems and Carter said he'd put me in a decent position. I wouldn't lose too much status." Carter was a bit immature, but when it came to working the computer networks, the man was a wizard. Although he was a few years younger than Matt and Angela, they grew up on the same level and were all close. His job creating new games for the Net meant he didn't have as much time to hang out any more. Apparently he had enough time to talk with Angela, however.

"Well, he certainly has the pull to arrange something like that. If he keeps working hard he'll make Head of Systems in a couple years. It would be quite an accomplishment to reach that position at his age, particularly in a field as popular as Systems." Every kid in Sanct had dreams of coding their own games on the Net, and the competition to just get onto that level was fierce.

"Not as young as you were when you became the Head of Supplies."

He blushed. "True, but nobody aspires to work on this level. If I'd realized you were so miserable in your current position, I could have –"

She threw her arms around his neck and kissed him on the lips. He was so startled he just stood there for a moment, not knowing how to react. Just as she started to pull away, he wrapped his arms around her and returned the kiss.

His phone beeped, breaking the moment. She pulled away. In a daze, he just stood there blinking. "You better get that and I better get going. I'll go see Carter. I think Systems might be the place for me."

He just nodded as she stepped onto the elevator. Just before the doors closed, she said, "You know, if I change to Systems you can ask me out..."

The doors closed and the spell was broken. Whatever had just happened still hadn't sunk in. He grabbed the phone, "Yeah."

"Are you gonna keep me waiting all day Matthew?" Tobias.

He turned toward the office and said, "Uh... Yeah, sorry Tobe, I got distracted with something. Give me five minutes."

~~~~

Matthew manipulated the spreadsheet with the mouse as he spoke into the speakerphone, "Consumption was down three percent in the last year, but production is down six percent. This wouldn't be so bad except we've been on this trend for eight years running. We're nearly out of reserves and the production is barely meeting the demand. Another year of this and we'll be in the red."

It was worse than he feared. For over three hundred years his predecessors had maintained a nearly perfect positive growth rate where food was concerned. Now it was going to hell on his watch.

"I'm not telling you anything new, Matthew." The voice coming out of the speaker was filled with static, but it had been that way his whole life, so he didn't even notice. "Maybe we've used the soil too many times. Maybe something in our water changed. I don't know. Something just isn't right, and our crops seem to lose a little more vitality each year. The oxygen and carbon dioxide levels are right, the nutrients in the soil are right, the sun lamps seem to be working perfectly, and yet the plants just don't thrive like they once did. Like everything else in this city, the dirt seems to be worn out."

"Come on, Tobe, it isn't like we can go topside and get some more. Even if it were safe up there, which it probably isn't, you have no idea what kind of bacteria and parasites are in that soil. One scoop of foreign dirt could spoil the whole crop and kill us all in a matter of months." He shivered at the thought. "Maybe it's the water? We don't know the real source of the water, maybe something changed that we haven't noticed."

"Bah, I've been looking at our water for seven years, and nothing looks any different than it did before."

"We need to find a solution."

There was nothing but silence on the other end. Both of them knew there was no answer, and both knew the consequences. The only real question now was whether to admit it to the population openly, or deal with it covertly. Seven years ago when the trend was first spotted, they decided to keep it from the population and convinced the medical division to help.

Medical controlled the rate at which the population expands and contracts. Once two people have dated for a long enough period, they are evaluated by the psychological department of the medical division. If deemed suited to raise children, the medical division would give them the go ahead to conceive one child. Every year the number of couples suited to raise a family changes, so some couples are allowed a second or third child, and others are only allowed one or none at all. Birth control was not left to the individual, but rather controlled by Medical. Very seldom was there an unplanned pregnancy in Sanct.

The adjustment in birth rate wasn't very big, only a small percentage to reflect the downward trend in production, and the general population was unaware. Not everyone's job was critical to the continued operation of the city, and over the many years jobs have evolved to fit the population. Everyone over the age of fourteen worked in some capacity, five days on, then Restday. The small changes in jobs went pretty much unnoticed.

All it would take now was another call to Alden, the head of Medical. His figures showed that a cut in birth rate of five percent and a drop in distribution of a quarter percent every forty days for the next year would stabilize things within a half dozen years. Changes that small wouldn't be noticed, and if the production rate didn't fall further, distribution could return to one hundred percent and birth rates could be stabilized. It was a big 'if', however. To date production was down almost twenty percent.

"You're the boss, Matthew, it's your decision." The line went dead.

He sat there for almost an hour, running the numbers through his head and verifying them on the computer. His encounter with Angela not forgotten but safely filed away for future analysis.

He punched a button on the phone. It rang twice. "What is it Matthew, you're supposed to be at home, hence the term 'Restday'."

"Dad, we need to put a meeting together." His tone left no room for wordplay.

"Give me an hour. We'll meet here at my house."

~~~~

Matthew put his thumb to the pad and the door opened. Only two apartments opened without announcement, his own and this one – his parent's. The apartment would be described by most as extravagant. The elder division leader was entitled to the best and biggest. In Sanct, extravagant meant a living room with seating for six, a kitchen two people could work in at the same time, a formal dining room which doubled as a meeting room for official business, three bedrooms, two bathrooms, and an office. In total it approached a thousand square feet, nearly triple the size of a standard family apartment.

As a head of a division, Matthew's own apartment was nearly five hundred square feet. It was a luxurious way to live, particularly as a single man.

His mother greeted him at the door. "Matthew! It's nice to see you, even if it is under pretenses."

"Hello mom. Good to see you too. Are they all here?"

She gave him a shameful look. "I haven't seen you in almost a month and you don't even have the decency to ask how I've been? I thought I raised you better than this, Matthew Miller."

He'd intended to save the small talk for afterward when he could focus on something other than the business at hand, but understood why his mother was upset. He should visit more often. "Sorry mom, I just have a lot on my mind. We can spend a little time after the meeting to catch up."

"Of course, I took the liberty of cooking dinner. I hope you can stay, I'd hate for it to go to waste."

He snorted at the irony, nodded, and made his way to the dining room.

His father was seated at the head of the table already, and all but one division head – his own – was present. He did a quick exercise to prevent any mistakes when greeting everyone. Going from the head of the table in a clockwise motion, he mentally named off each person.

His father, Jonathon Miller, was the head of the Laws and Justice Division and Elder Division Head. Next was the Head of Systems, Monty Phillips. Alden Karls was the Head of Medical. The next seat was empty, reserved for himself, Head of Supplies, followed by Margaret Johnson, Head of Education. To her left was Vernon Daniels, Head of Housing and Maintenance, and finally James Gilmore, Head of Security.

He greeted everyone appropriately and took his seat.

In the center of the table was a recording device and Monty reached over and pressed a button, signifying the official start of the meeting.

Jonathan stood up to announce the meeting. "Thank you all for attending, Matthew called this meeting, so without any preamble I will turn it over to him."

He stood as his father took his seat and began, "Thank you everyone for interrupting your Restday to meet. I apologize for any inconvenience it has caused.

"At the urging of our lead farm technician, I took the day to inventory our stores and analyze the usage."

His father broke in and said, "Isn't that what you enjoy doing on your Restdays anyway?" Chuckles all around, including his own. He knew the ribbing was just to loosen up the meeting a little and went with it, not bothering to defend himself. His life wasn't *that* boring. *Was it?*

"Unfortunately, the results are disturbing, and I can no longer decide the proper course of action without consulting everyone first."

The division heads all squirmed in their chairs. None of them knew what to expect in this impromptu meeting, but now it was clear the news would not be good.

"For the past eight years there has been a downward trend in crop production. Overall, production is down twenty percent over where it had been eight years ago, and this year saw the largest drop yet, six percent."

The mood in the room darkened and the tension grew. "How is it we're just hearing about this? I recall you reported crop production down, but you never told us it was this critical!" That came from James, Head of Security. Once he spoke, everyone started mumbling amongst themselves.

Jonathon rapped his fist on the table causing glasses of water to jump, and the room went silent.

"Seven years ago, when the trend just started coming to my attention, I searched the records for previous trends like this to see how the heads had handled it then. It turns out there have been many times in the past where adjustments needed to be made to fix a downward trend in production. To correct for this, Medical was called on to lower the birth rate for a short period of time, shrinking the population just enough to keep production in the positive. Adjustments like this take time, obviously, as babies don't eat as much as a teenager. Because of this, we produce an excess of food.

"The results of the changes we made back then are starting to be noticed in the consumption rates, but it isn't enough, and stores are down to the point where we only have about a year before we'll start running into a shortage, if the current rates remain the same."

"Is this legal? Can Medical adjust the birth rates without consulting all of us or at least the Elder first?" The question was posed by Margaret and directed at Jonathan.

Before the Elder could answer, Matthew said, "I researched it, and it is well within his rights to do so, as long as the rate change is no greater than five percent in any given year, or fifteen percent over a period of five years." Alden confirmed this with a nod.

Jonathan shrugged, "I've never run into this, to be honest, but I will take their word for it. Nobody knows better whether it is the right decision than Supply and Medical." That settled the matter and nobody questioned it again.

"So where does this leave us?" This was Margaret again.

"Well, here's the deal. If the decline in production stops where it's at, we can make another adjustment to birth rates and subtly ration the distribution of food over the next year. This will stabilize things enough to where we will be at a neutral production level again. However, this will leave us with no margin of error and if production drops any further, we'll be forced to actively ration food until a solution can be found."

The news was grim. Everyone in this room knew the consequences of openly rationing food, nobody more than James. "Anything we can do to avoid that must be done. Crime rates would climb dramatically as soon as any rationing went into effect."

Alden said, "The only thing I can think of here would be to make a dramatic drop in birth rates. Anything drastic would be noticed, however. We might even need to put a temporary hold on births altogether."

"That would be just as bad as rationing, Al." This came from James again.

"Wait a minute, what measures have you been taking to reverse this trend? I mean, there has to be a reason, right?" Monty was a computer guy, someone who thought in terms of logic. There was always a solution in his mind.

Matthew had expected this from him, and was prepared. He repeated everything that Tobias had said to him earlier. "Basically, everything we know about crop production says we should be doing fine. The best guess he has is that we need fresh dirt. There has to be something going on at a level we have never looked at to cause this sort of problem, and whatever is missing will probably never be found again. That is, unless we can compare it to soil that is still growing crops at a proper rate."

It took a moment for this to sink in. Jonathon was the first to speak. "I think what my son is saying is the only solution is to go outside and get some dirt."

The room erupted. Everyone was expressing their opinion at once and Jonathon was pounding on the table trying to call order to the meeting. A glass finally fell over and shattered, bits of glass and water going everywhere. The room went silent once again. Jonathon stood up, his face red over the disarray.

"I didn't say we were going to do it! It's an option on the table, and I think one that needs some careful attention. Matthew, how long before we *need* to make a decision?"

"If we wait more than a month, we will need to start adjusting the numbers I quoted. The requirements will climb exponentially the longer we wait, so it would be in our best interest to make a decision soon."

Jonathon mulled it over and finally said, "Alden, lower the birth rates five percent. That will buy us the time we need. The rest of you gather your thoughts and data and we will have a formal meeting on this in one weeks' time. Prepare well, we will not leave the meeting without a resolution."

Chapter 10

Wendy dropped the last crate in the cargo bay. Bart snored softly next to the cargo. The big man couldn't fit in the passenger seats, so he had to ride in back anyway. It was good he was resting, if the medicine did what it was supposed to do, he would be up and around in no time. She was still rattled from the encounter with the Hellcat. There was little doubt she would have walked away if it hadn't been for her giant friend. Even if she had a few regular soldiers with her, the chances of them taking that beast down before it killed someone would have been slim.

Bobby came up behind her and asked, "Got everything?"

"Yeah, let's just throw some straps on so none of this falls on Bart while we're in the air." Bobby got to work on that without another word. In fact, aside from expressing his happiness at finding what he said was one of the best amplifiers ever made, he hadn't said much of anything else.

Her PDP beeped and she looked at it. Chin was calling. It was getting close to her check in time, so she figured he was just getting antsy. She punched the button and said, "Hey, Chin, what's up?"

"Wendy, we have a… Holy shit! Is that blood?"

She put her hand to her face and felt something dry and rough on one cheek. Pressing a button on her PDP mirrored the camera output on the screen and she held it up to examine her face. Across her right cheek was a streak of dried blood. *I must have wiped my face after tending to Bart's leg*, she thought. She wiped it away with her sleeve and pressed the button to get Chin back on her PDP. "Yes, but it isn't mine, it's Bart's. We had a run in with a Hellcat. Bart tackled it and took some blows before fending it off. He's all patched up but he won't be running around for a couple days."

"A Hellcat? Like, a full size Hellcat? And you all survived?" He looked skeptical. "You sure it wasn't just a big mountain lion?"

Wendy sighed and punched a couple more buttons on the PDP, sharing the pictures she snapped of the fallen beast. "Yes, I'm sure." She punched the button again and his face reappeared. "Jesus, Chin, are you okay? You look like you're going to be sick."

"Uh, yeah, just… I ran into one of those beasts before, and I know just how deadly they are. Look, I'm sorry to have to tell you this, especially after you just went through an encounter like that, but we have a problem here."

Another spike of adrenaline caused her heart to pound. "What's wrong? It's not Jack is it?" she asked quickly.

He nodded grimly, "I lost communication with his team about fifteen minutes ago. It's odd, one minute everything was fine and the next I just had nothing. No visual, no radar, no link to the flyer. Could just be a glitch, but so far I have no idea."

Shit, this doesn't sound good. A feeling of dread swept through her already exhausted body. Her heart beat harder and she found it difficult to say, "Um, okay." She took another breath, "Did you, um, did you get a rescue crew out?"

"Yeah, they just dusted off. As soon as I lost contact I scrambled the team. Chuck is leading the crew. You were my next call."

"What can I do to help, Chin?"

"Nothing. Everything we can do is being done. Maybe you should get back here and have Teague check out the baby, you look a bit pale. There's nothing we can do other than wait anyway. Anton and his crew are the best we have, and Jack has proven he can take care of himself as well. I'm sure it's just a glitch and everything will be fine."

"I've got to take Bart home and make sure he's okay first. I think I would feel if anything was wrong with the baby, and I feel fine. Did you try to make contact with Camp Wisner? See if they know anything?"

"I sent them a message, but I haven't heard back from them yet."

She sighed, "Damn. Okay, thanks Chin, let me know the moment you hear something. Don't wait even a second. I want to be the first to know he's safe."

"Of course, Wendy. How much longer are you going to be?"

"I'll let you know when we get to Bart's place." She punched the button on her portable data pad and stood there for a moment, fighting off the urge to break down and cry.

Bart put a hand on her shoulder and said, "Don't worry, Little Red, Your man is smart and tough. Whatever happened he will be okay."

She jumped at the touch and his voice, not expecting him to be awake. Placing her hand on his she said, "Thanks. What the hell are you doing up? You need to get some rest and let that medicine do its thing. I want you thinking and feeling fresh when we get to your place. Let's see if your radios picked up any chatter about what might be going on with Jack."

The big man climbed into the cargo hold and hit the button to close the ramp. "Don't worry, Wendy, I feel fine, just get us back to my place. If there are answers there, we will find them.

~~~~

Caleb sat in the old council chambers feeling at once both at home and out of place. Around the table sat three others: Teague, Scott, and Thomas. "Teague, Jack sends his apologies for not personally asking you to be a member of this counc... uh... advisory board. Before we get started I want to get a formal acceptance from you for taking on the role of Head of Medical."

"Certainly. I am honored to take on this role."

"He left me with some instructions to carry out. The first was to make it clear that we are all equals. Individually we will each have the authority within our own departments to do as we see fit, and as a whole we act as the voice of leadership only when Jack is indisposed." Caleb wasn't sure this was a good idea, but it was no longer his show to run. Jack was elected leader, and he would respect that to the fullest extent.

"So this is sort of like a presidential cabinet?" Scott asked.

Caleb nodded, "From what I have read of U.S. History, yes, it will be much like a cabinet. In the coming weeks Jack intends to flesh this board out with a few more members and write up some official laws regarding our power of authority. He will also set up a succession of leadership, just in case something happens to him."

Thomas said, "So who here is going to lead the meeting? Should we have official minutes and all that stuff?"

"I suppose that is up to us to decide. When the council ruled, we simply recorded the sessions and executed any decisions made. I took the liberty of starting the recording once we were all assembled."

"Okay," Scott said, "so what now?"

"Well, we need to start hammering out some details. As you all know, I have been assigned Head of Security. That means anything having to do with the security and general peacekeeping inside this facility will be under my authority. Thomas, as Head of Defense, you will be in charge of everything outside of New Hope regarding the defense of our community and anyone venturing outside of the facility. Scott, you are Head of Systems and as such you will be in charge of anything having to do with maintaining this facility. We will be working closely when it comes down to protecting the more critical systems here, something Jack was particularly concerned about. I will be putting together something of a police force and perhaps we can work out a way to guard those things that are more important? We can go over more of that later. Teague, you are Head of Medical, which puts you in charge of everything from making sure our people are healthy to deciding who to bring back from the Freezer. If any of us have specific human resource needs, bring those to Teague, he will decide if he can accommodate you from the selection of people he can bring back.

"Are there any questions regarding your roles or your authority within those roles?"

Thomas asked, "What about community relations? Is Jack planning to handle that himself or is that something I will have to deal with."

It was a good question, and another one Jack had asked Caleb to discuss at this first meeting. "We will eventually add someone to this board to be in charge of that, but in the mean time you will have that responsibility. This might be a difficult position to fill because Theodore was the only one of the council to really have any kind of relationship with any other community leaders. We have to assume he will not be of much help in training someone new, so this will be new territory for whoever picks up the job. Jack was thinking George, our oldest and most experienced salvager, might be a good choice for the job. He has had more contact with communities outside of New Hope than anyone other than Theodore. If someone has a better suggestion, now would be the time to discuss it."

The room went silent while everyone pondered this. Teague spoke up first. "I am not sure anyone is more qualified, although frankly speaking I am not sure George is really suited for politics. I have had some discussions with Jack lately and while I don't want to speak ahead of him on this, his plans are to form a central government in which each community would have an equal representation. I imagine whoever we elect to take the community relations job will have to be capable of working with that government. Perhaps our best choice would be to look for someone with political experience from the Freezer. I recall there is at least one General we could bring back."

The idea impressed Caleb. He hadn't thought about this as an alternative and it showed a side of Teague he had never seen. Perhaps if he had shown this kind of critical thinking during all those years on the council he would have been regarded as more than Marcus' puppet. "Excellent idea. It would take some time of course, not just to bring him back but to get him up to speed on the politics. Thomas, what do you think? You would be the one having to deal with this in the meantime."

"I think it is as good of an idea as any. If Jack intends to put together a government reminiscent of the Federal government, there is little question a General would be equipped to handle that kind of politics. I would want to take a close look at his record first, and also look at other candidates of lower rank. There were a lot of really good officers in the Army who didn't move up because they pissed off the wrong person. Maybe we have a few of them in our coffers."

"Okay, anything else to add, Scott?"

Scott chuckled, "Nope, this stuff is way beyond my expertise. Give me something to fix or build and I'm on it, but this sort of problem solving isn't exactly in my wheelhouse."

"Alright then, I think it's settled. All in favor of picking the next Head of Community Relations from the pool of..." he didn't know the right word for the dead who had not yet been brought back.

"Corpsicles?" Scott volunteered. The men laughed.

Teague volunteered, "How about we just call them 'Unborn'?"

Nods all around. "Perfect. All in favor of picking the next Head of Community Relations from the pool of Unborn?"

All of them raised their hand and said, "Aye."

"Thank you, gentlemen, we have our first decision as the Executive Advisory Board." They mockingly patted each other on the back. It was a minor decision, but it was a good one. Perhaps Jack had the right idea here. Only time will tell.

"Okay, the next order of business primarily concerns me, but I believe each of you will have a role in helping to resolve this issue." The mood grew somber again after the brief celebration.

He continued, "Jack has informed me we have a problem with security. One of the... uh... Unborn, has disappeared from the coolers. Teague has evidence that it had been there, so it is unlikely it was a simple mistake during the transportation. The guards posted on that room all claim it couldn't have happened on their watch, and so far there is nothing suggesting when it could have occurred. We have been unable to find evidence of the remains being stored in New Hope. While it's possible whoever stole it is just letting it rot, I find it unlikely anyone would go through the trouble to steal it if they didn't understand its value. Most likely, it has already been smuggled out of New Hope."

The weight of this settled in on all the men. Thomas spoke first, "Any chance Theodore or Red could still be directing someone from jail?"

"As far as I can tell, no. I spoke with Tiny earlier and he insists that only a few people interact with the prisoners, and those are all men he believes are completely loyal to Jack. His policy is to not even allow them to speak with the prisoners."

"But that doesn't mean they won't know what's going on. Perhaps we need to interrogate them?"

"Good idea. What else?"

Now Scott spoke up, "Can't we just look at the footage from all the cameras and find who took the head?"

"So far none of the video I have reviewed has shown much, but I have not had much time to review the recordings. There is nearly four months of footage to look through. Since nobody even knows when this happened I am not even sure where to start."

"Can't Marcus work some of his computer magic and narrow it down for us?"

"Probably, but Marcus is… indisposed for the next several weeks. The only person here with even a fraction of Marcus' expertise with our computer system would be Theodore." Caleb wasn't going to bring it up, but he knew the man fairly well and it might actually be worth a shot talking to him. If he isn't behind this, he will want to know who is just as much as they do. Nobody here saw him as anything more than a treasonous criminal, however, so it was best to just keep his opinions to himself at this point.

Thomas said, "Indisposed? Where the hell is… Oh, never mind."

Even Caleb didn't know where Marcus had run off to, although he envied the man for finding a new path so quickly. "You sound is if you know where he is?"

"No. I mean, yeah, I think I do, but I can't talk about it. Even with you guys. It doesn't concern New Hope anyway, and I can tell you this much: If he is where I think he is, he's completely unavailable to us until he decides to come back."

Caleb made a note to talk to Thomas in private. Or perhaps talking to Jack would be better. He was curious where the former leader of the council had headed off to so quickly after giving up his authority.

Scott spoke up again, "It won't help find whoever's behind this, but I think it would be prudent to install a monitoring system to get in and out of the cold rooms. Maybe some kind of keypad entry? It would add another level of monitoring and who knows, if we don't catch this guy now, perhaps we will catch him if he goes back for more."

Teague said, "I think that is a great idea, just make sure it is an independent system and not tied in to our network. If whoever this is was good enough to cover it up, they will be good enough to bypass any surveillance."

The room fell silent again as each man pondered his responsibilities in the coming days and months. Finally Caleb spoke up again, "Jack talked to Chuck about this already, and Chuck was supposed to work on a list of names of potential people who could have smuggled something out of New Hope. What do you gentlemen say we call Chuck down here to talk about his findings?"

The men all nodded in agreement. Caleb pressed some buttons on the controls built into the table in front of them. Chuck's voice reverberated through the room, "Yeah."

Caleb looked toward Thomas. Technically Chuck was his man now. Thomas got the hint and said, "Chuck, this is Thomas."

"Hey, Thomas, any word there?"

"Excuse me? Word of what?"

"Oh, you aren't in the flight bay?"

"No, what's going on?"

"We lost communication with Jack's aircraft and we're on our way to investigate. I was hoping you were calling in to tell me you re-established communications and everything was okay."

"Uh, no, this is the first I heard. How long ago was this?"

"Oh, about an hour or so. I'm about forty five minutes to the clearing where he was supposed to meet Andrew from Camp Wisner."

"Roger that. Let me know what's going on as soon as you get there."

"Uh, how about you just go see Chin, he's running this show on your end."

"Will do, Chuck, thanks."

The room was silent. Thomas finally said, "Well, shit, I guess we better head to the flight bay and figure out what the hell is going on."

Caleb was concerned. Something didn't feel right about this, the timing was too critical. "Before we leave, I want to say something." The men all gave him their attention. "While we are legitimately in authority until Jack returns, we are the only ones he has told about this. Things could get ugly if we try to assume authority up there. Let's just go find out what is going on and try to help where we can." The men all nodded and filed out of the room.

~~~~

Wendy restlessly struggled to keep her attention on flying. The one hour flight to Bart's home was brutal. Bobby sat in the back and slept, leaving her without anyone to talk to. She checked in with Chin every five minutes, but each interval felt like an hour. She kicked herself for not insisting she be the pilot on his visit today. If she'd been with Jack, Bart wouldn't be injured and she would know what's going on.

Her landing wasn't smooth. She just wanted to get on the ground and see if Bart's equipment had picked up anything useful. As she rounded the back side of the aircraft, Bart stood there rubbing his head. "I thought you were a better pilot than that, Little Red."

"Shit! Sorry. Come on, let's get inside and see if there's been any chatter in the past hour. I was also thinking maybe we should try to raise Camp Wisner and see if they know what's going on."

"Didn't Chin say he already tried?"

"Yeah, but I'm guessing you have a better way to get their attention."

The big man smiled. "Yeah, but I'm not sure I should be letting them know how easy it is to break into their comm systems. Perhaps we should just listen in and see if there's anything going back and forth from their leader's aircraft to their home base."

They headed toward the house. The hair on the back of her neck stood up and adrenaline coursed into her veins. Something felt wrong and she froze, eyes scanning the area in front of her. The movement was barely perceptible but months of exploring dangerous areas had sharpened her awareness. She spotted the predator and breathed a heavy sigh of relief. Silver, Bart's new pet, had been honing his stalking skills lately, and seemed to enjoy practicing on Wendy. The wolf, or whatever species it was, was just a pup, barely three months old but still nearly as large as a full grown regular wolf. She relaxed, but not too much. Despite Bart's domestication of the baby beast, it was still a savage animal to her. "I just don't understand why you kept him."

"Silver? I don't know, we just seemed to bond. I did kill his parents, so maybe I just felt responsible. He's going to make a fine hunting companion one day. He's already better at tracking prey than I am."

After their encounter at the Warehouse, Bart had discovered the pup, newly born, alone in a little cave not far from the building. It seemed the cave had been home to the beasts and their attack was likely a response to Wendy and Bart's presence. She didn't feel bad, those were some vicious predators and if they hadn't killed them they would likely have been Silver's first meal. "And if he turns out to be too wild when he grows older? Are you going to be able to put him down?"

Bart nodded solemnly. "Yes, Little Red, I might have too much compassion for a Mute, but it doesn't make me weak. If I end up needing to put Silver down, I'll do so knowing he would have been dead if not for me taking him home that day."

"Come on, you know I didn't mean it that way, Bart. This is an animal that could rip your throat out while you sleep. I just want to make sure you don't forget that. And for the record, I think your compassion is what makes you stronger than your old clanmates." As if the pup knew they were talking about it, he gave up playing the stalking game and started playfully hopping around the two as they headed toward the house.

Bart kneeled down with a groan and Silver ran to him, licking his face. Then the animal sniffed Bart's leg and froze. His hackles went up and he looked around for danger. "Relax, Silver, it's just a scratch and the danger's gone." Bart's reassuring demeanor relaxed the pup again and he licked his face once more.

When Bart stood, the young beast ran over to Wendy, sniffing her left hand. Finding it empty, he bounded away. "Why does he always sniff my hand? Every time I come over that's how I get greeted."

"You fed him a snack once."

"Yeah, but that was when you first brought him home. I haven't fed him one time since then."

"He's an incredibly intelligent animal. He's been easy to train and in the forest his instincts are always dead on, even at this young of an age." He whistled; something Wendy had never heard him do. Silver came bounding back and sat obediently at his side.

"You've done a good job training him." She bit her tongue before saying more. He'd been without a family or friends for years, and Wendy was his only real friend. She spent a lot of her free time with him but she still lived in New Hope and that meant Bart spent far more time alone than with her. She couldn't fault him for wanting a companion and it was time she just accepted that his pet was going to fill that void. That thought made her pause. Aside from Jack and Bart, Wendy didn't feel like she had any friends or family either. People in New Hope were nice to her, but that had more to do with Jack than with her. In fact, she felt like an outsider in her own community, probably similar to how Bart felt about his own clan. Her bond with him was special, and perhaps the introduction of this animal was bothering her because she didn't want anyone or anything drawing attention away from that friendship. Suddenly she felt very selfish. Reluctantly, she patted the beast on the head and went inside without another word.

The main room of the small house looked something like an old military communication center. There were screens everywhere, boxes with lights and dials on them, a modified computer keyboard with giant keys to fit Bart's massive hands, and wires running to and fro. He sat down and started tapping away gently on the keyboard. Screens came to life with information Wendy could never have deciphered. "Well, there isn't much going on that I captured, let's see if any of it has to do with Jack." He tapped some more and then reached over and adjusted a dial. The speakers came to life.

"Base, this is Randall, we reached the clearing and there's no sign of New Hope yet. We will circle around and let you know if we spot any potential threats before landing."

"Thanks, Randall." The second voice was female.

"Base, Randall here, no sign of trouble. We landed and Andrew is out there getting some sun. I don't blame him. I'll check in in another hour."

"Sounds good, don't fall asleep again, you know how much that bothers Andrew."

"Yes, dear."

Bart turned the dial again and said, "That's it, I didn't pick anything up after that transmission."

"Shit. And it's been well over an hour, right?"

"Closer to two."

"So why isn't there another radio call after an hour?"

Bart seemed to ponder that for a moment before answering, "Good question. You'd think they'd have at least checked in, wouldn't you."

"Bart, do you think maybe something is just interfering with all the radios? If we didn't even pick up their attempts to reach their own people, maybe this is all a big communications problem."

Bart started typing away on his keyboard. "Well, let's see. I can reach the satellite just fine. But that's a laser link, not radio, and both New Hope and Camp Wisner should have been in range of the radios so there was no need for them to switch to satellite." He typed some more. "Hmm, there does seem to be some interference, listen to this."

He hit some buttons and the speakers came to life again, "Hey Briget, what do you say we take a break and fool around for a few minutes?"

"Sure, Hank, just let me... my... and we can meet..."

"What was that? You... little."

"I said... that... on the..."

Bart hit another key and said, "That's where it ends. That was picked up from somewhere near Deering, quite a ways away from where Jack was meeting Andrew but the line of sight between Deering and here is not far from their location. My equipment shows the signal dropped off rapidly and then nothing. That happened a little over an hour ago."

Wendy felt a trickle of relief. "So we probably can't get in touch with them because something's interfering with the communications. That probably means everything is okay. Now we just have to wait for Chuck to get there, if Jack is even still there. They might have finished up and when they figured out their radios weren't working, headed home."

Bart was typing away again. "Maybe, but I'm not so sure. It looks like whatever was causing interference is gone now. At first glance, the data suggests it ended about a half hour ago, although I can't be sure until I dig into this a little more."

"Would the interference cause any problems with communication between here and New Hope?"

Shaking his head, he said, "No, I don't think so, it looks like it was just affecting the area around where Jack was. I pick up all kinds of miscellaneous radio noise from all directions, and there is a blind spot centered pretty close to where he was last heard from."

"Okay, well, keep listening. I'm going to go call in and see if Chin has anything new."

~~~~

Chin sat restlessly at the command center. He hadn't felt this kind of anxiety since the events surrounding the Freezer. It made him question whether he should be here or out there with Chuck. He wasn't well suited to sitting here waiting.

Then again, the thought of Wendy facing a Hellcat reminded him why he was here and not out there. Ever since his last violent encounter with the horrors outside of New Hope, he had no desire to leave, even for a short time. He didn't feel like a coward – if he had to go out to protect his home he would do so without hesitation. Given the choice to go out or to stay here and direct those who went out, he'd pick staying home every time. Days like this, however, made that choice questionable.

The speaker beeped at him, and the screen showed it was Wendy calling in again. He punched the button. "Hey, Wendy, nothing new here, you get to Bart's place okay?"

"Damn. Yeah we're all here safe and sound. Listen, we checked Bart's surveillance network and found something interesting. It looks like just about the time you lost contact, there was some kind of interference centered fairly close to Jack's location. It's gone now, but whatever it was blocked all radio signals for a couple hundred miles all around western Colorado. Have you tried to contact Camp Wisner again?"

This was very interesting and it made sense. It would certainly explain how all communications had ended so abruptly when everything else seemed fine. "No, but I'll try again now. I'll call you back if I get anything. Chuck is almost there too, so we should know something soon."

"Okay, let me know." He ended the call with Wendy and started dialing in the ancient short wave radio to the frequency Camp Wisner listened on. The radio was tied into the computer, so he could send messages from his keyboard and they could be received on the other end even if nobody was actively watching. If Wendy was right, the message he sent earlier might not even have reached them. He typed in a message:

This is New Hope. We lost communication with our men while meeting with Andrew. Do you have any idea what happened?

He sat back, not expecting a response anytime soon. Almost immediately, the speaker beeped and a response came up on the screen.

New Hope, this is Camp Wisner. We also lost communication with our team. We just regained contact with them. They have told us all is OK, your men headed out when they discovered communications were dead. I imagine you should be hearing from them any time.

Relief washed through him. He sent back a quick 'thanks' and started trying to raise the flyer again.

The rail car pulled up and Chin turned to see who it was. So far nobody else knew what was going on. There wasn't anyone to alert other than Wendy. He was surprised to see Caleb, Thomas, Teague, and Scott get off the car.

"Hello, gentlemen, what brings you down here this fine afternoon?"

Caleb answered first, "We heard there was a problem and came down here to see what was going on."

Chin looked at each of the men, wondering why they had such an interest. "How did you find out?"

"We called Chuck and he told us what had happened. Is there any change? Have you heard from Jack?"

"No, but I just learned that there was some kind of interference that recently ended. Camp Wisner got confirmation that Jack and the rest of the team headed home when they lost communications. I was just trying to raise him again." He turned back to the controls and resent the handshakes that should reconnect him to the flyer's systems. Nothing.

He pressed some buttons and Chuck came on the speakers, "Yeah."

"Chuck, this is Chin, I just heard from Camp Wisner, they said Jack and the men were headed back this way, but I still can't reach him. Any signs on your radar? If he headed back this way you should've gone right past him a while ago."

"Nothing on this end. We're just about there, I'll report what I find when I get there."

He clicked off. "Shit! Where the hell are they?"

"Any chance whatever caused the interference burned out their radio?" Thomas asked.

Chin looked at him, annoyed. "Doubtful, those radios are pretty well shielded. Look guys, if you want to stay and watch, that's fine, but please just have a seat and let me work on this. The last thing I need is someone standing over my shoulder second guessing what I'm doing."

Caleb leaned toward Thomas and whispered something. Thomas nodded and Caleb headed back to the rail car without a word. The rest of the men pulled up chairs and took a seat. Chin just shrugged and turned back to the controls to call Wendy and let her know what Camp Wisner had to say.

Chapter 11

Caleb walked into Tiny's office. The big man boomed, "To what do I owe the honor, sir?"

Caleb smiled and said, "Please, Ezekial, you don't have to call me sir. Mind if I have a seat?"

"Not at all, and likewise, call me Tiny; when I hear someone say 'Ezekial', I feel like I'm in some kind of trouble."

Chuckling, Caleb sat and said, "Thanks, Tiny. Jack brought me up to speed on your new project. If it means anything, I think he made the right choices, not just in you to start a program to rehabilitate these young men, but also in choosing to give them another chance to prove they can not only be loyal, but worthwhile to our community."

Tiny nodded, "Well, thank you, I suppose. Is that why you came down here?"

"No, actually, I wanted to speak to you about something rather delicate. First off, I don't suppose Jack told you about the new advisory board?"

"Not that I recall."

"Well, just before leaving this morning, he asked me to be Head of Security. I accepted. Thomas, Teague, and Scott were also given positions."

"Congratulations. What does this have to do with me?"

"Basically it means you will be working under my authority now, at least in your capacity as jailor. We will have to work out who will benefit more from your retraining program before we make any decisions there. I do intend to build a police force, and I think you would be the perfect man to train them."

Tentatively, Tiny said, "My understanding with Jack was I would get full control over how I handle the program. Are you saying that will change?"

"No, not at all. Even if we decide your program falls under security and not defense, I will make sure you can run it exactly how you see fit."

"Great, so did you just come here to tell me things won't change?"

Caleb chuckled again, "No, actually I wanted to have a word with Theodore. Some things are going on within New Hope and I think he can shed some light."

Tiny leaned back in the chair, looking rather suspicious. "Jack was pretty clear on the point of nobody seeing Theodore. I don't want to come off sounding like I don't trust you, but I think I'd rather hear an approval from Jack before I start taking orders from you."

Caleb grimaced. He was afraid of this. "I can appreciate that completely, and under normal circumstances I would agree. However, it seems something has gone wrong and we lost communication with Jack. Chuck is already on his way to investigate and Chin is doing what he can to regain communications, but I believe Theodore might have some insight into what is happening. I hoped you would be reasonable under the circumstances."

Tiny looked concerned. He grabbed his datapad and tapped it a few times. "Tiny, I'm a bit busy here, what's up?"

"Hey, Chin, sorry to bug you, I just heard something was going on. Is there anything you need from me?"

"Not at the moment. If anything comes up, I'll call you."

"Okay, buddy, I'll be here." He clicked off. "He doesn't sound too concerned, but if there's something more going on with Jack, I want to make sure we're covering all our bases. How about we go talk with him together." The big man started to get up.

Caleb stayed seated. "Well, see, this is why it is delicate. Frankly, I do not believe he will open up to me if you are in the room. No offense, but I do not think he likes you very much. I have no problem with you listening in. I just feel it would be better if I spoke with him alone."

Tiny hesitated. He studied Caleb for a moment before finally saying, "I feel like I'm going out on a limb here. Fine. I have a screen right here and I'll watch the conversation. Just be advised, Caleb, if I see something I don't like, I'm simply going to leave the door locked until Jack gets back, is that clear?"

"Of course. I actually appreciate your loyalty to Jack and to New Hope. I think you would make a great security officer here." It might sound like he was buttering up the big man, but he was just being honest. Hopefully Jack would be back soon and could confirm his authority and allow him to start really getting down to the bottom of things. If something bad happened to Jack, this could get really ugly, really fast.

Tiny led him to the jail cell, which was really just a secure holding room. As the door closed, the lock clicked behind him. The room was not very large, maybe eight feet wide and ten long. One side of the room held a bunk, bolted directly to the wall, covered in what looked like a very thin and very uncomfortable mattress. Opposite the bunk, an uncomfortable looking couch occupied the majority of the wall. A toilet and a small sink completed the room's furnishings, residing on the wall opposite the door. Theodore sat on his bunk, staring at Caleb with a look of utter curiosity his face. The man looked haggard and tired, but otherwise in good health. He took a seat on the small couch. It was less comfortable than it appeared.

"Hello Caleb, did the council decide you committed some crime against the community too?"

"Stow it, Theodore, we both know exactly why you are here, so save the games for someone else. Personally I am sick inside for what you did, but I also know you well enough to understand why you did it. You have spent the past two centuries trying so hard to be better than Marcus, and it finally got the best of you."

Theodore scoffed as if Caleb didn't know what he was talking about. "I was trying my best to secure the future of this community. The reborn have been a threat in more ways than one and you all are too blind to see it. The very ideals that destroyed this world to begin with are the ideals they want us to follow. The last thing I want is for humanity to come back from the brink of extinction only to end up back at war, and this time because of some misguided notions of freedom."

Caleb knew there was no way to avoid this discussion, but in a way he welcomed it. Many years ago Marcus figured out the human brain was never equipped to handle hundreds of years of memories. Sooner or later one recurring idea or thought would turn into an obsession and overwhelm all other reasoning. Marcus saw this happen to Caleb and helped him get through it. It was obvious Theodore was going through something similar and it was Caleb's turn to try to help. He needed to manipulate Theodore into seeing for himself that his actions were the result of an obsession. His first step was to dispel the notions Theodore used to justify his actions. "This has nothing to do with how the reborn will change our world. We already failed, and when we got one last chance to bring humanity back from the brink of extinction, you tried to leverage it for some status with people who should no longer matter to you! You lost sight of all the reasons we built New Hope."

"Maybe I finally saw the direction Marcus had taken this place and decided I did not like it."

"You had just as loud of a voice in the council as any of us, including Marcus. I don't recall you ever standing up and making an argument for the general direction the community was headed. As a matter of fact, when we discovered the value of the facility in Montana, you got awfully quiet in the council. I just figured at first you were upset that your negotiations with the other communities would have to be put on hold. Now, looking back, I realize it was because the moment you saw that wealth you started thinking like you were back in Saber Cusp, trying to figure out a way to leverage our newfound wealth for more personal position."

Again, Theodore scoffed, "You have no idea what was going on back then. Once Marcus saw the wealth there, nothing I said or did was going to matter anymore. If you recall, I voiced my concern with the attention that wealth would bring us, and how it could end up being the death of this entire community! When you all ignored my concerns, I took matters into my own hands, and believe it or not, my actions are the reason this community is still standing!"

It was Caleb's turn to scoff. "How exactly do you think selling us out to Joshua saved us? If your plans had succeeded, you would now be in Cali, a mere pawn on his council, and we would be under their rule! You cannot see how your blind struggle for power nearly cost us everything we spent a hundred and fifty years building! All you had to do was work with us and not against us and you would not be in this cell."

This time Theodore sneered when he said, "I did not sell us out. There is far more going on than you can possibly understand. You have spent so many years with your head buried in the sand! If I had told Marcus the real situation outside of New Hope he would have risked too much far too soon. There is no sense in having wealth like that if we do not have the ability to hold on to it."

Caleb suspected he was being out-manipulated here, but at the same time he sensed there were some important truths in what Theodore was saying. "So, you lied to us even back then?"

"Of course I did. There was a very real threat to all the communities and I needed to keep everyone distracted so I could counter that threat before it became a problem for us."

"Distracted? From what?"

"Well, that is the question, is it not? What makes you think I am willing to cooperate with the people who have me incarcerated? Why should I help you? I am guessing you came here because there is a problem, probably with another community, and Jack and you and the rest of the council are standing around dumbfounded, searching for answers. Well, you are not going to get those answers from me, not unless you get me the hell out of here and start allowing me to go back to protecting this community, the way I have been trying to protect it for years."

Shaking his head, Caleb said, "You know, I came here thinking you still cared enough about New Hope to want to open up and help. Perhaps I was wrong; it seems all you want to do is try to manipulate me. If you are not interested in helping, this conversation is over."

"I am being sincere, Caleb. There are things the council needs to know, and the only way I am talking is if I can get out of here and in front of the council to say what I have to say."

Caleb's mind raced. While he was certain Theodore had latched on to the idea that he was the only man qualified to lead humanity out of extinction, it didn't mean he had suddenly become a blind fool. He could sense some truth in what the man was saying, although to reveal it he would have to out manipulate this master manipulator. He put a distressing look on his face and said, "There is no council. Jack disbanded it several months ago."

"What! And you allowed that? You cannot tell me Jack is making all the decisions without guidance. The man has barely been alive for a few months; he is hardly qualified to understand the complexities of our world!"

"Perhaps if you had not worked so hard to destroy his trust in the council with your treason, things would be different. This is mostly your fault, Theodore, and now you have a chance to make up for it, at least a small part. I need you to tell me the truth, not waste your efforts trying to manipulate me."

"My fault? Do not try to put this on me! Marcus is the one who decided to hold an election and nominate Jack, not me. And now you are saying he allowed the council to be disbanded? You are the ones who gave up all your power to an infant."

"But it was you who forced Marcus' hand. He always intended to put a Reborn in charge, and frankly I think it is the right choice. It was just premature because of your grab for power at the worst possible time! When are you going to accept that your blind desire for leadership nearly destroyed us all?"

Theodore seemed to deflate. Shaking his head, he said weakly, "If Marcus had not been so indecisive these past few years, I would not have had the need to make a play for his position. I did what I saw was necessary."

Caleb had won this fight. Now he had a choice to make. He felt he could press the issue and force Theodore into a corner where he would have to see how tenuous his justifications truly were, or he could try to extract more information on the threat the man had mentioned. He chose the latter. "I suppose it does not matter, your trial will be soon enough. Right now, I am the closest you are going to get to being heard by a council, so please, just tell me what you know."

"You said the council is disbanded, what good will talking to you do me?"

"Because I was recently made Head of Security, as well as a member of a new committee called the Board of Advisors. When it comes down to judging you for your crimes against New Hope, I will be an integral part of that process."

"And what role does Marcus play in this Board?"

"He doesn't. In fact, Marcus is not even here."

"What? You mean he left New Hope? Where did he go?"

"None of your business. Now, do you want to keep wasting my time or do you want to finish telling me about the threats to this community?"

Caleb waited patiently for Theodore to make up his mind. Finally, the man said, "Okay. Before I talk though, I want something." Caleb motioned for him to continue. "I want to be informed on current events. I will help you if you can get me information on what is going on. I cannot tell you what I think is happening if you cannot tell me what the state of affairs is."

Caleb shrugged. Despite his little victory here he still wanted Theodore to think he was getting what he wanted. If the man was somehow behind the disappearance of the unborn asset, he might try to use this as an opportunity to get a message to his agent. It was the perfect opportunity to set a trap. "I can arrange something. Now, tell me everything you have been lying about regarding the other communities."

~~~~

Chuck carefully circled the clearing, not wanting to land on anything that might prevent them from discovering what had happened. They scanned the area for life forms and found no heat signatures or signs of electronics. He punched the transmit button, "Chin, there's no sign of anyone here. I'm going to go ahead and set down and take a closer look."

"Thanks Chuck, let me know what you find."

When the engines had spooled down far enough, he reached to the back seat and grabbed his rifle. Emmet and Slick, the other two members of the team, jumped out, rifles ready. He took one final look around before exiting the flyer. After motioning the men to spread out and look around, he walked the perimeter of the clearing. At first there were no signs anyone had been here, but then he found the impressions in the ground left by a flyer. Nothing else stuck out, so he continued on.

On the opposite end of the clearing, he found similar impressions. Emmet shouted out, "Chuck, over here!"

He walked toward the center of the clearing where Emmet was staring at the ground. "What is it?"

"Not sure, but the ground is chewed up pretty good here. Look, it makes a pattern." He pointed to the ground surrounding the center of the clearing. Sure enough, there were six spots where the ground was torn up, evenly spaced around the center of the clearing.

Chuck pulled out his knife and got down on one knee in front of one of the spots. Digging through the loose soil, he found fragments of some kind of plastic casing. He put the fragments up to his nose and inhaled, smelling the familiar scent of explosive. He reached in his pack and pulled out a concussion grenade. The plastic looked similar. Without a word he showed Emmet.

"Well, shit, that can't be good."

Chuck shrugged. "Keep looking around. Slick! Get into those trees and make your way around the perimeter, tell me if you spot anything out of order."

Slick was about thirty feet away but there was no mistaking the expression on his face. "How the hell am I supposed to recognize if something is out of order?"

"Just do it!" The young man rolled his eyes and headed into the trees. "Jesus, Emmet, he's a good kid but I swear he was put on this earth just to piss me off." Emmet chuckled lightly at the comment, despite the heavy mood, and then continued to look for more signs of what might have happened.

A few minutes later, Chuck returned to the site of the second flyer. The sun was getting lower, and he caught a glint near the edge of the grass. It took a while, but finally he found the source of the reflection. A small piece of glass sat in the undisturbed grass, difficult to spot but resting high enough to catch the low sunshine. Normally he would dismiss it as random junk that could have been here for a hundred years. Unfortunately, there was blood on it. He put it in his pocket. If the blood was from one of their people, Teague could identify it.

A muffled shout put him on his guard. He once again went down to one knee, this time swinging his rifle off his shoulder. Scanning the forest in the direction of the shout, he signaled to Emmet to move in and investigate while he covered from his position. Another shout, this one he could make out. "Help, I'm stuck!"

Sighing, he took one last look around and then shouldered his weapon and plodded toward the tree line. About ten feet into the forest, he found Emmet helping Slick out of a hole. The hole was not wide, maybe four feet deep, and obviously recently dug. A pile of brush lay next to the hole, and Chuck picked it up. Held together by a thin green string, the bundle of brush, twigs, and leaves was the perfect size to cover up the hole. If Slick had not fallen in, nobody would have even found these holes.

"Emmet, as soon as you get slick out of there, go radio Chin and get him up to speed on what we have found. Slick you head that way and look for more holes. Try not to fall in another."

He didn't wait for a response or an excuse. As he made his way through the forest, he ran into another hole. On the fifth hole, he froze. The brush covering this one was propped up by a boot. As he pulled the brush away, he found the rest of the body, sans head, stuffed unceremoniously in the hole.

~~~~

Wendy put the flyer down in the flight bay, gently this time. Without hesitation, she shut everything down and jumped out, heading straight to the command center on the opposite end of the flight bay. To her surprise, Scott, Teague, and Thomas were sitting there too.

"What've you got, Chin? Any word yet?"

Chin swiveled toward her, a grim expression on his pale face. "Chuck just called in; he's on his way back. They found signs of a fight, some grenade fragments, a spot of blood, and some holes where soldiers could have been hiding. Chuck…" His voice caught and he couldn't seem to finish whatever he wanted to say. A chill ran up her spine and her heart seemed to pump harder.

"Spit it out, Chin. What else did they find?" She needed to know, regardless of how much she didn't want to hear.

"Um, he found a body."

The strength that had kept her going today finally failed. She started to collapse. Thomas seemed to appear out of nowhere, catching her as she fell. Instinctively she wrapped her arms around him in a huge embrace and completely lost control of her emotions. He didn't hesitate to hold her up and let her cry. She surrendered to the emotion, the rest of the world disappearing.

Chapter 12

Darkness became light, a hazy light, but light nevertheless. Full consciousness seemed to elude him despite his best efforts to wake up. The scenes playing before him were dreams, of that he was certain. Yet he had no control, no ability to interact, and no way to exit back to reality. One moment he sat with Jenn, watching Ally play with her toys, unable to tell them how much he missed them. The next, he stood over their graves, trying to find tears. Now he sat in a foxhole, chilled to the bone and scared for his life as he waited for friendly mortars to start exploding, tearing his men to pieces. Each scene felt as real and as painful as the day he experienced them for the first time. Now he was at the hospital, signing a form releasing liability for the procedure they were about to perform.

It seemed to go on forever, each scene familiar yet foreign in some way. Finally it was fear that pulled him out of the purgatory, a fear that he was dead, or worse… His eyes opened slowly. He looked around.

It took effort to focus, and the moment he relaxed, things went hazy again. He tried to move, but nothing responded. His breathing grew quick, the fear that woke him now gripping his heart like a vise. To his left, a medical monitor, to his right, a table with medical equipment. The room felt damp and musty, as if underground. The walls were plain concrete, and the lighting in the room unnatural.

A voice could be heard in the distance. It got louder. A man appeared in front of him, holding a clip board. "Welcome back, Jack."

Through the haze and confusion, he studied the face before him. Recognition was not comforting. "Teague?"

The man chuckled. "How are you feeling? Can you see things okay?"

His worst fears realized, he asked "What happened? How did I die? How long has it been since I left?"

"Don't worry about that, Jack, just answer some questions for me. What is your name?"

"Goddammit, Teague, you know my name, and you know I know it. Let's skip the bullshit! Where's Wendy? And what the hell happened?"

"If you aren't going to cooperate, I will have to sedate you some more. Was that pleasant Jack? Did you enjoy your dreams?"

What the hell is going on? "Come on, tell me what the hell is going on!" He didn't feel right. The last time he woke up in this room, things felt different. This time he felt *pain*. He closed his eyes and focused his breathing, slowed his heart, and swallowed his fear. He wiggled his toes. He could tell he was doing it, but when he tried to move his legs, nothing happened. He wiggled his fingers, and that felt right as well, but he couldn't move his arms. He opened his eyes and looked around, this time paying attention to the quality of what he saw. His vision was good, a little hazy but as long as he focused, everything was clear. Perhaps it was his mind that felt hazy.

"Don't worry, Jack, everything works, you are just restrained at the moment. The haziness you feel is from the drugs. You might even feel nausea and have a headache. That will get worse before it gets better. I could give you something for it, but frankly I really don't care if you are comfortable or not." The man worked some controls and the bed folded, moving him to an upright position. Outside the door, some people Jack didn't recognize were talking.

"Teague, I don't understand. What's going on? Why am I restrained, and why am I drugged?"

Teague pulled a chair over to the bed and took a seat. "Jack, what's the last thing you remember?"

He sighed in frustration. Whatever was going on, he had to play along if he were going to get any answers. "I remember talking with Andrew, then all hell breaking loose. I remember grenades going off, then a struggle, then nearly getting away, then nothing."

"The first time you woke up in our world, do you remember the last moment before your death?"

"Oh, come on, you know how much time I lost." He examined his friend's face, trying to understand why he was acting this way and why everything felt so foreign.

"Okay, but you remember being told why we don't bring back memories immediately before death, right?"

"Sure, it's so your body doesn't remember dying and spontaneously trigger the death mechanism. You told me all this. I can assure you, Teague, my memories are all fully intact and I am perfectly capable of thinking clearly. What I can't understand is what kind of game you are playing here!"

"Relax, it will be clear in a moment. Think about what you just said."

Jack closed his eyes again, practicing his calming techniques in effort to keep from losing his temper again. As he took a painful breath, he reviewed the questions, going backwards. *What happens when you are born with memories immediately before death. How much time did he lose when he was reborn the first time. What is his last memory.* "Wait. If you brought me back, you would have backed up a day or two to prevent me possibly remembering my death. That's what you're getting at? So I didn't die?"

"You are a very smart man, Mr. Taggart. Now let's see if you can figure more things out on your own."

Jack was elated to learn he hadn't been reborn, which meant he hadn't been killed. However, that didn't explain where he was or what was going on. Teague acted like a man who barely knew him. Nothing felt right. And he had been sedated. His last memories had been of a fight and subsequent capture. His eyes popped open again and he studied Teague. There was no question it was his friend's face, but something wasn't right. He looked younger, several years younger. And he carried himself differently. "You aren't Teague, are you? I mean, you are obviously his clone, but, how? And why?"

"My, my, Jack, you continue to impress me. I am starting to see why Marcus chose you to be his successor. Now for the trifecta. Can you deduce where you are?"

At first glance, it appeared similar to the room he woke up in several months ago. However, it wasn't quite right. The lighting was different, and the feel was different too. It felt mustier, more humid, and there was a different scent in the air. "I don't know, but I'm pretty confident I'm not in New Hope. I'm guessing, given how my meeting ended with Andrew, I am in a converted missile silo somewhere in Nebraska."

The man laughed. "Well, two out of three isn't bad. And frankly, that last one was a bit of a trick question. You couldn't possibly know where you are. Allow me to introduce myself, I am Sebastian. If you would like to get formal, my name is Sebastian Christopher Maddoxson. Contrary to your belief, I am not a clone of your friend Teague. In fact, he is my son."

~~~~

Wendy woke with a start. Looking around, she found herself in her own bed, yet she had no idea how she got here. Sitting up revealed three things: One, she had to pee. Two, she was wearing nothing but a t-shirt. Three, she was ravenously hungry.

She scrambled to the bathroom, catching a glimpse of her disheveled face in the mirror. Her puffy eyes indicated she had been crying a lot, reminding her of what Chin had said just before she broke down. Now she felt numb, no emotion and no desire to think about the news she received.

After taking care of her business and washing her face, she made her way into the kitchen. "Hey, how are you feeling?" She nearly came off the ground. Thomas sat on the couch, hair all messed up, no shirt on, and a blanket covering his legs.

Breathless from the shock, she said, "Holy shit, you scared the hell out of me. Why are you here?"

He stretched, joints popping. Stifling a yawn, he said, "You asked me to stay, so I crashed on the couch. I would've left but you were in quite a state and I wasn't about to leave you alone. How are you this morning?"

Confused about how she felt, she said, "I don't know. What happened?"

"Chin started to tell you that Chuck found a body and you collapsed."

Tears welled up as the barriers she had put up began to crumble.

"Whoa," he said, jumping off the couch and coming over to comfort her. "Take a deep breath." She tried to breathe but it caught. Gripping his hand, she took another breath. "There you go. Now, listen closely. You never let Chin finish before you collapsed. The body Chuck found was not Jack. It was Jerry, the pilot."

The barriers that held back her emotions collapsed and her knees went weak again. Thomas caught her, holding her tight. She took another breath, and then another. "Jack's still alive?" she cried.

"As far as we know. There is no sign of him, Anton, the other men, or even the flyer. There is sign of a fight but from there we don't know what happened.

The relief was short lived. Her man was still in danger. Pushing away from Thomas, she frantically looked around for her datapad. Locating it on the counter, she checked the time. 7:45 a.m. "We need to get out and look for Jack!" She pushed back the emotions and headed toward the bedroom to get some clothes.

"Whoa, hold on Wendy. We have two crews out there already, and I'm not sure I want you out there as well. You've been through a hell of a lot of trauma recently, and in your, uh, condition, the last thing you should be doing is running off to help. At least not until Teague can check you out and make sure the baby is okay."

Anger flared. "Don't think for a second you could stop me, Thomas!"

"Wendy, you need to calm down and get some food. You have a baby to consider. Just take it easy! I'll call Chin and see if there is any news, although he would've already called if there was."

As he walked back to the couch to get his tablet, she realized he was only dressed in tight boxer briefs. Looking away, she said, "Oh, Jesus, put some pants on." Then she looked down at herself, only wearing a t-shirt that barely reached her thighs. Her face burned with embarrassment. Slipping behind the counter that divided the kitchen and living spaces, she asked, "How did I get out of my clothes and into this shirt?"

He simply smiled at her and looked away, focused on calling Chin. She stomped to her room, only feeling mildly foolish at her crazy emotional swings. When she sat on her bed, she felt tenderness in her hips, probably from her tumble on the concrete floor of that recycling plant. Taking a moment to examine herself, she noted bruises on her knees, thighs, hips, and arms. And she stunk. Grabbing some clean clothes, she headed for the shower, purposely not looking into the living room as she quickly passed.

~~~~

After a refreshing shower, clean clothes, and a nice breakfast, she was starting to feel normal again. There was no question she was ready to get back out and look for Jack. Thomas insisted they stop by Teague's first, so they headed toward the elevators. "Look, I appreciate your concern, but I'm sure my baby is just fine."

"Wendy, did I ever tell you my first wife lost a baby once?"

"No, but I'm sure you want to tell me all about how she thought everything was fine and it turned out it wasn't. Well, I don't want to hear it.

What I want right now is to get my fat, pregnant ass into a flyer and get out there and see if I can find my baby's father."

"Your ass isn't fat, and this will only take a second."

"So you undressed me last night and checked out my ass?" She felt the familiar feeling of anger starting to rise.

He chuckled, "No, you undressed yourself last night, and if I had done it for you, I certainly wouldn't have done something as rude as admire your naked body while doing it."

"Oh, so now you don't want to look at my fat pregnant body?" She felt tears beginning to well up.

He didn't seem fazed by her emotional swings, frustration, anger, or even crazy sounding accusations. "I happen to think pregnant women are the most beautiful creatures on earth, but as tempting as it would be for me to look at your naked body, I wouldn't feel right about it. I have too much respect for you and Jack. Here we are." The elevator dinged and they stepped off, almost to Teague's office.

"Where the hell did you come from Thomas?"

He looked at her quizzically, "Montana, why?"

She laughed and entered the office.

~~~~

The rail car stopped and they climbed out. "See, I told you there wasn't anything wrong with my baby."

"Don't you feel better knowing everything is okay?" Thomas asked.

"Yeah, yeah."

He paused next to the rail car and looked at her uncomfortably. "I've been meaning to ask, did Jack talk to you about his plans for the Board of Advisors?"

"Yeah, we talked about it extensively, why?"

"Did he tell you he was going to ask me to take over the role of Head of Defense?"

"Yeah, and I agreed with him. I think you're well suited for the job. You obviously care about the people under your protection."

"Thanks. The reason I brought it up has to do with authority, however. Jack hasn't made our positions official in any capacity, yet he is… unavailable right now and that presents some issues. Technically this whole operation should be under my authority. None of us want to create an upset at the moment, not while in the midst of this situation, but if things get ugly, I think we need to be prepared."

"Well, I don't have any official authority either, so what are you asking me to do?"

"If you can back us up, it would go a long way toward legitimizing things. Assuming of course we don't find Jack today." He winced at the way that came out.

The look on her face spoke volumes. There was little question she wanted nothing to do with this conversation. He was talking about what would happen if they didn't find the man she loved. It needed to be asked though, and given the circumstances, anything she said would have more credibility than all four of the board members put together. She sighed, "There's an easy way to fix this, right now."

They reached the command station. Chin looked tired and haggard, but he didn't look ready to let anyone else take over. "Hey, Chin, how are things this morning?"

He stood up and walked close to her. "Oh God, Wendy, I'm so sorry. I didn't mean to lead you to believe the body Chuck found was Jack. Are you okay now? You collapsed before I could tell you more, and once we realized…"

"Don't worry about it, Chin," she interrupted, "just blame a lot of stress and my crazy hormones."

The relief erased hours of sleep deprivation from his face. "Is everything okay with the baby?"

"For Christ's sake! I'm fine, my baby's fine, and I just want to know if there's any news!"

"Sorry, I just…" He sat down, spun back around in his chair to face the control monitors and said, "Nothing much has changed. After Chuck called in about the body, I asked him to start searching the area, looking for wreckage. It is entirely possible Jack and his crew got away, but without Jerry there, it is just as possible they crashed, especially if there was a fight. So far we've covered about a hundred square miles of territory surrounding the clearing and there is no sign."

"Thank You. Now, I'm going to get in a flyer in and start looking for my man. If anyone wants to stop me they're going to get a lesson in how bad of an idea it is to mess with a determined woman!" She stomped toward the group of aircraft at the other end of the flight bay.

Pausing for a moment, she turned and said, "Oh, in case Jack didn't mention it, he assigned a new advisory board that can act with his authority in his absence. Teague, Caleb, Scott, and Thomas here are all members. Thomas is our new Head of Defense, so technically he's in charge of any operations outside of New Hope." Without pausing for a reaction, she turned again and headed toward her waiting aircraft. Thomas didn't try to stop her this time.

Chin signaled to two soldiers seated at a table not far from the command center. They got up and headed toward Wendy's ship. Then he looked at Thomas and then over at Scott, who was asleep in the chair. "Why didn't you say anything yesterday when you came down here?"

Thomas felt a bit embarrassed. "We figured it wasn't the time to talk about it, at least not until we knew what was going on. We didn't want to interrupt you from doing your job."

Shrugging, he said, "Whatever. Look, I was going to have Johnson take over for me for a while so I can go catch some sleep. Any issue with that?"

Thomas shook his head, "No, of course not… look, all this is just a formality. When it comes time to act, I just wanted to make sure – well, you understand." He paused then asked, "Which Johnson? The ginger kid? What's his name… Craig? Chris?"

Chin chuckled and said, "No… Johnson. That's his full name. I guess his father was named John. You've probably never met him, he isn't a soldier and he mostly hangs around the family levels doing odd jobs. He likes to jump around a lot, never sticks with the same job for more than a few months. The woman I've been bedding with lately took a liking to the guy and told me he's been looking for something more meaningful to do. Nobody else seems to be available so I figured why not? It isn't like sitting here is tough."

Thomas just shrugged. Aside from those guys sitting in jail for their role in Theodore's treason, he hadn't met too many native born men. The women were a different story – he'd probably met every one of them, at least the ones not pregnant or still recovering from pregnancy. It wasn't really all that surprising he hadn't met this Johnson fellow. "Where're we at with Camp Wisner? Anything new?"

Yawning, Chin answered, "Nope, same story. I contacted them three times." He reached over and tapped some buttons. Some text appeared on the screen and he read it aloud. "We had a nice chat with Jack regarding merging with New Hope then left shortly after discovering our communications were down. When we left, Jack and his crew were just loading up to leave. I hope all is well and please let me know if there is anything we can do for you."

Something tugged at his memory. "Wait, was that directly from Andrew?"

"I guess it was, I mean, the message said it was from Andrew, but I couldn't tell you for certain. We talk to them with shortwave radio but because we never know if they are actively listening, we both have computers connected to the radio and just type messages back and forth. The message comes up on the computer screen. Why?"

"I don't know. Something just doesn't seem right."

"You're just figuring that out now? Nothing about this whole situation seems right to me."

He ignored Chin's sarcasm. "Look, put together everything you have in a file and send it to my pad before you go on break. I'm going to get the Board together and figure out our next official move. In the meantime, just keep the crews out there searching, perhaps we're reading too far into this and Jack is just sitting in a busted airplane halfway between here and Colorado. Better to be covering all the bases, at least until the Board makes an actionable decision."

Chapter 13

Wendy dialed in a new heading and let the autopilot take over. Despite the desire to find Jack, she wasn't in the right place, emotionally or mentally, to spend hours circling back and forth. Besides, there was little doubt in her mind he hadn't simply crash landed somewhere without a radio. That was far too unrealistic and optimistic. Andrew had planned something out, and she intended to find out exactly what it was. She was going to need help, and not just the two men who came along to help scour the mountains around Colorado.

Last night's emotional break was evidence she couldn't handle this on her own. It wasn't just the hormones that caused her to fall apart like that. Nobody understood the despair she felt before Jack came along. Her entire life had been a series of disappointments and heartbreaks. Her very death was the 'coup de grace', like a punchline to the Devil's joke. To wake up in a world where she was expected to fulfill the desires of men, while setting aside her own hopes and dreams, felt every bit like Hell. She didn't even understand what sins she had committed to deserve such a horrible fate. Meeting Jack, particularly after getting such a vivid glimpse of his soul, changed everything. Her love for him saved her soul, and his reciprocation somehow turned Hell into Heaven.

Even without the baby, losing him would crush her. Their baby meant she had no choice but to survive that kind of loss. Without Jack in her life, she didn't want to bring a child into this world. That left one option: find Jack, whatever the cost.

"Excuse me Ma'am, why are we headed northwest? Isn't the search grid east of here?" one of the men asked.

Her first reaction was anger, but she knew that wasn't the right response. He had a valid question, one she would have to answer sooner or later. "Sorry, Jason, we're taking a detour. I hope you didn't have plans for dinner."

"No, Ma'am, but I would like to know where we're going."

"Please, call me Wendy. We're going to see a friend and see if we can figure out what happened to Jack and his men. This might take a few days, and it might get violent. Is this going to be a problem for you?"

She studied him carefully, wondering how he would react. It wasn't too much of a surprise when he replied, "None whatsoever, Ma... uh... Wendy. Tony's my friend, and Jack's a good man, I'm ready to do whatever it takes to help find them."

She smiled at him then looked behind her at a somewhat nervous looking fellow she had not met before. "And you? Do you have any problem with this?"

"No Ma'am. I sort of needed to get out of New Hope for a little while anyway. A few days sounds even better. Those women are fucking nuts!" He colored, "Uh, pardon my language."

She chuckled, "You're right, they are fucking nuts, and please don't call me Ma'am, I'm not your teacher or your mother."

"Sorry, Wendy. My name's Max. So where *are* we headed?"

Just then the radio squawked, "Wendy, I show you heading way off course, what's going on?" Surprisingly, it wasn't Chin.

She punched the button and said, "Who's this?"

"It's Johnson, Ma'am, Chin's taking a well needed break."

"Goddammit! Did I suddenly age thirty years?"

"Excuse me, I don't think I copied that."

"Never mind. Look, tell Chin I'm going to do some of my own investigating, I'll call if I find anything. Make sure a second search party gets out there when Chuck's crew gets back. And if you hear anything new, call me. Otherwise, don't bother me."

After a long hesitation, Johnson said, "Copy that. Be safe."

She punched the radio and said, "I hope you boys don't get scared easily."

~~~~

She didn't waste time with a graceful landing, kicking up dirt and debris that must have made an awful ruckus inside the large cabin. Bart would never intentionally hurt anyone, but there was a good chance he was still resting as his wounds healed, and barging into his cabin after a quiet landing might be too much like poking a hibernating bear.

Before she got out, the giant man was standing outside, a look of intense curiosity on his face. Silver stood obediently next to him, tail wagging. "Holy shit!" exclaimed Max.

"Don't worry; he's like a big teddy bear. Well, a big teddy bear that could crush your skull with the flick of a finger. Just don't tease him about his clothes. And mind the pup – he's still young and playful but his teeth are like inch long razor blades."

As she climbed out, she had to suppress a grin. It was always fun messing with people who'd never met Bart, and for some reason in this time of despair her dark sense of humor felt oddly comforting.

"Little Red, I didn't expect you back so soon. Did you find your man?"

"No, which is why I'm here. I need your help."

He nodded, "Of course, I'd be honored to help in any way I can. Who are your friends? Do they need a drink? They look a little pale." His deep chuckle could be felt more than heard.

"This is Max and Jason. Boys, this is Bartholomew."

"Holy shit," Max said again. Wendy couldn't hold back the smirk this time.

After introductions, they went inside. "I've been monitoring the air waves, but aside from your chatter and the conversations between Camp Wisner and New Hope, I haven't picked up anything unusual."

"Can you show me the conversations?" she asked.

"Sure. They're digital and had to be decrypted, which of course didn't take me more than a few minutes. You guys should really look into something a little more complicated if you want to keep your conversations private."

She scoffed, "What's the point, there aren't but a handful of people left on this entire planet, and—" she was about to say there wasn't a need for that kind of secrecy or security. Considering the current situation, even with only a few thousand people remaining it was apparent security would always be a concern. She didn't bother to finish her sentence as Bart was often one step ahead of her anyway.

She turned her attention to the screen and read through the messages. When she read their last transmission she flushed in anger. "Son of a bitch! I knew it!"

"Knew what? What are you seeing here that I'm missing?"

She pointed to the part of the message she had just read and said, "Jack had no intention of merging communities. He went there to propose something completely different. These guys are lying through their teeth, and it's time we find out exactly what they know!"

Bart shrugged helplessly, "Aside from the chatter I pick up from scavenging crews, these guys are pretty much radio silent. If they have a communication network within their community, it isn't connected to the computers I can hack in to from here. The best I could do for you is send a message the same way any other community would, but it appears that's a dead end. Whatever they're hiding, they aren't going to talk about it."

"Well, I'll be damned if I'm going to sit around and do nothing about this! I'm going to find out what Andrew knows if I have to go there and kick his ass myself!"

As stupid of an idea as it was, she found herself stomping out of the house toward the flyer. Somewhere in the back of her mind she knew they wouldn't make it within fifty miles of Camp Wisner without alerting them. By the time they landed there would be a welcoming party, complete with full armor and automatic weapons. Her emotions were in charge at the moment, however, and despite the futility of it, she fully intended to pay them a visit.

"Wendy!" the big man boomed. It wasn't the sheer volume of his shout that cut through her misguided resolve, rather his use of her name, perhaps the first time he had used it since they met. "Let's sit down and cool off and talk this through before charging in like a bunch of blood lusting fools."

From the doorway, she spun back around and said, "I'm tired of sitting around doing nothing! Everyone just wants to talk about things while Jack is out there, possibly being tortured!" Not wanting to cry in front of the two soldiers, she had to stop talking to hold it all in.

"I understand the feeling, but you're acting like my former tribe, following your anger and emotion and not stopping to use logic."

He was right, and her anger fled as quickly as it had arrived, leaving her feeling gloomy and powerless. Stumbling to an oversized chair, she sat down heavily. Nobody in the room said anything as she contemplated her foolishness.

After what could have been several minutes, Bart broke the awkward silence. "You understand," he began, "that charging in to Camp Wisner would probably result in getting shot out of the sky, right? And if not, they'll see us coming and just hole up in their silo and wait for us to leave."

Wendy simply nodded, wondering if her friend was still chastising her or if he had something relevant to say.

His chair groaned and squealed as he leaned back with a devilish smile on his face. "What if I said I have a way to disarm their defenses and unlock the front door?"

~~~~

"Let me get this straight," Caleb said, "you do not think Andrew is being straight with us? Or are you saying he is not in charge anymore?"

Teague shrugged, "I am just saying the message does not match what Jack shared of his plans."

Frustrated, Caleb took a deep breath, held it for a moment, and finally let it out slowly. He was tired and it took effort to keep the disdain out of his voice while asking, "Do you have any guesses as to who it might be sending us the messages?"

Teague's eyes narrowed, ever so slightly. Somewhat sarcastically he replied, "No, Caleb, I don't. Whatever happened in that clearing could have just as easily been targeted at Andrew as Jack. Perhaps a coup took place in Camp Wisner and our people were just collateral damage. All I know for certain is the message they sent sounds more like what they would say if they had never actually had the meeting."

Taken aback, Caleb nearly lashed out at Teague's insolence. Then he remembered they were *supposed* to be equals on this board. Besides, the man had a good point. When sending a digital message, there was no real way of knowing who was on the other end of the transmission. Before he could concede, Teague continued.

"Look, maybe Andrew has captured Jack and his men. Maybe the attempt succeeded but cost Andrew his life. Hell, maybe someone attacked them both and Camp Wisner thinks we are to blame! We just don't know, and in Jack's absence, it is left to us to decide the next course of action."

Thomas said, "Whether Andrew was behind it or not, we need to confront them and get some answers! I say we take a dozen men and a few flyers and go meet with them face to face. That will answer whether Andrew is
~~~~

the one lying or not, and perhaps a little intimidation will prompt them to tell us what happened."

Caleb shook his head, "Even if they were telling the truth, an action like that would be seen as hostile and they would have every right to shoot us out of the sky. The only way they would allow us to land is if they didn't feel we were a threat. A situation like that could explode way too easily and lead to a loss of life."

Thomas stood up and slammed his fist down on the table. "Well, we need to do something! I'm not going to just sit here while our elected leader could be in danger! We need answers, so unless you have a better idea, I'm going to go round up some men."

To Caleb's surprise, Teague roared, "Dammit Thomas, sit down! In case you haven't noticed, this isn't your world and we sure as hell can't start running around like a bunch of animals trying to establish dominance! This is a delicate situation, and if we handle it wrong it could end up costing us everything we built!"

Thomas flushed red and took his seat. Teague wasn't finished, however. "What if Cali is involved in this? Did you stop to think about that? Perhaps we could strong arm Camp Wisner into confessing what they know, but if other communities are involved, perhaps their intent is to flush us out, to get us to come out in force so they can ambush us and leave New Hope defenseless."

Weakly, Thomas retorted, "So what do you want us to do? Sit here on our asses hoping this whole situation is just a big mistake and Jack will come limping home in a few days with a grin on his face saying, 'you wouldn't believe what happened to us'?"

"No, but before we act, we *are* going to talk over all the possibilities and make a unanimous decision on *how* to act. Although I have never been to Camp Wisner, I *have* met Andrew before, and I can tell you he is not a stupid man. If he is behind this, he had good reason. If he is making a play for the wealth we recovered from the Freezer, I can guarantee he is not acting alone. On the other hand, I do not believe he would willingly enter into any kind of arrangement with Cali. He never got along with Joshua, and the threat Cali posed to us was well on the way to driving all of us smaller communities together, at least before our discovery in Montana."

Scott meekly raised his hand. Teague paused and looked at him questioningly and finally said, "You don't have to raise your hand here, Scott, if you have something to say, just say it. We're all equals here." Caleb couldn't help but wonder where Teague suddenly got this confidence. In over one hundred and fifty years he had never heard the man take on a tone of authority.

Scott smiled and said, "Sorry to interrupt, I'm not quite as up to speed as the rest of you here as this is a bit out of my area of expertise. Is Joshua the leader of Cali?"

Teague nodded, "Yes, he is. He's also the brother of our former leader, Marcus."

98

Thomas looked surprised. "What?" he asked, "You can't be serious."

Teague shot Caleb a meaningful glance and Caleb picked up on it immediately and said, "Joshua had a… disagreement with Marcus many years ago, before the fall of the Enclaves of Science. He moved on to San Cali, the former EoS city near the Pacific coast. When things fell apart, he and the survivors in San Cali were all but cut off from the rest of the continent and had few resources. It was actually Marcus who convinced us to use what miniscule resources we had to aide him in setting up a new community. He named it Cali after the city he had lived in for the better part of a decade. I believe Marcus' intent was to mend the rift between him and his brother, which seemed rather important at that time, considering our situation. Unfortunately, once things stabilized Joshua was able to hoard an enormous volume of resources, but he refused to show the same kind of generosity with other struggling communities. Instead, he used those resources as leverage to force other communities to join Cali. As you can imagine, this didn't sit well with Marcus or any of the other community leaders either. It is common knowledge that any community entering into an alliance with Cali will sooner or later end up under Joshua's rule. Camp Wisner would have to be in dire straits before even considering getting involved in something as potentially volatile as kidnapping or killing another community leader, even one as new to the stage as Jack."

Scott nodded but didn't ask any more questions.

"That still doesn't mean Cali isn't just as likely behind this as Camp Wisner," said Thomas, "perhaps Cali is working alone in this."

A chill went up Caleb's spine as he considered his conversation with Theodore earlier. As bad as the timing was, perhaps he should inform the Board of Theodore's request to be heard. Before he could speak, however, Scott asked, "Then how could Cali have known where to attack?"

Teague jumped in with, "Perhaps whoever stole our frozen treasure has been working with Cali all along. It wasn't exactly a secret Jack was heading out to meet Andrew yesterday. If this person has enough access to the flight bay to smuggle something out of New Hope, it is not a very big leap to assume they also didn't know exactly when Jack and his crew were leaving or where they were headed."

Thomas turned to Caleb and asked, "You went to visit with Theodore yesterday; did you get any kind of insight into who is behind the theft?"

"Funny you should ask, I was just thinking about that conversation. As a matter of fact, Theodore is pretty convinced he has some information that might shed some light on this situation."

"You told him about Jack being missing?" asked Teague accusingly, "You realize he could be in contact with whoever has been stealing from our coffers?"

"If he is, which I do not believe is the case, he would already know Jack is missing, would he not? No, I had a talk with Tiny, and there are only a few very trustworthy men who have any contact with him whatsoever. However, I did tell him about this Board, and he requested an opportunity to be heard."

"I have no desire to hear what that traitor has to say," said Teague dismissively.

"If all he intends to do is try to convince anyone here that he is innocent of the charges, I do not want to hear him either. However, I believe he has some information regarding the other communities that would at least be worth hearing. He was, after all, the only member of the former council to have regular relations with every community. Some things he said to me were quite discomforting and ring true to our current discussion. I would like to vote to at least to hear him."

"I'll second that," said Scott. This surprised Caleb. Scott's role here is strictly internal and as he had already admitted, this was way out of his wheelhouse. He noted that it would be a mistake to assume the man was simple just because of his ignorance of their history.

Teague sighed and said, "Well, let us put it to a vote then, all in favor of hearing what Theodore has to say?"

Caleb said, "Aye," at the same time as both Scott and Thomas. There was no need for Teague to vote against it. Caleb reached over and punched a button on the table.

A moment later Tiny's voice boomed over the speakers, "What can I do for you, sir?"

"Can you escort Theodore to the council chambers please?"

The hesitation was brief. "Sure, be there in ten minutes."

Chapter 14

Bart, Max, and Jason had all argued to wait until nightfall so they could assault the silo under the cover of darkness. Wendy had no intention of losing an entire day sitting around waiting. She figured she won the dispute because nobody wanted to argue with her. On the other hand, it was likely Camp Wisner's patrols and scavengers would all be out, leaving the main silo only guarded by the air defenses and perhaps a few men. At night there could be twenty armed men inside.

It only took Bart a few hours to assemble the electronic gizmos he would need to disarm their defenses, and long before dark they were up in the air heading east.

It was a cloudy day, so the plan was to go in at the max altitude of the flyer and drop in directly above the silo. It was entirely possible Andrew had all his forces patrolling the outside perimeter of their air defenses, just in case New Hope saw through the deception and mounted an assault. Even with Bart masking the flyer from their defenses, a patrol could visually spot them and intercept.

So far, it was going perfectly. They were forty miles inside the perimeter and they had not detected any kind of defensive activity.

Partly because she didn't want any argument, she didn't let Chin know what they were up to. In order to remain concealed, their GPS and radios had to be disabled, so if this mission failed, New Hope wouldn't even know she had gone to Camp Wisner. If she had even considered the possibility of failure she might have realized the strain her disappearance would put on New Hope.

"Tell Bart we're almost there," she said to Max. Even the radios they usually used to talk to the men in the hold of the flyer were shut off, so Max had to open an access hatch in the back seat and shout over the drone of the engines to relay the message to Bart, who sat calmly in the hold fiddling with his toys.

The hold was pressurized, but because of the size and the large main door, it wasn't as well sealed as the cabin. At this altitude, the difference in pressure was enough to make everyone's ears pop when the access hatch was opened.

A light came on and Wendy nosed the aircraft down, tilting the props to both slow the aircraft's horizontal speed and start dropping altitude. Jason shifted uncomfortably as gravity went from normal to near zero. The rapid descent was just shy of the same rate as gravity pulled objects down, and if you weren't used to it, the feeling was quite unsettling. "Hang on boys, wouldn't want you to float away."

Wendy loved this feeling. The first time a pilot had taken her up in a chopper and tried to impress her with some daring maneuvers, she was sold on flying. That love of flying is what killed her in the end, but with a second lease on life she seldom missed a chance to get back up in the air.

The clouds cleared and the ground grew rapidly. Jason gasped and looked away from the window, focusing on his feet. Wendy chuckled at this, but also hoped he wouldn't toss his cookies right now. At their rate of descent, uncontrolled vomit would fly everywhere.

The flyers were a cross between a helicopter and an airplane, which allowed them to maneuver in ways no aircraft from her time could have even considered. At five thousand feet she pulled back on the yoke and pedaled the aircraft back to level. This shifted gravity from close to zero to well over three G's. Jason moaned again, and she heard a thump in the hold. She winced, hoping Bart wasn't having too rough of a ride.

The buildings were well camouflaged from above, but Bart had provided some satellite footage of people coming and going, so she knew what to look for. At a thousand feet, she spotted the silo entrance and made some adjustments. "Hang on, were going in hot!"

The landing was within the tolerances of the landing gear, but only barely. Later she might realize a jolt like that was probably not good for her baby, but with the adrenaline in her system she really didn't notice. She punched the controls to open the back hatch and to put the engines on standby so they could make a hasty exit. Grabbing a rifle, she hopped out of pilot's seat and ran around to the back side of the flyer.

Bart was already climbing down the ramp, a pack slung over his shoulder. On his hip he wore an incredibly intimidating knife. Otherwise he wore his usual clothing which looked somewhat out of place on the massive Mute. The two ran toward the entrance door where Max and Jason already stood guard watching for any sign of attack from one of the nearby ranch houses. There was no activity at all, which wasn't completely unexpected. However, she was a little surprised at least one guard wasn't hanging out nearby. Hopefully this didn't mean they would find a whole lot of armed men inside.

The first plan was to have Wendy wait in the flyer and have Max, Jason, and Bart go inside. She quickly nixed that idea; there was no way she was going to sit this out. Besides, she figured a pregnant woman might be enough of a surprise to offset the appearance of a giant, bald, and leathery skinned man charging into their living quarters.

Bart pulled a device out of his pack and pressed some buttons. A keypad next to the door beeped and the sound of electric bolt locks moving could be heard over the mild whisper of the idling propellers.

Wendy grabbed the handle and pulled the door open while Max prepared to charge in. She half expected someone to be there firing and let out a breath as the chamber inside was eerily quiet. It was dark as well, beckoning her to explore much like the door back at the Warehouse had.

Turning on the flashlight on her rifle, she cautiously walked into the dark room. As she crossed the threshold, the outside world faded away and for a moment she felt like she had gone deaf. When she heard the shuffle of boots behind her, she knew it was just the sudden absence of sound.

The room was dimly lit, but her eyes had not yet adjusted and it appeared very dark. In front of her was a set of stairs. Through the holes in the metal stair treads she could see more stairs, so obviously the stairwell wound back and forth.

Max took the lead and started creeping down the stairs, reaching a landing and sweeping the next flight before moving on. Wendy looked back, expecting Jason and Bart to be behind her, but neither was there. "Hold up," she said quietly, although it seemed to echo down the empty stairwell.

She stepped back outside to see what was causing the delay. Bart stood there staring at the doorway, looking rather pale. "Is there a problem," she asked.

Jason said, "Yeah, he won't go in. Says he should just stay out here and guard the flyer."

This was unexpected but not particularly surprising. She should have thought about it when planning, but in all the excitement of finally doing something, it had slipped her mind. "Sorry, Little Red, I'm not going in there. It's too small, I will get stuck!"

"Okay, if anyone shows up, please don't kill them unless you absolutely have to. We'll be back as quick as we can, hopefully dragging that slimy, no good Andrew with us." She patted her big friend on the shoulder and signaled for Jason to head inside.

Once in the room, she said softly, "Don't chastise him for this later, if you were nearly three feet taller and two feet wider you would probably feel the same way he does."

He held up his hands and said, "I wasn't going to say a damn thing."

She chuckled and said, "Let's go."

They made their way down twelve flights of stairs. At the twelfth landing there was a door and another flight down. She cursed, having hoped the path to the living quarters would be straightforward. Making a split second decision, she passed the door and forged downward.

Each level had another door, and as tempting as it was to check behind it, she decided to go all the way to the bottom first. It took thirty flights in all, fifteen stories down before they reached the bottom. Going back up would be tough, especially if they were hauling a prisoner.

She motioned beside the door and Max once again took up a position, ready to go on the offensive if there were resistance behind the door. She grabbed the handle and pulled.

The door handle didn't budge. "Shit!" She looked for a keypad, but obviously the door was locked with a simple key. "I don't suppose either of you knows how to pick a lock?"

The men looked at her like she was crazy. She shrugged, figuring it was at least worth asking. Originally she figured Bart could open any door, if not with the finesse of some gadget he had built, then with brute force. Now she had three options. One was to go back up and try to convince Bart to come down and force the door open. Chances are that wouldn't work, and besides, they'd already been here nearly ten minutes. If they had been detected coming in, a fight would be waiting on their way out. If not, then the longer they were here, the higher the chance they would be discovered. Spending twenty minutes humping up the stairs to try what was probably impossible just didn't seem like a worthwhile use of time.

The second option would be to blow the door handle off. The rifles they carried fired armor piercing rounds and would make quick work of the door. However, if there were anyone in the levels above, or even anyone behind the door, they would be alerted and quite possibly armed and ready when they got to them.

The last option was a long shot, but she figured it wouldn't hurt to try. She knocked.

Jason said, "What the hell are you doing?"

She shrugged. Miraculously, the door opened. Stunned, Wendy stared at the little girl who had opened it. "Hello," was all she could think to say.

"Who are you?" the little girl asked.

Wendy shot Max a look that she hoped he would understand. He slid the rifle behind him and tried to not look menacing. Jason stood on the other side of the door where the little girl probably couldn't see him. She smiled and said, "I'm Wendy, is your daddy home?"

The little girl looked at her, then at Max, and back at her. "No, he isn't here, but mommy is, would you like me to get her?"

Again Wendy looked at Max who just shrugged. "Um, sure, that would be wonderful, thank you."

The girl turned and walked away from the door, leaving it open. "I'll be damned, I never expected that to happen," said Max.

Wendy pushed the door open and stepped into a fairly luxurious living room. It was nicer than the quarters she and Jack lived in, but somewhat sparsely decorated. She could hear faint voices in the other room. She signaled Jason to stay back around the corner and stepped inside with Max. She shouldered her rifle and waited.

A woman, perhaps in her late forties, rounded the corner and froze. "Who are you?"

Wendy smiled again and said, "I'm Wendy. You must be Andrew's wife?"

The woman's eyes narrowed. "One of them, yes. I don't recognize you, why are you here? How did you get down here?"

With no time to think, she said, "You know who we are. Where's Andrew?"

Looking downright scared now, the woman said, "You tell me. I haven't seen him since he left yesterday morning. Now please, why don't you just leave us alone?"

She started backing toward the rest of the apartment and Wendy kept pace with her, not getting closer, but not allowing the woman to get further away. "You haven't heard from him since yesterday? You mean he never came back after the meeting?"

"Dammit, I told you I haven't seen him, now please just leave me alone!" She backpedaled faster, glancing at a side table a few feet away.

Wendy signaled Max and he sprang into action, lunging forward and grabbing her. She let out a scream that he quickly stifled by covering her mouth. Jason entered and said, "Everything good?" Wendy just nodded toward him and he turned back around to cover the door.

She looked at the woman who was now terrified and said, "Is there anyone else other than you and your daughter in the apartment? Don't lie to me; I have no reason to kill you… yet." Obviously this was a bluff, she didn't think she could pull the trigger unless this woman was an actual threat, and right now she wasn't.

The woman shook her head, tears running onto Max's hand.

"If I have my friend here take his hand off your mouth, are you going to scream?"

Again, the woman shook her head.

"Hold on, Max, I'm going to sweep the place real quick." He nodded and she started by searching the end table the woman had been heading toward. Sure enough, there was a small pistol in the drawer. She couldn't blame the woman; if the tables were turned she would do the same. Of course if the tables were turned, she would have done her best to take Max down long before the man got a grip on her, but she supposed not all women had taught themselves to fight off a man. She continued to search the apartment.

The daughter was sitting at the kitchen table quietly. She looked scared and Wendy felt a little bad about that. This little girl was going to have a tough life though, so a situation like this was only going to help strengthen her. "Stay there and you won't be hurt and neither will your mommy, okay?" The little girl nodded.

There were three more bedrooms and a bathroom and Wendy carefully swept each room, checking closets and under beds just to be sure nobody was hiding. Satisfied the apartment was indeed empty, she returned to the living room.

"Okay, Max, take your hand off her mouth, I need some answers." He did so, but he kept a firm grip on the woman's arms. Wendy looked the woman in the eye and said, "Who did you think I was when I came in here?"

Confusion washed over the woman and she didn't answer.

"Answer me or my friend here will put a bullet in your little girl." Wendy glanced up at Max who gave her a look that clearly said 'screw you.'

The adrenaline was pumping hard, and mixed with the crazy pregnancy hormones, Wendy felt giddy, almost like she was high. It took effort not to smile or giggle, which was kind of sadistic given how badly they were scaring this woman.

"Please, I don't understand what you're asking, just please leave us alone!"

"Lady, I'm not who you think I am, but I want answers, and I want them now! Who did you think we were?"

"I don't know! Aren't you the same people who came here before and threatened Andrew?"

Wendy tried to look angry, but she wasn't sure if she was pulling it off. "Who came here before?"

"I… I'm not sure. I just know someone showed up and demanded Andrew follow along with their plans. They were dressed much like you, only their armor wasn't all black, it had some orange markings."

"Orange? That's Cali's colors," said Max. Wendy nodded in confirmation.

"What is it they wanted from Andrew?" she asked.

"I'm not sure. He didn't really talk about it. All I know is ever since they showed up, Andrew has been talking about how we will be able to stay where we are and not have to move in with those arrogant New Hope people."

The way she said it left no doubt she didn't think too highly of New Hope. This was interesting. When Teague had filled her in on the other communities, he made it sound like all the communities were friendly and even anxious to merge resources.

"Not a fan of New Hope, huh?"

The woman looked like she could spit. "Those pretentious bastards sit in the comfort of their underground city and let us toil away up here doing what we can to survive. Now they seem to have a way to fix the empties and they won't even share it with us. I'd rather wither away with my own people than have to suffer the tyranny of Marcus and his group of thugs."

Wendy looked at Max again, this time she was the one who was confused. Max didn't have anything to say about it. She decided not to press further. When they found Jack, this information would be helpful.

"So Andrew made a deal with Cali to ambush the meeting and take New Hope's new leader? It sounds like they double crossed him too, maybe killed him?"

The woman went pale and started to weep again.

"Is that what you think happened?" asked Wendy.

Lowering her gaze, the woman's shoulders began to shake as she wept, answering the question. Wendy believed her.

"Who else lives in the silo on the other levels?"

The woman sniffled and said, "Just the other wives and our only other seeder. Our community is dying, and if Andrew doesn't get back, I'm not sure we can survive much longer."

"Are your men all out on patrols today?"

"Yeah," she said, "Some of them are looking for Andrew, the rest are supposed to be out defending us. A lot of damn good they're doing." She had stopped crying and looked like she was getting angry again. This woman carried a lot of angst, but Wendy supposed it made sense given the situation. She never really realized how good she had things in New Hope.

"One last question. Who told New Hope that the meeting went well?"

The woman's head snapped up and she made eye contact with Wendy. The fear and anger returned to her eyes, seeming to be at war for dominance. "Son of a bitch, you're all hoppers aren't you? I never expected them to send a woman to do their dirty work. I'd say you must be barren but then that bump on your belly doesn't look like winter fat. Are you all so arrogant with your cure that you will send a pregnant woman to do your soldiering?" Before Wendy could reply, she continued, "Or maybe you're one of Jack's wives and the only one with spine enough to confront us? Well, if you're here looking for answers then you must be right. Those bastard Cali got your new leader and probably killed Andrew as well. It's a shame Marcus has been playing a pawn and wasn't there himself." This time she did spit, although she didn't come close to hitting anyone. Tears fell and her body deflated. Max had to shift his hold to keep her from sagging to the ground.

The gravity of the situation kept Wendy from reacting to the woman's insults. There was nothing she could do to this woman to bring Jack back home, and despite the woman's misguided vitriol for New Hope she felt sorry for her. She didn't even have the desire to try to defend New Hope and set the record straight. It was time to leave.

She pulled the pistol out again, ejected the magazine, and threw the pistol on the couch. "Let's go."

Max let the woman go and she crumpled to the floor. He kept his rifle on her as he backed out of the apartment but it wasn't necessary, the woman was too busy in her grief to do anything. They closed the door and headed up the stairs. "Are we going to check the other apartments?" asked Jason.

"No. I got what I came for here. That woman didn't lie to us. Her hatred of New Hope is as real as her tears."

It took a few minutes to reach the top, and Wendy's legs were burning. *At least it's good for my fat ass*, she thought. As they exited the silo, Bart asked if the mission was a success. She simply nodded and headed to the flyer.

Just as she was climbing in, there was a shout. A man came out from the silo entrance, carrying an assault rifle. Max turned and brought his rifle up, but Wendy put a hand on it, signaling for him to hold fire. Before the man could bring the weapon to bear, Bart turned around, drew the wicked looking knife, and roared a battle cry that could probably be heard for a mile.

The weapon clattered as it hit the threshold, and the man simply passed out from fear, not even making it back through the doorway.

Bart stood up straight and slid the knife back into his belt, a look of satisfaction on his face. Wendy smiled and Max and Jason laughed heartily as they all climbed into the flyer.

The adrenaline was beginning to wear off as Wendy punched the throttle and launched the flyer straight up. The acceleration was intense and the two men in the cabin were too busy holding on to notice the tears streaming down her face.

Chapter 15

Jack's eyes snapped open. A little unsure of his reality, he probed the room with all his senses. It was dark, probably night, although he was disconnected from any sense of time. All it really meant was nobody was around. The medical monitors cast an eerie glow on the rough concrete walls. The air still felt humid and cool, leaving a musty damp residue in his nostrils that didn't seem to fade. He was still bound, unable to move his legs or arms although he could distinctly feel every inch of his body. The haze of sedation was gone, replaced with pain – nothing sharp or defined, but there wasn't much of his body that didn't hurt in some way. He took in a deep breath and heard the creak of the restraints as his chest swelled with air. Whoever held him captive wasn't taking any chances, he wasn't just bound with some ropes, there was a full body restraint keeping him in place. He had a feeling if he could escape the restraints he wouldn't be able to move for several minutes if not hours just from being held in one position for so long.

It felt like he hadn't used his brain in weeks and frankly he wasn't entirely sure a few weeks hadn't passed. For a while he had held on to the idea that this was just an elaborate joke, but that was just his drug addled mind at work. Since he couldn't stretch his body, he might as well stretch his mind.

The first question didn't involve his location, at least not directly. He knew he wasn't in New Hope, and Sebastian had confirmed that much. Rather, he needed to know if he was in danger. On the surface, being bound to a gurney in a foreign environment might suggest danger was a given, but if they had wanted him dead, he would never have survived the clearing. They wanted something from him, and that brought him to the second question.

Perhaps it was as simple as his virility. Being one of the few men on the planet capable of fathering a child gave him enough value for any community to risk conflict and resources to capture him. If Thomas and his men were still alive, the rewards were quadrupled. This reminded him of the dead pilot.

He didn't know Jerry very well, but losing any of his people was disheartening. Losing one of the Reborn seemed to make it worse, although he cursed himself for feeling that way. The fact is, a virile Reborn is a lot more useful to humankind in this world, but his feelings had more to do with losing one more little bit of his old world.

Forcing himself to change his train of thought, he reviewed the last few moments before blacking out in the clearing. The memories helped him to understand why he felt so much pain. Even if these people had given him the drugs to accelerate his healing, which he doubted, he had taken one hell of a beating so it made sense he was in pain. He wiggled his pinky finger and winced. *Still broken.* There were probably some broken ribs as well, but the restraints prevented him from moving or even taking in too deep of a breath, so perhaps that was a blessing in disguise. It was impossible to tell if his leg was broken from the impact of the bullet or whether the bullet he recalled hitting his back had penetrated his undergarments, but even if they hadn't, the areas would surely be bruised severely.

At least he was still alive. The moment he woke up and thought he was reborn again made him realize just how much the idea of dying terrified him. For the first time in a long while, he had too much to live for.

Alive and not in immediate mortal danger was a relief, but it begged the question: to what purpose?

Perhaps it was time to answer the question of *where*. Most of the communities had some kind of underground bunker to hole up in if things on the surface got tough. He wasn't in Camp Wisner, or at least that was what Sebastian had said, but this still left several communities. Unfortunately he was unaware of any communities lead by a man named Sebastian. Of course, he had no idea if this man was even an authority around here, let alone a leader.

Leader or not, the man was right. Jack couldn't possibly know where he was. Even if he had enough information to figure it out, his knowledge of the other communities was simply too sparse to draw any conclusions. So he turned his attention to *why*.

Perhaps it was his ego, but he just didn't believe they only captured him for his ability to procreate. Andrew was obviously not in charge of the men who ambushed them, but he certainly knew it was about to go down. Hell, the man practically apologized for it.

The end of their conversation suggested Andrew really didn't want to end up merging with New Hope, but what would he gain by arranging the capture of its leader? And if he arranged it, why wasn't Jack sitting in a converted missile silo?

The only thing he could think of that made any sense at all was Cali. It didn't quite add up, but he had no other ideas. Cali has the resources to intimidate Camp Wisner into allowing an ambush like that, and they certainly have a reason to capture Jack. But if that is the case, why isn't Joshua interrogating him at this very moment? And from what Jack understood, they didn't have need for an underground facility, so why is he underground?

That left the question, if not Cali, then who?

He didn't get to finish this thought because right then someone entered the room, startling him. He could tell right away it was a woman, but in the dim light, he couldn't make out much more.

"I see you're awake." Definitely a woman, and by the tone of her voice she sounded friendly. This put him on the defensive.

Tentatively, he replied with a simple, "Yes." In effort to get a little more information, he asked, "Is it night?"

She walked right up to his bed before stopping to say, "Yes, in fact it is very late. Nobody will be up for several hours."

A chill ran down Jack's spine. It was one thing to consider the idea that his value to whoever his captors are is based on his virility. It is something else entirely to realize just how they can capitalize on it. Jack was all too familiar with the tone in this woman's voice. She was on the hunt. And here he was, strapped to a bed, completely unable to defend himself. Needing a way to turn her off, he asked, "Did Sebastian send you to seduce me? Are you his whore?" As the words came out of his mouth he felt his skin flush. He was normally not the kind of man who would be so rude to a woman, especially one who had not even given him a reason to speak so harshly.

He got the desired effect. Her face flashed anger and hurt and she took a step back. "How dare you! I am not Sebastian's whore, I'm his daughter!"

Well, shit, this just went from bad to worse, he thought.

~~~~

"Look, I need your help on this, but with or without you, I'm going." Wendy crossed her arms and sat heavily in the chair. Bart just stared at her while Max and Jason pretended they weren't a part of this argument.

"Little Red, you know I'd help you with anything, but I think you're being foolish and impetuous. What would you hope to accomplish by going to Cali? Even if you can get past their formidable defenses, which you probably can't even with my help, do you think you can just walk up to Joshua and demand he deliver Jack back to your arms?"

Wendy felt her face flush. He was right, but that wasn't going to stop her. Cali had Jack and she was going to get him back, regardless of how silly it sounded.

After a prolonged silence, Max said, "Look Wendy, me and Jason are going to crash in the hold of the flyer. It's late, why don't you call in what you learned to Chin and then in the morning we can head back in to New Hope and figure out the next step?"

She scoffed, "If I go back there and tell them we need to confront Cali directly, I won't be leaving there again. You and I both know it, so don't try to play dumb with me, Max."

"Well, perhaps that is what's best here. Last I checked, Cali had ten times the men we have, way more resources, and a chip on their shoulder for how our last conflict turned out. You're pregnant for God's sake, and you have three men to help you."

"Two men and one giant who could take on twenty men with his bare hands!" she replied.

Bart chortled at this comment. "Little Red, I could take on thirty of them if we were in the forest, but they have hundreds, and they're in the open in a land I am unfamiliar with, defended by weapons that can do to me what your friend did to that hellcat. It would be suicidal to try."

Again she didn't say anything. There wasn't anything to say. She had to try because life without Jack would be meaningless.

After another prolonged moment of silence, Max turned on his heel and left the house. Jason lingered.

"I suppose you're going to tell me I'm crazy too?"

"No," he said, "Actually I was going to tell you I admire you and will stand beside you if you choose to go to Cali. I agree with the others that it's a foolhardy mission, but I can see in your eyes that you will go either way, and I couldn't live with turning my back on a fellow soldier when they are in danger."

Tears welled up in Wendy's eyes. "Dammit, why would you have to go and get all honorable on me!" She buried her head in her arms and didn't see him smile and turn to leave.

When she felt a blanket being placed over her, she uncovered her face and smiled at the giant man standing over her. "Rest well, Wendy. Tomorrow we'll talk some more and decide what to do."

She fell asleep thinking about Jack and what kind of Hell he could be going through right now.

~~~~

Jack steeled himself for a blow, unable to defend himself. It never came. Instead, the woman stepped back to the bedside and said, "Do you really think if I wanted your seed I couldn't get it from you?"

Despite the dim light, he could see her face clearly now. She was actually very attractive. There was no question she was related to Sebastian and Teague. Where those men's faces were skinny and bony, hers was well defined but quite striking, perhaps even somewhat exotic, as if she had a hint of Asian or Polynesian in her blood. She leaned over him and he glanced down, somewhat involuntarily, and noticed her shirt was unbuttoned just enough to expose ample cleavage and the tops of her well rounded breasts. Quickly looking away, he said, "Nothing personal, but I'm not like the men you're used to. I have a lover, and I have no intention of being unfaithful to her." Even as the words came out of his mouth, the woman's forwardness, passion, and exotic attractiveness were sparking a battle between his mind and body. His breathing involuntarily quickened.

As a hardened soldier he had been prepared for the event of capture during the war, and although he knew every man would eventually break, he wouldn't allow any information to get into the wrong hands without one hell of a fight. However, he'd never been trained to deal with this kind of situation. In fact, he'd never even considered it. What kind of man would?

The woman laughed and stepped back once again. "I had heard that some of you practiced monogamy, but I didn't believe it. What kind of man would put a selfish woman ahead of the survival of our species?"

This piqued Jack's interest. "And where did you hear that?"

The woman laughed again. "Jack, please don't play me for a fool. If I want you to know something, I will tell you."

"I hope you want me to know then, because I'm really interested in what you have to say."

"You are pretty good at changing the subject, aren't you? Don't you want to keep talking about my lusty intentions?" Jack glanced over at her and couldn't help but notice she had a stunning figure. She was tall and slender, taller than Wendy, but quite a bit curvier as well. Wendy had an athletic figure, this woman was *voluptuous*. He chastised himself and looked away.

"No, but if you want to waste your time with it, feel free."

She once again stepped to the bed and ran a hand down his body. Even strapped down with what was effectively a full body length sheet of stout fabric from his shoulders to his ankles, he could feel her seductive touch. He tensed and then winced in pain, this time thankful he was so badly battered. The pain washed away any desire and he knew even if she unstrapped him from the restraints, any movement would prevent his body from winning the battle with his will.

Perhaps sensing this, she stopped touching him. "As much as I would love to copulate right now, I didn't come here for that. I would, however, suggest you get over this silly notion of infidelity through sex. You won't be seeing your lover anytime soon, if ever again, so there is no sense in fighting your situation."

Her words drove the reality of his situation into his mind with the force of a bullet through his heart. With effort he compartmentalized those emotions, choosing to deal with them later when he was more aware of his fate. Right now he needed to hold on to the belief that this was temporary, that he would find a way back to New Hope.

"So you're planning to keep me here for a while?"

The woman walked out of Jack's view and he heard wheels rolling on the smooth concrete floor. She slid back into his field of vision, now seated at a chair not unlike the one Wendy had been sitting in when they first met. He almost laughed at the familiarity of it all. Not more than five months ago he was in a room just like this, talking to another beautiful woman who wanted his body and his seed, late at night. In that situation he was not completely aware of how much his life was about to change. Now, however, he had a very bad feeling this familiar scene was going to lead to an equally different life. Only this time he wanted nothing to do with his life changing. He waited for a response to his question.

"Surely you didn't think we brought you here for a quick meeting before sending you home to your pregnant wife?"

Jack's mind reeled. While he had been asleep for what were probably at least a couple days, it had been a sleep forced with drugs and his mind was not feeling very sharp and well rested. *How did she know so much about him and New Hope?* He took a deep breath and focused. "Since I can't do anything about it, can you at least tell me who the traitor is who has been feeding you all this information?"

She chuckled. "It won't do you any good to know how we came about our information, but thank you for letting me know you have not yet discovered it."

Shit! He realized he was not well equipped for this kind of interrogation. "Since you aren't here to answer any questions, why are you here?" He watched her pretty face carefully, as if maybe he could get more answers from her body language.

She shifted once in the chair and didn't meet his eyes. "I've heard a lot about you, Jack, and I wanted to meet you for myself. Your story is… unusual. Not only are you from an era and a culture long extinct from this planet, but within weeks of being brought into this world you have already taken over a key community."

"I didn't take it over, I was elected to lead."

"But they already had a leadership. In fact they had perhaps the most competent leadership of any community, other than ours of course."

"Look, if you want me to explain you are going to have to answer some of my questions as well."

She appeared to mull this over for a moment before saying, "I am not at liberty to answer much, Jack, but feel free to ask."

"Didn't your father send you here to learn more about me?"

She laughed, "No, he doesn't know I'm here, actually. My turn."

"Wait! That wasn't my first question."

"But you asked and I answered. Now tell me why New Hope would give up competent leadership to such an unknown."

He sighed. This woman was sharp. He pondered his answer for a moment then decided it didn't really matter if he answered questions like this. He'd just have to be careful and not disclose anything that would put New Hope at risk. "Marcus knew he couldn't change the course humanity has taken. Humans are on the verge of extinction and as long as the people who created the situation are in power, he believed the fate of mankind was sealed. He hoped to derail our extinction by changing something big."

"But what made him think you could change anything?"

"Nope, my turn. Where am I?"

She shook her head. "You are in a room with me."

"You know what I'm asking."

"And now you know I can't answer that. Ask my father next time you see him."

"I suppose you can't tell me why I'm here or what's in store for me?"

"Nope, although I think you have a pretty good idea of what's in store for you." She said this with a seductive grin on her face.

He swallowed hard and pushed the nervous energy down deep. "Okay, then tell me about your father."

She rolled her eyes. "Come on, Jack, this isn't the game. Ask me a single question."

He sighed again. "Are my men alive?"

"Yes. You will see them soon. So what makes you so special over someone like Marcus?"

He shrugged, or at least tried to, which sent a wave of pain through his upper body. He took a slow breath, then said, "I was raised to believe in the sanctity of life. My moral base is different than the native born. Marcus saw this as a requisite for making decisions about our future."

"But you are a warrior, a soldier who has taken lives."

"Yes, in war and out of necessity, but I would also lay down my life to protect those who can't protect themselves, especially the infirm or elderly."

She scoffed, "And you believe that because we were raised to remove those who could no longer at least support themselves and had become a burden to society that we are a risk to the future of humankind?"

"Look where it got you so far."

"No! The wars that put us in this position were created by your generation, not ours. We only did what we could to survive."

"Not my generation exactly, but I see what you're saying. However, when the dust settled and mankind had another chance, you self-destructed again, even knowing exactly what the consequences were. You had a chance to start over and you nearly killed off the entire species instead. The men who ruled New Hope were born into the very culture that tried to extinguish mankind from the face of the planet. Surely you don't think they have the ability to bring it back from the edge?"

She didn't respond, seemingly lost in thought.

"Here we are, barely hanging on to existence and yet your own father, the leader of this community, has committed another act of war, one that could very well lead to conflict between my people and yours and possibly even lead to more death and destruction. How can you think for a second that people like that can keep their personal ambitions in check long enough for humanity to recover and flourish once again? You already killed one of my men, a virile man no less, someone who could have fathered a dozen children and contributed greatly to the diversity of our gene pool. You and your people are the reason New Hope elected someone like me to lead them."

Again she sat there, unable to respond. After a while he calmed down and began to relax. Exhaustion was slowly overtaking him, and his eyes began to feel heavy. He needed rest, not drug induced rest, but good old fashioned sleep so his body could heal.

As he drifted off, she finally spoke again. "You're on the east coast of the continent and your community refers to us as 'Yanks.' I'm not entirely sure what my father has in store for you, so stay on your toes and be cautious around him. I will see you again soon."

She quietly left the room without another word. Despite his exhaustion, sleep wouldn't come easily.

Chapter 16

Caleb sat up as the door to the meeting chambers opened, filling the darker room with light from the hallway. Tiny's silhouette covered the smaller man's shadow as the two men entered. Theodore stepped into the room and promptly entered the 'pit', the center of the room surrounded by the table at which the four men sat. The pit was where someone stood to address the council, but of course there was no council now, just this board, and while it wasn't quite the same, it had a strong sense of familiarity.

It was very late, but all four men had been adamant about working on this issue until they had some kind of actionable decision. Their elected leader, Jack, was missing, presumed captured or killed. Their former leader, Marcus, was completely unreachable; off pursuing a project he started nearly two hundred years ago and had to abandon in order to save what was left of humanity. Caleb sat on this Executive Advisor Board sharing his unofficial power and authority with three other men who have no real experience running a community, and who, without a clear order of succession, he might have to fight for the ability to make any truly important decisions. All this at a time when the tension between the native born population and the Reborn were at a critical juncture and even a spy for God only knows who is able to steal the most valuable item humanity has ever known right out from under their noses. Despite their willingness to sit here as long as it took to come up with their next move, they had stalled. Mostly this was due to a lack of information. Theodore had been the only man in New Hope who really understood the political situation outside of the community, and they needed a better understanding before doing something that could cause the already tense situation to escalate. It took some convincing to allow Theodore to address the Board, but with no clear course ahead of them, each man had conceded that they needed to at least hear what the traitor had to say.

Over the past century and a half, Caleb's greatest fear was failure. While there are plenty of people he could blame for the current situation, in reality he was equally responsible for laying the groundwork that allowed this to happen. He vowed to himself right then and there that if they made it past this challenge, he would not rest until he had made sure there was an infrastructure in place that would prevent this situation from ever escalating to this level again.

Turning his attention to the matter at hand, he said, "Theodore, you are not here today to defend your actions or plead your case. It is clear you have information regarding the political state of the other communities that is important to our current situation. Your honesty and thoroughness today will indeed weigh in on my future decision of your fate, so I beg of you to drop any subterfuge and ego and inform this Board with integrity.

"I am not here to plead my case, but before I can inform every one of my knowledge and give my advice I need you all to understand my position and why I took the actions I took."

Thomas spoke up and said, "As long as you aren't going to waste our time trying to justify your actions, we'll listen to what you have to say."

Theodore nodded and looked at each man in the room before continuing. "About a decade ago, it was realized that even with the ability to sustain the different communities; the gene pool was too thin for any one community to effectively bring humanity back from the brink of extinction. On paper it looked possible, but when you put it into practice the math failed to hold up. Inbreeding, accidents, and even bad luck turned what should have been a simple issue of time into a mess none of us could overcome. Even trading virile men between the communities was proving to not be enough to keep inbreeding under control. The only hope we had was to combine the various communities under one roof and coordinate all procreation in the most effective way possible.

"This is something I believe you all understand. However, what you might not know is that Cali was already just as large as all of the smaller communities combined, and even with all their efforts it was clear they would never be able to perpetuate our species on their own either. The only real answer was to merge all the western communities, if not under one roof than at least under one rule. I think it is safe to say we all know that New Hope would never have willingly joined leadership with Cali while Joshua had control. In speaking with other communities, it was clear none of them would live under Joshua's rule either. Furthermore, the longer we spoke of merging, the more obvious it became that none of the other leaders were willing to give up their own power. Even in the face of extinction, these men were unwilling to put the fate of their people in anyone else's hands."

Teague interrupted, "But you told us you were close to reaching an agreement, that aside from a few details, it was all but a done deal. Are you saying now that you lied to the council even before we discovered the facility in Montana?"

Theodore nodded grimly. "Yes. I had some ideas on how to make it happen but if I let Marcus know that the other communities were unwilling to negotiate much further I knew he would try to jump into the negotiations and make things even more complicated. See, the other communities hadn't stopped trying to negotiate some kind of agreement; they just made it clear that the agreement as far as we had worked it out up until then was no longer acceptable. I knew I could still make something work, I just needed more time. That was time I wouldn't get if the council knew how far we were from reaching an agreement."

Again Teague interrupted, "Don't you mean to say that if you had told us that your negotiations were failing you would lose respect and credibility? I have a hard time believing you withheld information like this strictly because the negotiations were so delicate that Marcus getting involved would destroy them."

Theodore's face reddened at Teague's words. Whether it was embarrassment or anger was difficult to say. He took a moment before answering. "Of course I was hesitant to admit to the council that I was unable to sway the other communities as much as I had hoped, but I assure you it was a delicate situation and Marcus would have only made it more difficult. As regarded as we all hold him, he is not seen as favorably by the other leaders." It was perhaps the most humbling thing Caleb had ever heard Theodore say and he was impressed that the man could even come this close to admitting he had been failing.

Teague didn't let up though. "Oh please, Theodore, if we had known that the situation was that tenuous then perhaps we could have acted more effectively and resolved the issues each community had with the negotiations. You jeopardized the entire community by trying to take on something that was above your ability when you had a council with a collective ability far greater than you alone."

This time Theodore didn't pause to collect his thoughts. "We? I don't ever recall you being more than a token member of the council," he scoffed. "In fact the only reason you sat with us is because you played a role in getting us out of Saber Cusp. If not for Marcus there would never have been a seat for you at this table. Why you are here today is a testament to Jack's inability to lead!"

"Enough!" Caleb slammed his fist on the table. "We aren't here to judge this man, Teague! And Theodore, you are in no position to speak poorly of Teague. This isn't the council, and here he has just as much power here as I do. If I were you, I would keep that in mind, particular as it pertains to your upcoming trial."

Theodore colored again. "My apologies, Caleb." He didn't apologize to Teague, however. "As I was saying, the situation was delicate. I needed a way to close the deal where we still had the largest authority or it would all be a waste of time anyway."

Thomas asked, "Why? The way I heard it, each community leader had more or less the same ideals as New Hope, so as long as all the communities were united, why did it matter so much who was in charge?"

"Because even combined, the smaller communities were barely the size of Cali, and they had already proven that a population of that size with so few breeders still wasn't enough to perpetuate the population. I saw that the only way to perpetuate humankind would be to have everyone under one rule, and that included Cali."

Teague scoffed and shook his head. "Like you already said, we all know that was not going to happen; at least not while Joshua was in power."

"Which is why I couldn't present my ideas to the council. I knew, however, that after a couple years as a larger community, you would be telling Marcus that we still weren't big enough, that we needed Cali to join up with us if we wanted to humanity to survive. At that point I would present a way to get rid of Joshua and open the path to bringing them into the fold."

"That's a bold plan, Theodore, but obviously it failed. You never got the other communities to agree to join us let alone to form an alliance," said Thomas.

"True. As I worked on negotiations, I got the feeling that someone was pulling some strings. The different leaders would all come up with the same objections around the same time. At first I thought it meant they were working together behind my back. See, we had the room to accommodate all the other communities, the most reliable food source, and are by far the most defensible location. That gave us the edge when negotiating and it followed that if we merged, it would be under New Hope's roof and New Hope's rule. If they formed an alliance without us though, they would have a unified voice and the power to negotiate more favorable terms for themselves.

"Unfortunately, I was wrong. I have some ears and eyes in some of the communities, and the information I was getting suggested someone outside of the other communities was talking to them, putting ideas in their heads that would keep them from making a deal with us. Naturally I suspected Joshua. Surely he too had some eyes and ears in the other communities and got word of a potential merging of communities and started his own campaign to manipulate the other leaders until things fell apart.

"I spent quite a bit of time and effort trying to verify that was the case. I actually nearly ended up in a brawl during one meeting with Deering when I probed a little too hard and they believed I was accusing them of colluding with Cali. I didn't realize how much they despised Cali."

Teague said, "Well, that explains why Glenn left so hastily."

Thomas looked at him questioningly.

"Glenn was a breeder from Deering," he explained, "He was part of an agreement to show up here and impregnate a couple of our women. This was just before we discovered the Freezer, and I think the last such arrangement we ever ended up making. He wasn't here for more than a few hours before he got into a fight with one of Red's men then left. Now it makes a lot more sense."

Thomas said, "What caused the fight?"

Teague laughed, "Well, the woman's name is Callista. After they copulated, Glenn was in the mess hall socializing and Red's man asks, 'So, do you enjoy being with Callie?' We never could figure out why Glenn got so upset at that comment." Despite the tension in the room, everyone got a chuckle at the revelation.

Caleb motioned for Theodore to continue.

"Well, I could never find evidence that Cali was involved in back channel talk with the other communities. In fact, pretty much every small community dislikes Cali as much as Deering. Before I could learn anything more, we discovered the Freezer."

Caleb already knew the story as Theodore had given him the basics earlier. However, this longer version painted a fuller picture of what was really going on, both with Theodore and with the other communities.

Theodore continued, "With the discovery in Montana, everything changed. We knew we couldn't continue to trade people with other communities as someone would talk." Everyone in the room understood just how dangerous the wealth discovered in the Freezer really is, so there was no need for Theodore to explain why the trade arrangements ended. "I couldn't even explain why we no longer wanted to trade virile men, so it was viewed as distrust. This ruined any chances of an alliance."

He paused to let it all sink in. "Then my spies started reporting some strange conversations. The leaders in nearly every community were questioning everyone about a new discovery made by New Hope. They didn't seem to know much, but they were asking a lot of questions, particularly to those who did patrols, scavenged, or traded. I knew whoever had been pulling strings before not only knew we had found something of value but also that they were still in back channel communications with the other leaders. It took me nearly a year but finally I got a piece of intelligence that confirmed what I had feared. It seems the person who had been manipulating the other communities all along was from the East Coast."

Teague exclaimed, "The Yanks? You told us they were too isolated from this part of the continent to be any kind of threat."

Shrugging, Theodore said, "As far as our research goes, they are a long way away and it is not a straight path. We never considered them a threat because of the distance and the fact that they simply never even tried to open up lines of communication with us let alone bother us. Four decades ago three communities we knew about went dark. All were on the eastern half of the continent. Shortly after, we came across a lone survivor making his way west. Most of what we know came from this man and our satellite imagery seemed to back it up. They have at least a couple thousand people and now it seems they have an eye on the western communities. That's why I ended up doing what I did."

"You mean that's why you committed treason and tried to leverage New Hope for a place in Cali's council?" This again came from Teague who seemed to really have a chip on his shoulder about Theodore. Caleb couldn't blame the man really, if he hadn't known Theodore so well for so many years he would have just written him off as a traitor and felt the same way as Teague.

"That's why I formulated a plan to protect New Hope from the greater threat and try to secure the future of humanity." The way Theodore said it sounded like he was convinced he was telling the truth. "See, with no hope of uniting the other communities under New Hope's rule and then taking Cali by force, the only option I could see would be to have a seat on Cali's council after making sure all the communities were united under their rule. I knew it meant sacrificing the sovereignty of each of the smaller communities, including New Hope, but it was far preferable to the alternative."

With a bit of disgust in his voice, Teague asked, "Did you ever think to bring any of this to the council?"

"Why bother? I already knew how Marcus would react. There was no way he would give up the resources we found in Montana. And there was no way he would join Cali, particularly if it meant Joshua would share in those resources and have the tools to strengthen his position of power, even if he could have a seat on Cali's council. And we all know Marcus would never consider trying to take down his brother. That's how wars are started, and he would have avoided that above all. Marcus would have played it safe, continued on the path he had already chosen, and perhaps tried to warn the other communities of the folly of negotiating with the Yanks. This would have let the Yanks know that we are on to their manipulation and the kid gloves would have come off. They are toying with us right now, biding their time before they strike. In fact I would be surprised if they didn't already have at least one spy in our community, someone reporting our every move to whoever is in charge on the East Coast."

At this each of the men shifted in their seats. Theodore obviously picked up on it and said, "So something has happened already? I cannot help you if you hold back even the smallest of details. I realize you have reason to distrust me, but all along my intentions have been toward keeping myself and the human species alive. If you do not believe in my loyalty to New Hope, at least believe in my loyalty to survival. Without my help you are running around blind and deaf. Let me help."

~~~~

Caleb sent Theodore out so the Board could discuss what they learned.

Teague spoke first. "I am having a hard time trusting him. He has proven to be a master at manipulation and in the several weeks he has been incarcerated he could easily have come up with a justification for his actions that sounded both plausible and for the greater good. For all we know, Theodore has been receiving information while in holding and is using it to craft his current story. Even if he is telling us the truth this time," he put the emphasis on *this time*, "it is quite a leap to assume the Yanks are involved in whatever happened with Jack."

Thomas nodded and added, "I would have to agree with Teague here, I simply don't trust Theodore at all. If the man is speaking the truth today, it isn't for the good of New Hope; it's for his own benefit in some way. On the other hand, I can't see how it would hurt if we shared the details of the current situation and see what he has to say. Perhaps we can probe a little more into whether he is involved in the disappearance of the unborn asset."

The three men turned to Scott. He almost seemed surprised they were looking at him. "Uh... if you're looking to me for advice on matters of intelligence and spying, you're looking at the wrong man."

Caleb asked, "I understand, but I would still like to know your opinion on the matter."

"My opinion is that it sure feels like we aren't doing much to find Jack. We know some kind of violence took place and we know Jack and three other men are missing along with their aircraft. We know who saw them last and we asked and got a response that's obviously a lie. If what Theodore is saying is true, now we at least have an idea of why Wisner Camp would be lying to us. Whether or not the Yanks are behind it is beyond me, but if we don't start by speaking with someone who we know is involved then why are we even here debating this?"

The men all fell silent. Caleb finally said, "I've known Theodore for a long time, both before the fall of the EoS and of course in the many years we have sat at this very table and made the decisions that got us to where we are today. I know him as someone who desires to be in charge, someone who has always resented being in Marcus' shadow, and someone who would never do something that would put humanity at risk. I believe he is at least being honest with the information he is providing today. I cannot say he isn't using this knowledge to paint himself in a better light with the four of us, simply because he knows his fate rests heavily in our judgment. However, I believe he is the only man in this community who has the first-hand knowledge to assess the situation and advise us on our next step. I believe Thomas has a good point: he is in our custody and regardless of the information we give him he is powerless to act on it any capacity. Tiny has assured me that nobody he does not trust implicitly has had contact with Theodore during his incarceration. I believe we should give him all the important facts and see what he has to say. We are all very intelligent men here; I believe we will be able to make the right decision even if Theodore is trying to manipulate us."

With heavy eyes, Teague said, "Okay, but we should at least do this with a well-rested mind. I move that we go get a few hours of sleep."

Thomas and Scott both nodded eagerly. Caleb understood, even he was not feeling as sharp as he should be. This gave him an idea. "Perhaps we should deprive Theodore of the same. Have Tiny take his time getting him back to his cell, then have the next shift get him up and have him waiting when we get back here."

They quickly voted for both and adjourned for the night.

Chapter 17

After a restless night, Wendy paced, trying to decide on what course of action to take. Every ounce of her body wanted to already be behind the controls of the flyer, on the way to Cali to rescue Jack. Her mind, on the other hand, was asking too many questions. The first and foremost being *what exactly do you hope to accomplish by flying straight to the enemy?* She didn't have an answer yet, but she also knew sitting here thinking wasn't going to get Jack back.

The second question in her head had to do with whether she should head back to New Hope and rally some more soldiers. Cali was rumored to have over three hundred people, and their air defense system was second to none. The radiation patterns meant a ground approach was difficult if not nearly impossible, and even if they had an easy way in, this wouldn't be like waltzing into Camp Wisner and confronting a lonely housewife. They've captured the leader of New Hope and they will be on high alert. The fact that they haven't reached out to barter for Jack's return or leverage him in some way probably means they just figured it would be easier to torture what they need out of him and the other men. Another wave of anxiety coursed through her body, pushing her to do something besides wait.

She was convinced that without a clear chain of command, New Hope would just waffle, delaying any kind of response. Even knowing Cali is behind this will mean a lot of debate followed by what will likely be a lot of inaction. Furthermore, while she has a lot of leeway in what she can do right now, that could change the moment she came back and reported her actions. Between being pregnant, her closeness to Jack, and her rash actions up until now, it's highly unlikely they'll let her leave again once she returns. *That just won't work*, she thought. Her emotional break the other night was a warning. If she's forced to sit and wait for the worst news, it will break her even worse, and she can't have that.

"Little Red, your pacing is loud enough to wake the dead."

She started. "Jesus Bart, I wish you could be a little noisier so I could hear you coming."

The man chuckled, a sound that practically rattled the windows. "Are you kidding? Every rodent for a mile heard me get out of bed and tromp out here." The gentle giant went to his kitchen shelves and prepared a morning meal. "Would you like something to eat?"

Wendy's mind was still reeling as they ate, but Bart wasn't about to leave her to her thoughts. "So what have you decided after some sleep? Have you come to your senses here or are you still hell-bent on a suicide mission?"

"Suicide would be returning to New Hope and being sent to my apartment to rest like a good little pregnant woman while a bunch of men who can't make up their minds sit around and debate about the next course of action as some sadistic sonofabitch in Cali works on beating some answers out of Jack."

"Oh, come on now, your imagination is getting the best of you. What would Cali have to gain from torturing someone? You don't understand the people in this world, Little Red. Whoever took Jack is after something more valuable than a little intelligence on New Hope."

"You mean like the location of a veritable gold mine of DNA diversity?" she replied with a snide tone.

Bart shook his head, "Cali already knows where the Freezer is, and torturing Jack isn't going to get them inside. Besides, the majority of the value from there is safely stored in New Hope."

"But they don't know that!"

"Sure they do. They watched you fly in with a dozen aircraft and twice as many men and clean the place out. You haven't been back since and it's been months. It doesn't take a genius to figure out that whatever was valuable in there is no longer there."

"There's still value there, we just scooped the cream off the top. At the very least it's an underground facility that could be turned into a home for a moderately sized community. And while I don't know much about cloning and genetics, Teague told me we haven't even begun to tap the value of that place."

Bart shook his head, "You're missing the point. They know where the facility is and they know New Hope is no longer all that interested in it. Surely by now they've tested the defenses we left in place and found them to be formidable. At the most they're watching to see if we start going back; otherwise it isn't worth the effort or the lives it would cost to get in."

Her anger flared. "Then why in the Hell would they take Jack? He'd never cooperate with them, so anything they get from him they'd have to beat out of him. I'm not going to sit here waiting for someone to debate the issue while that could be happening!"

Bart held up his hands in surrender. "Okay, Little Red, Okay. I understand. I just think it is highly unlikely they're torturing him. Jack certainly has value to New Hope, and perhaps they're planning to leverage him to gain some of the wealth from the Freezer. All I'm saying is perhaps the best course of action is to wait to see what they do next."

She stood up and started pacing again. "Dammit, what part of this don't you understand? I can't sit here and wait any longer. I need to do something about it."

"How about you start with calling New Hope and telling them what we found?"

"I'm going to. Then we're going to pack up some of your fancy gear and head west. We aren't going to learn anything more here, and I'm not going to sit around waiting. I'm sure as Hell not going back to New Hope to wait. I'm going with or without you. I hope it's with."

Bart sighed. "You know I'd never let you go alone."

~~~~

After waking the men and telling them to get up and get ready, she climbed into the cabin of the aircraft and turned on the radio. "Chin, this is Wendy, are you there?"

Almost immediately Chin's voice came on, "Wendy, how are things going? Learn anything?"

"I think so but I need more time to confirm it."

"What exactly does that mean? If you heard anything, tell me."

This was a tough call for Wendy. She wanted to share what she knew but didn't want to confess how she had come to know it. "We uh... overheard some chatter between Cali and Camp Wisner. Nothing specific but if they're talking then I'd bet money Cali is involved in this."

"I suppose that doesn't surprise me much, they lost a lot when you... I mean when they attacked our aircraft and that computer took most of them out. We beat them in an expensive game of chess and I've been expecting some kind of retribution. But are you sure it's Cali whose behind this?"

"Pretty sure."

"Okay, I'll get this to the Council. I mean to the Board, or whatever. They've been in the meeting chambers since last night trying to decide what to do next."

Wendy scoffed, "Typical. Any new information from the patrols?"

"Not a thing. This is the first bit of information I've heard since we confirmed the body we found was Jerry. Are you heading back here today?"

Wendy paused for just a moment before answering, "No, I... I can't be there right now. I need to be doing something, and right now the only thing being done there is sending out people in hopes of coming across Jack and his crew. I honestly don't think this is some malfunction in Jack's aircraft, so spending hours looking for a ghost would be worse than sitting in my apartment waiting for news."

"I don't blame you, but we have to be sure. You of all people should understand that."

"Yeah, I get it. I'm just not holding my breath waiting for the patrols to come back with Jack. I'm going to hang out here for a few days with Bart. Maybe we'll catch some communication that gives us more information. We might head to the Warehouse and set up a listening station to see if we can intercept some of their chatter." Lying didn't feel good but it would keep them off her back long enough for her to find out what she needed. Sharing the information she got in Camp Wisner might not be the best thing anyway. What could New Hope do with the information she has? It wasn't like they were going to mount up an attack against Cali, and from what Jack had told her, Cali wasn't exactly answering the phone these days.

"All right, I'll let everyone know where you are." He paused before adding, "Look Wendy, I know you're restless and looking for some action, but please don't go looking for a fight. The last thing we need is to find Jack and have to tell him we lost you because you went off to capture a Cali patrol and got shot down. The Board will decide how to proceed from here. Check in with me later and I'll let you know what they decide."

"Roger that, Chin. Thanks." Chin was just looking out for her. He didn't have any real authority, so if all this went sideways, at least she couldn't say she defied orders. *Better to ask forgiveness than permission, right?*

She went back inside to see if Bart was ready.

"Okay Little Red, here's the deal. If I go with you, we're only going to scout things out. No starting a fight and no infiltration. We'll probe their defenses and observe only. If things get hot, we get out of there fast."

As much as she wanted to confront those people directly, her common sense seemed to prevail. "Deal. Let's get going."

~~~~

Theodore looked positively rough. Caleb felt bad for treating him this way, but it felt like it was necessary. Besides, he could sleep all he wanted to when this was done.

"You look tired, Theodore, would you like a chair?"

"Please," the man croaked, "and a glass of water would be nice."

It was early still, but all four men sitting at the table got a few hours of needed sleep and filled their bellies with some food. Caleb was still a little tired but felt far more refreshed than he had earlier. "Thomas, would you like to explain our situation?" Just before letting Theodore in they discussed what to share and what to hold back. They all agreed that he didn't need to know about the missing head, but the rest was vital to gaining a true understanding of the situation.

Thomas cleared his throat and said, "Well, your suspicions last night were correct, Theodore, something has happened and we are not sure how to react yet. Jack has been working with the other communities for several weeks now to finish the agreements you started, or rather what you told us you had started." Caleb watched Theodore closely, but if there was any regret for his actions he hid it well. "Two days ago he went to meet with Andrew from Camp Wisner at a neutral location about halfway between here and there. Not long after he arrived we lost communication with Jack's aircraft and with the men there. We investigated the site and there is evidence of a fight and one of our men was found missing most of his head. Camp Wisner has told us that Andrew returned from the meeting and said all had gone well."

He continued to fill in all the details, including how Teague was aware of Jack's plans to form a central government rather than to just get the other communities to join New Hope, and how whoever sent the message from Camp Wisner didn't seem to know that. When he was finished, Theodore just sat there, looking lost in thought.

Caleb began to wonder if the sleep deprivation had been too much, if maybe the man had zoned out due to exhaustion. Then Theodore looked at each man and said, "Well, we certainly are in a bad situation, aren't we." He didn't sound completely upset about it. "Can I ask who is officially in charge in Jack's absence?"

Caleb snorted, "We have all the authority we need here, so don't get any ideas."

Putting up his hands, Theodore said, "Slow down, I am here to help, nothing more. I had feared something like this could happen but I did not realize how bad it really is. I am very relieved that you at least had the sense to talk to me about it."

Teague said, "We aren't here to listen to you gloat or chastise us. We are merely looking for your opinion of the situation."

Nodding, Theodore said, "I understand, I apologize if I am coming off the wrong way here, I have not had much sleep. The point here is we are indeed in a dire situation. At least Jack had the foresight to leave a solid chain of succession in place in the event something like this might happen."

Caleb managed to remain still, but Thomas and Scott shifted in their seats and glanced at each other. Theodore didn't seem to notice. "As I said last night, I suspected the Yanks had convinced each of the small communities that merging with New Hope was a bad idea for them. In fact I am positive they would never agree to a merger with New Hope at this point." He paused to take a drink of water. "From my experience with those communities, I would not be surprised if they met any kind of meeting meant to sway them toward a merger with hostility."

Shaking his head, Teague said, "But Jack had no intention of trying to form a merger, he was proposing a central government, one where each community would have equal representation."

"Are you sure they knew that? Did he open up with that or was he just trying to feel them out before proposing his plan? Keep in mind, for many years we have been talking about an alliance that would result in a merger. They would have no reason to believe that even a new leader from New Hope would be after anything different. In fact, it would be rather insulting if someone they had never even met came strutting in talking about saving everyone."

Teague colored slightly and said, "Keep your contempt for Jack out of this, Theodore. Jack would never have strutted into a meeting like that. I understand your point, and while I am unsure of the details, I believe he had been just opening up communications. However, even if any one of the other communities were offended by the offer Jack was making, I cannot see any of them risking conflict with us. They all know something is going on. Every single fertilized egg we have traded with them in the past four years would have resulted in a successful birth, and we were never asking for virile men in return. If anything I would assume they think we discovered a cure to the virus. If they think that, then surely they would think our numbers have swelled in the past few years. Nobody was going to start a conflict with a community who potentially had the cure, no matter how offended they were with us."

Theodore appeared to mull this over then said, "That could very well be. The alternative then would be that either the Yanks threatened Camp Wisner into ambushing Jack and his men, or they did it themselves."

Thomas said, "Why are you so sure it was the Yanks? Couldn't Cali have been behind this? We aren't a threat to the Yanks, but between the recent conflicts with Cali, your own treason, and the fact that by now they must know what we got from Montana, it would seem they have a lot more reason to do this."

"Anything is possible," Theodore said, "but I don't think so. Unless they have managed to get into the facility in Montana, they don't know exactly what we found there. Well, that is unless they have a spy here."

Thomas interrupted, "I don't think they will be getting into the Montana facility any time soon. We locked it up pretty tight, put some stronger defenses in place, and even set some traps that will discourage anyone who gets close from trying too hard. They would have to lose a lot of lives to get into that place. If they had, we would have been alerted and so far none of the final defenses have even been triggered yet. We still hold that facility, at least for now."

"Good to know. There is a lot more value there that we haven't tapped." He looked at Teague when he said this.

Caleb made a mental note to ask later what that exchange was all about, then asked, "Speaking of spies, Theodore, is there anyone here in New Hope you would suspect of being a spy for another community?"

Theodore shook his head, "I would think if anyone could answer that one, Caleb, it would be you. After all, internal security was your area of expertise."

Caleb flushed a little, both at the insult and at the fact that it was indeed his job to watch for that and he had not only missed whoever had stolen the head, but also that Theodore was passing information to Cali. Perhaps he wasn't as dull from the sleep deprivation as they thought. "I never detected anyone, but it seems you are better at this sort of thing than I am, so I figured it was worth asking. You were saying why you do not believe Cali is behind this?"

"Yes," Theodore showed a hint of a smug grin but hid it fairly well, "as I said before, none of the communities trust Cali. I would go so far as to say I think they despise them. And while they are larger than all of us combined, I don't think they have the resources to threaten anyone enough to create a conflict like this. As Teague said, it is likely the other communities know we have something that could help everyone, so it would take quite a threat to take any action against us, and I just fail to see how Cali could push any community that far."

Everyone in the room seemed satisfied with the answer. Nobody seemed to want to ask the next question, however, so Caleb spoke up. "So

Theodore, if you were still in power, what would you propose to this board that we do about this?"

This time there was no smug grin to hide, he simply replied, "You need to pay a visit to Camp Wisner, preferably with a few dozen men and some overwhelming force."

Thomas narrowed his eyes and said, "Even after all you have been through, you still believe violence is the answer?" Caleb wondered if the man was forgetting he had proposed the exact same response less than a day ago.

"No," Theodore replied grimly, "violence is the very last resort. However, I believe it was one of your very own presidents, ironically a Theodore, who said 'speak softly and carry a big stick.'"

The message was clear. You can't keep peace unless you have a way to enforce it.

Theodore asked, "And if the Yanks are the ones who ambushed Jack?"

"Then it is time to hold another election."

Chapter 18

Jack woke to the sound of footsteps. He'd been asleep but given the situation, his body was on alert. It was Korea all over again and nobody was going to get within ten feet of him without waking him up.

A nurse, or maybe a doctor, quietly started unhooking the restraints. She didn't speak and there was no need to warn him not to try anything; after so many hours being held in this position she knew as well as he did that he wouldn't be able to move without severe pain for at least an hour or two. With his body healing the stiffness would be even worse.

The restraining sheet came off and his left arm rolled off the table. Pain surged through his body and he gritted his teeth in effort not to show it. He tried to lift the arm back onto the narrow bed, but not only did he not have control of the appendage, the effort to move it just caused more pain. He gave in and some moans escaped his lips. He wouldn't let it turn into a scream or a cry, however. He wouldn't give them the satisfaction.

The nurse said, "I would give you something for the pain, but right now you aren't worth as much to me as a good painkiller." That was it, and she didn't look sorry. She adjusted the table to a sitting position, causing another wave of agony to rip through his body. At least now he could examine himself. It wasn't a pleasant sight. His naked body was covered in purple and brown bruises. At least he didn't see any holes. The woman began to examine him, starting with his feet. As she probed and poked he winced but with clenched teeth he managed to endure it without uttering a sound. He wasn't sure why he wanted to make her believe it didn't hurt; surely she knew how much pain he was suffering. He closed his eyes and focused on breathing.

"I have to be honest, Jack, I'm impressed with my brother's work." A familiar voice and one that was not exactly welcome at the moment. "There isn't a natural born man on this planet that's made it twenty five years without the scars to show for it. Despite the bruises your body is pretty much flawless. I'm actually quite turned on.

He dropped the charade of indifference and opened his eyes. She stood at the doorway, eyes clearly taking in his naked body. "Does it excite you to see a man so battered and bruised?"

Despite her revelation the night before, he still didn't trust her, and keeping her distracted with anger might keep her off guard. Unfortunately the comment didn't seem to faze her. "Frankly speaking, Jack, I am quite used to battered and bruised men. The world is an ugly place with little room for vanity or even hygiene. Even those who have it pretty easy are usually in far worse shape than you. Only those who have been fortunate enough to go through renewal have a body as flawless as yours, and I have never had the opportunity to bed one of them." She still didn't meet his eyes, which had the desired effect of making him uncomfortable.

"Something tells me you aren't here to untie me, apologize for the inconvenience, and let me go home."

She laughed, not an altogether unpleasant sound. In fact, with the lights on she was even more striking than the night before. Her clothes weren't typical of what a New Hope citizen would be wearing. They had more style, more flair, and showed off her voluptuous curves without leaving much to the imagination. He purposefully twisted his torso to replace those kinds of thoughts with some pain. It worked.

"Unfortunately for you, I'm not. I am, however going to move you to another floor. It won't be quite as comfortable but I think you will enjoy the company." She tossed some clothes onto his naked midsection and said, "Get dressed."

He looked at the clothes lying on his lap. Even the thought of trying to put them on was almost comical at this point. As if to emphasize, the nurse took his right arm and began to move it around. The agony was almost too much, but he pushed through it and put all his effort into relaxing. After a few minutes the pain eased and he started to feel the blood flowing into his muscles again. The nurse moved on to the other arm and the pain started again.

~~~~

It took over an hour, but eventually he could move on his own once again. The stiffness and tenderness was still present but as long as he kept moving it didn't hurt quite as bad.

By the time he was on his feet and able to walk, the woman returned. She walked up close, took his arm almost intimately, and smiled. "This way."

She led him out of the room and down a hallway, matching his slow pace and not rushing him along.

It was very reminiscent of the medical level in New Hope, but there were differences. The musty air had a hint of saltiness and the concrete walls were blotchy with moisture. The ceiling was lower and everything felt heavier, more like the bunkers he had built. "Where are you taking me?"

"Does it matter?"

It didn't, but he had to ask. There were a lot more questions though, so he just moved on. "Do you have a name?"

She smiled and said, "Trystana." She pronounced it like 'tris-donna'. "You can call me Trys."

"I would say it's nice to meet you, but you'll understand how I don't think any of this is nice."

She just laughed lightly as if he had said something whimsical and witty. "It's a pleasure to meet you, Jack. I realize you aren't happy with the situation, but nevertheless, I'm glad you're here, alive."

They came to an elevator and stepped on. To his dismay, they went down, not up. He knew there was little hope of escaping, but for some reason he felt like if he made it to the surface he would at least have a chance. As long as he was stuck down here he was a prisoner without hope.

"Tell me about Wendy. You made it sound like you love her, but you've only been around for a few months. She must be pretty special to capture your heart so quickly."

The mention of her name stabbed him in the heart. He didn't expect a question like this. "How do you know her name?"

"I know a lot of things about you."

"Are we still playing our question game?"

"If you'd like."

There wasn't much sense in evading the question and perhaps explaining his feelings would grant him some reprieve from what was surely expected of him. "Wendy is... I don't know, she's just a good woman. We clicked. Haven't you ever just met someone and you knew right away you'd like to know more about them?"

She smiled coyly. "Yes."

"Well, there you have it then, we clicked. The more I got to know her, the closer I felt."

"So it didn't have anything to do with your young body? Or your lonely heart? Or being in a foreign world and seeing a beacon of familiarity?"

He wasn't sure where she was going with this, but the questions were a little uncomfortable. "Are you suggesting my feelings for Wendy are just a reaction to being in this world?"

She shrugged, "I'm just curious what it takes to make a man want to give up all other women, and more importantly, the opportunity to father more children with those other women. I've never met a man like that, and surely the woman who has that kind of hold must either be someone special or someone very selfish."

"She *is* special, to me at least. But that isn't why I'm monogamous with her. I was raised to believe that you choose a woman, you stay true and loyal to her. Besides, it's a mutual agreement of sorts. I'd be hurt if she chose to pay intimate attention to someone else, and she'd be hurt if I did the same. There's a certain level of respect for each other's feelings."

"So it's your morality that leads you to ignore other women and only bed this one?"

He thought it over briefly. "I suppose that plays a role. I also think it's human nature though. When a relationship gets to a certain point, you open up to each other. You don't just give your body to them; you drop all your walls and let them into your heart. You share everything about you with the other person, and they share everything about them with you. But people are possessive by nature, so when someone gives you something you covet so much, you'd be hurt and maybe even angry if they went and shared it with the next person. If you really care about someone, you don't want to hurt them, so being monogamous is also about respecting each other's feelings and being able to trust that the other won't hurt you."

"So what you are saying is sex is tied to that emotional connection. Does that mean that in order to have sex, you have to have strong feelings for someone and trust them implicitly? Or just that once you have sex you will have feelings for them?"

"Well…" he faltered, "Uh, no, you can have sex even if you don't feel for someone. And sex doesn't automatically lead to caring."

"So sex isn't about emotion?"

"Not the act itself, I suppose, but the meaning behind the act is."

"But you just said you can have sex without having an emotional connection. So do you just pretend to have feelings for someone when you have sex with someone you aren't in love with?"

"No! I mean… Look you're twisting this around. The point of monogamy is that you trust each other enough to know that they won't do something that hurts you."

"Is it their act of sex that would hurt or that person feeling something emotional for someone else?"

"By having sex with someone else it means she feels emotion for someone else, and that would hurt."

She chuckled, "But you just said that sex doesn't have to involve emotion. Why would you think that by her having sex with someone else she would feel something for the man? Or that she would stop feeling that way about you?"

"I don't know, maybe it would just be the jealousy I felt for having to share her with someone else."

"Jealousy? So what you're saying is that when it comes down to it, monogamy is just about possession. About owning the person you are with and being selfish and wanting them all for yourself."

He felt like he had lost this argument, only because she clearly didn't have the same kind of upbringing as he did. She just wouldn't understand because she had been taught from day one that sex has nothing to do with intimacy or emotion. "I suppose that's the easiest way to describe it, although I don't think it's a very fair assessment. Monogamy is part of a commitment born of emotions so strong that no other person can tempt either one of you, either physically or emotionally. If they can, it's a sign that your commitment is not as strong as you thought."

"So you have never been tempted? No woman has ever caught your eye and made your loins stir with desire while you have been in a relationship?"

The elevator had stopped and now he stepped off, wanting to walk away from this conversation. She didn't follow immediately.

"Answer the question," she said, "and I'll stop asking about this."

He turned and sighed. "Yes, sometimes I get tempted. It doesn't mean I don't love Wendy though, it just means my body wants something my heart doesn't. My commitment to her means I wouldn't do that though, and I trust that she wouldn't either. I know it sounds hypocritical, but it's just the nature of mankind. We want things that are in opposition. Whichever thing we want

more tends to win out. Some would say that is where religion comes from – good versus evil, the devil trying to influence us from straying from the path of good."

"Are you a religious man, Jack?"

"Not particularly. I was raised to believe in God, and I still do. I'm not so sure about religion these days, however. Why?"

She shrugged, "I just don't want you to think of me as the devil. Can I ask you one more question?"

"Sure."

"Were you married in your former life?"

The question intrigued him. "Yes…"

"And how long after she was lost to you did you allow yourself to stop being monogamous to her?"

The question stung a bit. Not only did it bring back some of the questions he had when he first met Wendy, but it also drove home what was surely her point: he wasn't going to be seeing Wendy anytime soon, if ever. If she is truly lost to him, how long before he accepts it? "You said one more question, and I already answered."

~~~~

Trystana pressed her thumb to a panel and the door opened. "This is your new living quarters. It's the old barracks, so you'll be sharing with several others. I trust you'll be okay with that, however. Food will be brought a few times per day. For now you won't be allowed to leave this room, but depending on how well you cooperate that might change. Thank you for the conversation. It was very enlightening." She turned away before he could say anything.

"Jack!"

He turned to the voice and stepped into the room. He didn't hear the door close behind him. "Anton? Thank goodness you're okay!" Anton and his three men were standing, looking at him as if they had expected to never see him again.

Anton walked up to him. Smiling he said, "I told you, call me Tony." His smile faded, "Jesus, you look like hell. They really did a number on your face. How about the rest of you? I heard the shot and saw you go down. I feared the worst."

Jack shrugged painfully and said, "I'm a little bruised up but as far as I can tell there aren't any holes in me. I'm thankful I was wearing that under suit. How about you? One of your men looks like he took a few blows to the face. Everyone okay?"

Anton nodded slowly. "All except for Jerry," he said solemnly.

"Yeah, when I saw his body lying there I knew we had to fight for our lives. I honestly thought I was dead."

"Well, I'm glad you aren't. You sure gave them hell going down though. Come on, let's get you settled in and have a talk."

The room was large, perhaps fifty feet wide and twice that in length. Unlike the larger rooms in New Hope, this one had beefy concrete pillars every twenty feet supporting the ceiling, further proof that this was more like a bunker he had built. If Trystana had been telling the truth, they were on the East Coast, and he had never built anything over here, so it definitely wasn't one of his. It might aid him in coming up with a way out, however.

There were several partitions, all about five feet high. They divided the room up into cubicles. He could see that they each contained two bunks. It looked more like a prison than a military barracks. Several other people were in the room with them. The ones he could see standing around were haggard looking men. He wondered if Andrew was here or if they had let him go. The last glimpse he had of the man and his guards looked like they weren't exactly feeling safe.

Anton showed him to an unused bunk. "If you don't mind, you can bunk in this cube with me. We've been taking turns keeping watch at night. So far nobody else in here has given us trouble, but I'm not about to let my guard down." The bunk was sparse and looked uncomfortable. He sat down, feeling exhausted from the walk down here.

"Thanks. I'm not sure I'll get much good rest here for a few days while I heal, but I suppose it could be worse. I've been restrained for the last day or two, maybe longer. My body is pretty unhappy with me right now."

Anton snorted. "It couldn't have been for more than two days, that's how long it's been since we arrived. In fact, lunch should be delivered pretty soon." He rubbed his belly. "Have you learned anything about where we are yet?"

Jack shook his head. "Not really. The woman who brought me here said we're on the East Coast, but I'm not sure I trust her enough to believe her. Her father seems to be an authority around here, if not the leader. And get this: he's a spitting image of Teague. When I woke up I thought for sure I'd been killed and was back in New Hope, fresh out of the tank."

"No shit? That must have been a real trip. Is this guy some kind of clone of Teague's then?"

"I don't think so; I think it's the other way around actually. I got the feeling this guy is old school, as in one of the founders of the EoS. He has the same kind of mannerisms as Marcus, only he seems somewhat demented."

Anton frowned. "I don't get it. If Teague's father is the leader of another community, why didn't he say anything?"

"Probably for the same reason Marcus never shared that Joshua is his brother. A lot of strange shit went down in the Enclaves of Science, and I'm willing to bet we will probably never know or understand half of it."

"So the good looking woman who dropped you off here is Teague's sister? That blows me away. Well, you certainly learned more than we did. All I can tell you is that we've been stuck in here since we arrived. The flight was fairly long, so East Coast wouldn't surprise me much, although frankly I figured this was the West Coast. Some of the guards are wearing orange markings on their armor. They had us in the hold, so we never saw any landmarks that could tell us where we are or what direction we were going. When we landed it was getting dark and I think we landed inside a hangar or cave or something. I couldn't see stars. They moved us right in here and we've been here since."

"Have you made any friends in here yet?"

Anton poked a head above the partition and scanned the room. "Not really. We tried to chat with those other men but they didn't seem too friendly so we've been giving them some space. However, we have made some other friends it seems."

"Oh yeah? Let me guess, some female visitors?"

Anton chortled. "Oh yeah. Every night several women come down. The guards let them in and they come around looking for some attention. They're pretty persistent but so far I've been able to keep them off me. My men aren't exactly unhappy though. Things could be a lot worse. They do pay attention to a couple of the other men in this room, so there must be some other virile men here as well."

This was all very discouraging. It seemed Sebastian, or whoever was running this place, expected them to contribute to the gene pool. This was perhaps Jack's greatest fear. "How do you feel about all this?"

"The women?" Anton asked, "Well, I'm happily married and have no desire to have any kind of sexual relations here. Besides, each child we give them could end up being an enemy one day. That wouldn't sit too well with me."

"You married a native, right?"

"Yeah. I know her well enough to know she would never care about me having sex with women here. In fact she would encourage me if she could, just to spread my seed. Even having permission though just feels wrong. I feel sick just thinking that in a few months she could be with another man, assuming we're stuck here for a while. Do you know what I mean?"

Jack nodded, "Yeah, I do. As a matter of fact Trystana, that woman who brought me in, was just talking about the same subject. She just didn't understand though. We come from a different world and I guess our minds just work in a different way. Good luck trying to explain it to any native born. And good luck trying to understand it yourself. I hate to say it, but we might be stuck here for a while. I'm not sure what Sebastian has in store for us, but whatever it is I don't think we'll be getting out of here easily. He wouldn't have gone to the effort and risk if he didn't have big rewards in mind. Let's keep our eyes and ears open, try to get friendly with the others in this room and try to get as much information as we can. If the men are sleeping with the women they send in, have them drill the women for information. Maybe we can figure out a way to get out of this place."

Chapter 19

Wendy eased the flyer down onto the makeshift pad. In the weeks since they discovered the Warehouse, the other scavenging crews had made some major progress. A landing pad was created close to the building, and an actual air strip was cut into the forest. A few weeks ago Wendy flew their big transport plane in and hauled all the machinery they could fit back to New Hope. Once that machinery was made functional, they had planned to come back for more, but that wouldn't be for a few more weeks. Aside from some remote sensors, the place was left unguarded. Chin would know she was here, but then he would already expect that.

Everyone got out, stretched their legs, and took care of any business. Silver was running around, obviously excited to be somewhere he recognized, even if he was just a newborn pup the last time he was here. "Still not sure why you brought him," she said.

Bart shrugged. "I wasn't going to leave him if we were going to be gone for more than a few days. Besides, he'll end up being an asset if we run into trouble."

"Okay, but if he shits in my aircraft you're cleaning it up! Stretch your legs everyone, we're heading back out in ten minutes!"

Jumping back into the cockpit, she called in to New Hope. Johnson answered, and when she asked where Chin was, he replied, "He needed a quick break. Said something about looking at a board?"

"What the hell are you talking about?"

"He said he had to see a board. I figured he was just tired and mumbling nonsense to himself."

"Oh, he must be meeting with the Board. Look, just tell him I'm up at the Warehouse, but I'm going to scout a little to the South. My radio is going to be off so I don't attract any attention, so if he needs to reach me he can contact me later tonight after I can get the laser radio set up. You got all that?"

"Yeah, yeah. At the warehouse, no radio, doing some scouting. I'll tell him."

She signed off and then reached under the dash of the controls and disabled the radio and tracking. If Cali's air defense was half as good as she had been told they would surely pick up any kind of signals coming from her aircraft. The only part of her communications system left on was the open channel radio, and it was just listening, not transmitting any signals.

Three minutes later she fired up the propellers again and prepared to head out.

~~~~

"Max, do you have a woman back at home?" Despite her anxiety, she couldn't make time go by faster. They were scouting the northern airspace around Cali and it was quite boring. Wendy needed conversation to keep her mind off Jack.

"I have too many, but none I like enough to settle down with. I'm not sure any of them are too interested in settling down anyway, so it's probably good."

Wendy stifled the urge to scoff. She didn't have much respect for the women of New Hope. Not that she had a lot of respect for most women from her own time, but these women were worse by far. At best they had one skill: seduction. *Or perhaps two*, she thought. They seemed to be pretty good at being mothers too, but she wasn't really sure that was a skill she could respect. She reserved judgement until after she had her own child since she didn't really have any experience in that field. As for their first skill, she didn't exactly have disrespect for them; it was more like she simply disregarded them. They were just another factor to deal with in this new life. Very few of them could do anything of real day to day value. Sure, procreation was important, now more than ever, but women were in abundance, and in fact Teague had told her it was common to abort pregnancies where the baby would be female.

The women here just seemed to have it too easy. They seldom had any real responsibilities and all they seemed to do was wander around looking to get pregnant. Wendy had never been in a situation in her life where she didn't have to work hard for everything she had. In the Army, she had to work twice as hard to gain the respect of the men, and even then it only went so far. Women who used their vaginas to get ahead were always regarded with animosity in her life.

Despite bringing the subject up herself, she wanted to change it. "So what was your MOS in your old life?"

"I drove a Bradley mostly. Spent some time behind a gun in Iraq. Nothing too special. Really just wasn't sure what I wanted out of life, so I stayed enlisted until I could figure it out. Didn't mind the fighting or the heat, never lost a night of sleep over the shit I saw, so it seemed like a good fit. The pay wasn't great but back home in Detroit there wasn't much for jobs anyway. Not that I would have wanted to go back home. That wasn't exactly a great life either."

She nodded, more because she had heard the same story a hundred times while in the Army. Her own life wasn't quite the same. She had plenty of ideas of what she wanted out of life. She didn't really know where to take the conversation from there, but he seemed okay just talking, which was good as far as she was concerned.

"I got to visit a few interesting places. Spent a year in Germany, a year in Korea, was in Iraq twice, both in the second war. I lived on both coasts in the U.S. and even did a tour in Egypt. Would have been headed for Afghanistan if I hadn't..." He let that trail off without another word.

"It's okay if you don't want to talk about it," she replied.

"No, it isn't that, I just feel like I was expendable. I had no direction, wasn't exactly skilled. I was a soldier, never had the desire to command or anything like that. I just can't see why the Army would choose to put me in the Freezer. I wasn't much value to them back then."

She shrugged. "If they didn't see value you wouldn't have been allowed to re-enlist, at least not toward the end. Besides, you're pretty darn valuable now."

"My sperm is valuable, I'm not so sure about the rest of me."

"Oh come on. You're a soldier who's seen combat; that puts you above half the men Teague has brought back. You aren't exactly hard on the eyes, and I suppose that's a plus these days. You take orders and don't shy away from danger, and that's a big bonus in my book, particularly since you're with me. I'd say New Hope is pretty lucky to have a guy like you."

Max smiled shyly. "Thanks Ma'am. I mean, Wendy. Sorry if I'm being a downer, I always seem to get this way when I know I might end up fighting. I guess it's my way to react to the idea I might die."

Wendy could understand that. "Don't worry about it, I get it. Just keep your helmet on and don't get shot in the head and chances are you will be brought back if you die. These days immortality is cheap."

Max laughed. "Too cheap. I can't even imagine what living for more than a hundred years does to these people. I was barely in my forties and had lived enough to not be too sorry to get my ticket punched."

Wendy was surprised at how profound his simple statement was. Jack was having such a hard time understanding the native born. Some of them had been cloned, particularly the leaders. Perhaps part of the disconnect in cultures had to do with what effectively was immortality. How do you even begin to understand how someone who is approaching two centuries of life sees the world?

A light flashed on the instrument panel, interrupting her train of thought. Curious, she looked at one of the display panels to see what was up. The radar panel showed three aircraft heading straight at her. "Strap in!" she shouted to the men then turned the craft east while assessing the situation. They were about a hundred miles north of Cali, and she hadn't expected to run into any patrol craft for at least another twenty minutes. She certainly didn't expect to be spotted before she saw one.

Another light came on; this one signifying there was a hailing signal on the open channel of her radio. She punched the button and the speaker crackled, "Unknown aircraft, you have entered Cali airspace. Turn to the following coordinates and prepare to be escorted to a landing site. If you turn and flee we will run you down. You are surrounded on all sides. You have sixty seconds to comply."

"Oh shit," she said. Her mind raced. She turned again, heading back the way they came. Surely they were bluffing about being surrounded. Her radar should have picked up anyone for dozens of miles, and she hadn't spotted so much as a large bird, let alone several aircraft. At full throttle the medium flyer was fast, but not as fast as the smaller two seater flyers that were showing on the radar. She was making just under 450 miles per hour airspeed, but even at this rate they'd be in range to fire on them in a few minutes, at which point she would be forced to comply or fight. She had no intention of getting into a dogfight when she was in the slower and clumsier aircraft. Then the radar beeped and dead ahead of them two more aircraft showed up. At her current speed they would be in visual range in less than a minute.

Fear and regret overwhelmed her and she nearly shut down. Floundering under a wave of guilt and shame, she struggled to get it under control. Her need for answers had overridden her common sense and now she was cornered, caught in a trap she should have seen coming. With effort she swallowed the fear and compartmentalized the rest of her emotions. Quickly assessing her options, she ran the scenarios through her head hoping one would be preferable to another. Escape from this trap looked grim. If she landed and tried to play it off like she was just trying to make contact to trade, they would inspect her hold and find Bart there, and that wouldn't end well. If she fought in the air, they would surely win. If she ditched the flyer and headed out on foot, they could at least fight and run under the cover of trees, but with air support and superior numbers, even Bart's superior fighting ability might not be enough to keep them from being captured.

"Shit!" She exclaimed in frustration. So far there wasn't anyone on the radar to the north or south, but since they managed to sneak behind them there was no reason to believe they were bluffing any more.

Something Jack said to her before he left came to mind. She was too valuable of a prize to go with him. If she followed their direction she would end up the newest citizen of Cali. And if they figured out who she was, they would use her to get Jack to tell them anything they wanted to know and maybe even to help them infiltrate New Hope. "Open the cargo hatch!"

Jason turned and quickly opened the hatch to the cargo bay.

"Bart! Hold on, this is going to be a hard landing!"

"What? Why? What's wrong?" The big man could easily be heard over the whine of the engines running at full speed.

"Cali spotted us and set a trap. They're closing in on us from all sides and if they catch us they'll kill you and Silver and take the rest of us. I'm going to drop us to the tree line and then put us down and it might get really rough. The moment we land we'll only have seconds to get to cover and camouflage ourselves from their sensors. Get ready!"

Turning back she analyzed the landscape once more, and then started her rapid descent. The Cali aircraft would have a visual on her in just a few more seconds, and if they saw everyone exit the aircraft before finding cover they wouldn't stand a chance of getting away.

They were on the western edge of the Cascade Mountains in the northern part of what used to be California. To the west was the Sacramento Valley, but it was a ways off. Thankfully they were over a few thousand acres of forest land that wasn't an irradiated wasteland. She only hoped it wasn't boxed in on all sides, or worse, home to latent biological weapons. Spotting a small clearing surrounded by thick trees, she dove quickly, nearly as fast as her dive into Camp Wisner.

A hundred feet above the ground she leveled out, aiming toward the clearing. The treetops here were almost brushing the bottom of her flyer. As she crossed the threshold of the clearing she stalled the aircraft on purpose, dropping nearly eighty feet in about a second and placing everyone in the craft at zero gravity. As quickly as she had stalled it, she swung controls the opposite direction throwing the propellers into full thrust and creating a cushion of high pressure air under the aircraft that acted like a giant pillow. Despite the cushion the occupants would feel around seven times the normal pull of the earth. The skids slammed into the ground, but they were still moving forward at nearly eighty miles per hour, skiing across the clearing. She reared back on the controls, trying to stop the craft before the clearing ran out of room. She was almost successful.

The craft jolted as it wedged between two ancient cedars and came to an abrupt stop. Max wasn't completely belted in and his head slammed into the dash of the cockpit. Wendy punched the controls to open the hatch and only paused long enough to see if Max was still conscious. He was, so she grabbed her pack and threw her door open. "Get out! We need to get as far from here as we can!"

Bart appeared in front of the craft, scanning the forest ahead of them while waiting for the others to get out. Without a word, he plunged ahead, Silver at his side. Within moments Wendy couldn't see or hear him, but she kept forging ahead, trying to spot the path the big man took. The forest was thick through here, if she hadn't spotted the clearing she would have ended up fifty feet up in the trees. Glancing back, the flyer was already out of sight. Max and Jason looked at her for direction and she simply nodded grimly to both men before turning back toward where she had last seen Bart. It took effort not to think about their dire situation.

Part 3

Chapter 20

Matthew paced nervously as he went over his notes for the hundredth time. The apartment was small enough that he could only take five or six steps before having to turn around again. It wasn't presenting his arguments to the rest of the council that gave him the anxiety but rather what he was proposing. There were so many unknowns. Nobody had stepped foot outside of Sanct in nearly three hundred years.

Yet he believed this was the only option available. The failure of the crops would continue, of that he had little doubt. If there were something they could do to reverse the eight year trend, they would have found it by now. It was simply beyond their capability to fix. For the fifth time in the past three hours, he threw the notes on the chair in disgust and fell into the couch with a heavy sigh.

There was still over an hour to kill before the meeting. If he went to his parent's place early he would have to endure an interrogation from his mother. He and Angela had only been on two dates, yet his mother was already heavy handedly hinting about how nice it would be to have a grandchild. Anxiously pacing his empty apartment seemed like a far better idea.

He made it thirty seconds before he felt the urge to pace again. As he stood, his phone rang. Desperate for any kind of diversion from his anxiety, he pressed the answer button without bothering to look who was calling and simply said, "Yes?"

"Hey Matt. What's shakin?"

"Oh, hey Carter. Nothing much, just hanging out. You?" Carter may be an up and comer in Systems, but he wasn't a leader yet. That meant he wasn't privy to the meeting this afternoon, so Matthew couldn't talk about it.

"I just finished a marathon coding session and launched a new mini game on the Net. I'm about ready to crash and get like fifteen hours of sleep."

"Geez, that's like the third new game in a month. You're on a mission." Matthew kept up with current Net events just enough to be able to stay relevant in conversations. He was one of the few people who had little desire, or time, to get too involved.

"Uh, more like the fifth! What, have you been hiding in a cave?"

It was a lame joke that Carter overused, but Matt laughed anyway. "Sorry, the past few weeks have been crazy. Congratulations, you're really rocking the system with your code."

"Thanks! I hear you've been busy. I also wanted to say congrats. You owe me one big time."

"How's that? What the hell are you talking about?"

"Don't give me that shit, you know exactly what I'm talking about. I did you a solid, bro, and you owe me."

"Is this about Angela? How is it I owe you anything?"

"Oh come on, we've been friends since we could talk, I know you've always had the hots for her, and your position there meant you would never be able to ask her out. I finally convinced her to move to my level so you could finally ask her out. Frankly though I'm surprised you actually did it on your own. If you hadn't pulled the trigger on this, I was going to call you up and tell you to shit or get off the pot."

"Oh, don't give me that bullshit, Carter, you've had just as much of a thing for her as I have. You moved her to your level so you could be closer to her, and you know it!"

Carter laughed, "What! Why would I bring her to my level? I'm not far behind you in becoming Head of Systems, and I'd end up in the same boat you've been in."

This was true, but Carter was always trying to work an angle. There was no way he'd offered her the job just for Matt's sake. "Well, whatever the reason, you sure as hell didn't move her to your level because of me. I know you too well."

"I'm hurt, bro. Why wouldn't I do something for my two best friends? At least give me the benefit of the doubt."

"Okay. Fine. So maybe you did offer her the job for me. And I can't say I'm not unhappy about it. I'll get you a round the next time we're out."

"That's cool, Matt, but you owe me more than just a round."

"Don't push your luck, Carter."

"Oh relax. There is something you can do for me though."

Always an angle. "Yeah, what's that?"

"Give me the skinny on what's going down today. Monty is too quiet lately, and rumor is there's a big meeting this afternoon at your place. I just want to know what's happening."

Shit. This was all Matthew needed, someone out spreading rumors. "I don't know what you're talking about. What did you hear?"

"Come on, man, I'm practically in charge of the Net, I hear everything. Between Monty being all hush-hush, you being non-existent in the Net, and Vernon's kid Mike talking about how his dad's been a real asshole lately, it isn't tough to figure out there is some kind of important meeting going on soon. All it took to confirm was overhearing a couple of your minions complaining about how they had to deliver a bunch of food to your pop's house on Restday."

The man was too smart for his own good. "Listen to me carefully, Carter. You don't need to concern yourself with what goes on with council meetings. Trust me, it hasn't got anything to do with you. And I better not find out you're spreading rumors." That wasn't entirely true, of course, it had to do with everyone in Sanct, but if word got out about what they were talking about, it would cause unrest, and unrest was bad.

"Alright. No need to get your panties in a bunch. The truth is, Monty's lost his edge, and I'm hoping he'll be retiring soon. I just figured maybe this meeting was about him officially announcing retirement and the council voting on his replacement. I've been working my ass off to get set up for this position. I know I've got your vote, but hey, not everyone thinks I am best suited for this job."

"Wait, is that why you offered the job to Angela? To score some points so I'll be there to speak for you if the head position opens up?"

"No way, Matt! Geez, do you really think I'm that self-centered?"

"Well…"

"Oh, come on!"

"Okay, maybe not, but don't hand me this line of bullshit about you convincing her to transfer just for me."

"Damn, you must be wound tight right now! Whatever, you can believe what you want, but I was thinking of you when I offered her the job. Besides, there wasn't a chance of me and her ever happening. I've been asking her out for years and she always shoots me down. She's always had a thing for you." This comment left him stunned. He had no idea she ever had a thing for him. It explained so much. "You still there, dude?"

"Uh, yeah. Why didn't you tell me she had a thing for me?"

"Are you serious? I thought you knew! Hell, I figured you guys probably hooked up back when we were teenagers and just backed off when you both got assigned to the same level."

"Nope, I never thought she would go for a guy like me. Hell, I was starting to feel guilty about asking her out during this transition. You know, like I was taking advantage of her feeling vulnerable or something."

"Hah! For someone as smart as you are, you sure are stupid sometimes. Look, are you sure this thing today isn't about Monty retiring?"

"I'm sure, and I was serious when I said you need to keep your nose out of it. It doesn't take much to start rumors with no merit that can lead to unrest. If you cause some unrest here you could end up in jail and then you could kiss your hopes and dreams goodbye. Just stick to what you do best and things will come around for you. I *do* have your back if the position becomes open."

"Okay, bro, I appreciate it. Let me know if you want to get a first look at the new game I finished earlier. I'm gonna go crash for a while."

"Hey Carter? Thanks. I mean that. I've only been on a couple dates with Angela, but things are going really good, and it means a lot to me that you might have helped that happen. Even if you did it as much for you as for me."

"My pleasure bro. I will take you up on that drink sometime too."

~~~~

The conversation had done a lot to take his mind off the seriousness of the meeting, but as he entered his parent's home, the weight of it came back just as strongly. He was well prepared, but this was the part of the job he really didn't like – being responsible for so many people's fate.

After pleasantries with his mother and a promise to stick around after the meeting to talk, he sat down at the table.

He expected it to be chaotic from the start, but to his surprise the mood was somber. His father stood up to announce the start of the meeting.

"Gentlemen, and Lady, we are here tonight to decide if we should take a monumental step. For nearly three centuries the city of Sanct has endured. Our forefathers were tasked with saving humanity from the devastation of an apocalyptic war. For all we know, we could be the only humans left in the universe. Returning to the surface has always been left to our discretion as the creators of this city knew they would never be able to foresee exactly what circumstances forced us to close ourselves off from the rest of the world. Tonight we will decide if that time has come. Since he is the one who brought this option to the table, I will start the meeting by giving the floor to Matthew."

Matthew took a deep breath, glanced at his notes one more time, and stood up. "Thank you, Jonathan." It always felt weird to call his father by his formal name. "I have spent the past several years analyzing numbers, and the recent data I brought to your attention three weeks ago has made it clear to me that Sanct is in trouble. Barring some kind of miracle, I can't see how things will suddenly get better without intervention. It is true there have been declines in production in our history, but never for more than a few years, and never to this extent.

"If we don't seek answers on the surface, here is what will happen: Within a few years we will be forced to drastically slow, or even stop reproduction. Setting aside the ancillary effects that decision would have on the peaceful state of our population, the future of our city would begin to look very grim. Adjusting the population down so dramatically has quite a few consequences. First and foremost would be the necessity to ration food. Second, the older generation would have to work longer before the potential for retirement. Third, work hours would have to be extended and jobs consolidated. It would take several years before enough elderly have died off and we could resume a more normal birth rate. That would leave a generational gap that could cause other problems."

As he said the next sentence, he turned to Monty. "Fourth, as the population declined, so would the workforce, meaning certain types of non-critical jobs would have to be eliminated. Jobs like maintenance of the Net." He watched the old man pale as he said this. The Net wasn't just a game, it was the only escape people had. Sanct was a massive city, but it was still a cave, and the only way out was through the door to the surface. Humans were never meant to be caged like this, and while people were, in general, happy, the Net had an incredibly large influence on that happiness. Just as a plague could quickly wipe out an enclosed population like theirs, dissent and unrest could destroy the city in short order.

He continued, "Furthermore, there is no guarantee the rate of decline in crop production would not continue, or worse, accelerate. Even if we halted population growth completely, unchecked acceleration in that rate of decline would mean starvation within two decades, possibly sooner."

Before he could continue, a murmur rose in the room. Jonathan rapped his hand on the table to remind everyone that Matthew had the floor, and it was disrespectful to interrupt whoever was speaking. Everyone here would have their say before the meeting ended.

"I don't think it is necessary to speculate further on what we don't know for sure. Best case scenario here is we stick to the adjustments we made three weeks ago and hope production doesn't continue to decline. Worst case scenario, Sanct will no longer be a viable home within a couple decades. I understand many of the risks involved with going topside even if just to collect samples, but it is my opinion the risk is necessary. Thank You."

He took a seat but his anxiety didn't ease up with the conclusion of his speech. Once everyone here had a chance to say their piece, they would vote. Unfortunately, the vote was just the beginning, and either way it went there wasn't an easy path ahead.

Chapter 21

The meeting was called to order. Not everyone from New Hope was in attendance, but the meeting room was fairly full. Twenty Reborn soldiers, another dozen scavengers and maintenance crew, and the few native born men who weren't currently incarcerated but willing and able to fight were all present. For the most part, this was the remaining fighting force of New Hope. If it came down to it, another three dozen people could be armed to defend their home, but most of those people would have little to no experience with conflict and even less desire to engage in violence.

A few of the native born women were here, more out of curiosity than necessity. Every detail of what was discussed today would be spread to the rest of the population, probably with some inevitable inaccuracies. It was an open meeting though, and the intent was to dispel rumors and relay only the hard facts.

Of course, the four members of the Board were seated at the table in front of the auditorium style room. Caleb opened his mouth to start the meeting, but Teague took the lead before he could say anything. He felt his face turn red, but he wasn't sure if it was annoyance or just embarrassment over assuming he would take the lead.

"Ladies and Gentlemen, I appreciate you all coming to this meeting," Teague announced, "I'm sure there are plenty of questions; hopefully we can answer most of them. First, I and the three other men before you are part of a group Jack put together just before leaving a week ago. We are his Executive Advisor Board, and in his absence, we have been placed in charge of New Hope."

One of the native born men stood up and said, "I think I speak for most of us here when I ask: How do we know you aren't just taking advantage of Jack's absence to seize power? It seems mighty convenient that he headed off without a word and didn't come back. Now you four are saying he gave you authority. It sounds a bit fishy to me." Quite a few people in the room nodded and murmured their consent.

Expecting this, Caleb jumped in. "I will admit the timing is less than ideal, but Jack only asked us to join the board mere hours before leaving. He was planning to make an official announcement when he returned, which of course never happened. Hence the reason we're all here right now. However, as you know, I spent nearly two hundred years of my life as a part of this community's leadership and am one of the founders. In fact, I remember very well the day we opened our doors to you and your family, Josef. If you truly believe me to be lying about this then I must have failed you all during that time."

Josef looked away from Caleb's eyes but still replied, "I used to place all my trust in the council but you know as well as I do why that trust is now questioned." Several of the men around him agreed, both native and Reborn alike. He looked back up and asked, "How about his woman? I wouldn't question your claim if she backed it up. Conveniently for you I haven't seen her around lately either. Any insight there?"

Chuck, sitting in the front row, stood up and turned to the noisy crowd. "If it's any help, Jack asked me to be part of this Board and I turned him down. I actually recommended he ask Caleb to join, so I believe they're telling the truth here. Besides, what does it matter? The council didn't really hold this place together while it led just like Jack isn't the only reason you are all alive today. We're a small community that's pretty much self-sufficient. We only need a leader because of things like dealing with outside communities or having someone to settle the inevitable disputes within our own community."

"Before the election I never would have questioned who was in charge, or even cared much for that matter. I guess having a role in deciding who makes the decisions around here changed how I look at things." Josef's reply gave Caleb new insight into the population of New Hope. Even such a small change had impacted the way the citizens view their community. Whether this was a positive change or not was still open to interpretation. He filed it away for later.

"Well, Jack's not here and right now we have a situation that requires someone to make the hard decisions," Chuck continued, "If, and as far as I'm concerned this is purely hypothetical here, the worst case scenario plays out and our elected leader isn't back soon, then we can just hold another election and officially decide who we want to run New Hope." He turned back to the Board and said, "I'm sure if we give these men a chance to speak we'll all get the answers we're looking for, including the whereabouts of Wendy." The last comment sent a spike of anxiety through Caleb's belly. Chuck had purposely been kept out of the loop on that situation, and there was no telling how he would react to learning the situation.

The room settled down and Teague continued as if he hadn't been interrupted the first time. "Thank you, Chuck. The purpose of this meeting is indeed to inform all of you of the current situation, end any rumors, and decide our next course of action. If you haven't all heard yet, Jack went to meet with the leader of Camp Wisner a week ago and didn't return. What you probably don't know are the details regarding the past week and what we have done in effort to find him."

The door to the conference room opened, and all eyes turned to see who was entering late. Caleb was surprised to see William walk through the door. He hadn't spoken to the man since the council was disbanded and the rumors suggested he had been somewhat of a recluse since Jack took leadership. "Sorry I'm late, please carry on," William said quietly before taking a seat near the door and away from the rest of the crowd.

Teague glanced at Caleb briefly before continuing, a look that said he was just as curious about the late attendee. "When we first lost contact with the flyer, we sent out a patrol to investigate." Now he looked down. "It appears some kind of fight took place at the meeting location. One of our men, Jerry, was killed in the fight. We recovered his body."

A few murmurs and sobs were heard from the crowd and Teague took a moment before continuing. "The past week has mostly been spent trying to put the pieces together and gather enough intelligence to decide on our next move. We've officially ruled out any accidents and completed a very thorough search of the area between here and Colorado where Jack and his men were last known to be. At this point we are confident he was ambushed and did not escape."

"Who's behind it and when do we strike back?" Caleb didn't notice who asked the question – he was too busy watching William, trying to decide of the man's sudden appearance meant anything. He shifted his attention to the soldier who spoke. He'd never met him, which wasn't particularly surprising. They'd brought back well over a dozen people he hadn't even seen, let alone met formally. In the century leading up to the discovery of the Freezer, Caleb could barely count on two hands the number of new people who had joined New Hope's population, and he knew every one of them very well. In recent years he had lost count and now he hadn't even met half the Reborn. How was he supposed to ensure the safety of all these people if he didn't even know them? It had been weighing heavily on his mind this past week, more so than it ever had while the council ruled.

He pushed those thoughts aside to focus back on the meeting. Thomas addressed the soldier. "Not only are we in a poor position to be going on the offensive, we wouldn't even if we could. I realize for those of us who were not born into this new world naturally it might seem like we're just wasting time and maybe even cowering in our bunker here. However, the last thing this world needs, or humanity for that matter, is another war. We can't solve everything with violence."

"Then why call us all together?" the same man asked, "It looks to me like most of the soldiers we have are in this room."

"Sometimes to avoid a fight you have to flex your muscles and intimidate your opponent."

"What Thomas is saying," Teague cut in, "is we have a pretty good idea of who is behind this, but we want to be sure. Camp Wisner has been avoiding us for the past week but just this morning they finally responded to our calls. They have invited us to visit and see for ourselves that they don't have Jack or the other men. Obviously this is suspicious, to say the least. We believe if we show up in force, prepared for anything, we can get the answers we want without conflict. Plus if this is just another ambush, we can be ready for it this time."

"Come on, we all know it's Cali behind this!" This came from Josef again. "Those sonsabitches have just been waiting for a chance to get back at us."

Teague nodded and said, "At first we thought that was the case. In fact Wendy intercepted some radio chatter that convinced her they were involved. Unfortunately she hasn't checked in since so we can share our new insight."

Caleb groaned. *This is where things might get ugly*, he thought. "Where exactly is she now?" Chuck asked, "And why haven't you shared this with me?"

Teague stole another glance at Caleb, again as if checking to see if they were thinking the same thing. "Well, to be honest we're not sure. She headed to the Warehouse in Oregon so she could set up some surveillance with two of our Reborn and her... friend." While there were likely rumors of Bart, there were a lot of people here who would never accept a Mute as an ally to New Hope. This wasn't the time or get into a discussion about it, so he was happy Teague glazed over her companion. "We know she arrived at the Oregon site, but we haven't heard from her since."

"And you had me wasting my time searching for wreckage even after it was obvious Jack and his team were ambushed and captured? One of our own could be in trouble and you've done nothing?"

Caleb spoke up, "It was my choice to keep you searching, Chuck. We had to be sure. Nothing we have found to date tells us for sure Jack was captured. We are down to just a few good pilots and we couldn't afford to have you chasing after Wendy, who is most likely hiding somewhere on the outskirts of Cali territory listening to the radio chatter and trying to find out more about her man."

"The chances anyone got away from that clearing but were unable to radio in were slim! The only reason I agreed to be out there looking is we didn't have anything else better to do. Meanwhile Wendy is out there with proof of who took Jack, putting herself in danger while you keep that from me?"

Not wanting to blow this up in front of everyone Caleb tried to reason with him. "Wendy made her decisions despite orders to head back here. Sending our best pilot to retrieve her when there was still a chance, however slim, that our leader might be found was a distraction we couldn't afford. There are bigger problems than chasing after an impetuous and irresponsible woman who is clouded by emotion."

"She's clouded by emotion because she's pregnant and the man she loves is captured and most likely being tortured for information! Just because she's not thinking clearly doesn't give you the right to place a lesser value on her life! After all these years you still don't get that, do you?"

This was going poorly and he needed to take this discussion behind closed doors. "Listen, Chuck, I understand your anger here. I care about Wendy too, even if I had to make the decision to leave her to her own resources, of which she has plenty. I want to remind you that you didn't want the responsibility for making these kinds of decisions. Now that you forfeited that responsibility, you have no right to second guess the decisions of those of us who didn't. We can discuss this further after this meeting." He turned to Teague and said, "Please, Teague, carry on."

Red with anger, Chuck opened his mouth to argue, but then stopped, narrowed his eyes, closed his mouth, and sat down. Caleb sighed but the anxiety didn't relent – there was little question this argument would resume the moment the room was cleared.

An uncomfortable silence lingered before Teague finally said, "As I was saying, we do have reason to suspect Cali, but new information has come to light regarding the political landscape between the communities. We don't believe Camp Wisner would ally themselves with Cali, even under threat of force. Andrew has nothing to gain from such an alliance and all he would have to do is call one or two other communities to help if Cali tried to strong arm him."

"So who the hell is behind this?" Joseph asked.

"Well, we believe the Yanks have been meddling behind the scenes for a long time," Teague replied.

"What the hell do they want with us? We aren't a threat to them and they're too far away to even trade with."

Chuck cut in again, "But we are a threat now, for the same reason we're a threat to everyone. They just aren't supposed to know it yet." He then turned to the crowd. "We should have expected something like this. We have the most valuable commodity on the planet right now and this is going to make us a target. Look around you, we aren't exactly an army. If it weren't for this hole we live in, we wouldn't have a chance. Give us a couple years and we might have the manpower to overcome any of the other communities. To those in a position of power right now, that makes us a threat."

Caleb held his breath, hoping nobody would ask the kind of questions he didn't want to answer yet, like how would anyone else know what they had. As head of security he still hadn't been able to devote much time to the investigation into the missing assets. If the entire community knew there was another traitor in New Hope then distrust would grow even worse than it is now. It would be a bad time for that, to say the least.

Seeming to read his mind, Thomas stood up and said, "We know other communities suspect we have something of value. Cali knows we do, even if they aren't sure what it is. Most communities believe we have a cure to the virus. But this ambush on Jack could lead to the impression that we are weak and vulnerable, which could lead one of them to attack. We all know how safe we are down here in our homes, and most of you are well aware of how solid our defenses are. You know what a slaughter it would be if a community forced us to defend ourselves. I don't want that to happen, so we need to reinforce our image of strength and security. I think showing up in Camp Wisner with a dozen men and a few flyers will do the trick nicely. We have a right to answers and nobody could deny that. If other communities know what is going on already, they will also end up hearing about this, and that's what we want. So I need volunteers."

Instantly most of the people in the room raised their hand.

~~~~

Chuck waited for the room to clear before confronting Caleb. It took a lot of willpower to shut up during the meeting. Besides, he simply wanted answers, not grandstanding or popularity. When Teague, Chin, and Caleb were the only ones left in the room, he stomped over to them.

"Why the hell didn't anyone tell me about this? I told you we were wasting our time searching for a down aircraft after the third day! We wasted three more days scouring every inch of safe soil between here and Colorado with nothing to show for it! Now Wendy's missing and probably starting a war with Cali while you guys have been sitting on your asses pondering your next move?"

Caleb said, "Please calm down, Chuck. There have been plenty of times Wendy has turned off her radio and not checked in for several days. You know that just as well as I do."

He was right, but that was when everything was calm and peaceful, not when her man was missing and she was several months pregnant. These men didn't understand how volatile that woman could be. He shook his head, "You don't know Wendy. If you haven't heard from her at a time like this it's either because she's doing something she knows you wouldn't approve of or something happened to her. You should have told me."

"We needed everyone we had out searching for Jack. With Jerry dead and Wendy off doing her own thing, that left us with three competent pilots including you. We needed to be one hundred percent sure Jack didn't manage to get away and crash trying to get home. His pilot was dead, so even though logic would suggest he was kidnapped, the idea that he got away but crashed was still a viable option, one we had to rule out before deciding our next move. If we'd told you about Wendy not checking in you would have abandoned your duty and run off to find her. If she's in trouble with Cali there isn't anything we can do about it right now anyway. In case you didn't notice, that room was practically our entire military force, and it was not very full. If we lost our last good pilot right now we wouldn't even be able to go to Camp Wisner."

Caleb was right, even if it were for the wrong reasons. "The moment we get back from this mission I'm heading up to the Warehouse and I dare anyone here to try to stop me." He studied each man in front of him but didn't get an argument.

~~~~

Caleb turned off the lights and walked out of the room. When he turned the corner, he almost walked right into William. "Hello Caleb."

"Hello, old friend. I have not seen you around much since the election. How are you adjusting to life as a civilian?"

"Frankly? I am bored. I have tried to start hobbies, tried to lose myself in literature, and even tried to sit and write my own memoires, all to no avail. Marcus has his pet project and you have this council. The only one of us who is probably more bored than I am would be Theodore."

Caleb chuckled. "Theodore could keep himself occupied in his own mind for a century before he would be bored."

"True." They shared the humor of that statement.

"So what brings you to the meeting? I expected you to speak your mind at the very least, yet you were quiet the whole time."

He shrugged, "I just wanted to see what was going on. I was spending some time in the park level and overheard a couple mothers going on about how Jack was missing and nobody was even sure who was in charge. I guess now I know."

Caleb studied his old friend then said, "Now you know. Are you intending to do something about it?" He couldn't imagine William doing anything without a very specific purpose.

"No, I think you have it well in hand. However, if Jack does not turn up soon I would think it prudent to hold another election. Not that I think you are doing a poor job, just that I believe Jack was right in pressing for an elected official. The Reborn do not seem to be the type who take orders from somebody they did not choose to lead, at least not for very long."

"So if we hold another election I can expect you to run again?"

"Do you not think you and I are best suited to lead this community? I mean, I was surprised at how much backbone Teague was showing in there. Far more than he ever showed in the council, but I am not sure I would want to rely on him to make the difficult decisions."

Caleb nodded, "I have been seeing a side of him I am not sure any of us are familiar with, but I think you are right about him. My question would be whether you are asking me to back you or feeling me out as an opponent?"

"Oh, drop the cynicism, Caleb, I told you why I was at the meeting and I am not being deceitful. As bored as I have been, I sincerely hope for Jack's safe return. If the time comes that you are certain he is not returning..."

"Then you will reluctantly throw your name in the hat?"

"Then I would be happy to help you scout out another Reborn to run."

This took Caleb by surprise. "So you would not run?"

"Only if they needed someone to run against to make it seem like they are making a decision for themselves."

"I am not sure I understand your motives, William."

"All this free time has given me opportunity to ponder our past. Two centuries is a long time to be alive, and unless some sort of accident happens, it could easily turn into a dozen more. My new perspective has helped me to see what Marcus seemed to have figured out long before us."

"And what is that?"

"Immortality and absolute power do not mix. The longer we live, the more we believe the conclusions we have drawn over time are not just opinions or ideals – we begin to see them as unwavering facts. This limits us, and when we have ultimate authority over others, we create a culture that cannot adapt to changes in the environment. When any culture cannot adapt, it will eventually self-destruct. If I took power again and saw the potential we have right now through to fruition, I am quite sure I could never give up that kind of authority again. I am also quite sure it would mean the eventual extinction of our species."

Caleb stared at his old friend but didn't respond.

"Listen, you seem to have your hands full so I will let you go. If you need any help, please do not hesitate to call. Just because I have no desire to lead again does not mean I am not willing to offer up my considerable insight."

"Thanks, William. I will keep it in mind."

Chapter 22

The main door at the far end of the room opened. Nobody appeared to stop what they were doing, which was mostly sitting around, but everyone in the room noticed. When several armed men entered the room, most conversations ended immediately and people scurried back to their bunks. Whatever was going on wasn't going to be pleasant for someone. To Jack's surprise the next person to enter was Trystana, dressed in her usual form fitting clothing. He sat up and motioned for his men to go back to their bunks.

As he suspected, Trystana and her entourage of guards headed straight toward his cubicle. In the past several days she had visited a few times, although usually she was only escorted by one guard and that guy stood at the door while they chatted privately. On the surface she appeared to just want to socialize, and the conversations were not unpleasant. Mostly they played their question game, trading an answer for an answer. Oddly, most of her questions were about his past, and almost nothing she had asked had anything to do with his life since being reborn. He kept his guard up waiting for questions about New Hope's defenses, weaknesses, or the spoils from the Freezer. With little more to offer other than sensitive information about New Hope, it was a matter of time before they revealed the true intentions behind his capture.

"Hello Jack, I trust you are feeling better today?" He felt a little better every day, although without the medicine to accelerate healing he wasn't going to be without some residual pain for several more weeks.

"Sure. Why the extra guards today? You worried someone here will hurt you?"

She laughed, "Of course not. Every man in this room knows perfectly well that laying a single finger on me would result in a long and drawn out death that wasn't particularly peaceful. In fact, the only reason I have a guard with me at all is to make my father happy."

She hadn't answered the question, and he wasn't going to ask a second time. To ask would mean his first question was answered, and as tedious as it could be, that was how the game worked. "Look, I'd love to sit and chat some more, but I came here to get you. The guards probably aren't necessary, but my father insisted. So let's go."

Jack glanced toward Anton's bunk and saw the man looking at him questioningly. The question was simple: do you want us to stop them from taking you? His answer, of course, was no. A fight now wouldn't do anything but potentially end with another of his men dead. Standing up, he followed her without hesitation.

Once clear of the room, he asked, "Where are we going?"

"To see my father. He wants to have a chat."

"Any idea what he'd like to talk about?"

She didn't respond but he noticed her sideways glances at the guards. However silly the notion, he wanted to believe she didn't approve of her father's actions and that everything she had shared with him had been in confidence and not things her father wanted him to know. When the guards weren't around she seemed more open and friendly, but the cold fact of the matter was that he was being held against his will by people who had no qualms about committing violence. It was doubtful his capture and incarceration was committed just so Sebastian's daughter could have someone to talk to at night. If the tables were turned and he needed something from a prisoner, it seems like the best way to get it would be to gain their confidence and friendship. He couldn't think of a better way than to use an attractive woman with a charismatic personality and a great rack. He had to keep his guard up around this woman, something he recognized he could easily forget.

Without another word, she led him down one hall, and then around a sharp right turn down another straight hall before they came to the elevator. The more he saw of this place, the more convinced he was of the approximate date of origin.

The ride lasted longer than he expected. When the doors opened to a cavernous room, a small rush of adrenaline raised his heart rate and his anxiety level. This was clearly the top level of the bunker, possibly even above ground, although it looked mostly like a natural cavern, similar to the flight deck at New Hope.

"If you're wondering, the answer is yes, this was built before the turn of the century but long after you had died." Jack had been busy studying the architecture of the room and Sebastian's voice startled him. Already a little jumpy from the adrenaline, he actually flinched before forcing himself to relax and appear nonchalant.

The man was either very perceptive or he could read minds. He filed yet another tidbit of information away to add to what little he knew of the man. "Actually I was wondering if you were taking me out of the bunker to let me go. I already knew the building was built after my death, but not long after."

Sebastian looked intrigued and asked, "You live up to your reputation, Jack. Tell me, what made you so sure."

"Well, the elevator controls are more modern than what I would have used in my time, and while they have obviously been repaired multiple times by someone with little skill, they are undoubtedly still the original controls. The architecture and layout are very similar to the bunkers I had a hand in designing and building and even the walls were constructed with the same form designs I came up with. That tells me that whoever built this facility didn't come up with much of anything new, so it couldn't have been long after I was gone." He could have added that New Hope was an example of something built after the turn of the century, but he wasn't going to give anything regarding his home to this man.

Sebastian nodded. "I am impressed. You certainly know your bunkers. And while you are correct that we are about to exit this bunker, we have a lot to do before you gain your freedom to leave."

"So you are planning to let me go back home? And my men?"

"In time, although I'm not sure you will still call it home by then. Let us leave that for another discussion on another day. Right now I want to show you some things." Without another word, he turned and walked away from the elevator toward the other end of the cavernous room.

One of the guards, positioned just to the right and behind Jack, nudged him forward to follow. He took two steps then placed his next step in the path of the guard. Pivoting slightly, he shifted his body closer to the man and then swung one arm behind the guard and pushed. In one graceful move the guard went down. Jack followed the man down, driving his knee into the man's solar plexus. Air whooshed out of the man's lungs and his face turned red. Jack stood up and said, "Oh goodness, my bad. Here, let me help you up." He grabbed the guard's hand and started hoisting the man to his feet. On the way up he got close and whispered, "Push me again and you won't be getting up." The guard was too busy trying to take a breath to respond.

Sebastian turned toward the commotion and said, "Is everything okay?"

"Yeah, sorry," Jack said, "I was looking around and I guess I stepped in front of your guard here." The move was childish and his body was still stiff and sore and had hurt performing that move, but it gave him great satisfaction and helped to ease his tension.

Sebastian glared at the guard for a moment before turning back. Jack nudged the wheezing, red faced guard and then followed.

The room was not empty. Dozens of vehicles, mostly the type Jack knew came from the days of the EoS, were lined up in neat rows. Some were simple four seater models like the collapsible ones they kept in the flyers, and some were heavier models built like they could handle any kind of terrain. There were even a few that looked a lot like armored transports. Further toward the opposite end of the massive room were aircraft. Again, most were similar to what New Hope had – small, medium, and large flyers. There were a few that looked more sinister, like they were built for speed and combat. Jack took a mental inventory of everything he saw. There were easily ten times the number of vehicles and aircraft his own community had available, and the room was full, so more could be stored in another location.

As he walked, his heart sank. It would take all the western communities, including Cali, to even come close to matching this kind of military strength. The only question that remained was whether Sebastian had the trained manpower to pilot them all at the same time. He knew they had the numbers, but whether any of them were capable of flying or fighting was a whole different subject.

They reached the main door to the cavern, a massive entryway with an equally massive stainless steel door closing it off from the outside world. Sebastian motioned to one of the guards and he rushed over to a control panel and started working the controls. The door whirred with electronic motors and gears for over a minute before a final thump rumbled through the room. Then as if in slow motion, the door swung open. Sunlight poured in around the opening. Jack had seen doors similar to this, but he never got tired of the sight of such mass moving so elegantly. He watched as the door moved aside to reveal blue sky, white clouds, and a concrete clearing several thousand feet in dimension. Dozens more vehicles and even a few aircraft were parked out here.

The guard caught his attention and motioned toward a medium sized flyer, similar to the one Jack and his men had flown in to meet Andrew. The guard didn't lay a hand on him, but it was clear he was supposed to get in. Sebastian was already in the back seat.

Once seated, the pilot eased the craft off the ground and out the massive door. As he picked up altitude, Jack got a glimpse that was a little more familiar. It confirmed that they were indeed on the East Coast, not that he had reason to believe Trystana had lied to him about it. He had seen satellite photos of this very location. Along with a photo of a mass of people gathering in some kind of town square, it was one of the only pieces of intelligence they had on this community.

He counted the aircraft and vehicles outside as they took off. There was no question now that if Sebastian had the manpower to drive and fly all these vehicles at once that they could easily overwhelm even the combined strength of all the western communities.

"Do not worry, Jack," Sebastian said, "I lost my taste for war just like everyone else did. I have neither the desire nor the need to engage in mass conflict with other humans."

"So why ambush and capture me? That act alone could cause mass conflict."

"You are a special man, Jack. People follow you, and will fight for you if you ask it of them."

"No different than any other community leader."

Sebastian turned to face him. "But you are, Jack. You are a fighter, a man born of war. The other leaders will struggle to protect their communities. Some will even struggle to increase their own sphere of power. This is something *we* were born into – the desire for status. Some of them might even be willing to sacrifice a fellow human, as long as the sacrifice gains them more than that person could give them in life. But none of these leaders will go to war. They might posture, but everyone knows when it comes down to it, they will never start something that causes unnecessary loss of life. You do not have that reservation, Jack. That makes you different… both special and dangerous."

Jack shook his head. "You don't know me. Yes, I've seen war and the devastation it causes, but I have no desire for that kind of conflict."

"Desire and potential are two different beasts. Tell me, if you were still back in New Hope and someone else, one of your friends perhaps, was taken in the same manner, what would be your response?"

Jack opened his mouth to respond but realized where this was headed. He would indeed mount up a force and go on the hunt for whoever was responsible. "My people will respond the same way I would. They wouldn't take this lying down, but they won't escalate it into all-out war. Neither would I. Besides, you are the one who captured me, so it is your instigation that would cause the response."

"It is that attitude that starts conflict, Jack. Someone else does something you do not agree with, so you exert your strength in retaliation and you believe it is justified and therefore the right thing to do. But who did you leave in charge? Marcus? One of the other original council members? See, those are all men who would weigh the cost of finding you versus the cost of losing you and then decide on the best course of action for the community. Justification for the wrongdoing does not play into the equation for them. At the most they might send some men to question Andrew, but then what? What can they do without losing far more men than they can afford?"

If he had left Marcus or Caleb exclusively in charge, then Sebastian would probably be right. With Thomas in the mix, it was possible they would be doing more than just questioning Andrew. This added to his anxiety. There was nothing they could do to rescue him at this point, but they didn't know that, and the Reborn would be crying for retaliation. This was assuming the Board was able to assume authority too. It was entirely possible that because of his indecision over the past few months people were questioning the authority of the Board. Again his anxiety rose and he started to feel claustrophobic. There was no telling what kind of chaos was going on back in New Hope. Wendy would be crawling up the walls wanting action, and several of the Reborn would be ready to lay down their lives to find him and save him. The situation was even more dangerous and volatile than he had realized before this conversation. With effort he tried to keep his breathing normal even though he felt close to sheer panic. He knew he wasn't covering up his discomfort very well.

Sebastian smirked. The man probably thought he had read the situation perfectly. He hadn't, but Jack wasn't about to correct him. Let him go on thinking he has all the answers. He was a smart man but not quite as smart as he thought he was. The wave of anxiety eased up and Jack tried to appear more relaxed.

"So you see me as a threat to the status quo? Why capture me then? Why not just kill me?"

"I see you as a threat to the western communities. Overall you are a merely a bump in the grand scheme of things. The Reborn, as you call them, are the real threat. The DNA they are bringing to the pool is welcome, but their ideals are not. I cannot have a world full of people who still believe war can solve problems."

"But they don't just bring the ideal of war; they also bring the ideal of the sanctity of human life beyond material value. They bring a morality that seems to have died with most of the people of the world."

"We value life, Jack, and don't throw it away to defend some outdated sense of morality."

"You place a value on life, but it scales with the value of other objects. My men would put themselves at risk to save a soldier who is wounded to the point where he could never contribute productively to society. They would do the same for a group of old people, or even to protect someone who doesn't share their own moral values."

"Sacrificing productive lives to save the lives of people who will only drag their society down? I simply don't understand the logic in that."

"That's because you are trying to use logic to measure the value of a human life. Even a grandfather with nothing left to give his community is valuable to the people who care about him. If your daughter suffered an accident and could only lie in bed, reliant on others to feed her and keep her alive, would you be so quick to measure the value of her life?"

"Without hesitation."

"And that is why you don't see the value in the Reborn. I would die before allowing any harm to come to my daughter, or anyone I care about for that matter."

"And you would kill for them too, right?"

"If need be, yes."

"And you do not see the irony in that, Jack? You believe in the sanctity of life so strongly that you would take a life to defend the value?"

"To save someone I care about or to protect those who can't protect themselves, yes, I will take lives for that. If someone threatens my freedom or that of my country, yes, I will take lives. At least when I take a life it's for a moral reason, not simply based on a mathematical equation. The thing about violence is very few people have the capacity or tolerance for it. Show them what happens when they infringe on other people's values and chances are they will respect the response and think twice about infringing."

"But what happens when they don't back down? Or how about when the people you are fighting believe even more strongly in their own morals and values? Do you think the world got this way because everyone respected the danger in infringing on other people's values?" Sebastian gestured out the window. Engrossed in the argument, Jack hadn't been paying attention to where they were going. He looked out the window to see a sight he had not experienced. The landscape was a wasteland. Nothing grew on the dark gray dirt. Every so often he could spot what might have been the outline of a building, but otherwise it was like a gray desert, devoid of all life. It could have been a picture from the moon.

"The world got this way because of greed, because of blind faith toward a higher power whose words convinced masses that they needed to kill other humans until only those with the same blind faith remained. It got this way because people believed violence against others could solve disputes or keep one set of beliefs from imposing on a different set of beliefs. In the end, war is war and the result is destruction."

They travelled across this wasteland for dozens of miles. Every so often there was a patch of a few miles of green land, sickly but not dead like the rest of it, and certainly not the lush forests he had visited around Idaho and Oregon. The comparison to this landscape was sobering. Jack had flown over zones that were unsafe but they always traveled up at a safe altitude, never so close where he could see the devastation first hand. He had seen satellite photos and even caught glimpses out the window when the clouds cleared, but from way up it just looked like dark patches of land, and he never got the true sense of what the world had become.

Without a word, Sebastian pointed to the other side of the aircraft. Jack turned and looked out over a crater easily two miles wide. "Welcome to Washington D.C., Jack."

Chapter 23

Carlos climbed into bed and snuggled up to his wife. "Hey, baby."

Sannie pressed her warm naked body into his spoon. "Hey to you too, lover. How was your day?"

He sighed. "Not good. Word is Joshua might cut me from the patrols. I really don't want to go back to the fields."

"Oh come on, that's just the guys talking trash. They're just yanking your chain."

"You think so?"

"Look, you brought back that big flying machine. That's huge and Joshua isn't going to just cut you from the patrols just because you got scared off. A lot of men run into things out there that scare the shit out of them."

"Baby! Come on." He was already sensitive about his reaction to that beast, he didn't need his woman reminding him, even if it wasn't intentional.

She laughed, "Sorry, you know I didn't mean it that way." But she laughed anyway, and that bothered him.

She reached behind her and took hold of his member. "Let's not talk about it, just make love to your wife and then get some sleep."

He let her do her thing for a few minutes before sighing in frustration. Ever since he'd run into that... giant, he couldn't relax enough even to have sex with his wife. It certainly hadn't helped that the guys never relented on giving him grief for losing control of his bowels.

"Come on, Carlos, you have to let this go. It's been a week and I need some real attention. I know what kind of man you are or I wouldn't have married you. If that beast was big enough to scare you off, he would have done the same to *any* man. Now quit being such a pussy and get over it!" She slid down under the covers and took him in her mouth, but it was a wasted effort. Every time he closed his eyes he saw that giant mute appearing out of nowhere, charging at him with a roar that he could still hear. He almost felt sorry for the dumb Hoppers who'd run off into that forest trying to get away. If those idiots had just landed they would have probably been home by now, relieved of all their cargo of course, and possibly their aircraft as well, but at least they'd be alive. Much better to get sent home with your tail between your legs than to get mauled by an eight foot tall Mute.

He'd never killed anyone before, and although he didn't pull the trigger, he felt like he'd caused their death. After all, it was his idea to pin them in and not give them an option. He never expected them to crash their aircraft and run off toward certain death in those Mute infested woods. Maybe he didn't have what it takes to run patrols. What if one of the small communities attacked Cali? Could he shoot them down, or worse, put a bullet in them face to face? He always thought so, but between the nightmare that literally scared the shit out of him and the fact that at least two, maybe more men had died because of something he did, he was no longer sure. Perhaps the best place for him was in the fields, picking crops and pulling weeds.

At some point Sannie realized her husband wasn't going to be able to perform and she stopped trying. Carlos didn't even notice until she got out of bed. "What's up, baby? Where you going?"

Her beautiful face scrunched up in frustration. "Nothing's up, and that's a problem because I need some attention. First you're out for over a week leaving me all alone here, then you get back and are too freaked out to service your wife, and it's been a whole 'nother week! Well, I'm sick of taking care of myself, so I'm gonna go find someone who can."

He couldn't blame her. If the tables were turned and she wasn't putting out, he'd go find some tail somewhere else too. He'd really like to just hold her right now but obviously she wasn't going to be too emotionally supportive, so maybe it was for the better. After she got what she needed she would be satisfied to give him what he really needed. "Fine, go see Mikal; he's been complaining that his wife hasn't been in the mood lately. But just do me a favor and don't tell him why you needed someone else. I already get enough grief for what happened; I don't need the guys making fun of me for not being able to get it up too."

She rolled her eyes but her expression relaxed. "Don't worry, I won't say nothing. I love you and I'll be back in an hour or two. Try to get some sleep or something." She bent over the bed and gave him a kiss.

"Thanks, baby. Love you too." He didn't fall asleep though, not even after she got back.

~~~~

Wendy crawled out of the small tent and stood up, putting her hands out wide to stretch. A sudden jab of pain in her lower back stopped her and she reached back to massage the spot. These tents weren't all that comfortable, even with the bed of leaves and needles Bart had prepared for her. Her baby bump made it even more difficult to sleep, and having to get up three times a night to pee didn't help much either. She certainly didn't feel relaxed.

"Good morning." She turned to see Max sitting by the fire, a pot of coffee steaming on top of the rack over the small flame. She felt a moment of self-consciousness at only wearing her skin tight and very revealing under suit, but then he was dressed the same, and after a week there wasn't much he or Jason hadn't seen of her. Besides, it wasn't like he would be interested in looking at her bloated ass or her swollen belly. She stepped over to the fire and took a seat next to him, legs spread apart in a comfortable but un-ladylike position.

He handed her a cup and she took it in both hands. "Thanks." She inhaled the aroma then took a cautious sip. Thankfully, coffee was one of the few luxuries from her old life still in abundance. Half the communities had some kind of coffee crop and it was almost a currency when trading. There was little better in the morning than a hot cup of java, especially when surrounded by fragrant cedar trees. The air was a bit chilly as it was late summer. If anything, that added to the wonderful feeling of the warm coffee cup in her hands. "Is Bart up yet?"

Max shrugged. "I didn't check on him." The big man was usually up long before anyone else woke up, so Wendy assumed he was already out looking for some breakfast.

She sat and enjoyed the silence of the early morning, completely at peace. As the sun warmed the trees, she could hear distant pops and cracks. She never expected she would enjoy being outdoors as much as she did. It was never really her thing. Then a few months back, when she had been stranded in Idaho and met Bart for the first time, she started to fall in love with living out here. The bed situation could be better, but the early mornings like this when everything was so peaceful and there were no walls or ceiling above her head were pretty fantastic. Perhaps it had more to do with living in a bunker underground than really loving being outdoors, but either way the mornings out here made the other hardships worth it.

It wasn't like she'd want to live outside of New Hope permanently. After all, the dangers out here were very real, and without someone like Bart around, she probably wouldn't last long. But perhaps one day they could build a life outside of a bunker, someplace like this where she could have a nice deck to come out and enjoy a cup of coffee while the sun rises.

Thinking about her future brought home a cold reality. Unless she made it back to New Hope, there was little chance she would ever see Jack again, let alone live out her later years in a place like this.

"Think we'll make it far enough North today?" Bart had a radio in his bag, but it wasn't very powerful without an antenna array. They'd brought one along but in their haste to get away it was left behind in the hold of the flyer. Their goal since escaping capture was to make it far enough North to get in range of the radios in Bart's home. Once they could pick up those radios he was certain he could relay a signal to his makeshift laser transmitter and contact New Hope. After nearly a week they hadn't made it very far. The forest was thick and sometimes impassible, and at least a couple times per day they would run into dead ground, a sure sign of radioactive fallout and that meant taking the time to skirt around it.

Max shrugged again. With a smirk he said, "Are you saying you're getting tired of hiking through the forest? Where's your sense of adventure?"

She scoffed. "You can kiss my fat, adventurous ass."

He rolled his eyes, "You know, you keep talking about your fat ass, but I know you aren't fishing for compliments like most women who make comments like that. That means you really think you have a fat ass, and frankly that just isn't true. Besides, who cares if it was? Even if your ass was fat, which it isn't, you're still the most beautiful woman in New Hope."

She looked away, a little embarrassed but also feeling disappointment. Max seemed like a nice guy, but with men it always came back to sex and how good a woman looks, no matter the situation. "Don't be that guy, Max. It doesn't work on me. And quit looking at my ass." She got up to go put some clothes on.

"Wait, that's not the way I meant… Dammit! You know, you aren't the only one who's been hurt before, Wendy. At some point those big walls have to come down and you need to get rid of that massive chip on your shoulder. I've seen some glances of the real you behind that cold exterior and I think you're pretty great. For such a strong woman, you sure do have a lot of insecurity and angst."

His words hit her like a freight train. Before she could really process it, anger flared. "Where the hell do you get the impression you know me?" She tossed the last of her coffee toward the fire, creating a burst of steam and an angry hiss that reflected her sudden anger. Intending to stomp off toward her tent, she somehow ended up turning around and saying, "You know, I *have* been hurt, mostly by men like you who see this body and make assumptions about my personality. The ones who don't just decide they can take what they want from me somehow think they see something in me that they like, but it's always just their little heads telling them that I'm this wonderful person so their big head will want to talk to me. Well, let me tell you about the real me. Deep down I'm just a selfish bitch who can't control her impulses. We're stuck here in a forest in California of all places, cut off from our own people because I was too stupid and impetuous to believe anything bad could happen to us as long as I was at the controls. Well, guess what, I'm the reason we might never see our home again. I'm the reason I might never see Jack again."

She was crying now, and she couldn't stop talking through the sobs. "I'm not strong, I'm just stubborn. And… and the *one* man whose seen me for who I really am and still puts up with me is *gone*, and I don't know if I'll ever see him again! You're damn right I'm insecure about losing him because in this world, without him I'm just a community garden everyone wants to leave out for any man to come along and plant their seed."

Arms wrapped around her. Confused, she struggled to break loose. The embrace didn't relent and she heard Max's voice in her ear, "Shhh. Just relax. It's okay. It'll all be okay, Wendy." She started to push away again, but he only held her tighter. Finally she stopped struggling, settled into him, and just let the tears flow.

When the anger, fear, anxiety, sorrow, and confusion passed, she pushed him away and he let go immediately. Without another word, she retreated to her tent to be alone. Once safely closed off from the world, she curled up into a ball and closed her eyes.

~~~~

High up in a tree, Bart watched the drama unfold. He cared deeply for Wendy but didn't quite understand the woman. Her personality was as fiery as her hair, but she had a deep set insecurity that sometimes showed itself. In her pregnant state her emotions were all over the place, but that was to be expected. A pregnant woman in his clan made Wendy's recent actions look normal.

He was glad the smoothskin men were there; at least they seemed to know what to do when her mood swung like that. He could defend her from any physical threat, but there wasn't much he could do to help her with her emotional struggles. When the drama ended in such a curious fashion he turned his attention outward of the camp site. He couldn't spot Silver through the trees, but he could sense the animal was stalking something not far to the east.

The reason he had climbed so high up this ancient cedar was to get an idea of the landscape ahead. Several times since starting this journey they had run into wasteland and were forced to divert course. It had cost them a lot of time and he figured they hadn't even made it fifteen miles yet. He could probably forge straight through and make much better time, but certainly Wendy, and more importantly, her fragile baby, would be sickened by the radiation. From up here he could see for dozens of miles in every direction and could spot the clearings that were most likely caused by dead ground.

The area they were in was just north and east of what Wendy called the Sacramento Valley. The terrain was hilly but not quite mountainous, at least not yet. About a hundred miles to the south was the Community of Cali. While their original goal had been to try to get close enough to spy on them, without the equipment they had left behind in their flyer there was no way to send what they might find back to New Hope. Besides, there was no ground cover down there and that close to Cali they would be spotted and captured long before they got close enough to find anything of value.

Bart knew the entire mission had been a fool's errand, but he figured as soon as they got too close Wendy would be warned off and they would return home to come up with something more productive. He did intend to set up a discreet relay station so he could more effectively listen in on the latent radio waves bouncing around this valley. It was a shame things went sideways so quickly. They were safe, for now and the only thing pressing him to make good time getting back home is Wendy's pregnancy. If she were an Evolved woman he wouldn't worry about it, but regular humans were so fragile and barely capable of staying alive outside their safe and comfortable homes. They didn't have the knowledge or experience to go through a birth in the wild. Thankfully he had at least a couple months before she was too pregnant to travel, and that should be more than enough time to get them over these mountains and back to his home where he can contact New Hope.

He consulted the data pad he had brought along. He loved gadgets like this, and this one was proving quite useful lately. The humans wore miniature versions on their forearms, so he had crafted a sling to hold his full sized datapad on his arm in similar fashion. The size was perfect for his meaty fingers. Jack had shared everything he had concerning the known satellites still functioning in the sky above, so Bart knew there was only one Global

Positioning Satellite in range and it wasn't terribly accurate. It gave him a general idea of where he was on the map, and that made the maps stored in the device useful.

If they headed east, toward Nevada, they would run into mountains. Even if they could pass those mountains and head southeast toward New Hope it would be a journey of several hundred dangerous miles. Nevada was a desert wasteland, incredibly dangerous to cross even without the fallout, and who knows what kinds of mutated beasts they could run into out there.

To the west they would run into the old main highway and have a path straight north toward Oregon. The terrain would be easy and they could make good time, but the forest ended in that direction, leaving them exposed to any air patrols. There was also no doubt that the way would be blocked by massive amounts of scorched earth. That part of California took a beating in the war, and even Bart's tolerance of radiation wouldn't be enough to survive. That left really only one choice.

The path to the north was not the easiest, but there were several advantages. First, they could remain under the cover of this forest until they hit the bigger mountains. By then they would be well out of Cali's territory. Second, the area to the north did have several smaller highways, which meant paths through the mountains. The area was less populated during the wars and less likely to be blocked by swaths of fallout. Finally, it took them very close to the Warehouse site. There were secure radios stashed there that they could use to contact New Hope. They'd have to climb a mountain to reach it, but he was confident he could at least get Wendy there.

There was a chance, however slim, that as they made their way North they could get within range of his radio equipment back at his home. It would be possible to trigger a relay he had set up and get a message to New Hope. However, without the proper antenna for his radio it could take hiking a few hundred miles before getting in range. He hadn't told Wendy or the men yet, but there was one more downside to using the radio like that: if he transmitted, Cali would pick it up before New Hope would get it. He kept this information from them because he knew for people who weren't used to travelling by foot, a journey of several hundred miles would seem impossible. If they gave up now he wasn't sure he could get them all to safety, so he told them just enough about the radio idea to keep them motivated. He could carry Wendy the whole way if he really needed to, but the men would need to pull their own weight.

Putting the datapad away, he scanned the landscape once more looking for potential hazards in the direction they would travel. His gaze lingered on an area to the east. Several miles out the air looked hazy. This could be some morning fog or even a natural hot spring. It could also be smoke from a campfire. A very large campfire. Whatever the cause, he would avoid that area.

His keen ears picked up the sound of a brief struggle and the cry of prey caught in the jaws of a predator. Sounds like Silver had caught them some breakfast. He put his fingers to his lips and let out a sharp whistle. If he didn't call the young beast back to camp there might not be any of whatever he caught left for everyone else. With a grace that belied his size, he half slid, half climbed rapidly down the tree, landing silently on the soft bed of leaves and pine needles at the base of the large tree.

Just as he landed, Silver cleared the trees in front of him, dragging a small deer. Bart smiled and cautiously approached the beast. Despite their friendship, Wendy was right, he was still a wild animal and taking his kill required some finesse. With one hand he rubbed Silver's head, just behind the ear. "Good boy! You did well!" He carefully pulled on the carcass, letting Silver let it loose, not forcing it from the animal. Silver held on for a moment and growled, but then stopped and opened his jaws. Throwing the deer over his shoulder, Bart patted the wolf once more and said, "Let's go have some breakfast."

Silver yipped at this, and ran excitedly back toward camp a few hundred feet away. As Bart waltzed into camp, Max didn't look up. He was sitting by the fire, staring at the small flames and smoke, not seeming to even notice the big man arriving. *This one wouldn't make it a week out here on his own*, he thought.

"Good morning, Max. How about some venison for breakfast?" Max finally looked up and smiled.

"Ooh, that's a nice kill. Did Silver catch it?"

Bart nodded proudly. "All on his own. And he didn't even eat any before returning."

Jason's tent moved and a head popped out. "Did you say breakfast? I'm starving." He climbed out and headed straight for the coffee. It was well past dawn but Bart didn't say anything about the late sleeper. The man had stayed up late watching over Wendy and Max, and even though Bart told him it was unnecessary, he insisted.

Max walked over and started helping Bart to dress the carcass. Quietly, Bart asked, "Is Wendy okay?"

He nodded and looked toward Wendy's tent. "I think so. Our conversation took a turn I wasn't expecting. I'm good at saying the wrong thing at the wrong time, or at least that's what women have told me in the past."

Bart chuckled, "I wouldn't worry about it. Wendy's under a lot of pressure and I think she just needed to vent. Maybe it's even a good thing. She never wants me to see that side of her, so she keeps it bottled up around me."

He shrugged, "I don't know. I don't understand women at all."

"You seem to understand her more than you think. I was watching your interaction from up in the trees and I saw how you were able to comfort her like that. I'm sure she appreciates it."

Wendy's tent moved, and both men stopped talking, busying themselves with breakfast.

Chapter 24

Jack didn't say much for the next half hour of the flight. He just took in the bleak and devastated landscape. A lot of emotions passed through him in a jumble: anger at the people responsible for this kind of destruction, sorrow for the billions of lives lost, fear for what the future holds for his child. If he'd grown up in a world like this he'd probably see the Reborn as a threat just as Sebastian does.

"I get it," he said, finally breaking the silence. "But I still think you're wrong. The Reborn might be from the generation that started all this, but you don't understand something here: there were some seven billion people in the world back then. With so many people, you couldn't point at everyone and blame them. Just one city back then could house a dozen different cultures all trying to live life the way they felt it should be lived. Most of them were incapable of committing violence even on the smallest scale. And most of the people who were capable still abhorred it. A lot of these people became policemen and soldiers, men and even women who would stand up for those who couldn't defend themselves. None of them had any interest in War."

Sebastian studied Jack's face and finally replied, "You make a good point. There *was* an abundance of human life at that time, and any time there is an abundance of something, people will take it for granted and not value it as much. The individuals might not be interested in War but as a whole, those nations in power craved it. They either wanted to flex their muscles and show the rest of the world how strong they were or they wanted to force others to live the way they do. Maybe they didn't want to be the ones fighting the actual fight, but there were so many people it was easy to send thousands to their death. The Reborn lived in a world like that; where as a whole people were willing to go to war to protect their lifestyles and ideals, and as a whole they would sacrifice individual lives to accomplish it. I have read the history books, Jack, and I have seen how even the soldiers willing to lay down their lives to protect their country were treated when they returned. In their homes they might value life above all else, but as a people they were always willing to sacrifice human life to keep what they had."

His words were like blows from a fighter, wearing Jack down. He was already worn down from their first exchange, and their tour of desolation had been a massive blow that left him depleted. Always the fighter, he summoned his reserves and threw back another volley. "Fighting to keep what you have and hold dear is a part of the Human Condition. But there is a difference between fighting and war. I lived through the Second World War, and my generation lost the taste for it just as you have. It wasn't caused by two cultures fighting to keep what they hold dear, it was caused by a single person who was hell bent on killing everyone who didn't fit his idea of a perfect human. The battles I was in afterward were chess matches between two nations capable of destroying the world, fought with the desire to prove to the other that any real war would result in what you have just shown me. Neither of those nations really wanted to destroy the world even though they poked and prodded each other to look for weaknesses. I too read the history books of what happened after I passed, and those people who were willing to sacrifice the soldiers and then shun them for their actions were the ones who grew up not knowing war, not knowing what it's like to have to pick up a rifle and fight for your life. They were the generation who lived through peacetime, and they are the ones who hungered for conflict. Just as those who lived through the peacetime in the Enclaves of Science were so quick to go back to weapons of mass destruction the moment they became available."

Sebastian scoffed, but Jack could tell it was a solid blow. "You know nothing of the EoS, Jack. Whatever Teague or Marcus might have told you of that time was most likely spun to paint a picture that suited their opinions. What happened there happened because of *religion*." He nearly sneered when he said the word. "The moment the churches gained power again, humanity was doomed."

Jack felt the weak response was a sign his opponent was on the ropes so he went in for the knockout. "Those weren't churches – they were facades used by power hungry people with no sanctity for human life to drive a mass of people who had never experienced war first-hand to fight for something they didn't truly understand. In my time we had one man who was capable of convincing a nation to follow him in his desire to commit genocide. From what I have read, the EoS was filled with men like that. Why do you think the Reborn are a bigger threat to humanity? My people never created a virus designed to kill off the entire human race. You can point your finger at whatever you want, it won't change the fact that humans who know only peace will eventually end up in a fight and humans who don't respect every life lost in those fights will end up escalating it until it consumes everything."

Jack was so confident in his reasoning he couldn't see how Sebastian could counter it. All those hours of studying the history of the native born population seemed to pay off. However, without hesitation, the man surprised Jack and fired back, "I agree, which is why my people will never forget the atrocity of war and never get the opportunity to let someone capable of genocide rise to power."

The sheer certainty in his voice sent a chill down Jack's spine. "And how exactly are you planning to ensure that?"

"Because I will always be there to remind them."

~~~~

Anton paced nervously. Jack had been gone for several hours now, and it had him on edge. It wasn't like they could do anything to stop him from being taken, but it felt miserable to have let those guards just waltz out with the man he had been tasked to protect. For the fifth time in the last hour, he tried sitting on his bunk.

"You're going to wear a path through the floor if you keep that up."

He turned toward the voice. A woman stood at the cubicle entrance, leaning casually against the wall. The last thing he wanted right now was to fend off another female looking for his seed. He opened his mouth to tell her to leave but hesitated. Maybe some company right now will keep his mind off Jack. Besides, Jack had told them to drill the women for... uh... information.

She took his non-answer as an invitation and took a seat on the bunk opposite his. "Don't worry; your friend will surely be back."

"Do you know where they took him?" he said, surprised she knew why he was anxious.

Shaking her head she said, "No, sorry. I've been watching you lately and I see how protective you are of your friend. I just spotted him earlier with Sebastian, so I knew he was safe. Sebastian doesn't kill people unless it can send a strong message to his Bastards, and almost none of them are even aware of you and your friends. Hence, killing any of you would be pointless."

"Wait, who are you calling bastards? And why would it matter to them if we were alive or dead?"

She looked at him funny and said, "You're not familiar with the term?"

"No. I mean, yeah, I know what a bastard is, but I'm not sure who you're referring to."

She giggled, "We're the Bastards. All of us, here in this community."

"You're all bastards?"

"Yes. Well, no... I mean, yeah I guess most of us are." She laughed.

"You're just messing with me, aren't you."

Shaking her head, she said, "No, I think we're talking about the same thing here. This community was named 'Bastion' after our founder, Sebastian Maddoxson. So all the citizens are Bastards."

Anton chortled, "And that doesn't offend you?"

"The meaning of the word bastard? No, why would I be?"

"Because it's usually used to insult someone. You know, call them a dirty bastard when you want to get a rise outta them."

She giggled, "You have a funny accent. I've never heard anyone talk quite like you before."

He did have a bit of his Brooklyn accent but he never felt like it was very strong. During his life in the Army he had traveled a lot and most of his squad were from the Midwest and didn't have much of an accent. When he would visit home everyone would look at him funny because his accent had faded so much. "I could say the same about you. Most of the native born people I've met are either super precise with their words, or speak in some kind of hillbilly slang. You sound educated but a lot more relaxed than most."

"What's a hillbilly?"

Her expression was so innocent he nearly laughed. "Sorry, I guess you wouldn't really understand. It's just a word we used to use to refer to people who lived up in the hills in the southern states. Kind of a backwards people, usually inbred so badly they didn't have a full deck of cards, if you know my meaning."

She shook her head, "I don't, but I enjoy listening to you. You're kind of funny. But I'd be careful when talking about inbreeding; it's a bit of a sensitive subject with a lot of people. Not the Bastards, of course, but a lot of the outsiders we bring in."

"You never answered my question. Why aren't you offended by that term?" In fact, she hadn't answered most of his questions.

She shrugged, "Bastards? With only a few men in the whole world who can father a child, most people left on earth are bastards. No father. Or in the traditional meaning, our mothers never married our father. At least for those who have a father at all, of course."

"How could you not have a father? Everyone has a father, you can't make a baby without one." Anton had been friends with Chin for a while now, and he knew a few other native born men and most of the native born women in New Hope. They all confused him, but this woman made it feel like he understood his friends back home perfectly.

For the first time in the conversation she looked upset with him. Looking away, she said, "Not all of us have a father. Sebastian made us and put us in our mothers. It's how we avoid inbreeding."

"I'm sorry, I wasn't trying to insult you, I just never heard of anything like that."

She smiled and looked embarrassed. "It isn't your fault then, so don't worry about it. I'm Andrial." She held out her hand.

He shook it and said, "Anton, but you can call me Tony."

"Pleasure to meet you Tony. Would you like to have sex?"

He sighed and shook his head.

Andrial's frown actually made him feel bad. "Look, it's nothing against you, I just have a woman back home who I really love, and I don't feel right screwing around with other women."

Looking away, she said, "That's the most ridiculous thing I've ever heard. If you don't find me attractive, just say so."

He did find her attractive. In fact, she was just his type of woman – Long curly brunette with some hints of Italian in her face, slender waist but not too skinny where it counted the most and her laugh had sent chills down the back of his neck. "I'm not lying, and anyone who thinks you're unattractive is an idiot. I just happen to really love my wife."

She smiled and looked him in the eye, "I like you, Tony. I think you're weird, but in a good kind of way."

"Yeah?" he said, smiling, "Well I like you too. I hope you can stay and talk some more. I'm glad you stopped by, I guess I really needed someone to talk to."

~~~~

"What exactly is that supposed to mean?" Jack was pretty sure he picked up on the meaning and it had chilled him to his soul.

"I've been alive for close to two hundred and fifty years, Jack. Nobody on this planet has lived to see as much as I have, and nobody is better suited to bring humanity back from the brink of extinction to reclaim our place at the top of the food chain. Who better to be a leader than someone who can honestly claim immortality?"

Jack shook his head. "You aren't immortal. You haven't lived more than a few dozen years. You just have the memories of the last Sebastian in your head. That man died, and some day you will as well. Don't you understand that?"

Sebastian shrugged, "The body is just a vessel, Jack, but this isn't the time or place to discuss the metaphysical. Even if you were right, what does it matter? Inside I still feel like the same man. As far as I can tell, I'm just one man who's been renewed several times over. My next incarnation will remember this conversation as if they had it. Perhaps they will even use our conversation to make an important decision one day. After all, this has been very enlightening. Even after this many years I can still learn new things about people. I think you are right, Jack, the Reborn aren't specifically to blame for the wars. However, I still believe the ideals they have can cause destruction if allowed to be passed on to peaceful generations. I will allow them to live, under the condition that we separate them all, spread them out amongst the different communities so they can learn our ways and integrate into our culture."

"You say that as if you believe you are already their leader and have some kind of sway over them."

Smiling, Sebastian leaned back in his seat and said, "But Jack, I don't need to be their leader. I have their leader right here, and in time you will come around to see that I am the rightful heir to humanity. Without me you would still be a frozen corpse slowly rotting away in a hole in the middle of nowhere. Without me, humanity would have ended over a century ago. I cracked the code, I figured out how to bring people back, memories intact, and I will be the real savior of humankind."

This man is completely off his rocker, he thought. "And what if I tell you right now I will never see eye to eye with you, and that I certainly won't help you tear my community apart or rule over even one of us?"

"Oh, I'm confident you will, Jack. You're a smart man, extremely sharp witted and quick on your feet. I see great potential in you, and as my right hand you will eventually have more power than you can ever imagine. You will have the freedom to accomplish whatever your heart desires, as long as you don't do anything to risk the future of humankind. Of course, with that being said, if for some reason you don't come around it is quite simple: I will spend the next several years capturing every Reborn on this planet. First I will clone them as a newborn so they can be raised properly without the taint of their past in their heads, then I will put a bullet in each of their heads. I will start with Wendy, after she has your baby of course."

Chapter 25

The forest thinned out enough to make the next several miles go by quickly. Wendy was thankful. Those first few days had been brutal, although she hadn't let anyone see how much pain she had been suffering. By the end of each day, her lower back had felt like it was on fire, and she nearly had to cut her shoes off after the first day because her feet had swelled up so much her laces wouldn't budge. She was used to hiking, but pushing through dense forest for twelve hours a day with only a few short breaks had made her regular day to day scavenging hikes seem like a short walk in the park.

The ground had a soft layer of pine needles that cushioned each step, kept them quiet as they marched forward, yet provided enough support to not add to the fatigue. It also acted to damp the sounds of the forest, which was both good and bad. She didn't have to tread lightly to remain quiet, but then neither did any potential predators.

Nobody spoke as they forged ahead. After nearly a week out here everything that needed to be said had been said, and since they almost never lost sight of each other, there was nothing new to share. This too was both good and bad. It was nice to just lose yourself in the hike, look inward and get a chance to just ponder whatever comes to mind without interruption. On the other hand, it left her with a lot of time to think about Jack, the baby, and her future. She tried to tune it out but it was haunting her steps more often than not.

A very subtle shift in the quiet shuffling of the group caused her to snap out of her inner contemplation and take an inventory of her surroundings. Bart was nowhere to be seen. The giant man usually made less noise than even she did, despite weighing ten times as much. It was the absence of his whispery footsteps that caused her to take notice. She stopped walking and held her breath, listening to the forest around her.

The men in front of her both stopped after a few more steps, most likely sensing the same thing she had moments before. Something was definitely wrong. Wendy felt like the air pressure had suddenly changed and plugged up her ears. The snap of a twig to the right dispelled that notion and let her know her ears were working fine; there just weren't any other sounds in the forest. No birds whistling in the branches, no insects buzzing around, no squirrels scurrying from tree to tree.

Her first horrible thought involved the remains of a weapon of mass destruction, something that had killed everything that moved, and they had walked right into it. But that didn't feel right. Bart wouldn't have just vanished if he sensed they were in danger, he would have warned them first.

She eased the strap of her weapon off her shoulder and bent her knees slightly, preparing for anything. Before she could swing the weapon to the ready, several shapes appeared from behind the large cedars. It happened so quickly she felt like she blinked and they just appeared.

Max dropped to one knee and in a flash his weapon was ready, pointed at the Mute fifty feet in front of them. Jason was a step behind him, rolling to the ground and coming to rest on his belly, his weapon shouldered and pointed to the left toward two more hideously muscled Mutes. Wendy was already looking to her right, but felt the hair on the back of her neck raise up. She wasn't sure how, but she knew there were more behind her. "Hold fire!" she whispered fiercely, "We're surrounded."

She turned to face the Mutes she was sure were behind her. Sure enough, one more was standing next to a tree not thirty feet from where she stood, and one more was twenty feet to his left. She waited tensely for them to make a move or say something.

Oddly, they didn't seem to pay attention to her or even the other two men. Their eyes scanned the forest, perhaps sensing that the three small humans weren't alone. They all remained for what could have been a full minute, standing off silently.

"RAAAARRRRG!!!" roared Bart from above, louder than any beast Wendy could imagine. The giant Mute jumped from an old cedar a dozen feet away and landed to the right of her with a resounding thump that seemed to shake the very earth. It took everything Wendy had not to scream. Max snapped his head around to see what landed next to him, but to his credit didn't move his aim off his target. Jason was already prone but Wendy still heard him whisper a curse.

The Mute men in front of her tensed. One of them roared his own battle cry, pathetic in comparison to Bart's but still terrifying to Wendy, and charged. A flash of gray and the Mute went down not ten feet from her, Silver's jaws clamped around his throat. The beast was growling low but didn't rip his throat out quite yet.

"We don't want a fight, but if you take another step closer I can assure you none of you will walk away," Bart said loudly in a voice that would turn any man's bowels to liquid. "We're simply passing through; we'll be gone from your territory by nightfall."

"What kind of man travels with puny smoothies?"

Wendy couldn't see which had asked the question. She remained tense, body coiled tight and ready to swing her rifle the rest of the way off her shoulder if another of them made a move.

"What kind of man would allow a lone wanderer to not only hear your approach but have time to observe and plan a counterattack? I know there are four more of you there, there, and there." He pointed out three other trees, two in front of him and one to his left, just off to the right of the one Max had his sites on.

"We knew you were here."

"But you couldn't spot me or I'd be dead. And my pup slipped right past your guard. Pathetic."

Why was he insulting them? She wanted to turn around and smack him and tell him to shut up but she needed to let him handle this. It seemed to be working – at least they hadn't attacked yet.

"Enough of this chit-chat! We'll agree not to attack, but you will come with us and meet our clan leader before you will be allowed to move on. Even if you got lucky enough to best us in battle, I can assure you that you wouldn't survive the next encounter. Our clan is stronger than any in history and a few smoothies would never escape their numbers, even with a warrior such as yourself aiding them."

Wendy looked at Bart to see his response. The big man's eyes narrowed and then he looked at Wendy. "Do you trust me, Little Red?"

"Of course. This is your show, Bart."

He whistled sharply and Silver released the Mute he had pinned and sauntered over to Bart's side. "Relax, men, they aren't going to attack, you have my word."

Jason rolled over and sat up, but didn't take his eyes off the Mutes in front of him. Max held his rifle on his target for another heartbeat before lowering it. "Like Wendy said, Bart, it's your show. Just don't fuck us over or I'll make sure you pay before I breathe my last breath."

Bart turned to him and grinned. "I like you Max," was all he said in response.

The Mute who'd been talking approached and stopped about ten feet away. He was pretty big even for a Mute, which meant he stood a little over six and a half feet tall and probably weighed in at close to four hundred pounds. The others quietly disappeared into the trees. If Bart said they wouldn't attack, she believed him, but it still made her nervous knowing so many violent men were hidden in the trees. She tried to shake it off – it was better to be alive and nervous than in a fight where you might die.

"I'm humbled by your stealth, especially given your size. And your pet is a fine looking animal. I bet he's a fine hunter. I'm Thran, son of Bron."

Bart stepped over to Thran, making him look small in comparison. He studied the Mute's face fiercely before finally patting the smaller man on the shoulder and saying, "I'm Bartholomew, pleased to meet you, Thran."

Thran nodded and said, "Funny, our clan leader once had a brother named Bartholomew. He tells stories about his incredible size that matched his incredible ineptitude and clumsiness. He even jested that this big man wore clothing like a smoothskin. Surely that wouldn't be about you, but the irony of meeting another man as large as you with the same name and description is profound."

Bart grinned. "Surely."

Wendy saw something in his eyes she'd never seen before. She verbalized her only thought. "Oh, shit."

~~~~

The hangar at New Hope had seldom seen this much activity. A dozen Reborn soldiers stood at attention in full armor, armed to the teeth, and ready for action. Tiny had come down to make sure the men were fully aware of the mission at hand, even though he wasn't going. His new boot camp was in full swing and as he spoke to the Reborn soldiers, Red's former men were running laps around the flight deck. One of them had nearly quit already, not even a full week into the program, but Tiny had reminded him what his fate would be if he chose to drop out of the program. The motivation was quite effective.

"Men," he boomed, "I want to make it perfectly clear that this is not a chance for you to exert your frustrations on the enemy. While it's likely Camp Wisner played a role in the recent disappearance of our leader, ultimately we want them to join us as an ally. So if any one of you steps out of line and even so much as looks at them offensively, I will have you running laps and going through the same training program those men you see sweating their balls off are going through! Is that perfectly clear?"

In unison, the dozen soldiers cried, "Yes, Sir!"

Tiny paced back and forth in front of them, massive arms clasped together behind his back. "That being said, you will be ready at all times. If the order is given to strike, you will strike hard and fast. If chaos breaks loose you will secure it and bring order. Is *that* clear?"

"Yes, Sir!"

"Good!" He turned to Chin and asked, "Are you ready to go?"

Chin spun his chair around and stood up. "Yes, Sir!" he said, somewhat mockingly. He managed to keep a straight face and even snapped a sharp salute. One of the soldiers snickered, but Tiny didn't catch who it was. He grimaced, but it was as much to keep from grinning as from being upset.

"Mount up!" The soldiers filed toward the aircraft, splitting up and piling six at a time into the holds of each of the two medium craft waiting. Turning back toward Chin, he said, "I realize you were never properly trained. Perhaps you need to join the men running right now so I can whip some respect into your scrawny ass?"

Chin sat down and spun around to look at his controls. "Just pulling your leg, Tiny."

Tiny chuckled and headed toward the outside perimeter of the cavernous flight deck to yell at his new recruits when they passed. Chin was a little sonofabitch sometimes, but the man was loyal to New Hope and would do his job with as much dedication as any of those soldiers.

~~~~

Thomas nervously shifted in the seat. "Relax, Thomas, we're almost there and this should be a piece of cake. Nobody's gonna do anything stupid," said Chuck.

"That's not what I'm worried about, Chuck."

"No? Well what's got your panties all twisted up?"

Thomas shrugged. "I guess… I don't know, I'm just worried about our next step. I mean, the best case scenario we learn everything we need to know about what happened with Jack, but then what? This is like… our one and only play." He stumbled through the words, paused to review what he had just said, and decided it fit his feelings. "I hate to say it, but whether we get an answer today or not, we're better off just holding a new election and moving on. Jack's… well, Jack's a good guy and he came through for us in a pinch. Marcus seems to think he's our best shot at making all this work out, you know, with the Reborn coming into such a different world at such a critical time, but at some point we have to cut our losses and run, don't we? Hell, I just don't know. I don't want to be the man to make that decision."

"I can tell you our next move. We finish this operation then we mount up and go make sure Wendy's okay. After that we'll worry about Jack. It's all we can do."

He shrugged. "I don't know, Chuck, maybe it'd be best if we don't find Wendy."

"What the hell is that supposed to mean? Wendy's not just one of us, she's a good woman and a hell of a pilot. Even if she wasn't a friend nobody's going to stop me from going out looking for her after this."

"Whoa, I'm not saying we shouldn't look for her. Just that if we find her but have to tell her Jack's gone for good, she might completely lose it. Do you realize how fragile she is right now? I would've confined her to her apartment if I hadn't been so sure it would send her over the edge. What good is she to anyone, including her baby, if she just ends up shutting down and going catatonic?"

Chuck scoffed, "Don't be ridiculous, she's stronger than you think. She'd be hit hard if Jack's gone for good, but she'd recover."

"I'm not so sure. You didn't see how she reacted when she thought we found his body. I've never seen someone shut down like that. I'm just saying, maybe if something's happened to her it would end up being the more merciful way to go."

"That's pretty cold, man. A week hanging out with Caleb and Teague and you're starting to sound like one of them. I'm just glad it's not me missing, stranded out there in the wasteland waiting for you to send some scouts to look for me."

"Oh, come on Chuck, I said I didn't mean we shouldn't look for her. And it isn't easy trying to make decisions that affect so many lives. In the last week we've lost nine of our people, eight of them are capable of fathering a child. There probably weren't eight virile men between all the smaller communities before we came along. Do you have any idea how much of a blow this is? The last thing I want is to make a decision that only costs us more people."

"One."

"What?"

"One. We lost one person. Eight more are missing but presumed alive. We're about to learn what might have happened to five of them, and after this we will find Wendy and the two men with her and recover three more. And if we've lost Jack for good, it'll be tough on her but she's strong, she'll recover. We'll all recover. I know far better than you exactly how much of a blow losing them all would be, and how important it is that we do everything we can to get them all back. If you've lost sight of what we're fighting for, then you have no right to be making any decisions at all." Before Thomas could respond, a light flashed on the instrument panel. "Hang on; we'll be on the ground in a moment."

As they dropped down to land, Chuck's words resonated in his head. He was short sighted but ultimately he was right. Nothing ahead of them would be easy but they would do what they had to do to survive. There was no sense in worrying about the next step until they finished this one.

~~~~

Three men were waiting, armed and armored, at the landing site. The town of Camp Wisner, if it could even be called a town, wasn't much more than a few outbuildings, a large clearing with three small flyers parked in a neat row, and a squat structure that looked like a tiny military bunker sitting right in the middle of it all. A sturdy looking wall, perhaps eight feet tall, encircled the buildings, giving it the appearance of a fortified military camp.

A sturdy looking door on the otherwise nondescript structure swung open just as Chuck set the small flyer down in the center of the clearing and the two medium craft followed his lead, one landing on each side. Through the dust and debris the three aircraft kicked up, Thomas watched two more men step out to join the others. These men were younger, probably late teenagers, and neither wore any visible armor. They had the same M74 assault rifles slung behind them that everyone else carried. A lone woman followed the two young men out. She looked to be about middle age but looked frail and as if she hadn't seen much sunlight in about a decade.

Thomas opened the passenger side door and jumped out. He was armed with only a sidearm, and otherwise dressed not unlike Jack had been when he left a week before. Of course he had on his bulletproof under suit beneath the clothing, but that was just a precaution.

The holds on the two larger aircraft opened and the soldiers marched out, single file, and then took up two positions, one on each side of the cluster of three aircraft. They clearly outgunned the men here, although Thomas suspected there were more men waiting both in the surrounding buildings and probably in the air not too far out, just in case things went sideways. Trying to appear calm and confident, he approached the welcoming party. "Good afternoon. I'm Thomas. Which one of you is Andrew?"

The two young men looked at one another, then toward the woman. She stepped forward and said, "I'm Andrew's first wife, and I will speak on his behalf. Unfortunately I haven't heard from him since the day your own leader disappeared."

This sounded suspiciously like a load of crap. "Really," he stated, "so why did you tell us he had returned safely a week ago?"

There was a shadow of defiance in her eyes, but he could see it was weak and lacking resolve. This is what pride looked like after all hope was lost. She shrugged, "I was scared. I knew Andrew was about to do something he didn't want to do – something that would really upset your community – but I figured he would have a way to keep you from coming after us. When he failed to return and you were still insistently trying to contact us, my only play was to stall you, hoping my husband would return eventually. I think I have to face the facts, the first being that he isn't coming back, and the second being that I can't defend myself against you if you are looking for retribution. The men you see here are all we have left, with the exception of our largest flyer filled with our women, children, and our only adult seeder parked a few miles away. Their orders are to run if you came here looking for retribution. All of us are prepared to die for whatever my husband did. We have no value left to humanity anyway. The men here are empties and I tried and failed for years to give us another breeder. I'm too far past my prime to be of any value." She hesitated only long enough to glance around at the armed men lined up in a show of force, and then continued, "From the looks of your men, I'd say it was wise of me to send them away. That seeder is valuable enough to buy sanctuary for our refugees at any of the communities, and the two young male children will be virile as well, and that will ensure good lives for everyone on that aircraft. We have nothing left, so do what you came to do and get it over with."

Her monologue took him off guard and he wasn't quite sure how to respond. "Look… We aren't here for retribution, we just want answers. If you'd been honest with us from the start we wouldn't even be here. I… I didn't realize you were in such dire straits. Tell us what we need to know and we can talk about doing what we can to help."

She scoffed, "New Hope has already done enough for us, thank you." Before Thomas could ask what that was supposed to mean, she continued, "I already told the woman you sent everything I know."

This came as another surprise. He almost asked her what woman, but before he could ask it became clear why Wendy was so adamant that Cali was involved in Jack's disappearance. "Why don't you go over it again. Perhaps we can make more sense of the situation."

She shrugged and said, "Some men showed up here a while back, armed and not afraid to push us around. They've been here before, but it's been years. Your woman seemed interested that they had orange markings on their armor. They met with Andrew and he was stressed out about it but didn't tell me what was going on. Andrew wasn't interested in merging with New Hope, but he was certain you guys had come up with a cure for the virus and would hold it over our heads, so I wouldn't have been surprised if he made a deal in exchange for whatever it would take to get a hold of that cure. Since he never returned I guess they double crossed him too. Whatever's going on, it's too late for us."

"Why's that?"

"Yesterday one of our scouts spotted a group of Mutes heading this direction. Dozens of them and they'll be on us in a matter of weeks if not sooner. We just don't have the manpower to fight them off. Half our farmers already disappeared or wandered off, and I'm not even sure we will have the food to last us through the winter. Camp Wisner is dead." A tear slid down her cheek. If this was an elaborate deception, this woman could win an award for her acting. As far as he was concerned, she was telling the truth.

Before he could respond, the small flyer he had arrived in spun up the motors and took off. The men were instantly on their guard, rifles unslung but not shouldered or pointing at anyone – yet. He signaled for them to stand firm and then tried to catch Chuck's attention as he piloted the aircraft several hundred feet up.

The pilot of one of the medium craft opened his door and ran toward Thomas. "Sir, an aircraft is headed this way. It appears to be a medium sized flyer. Chuck lifted off to intercept and protect us." Thomas nodded and the man went back to his cockpit to await instructions.

Turning back to the woman, he said, "What the hell is this? I thought you were being sincere! You think you can ambush us like you did Jack and his men?"

A look of horror on her face, she cried, "NO! This isn't my doing! Please!" She turned to the three armed men next to her. They looked nervous but ready to fight if need be. "Drop your rifles, men! Show them we aren't looking for a fight." The men instantly complied, setting their weapons on the ground and showing their hands. "See! I don't know what's going on. I told our women to get out of here and not come back unless I called for them later. I'm not sure why they would come back but please don't shoot them down. They are all innocent of whatever foul plan my husband had for your leader."

He pulled out his PDP and punched up Chuck's radio. "Talk to me. What's the situation?"

Chuck's voice squawked over the tiny speaker, "It looks like a lone aircraft, about five miles out coming in at normal cruising speed. I tried to hail him but got no response. I'll pull back and keep him in my sites. If he accelerates to an attack speed I will light him up. You might want to take cover."

The woman and her men nervously scanned the skies, waiting for fire to rain down on them. "Please," she pleaded, "let's go inside, we'll be safe in there if whoever it is attacks."

Thomas frantically processed the situation. He was usually calm and sharp under pressure but this whole scenario had him feeling muddy. He usually had a clear enemy and a clear mission, but this time he had decide on the fly who to even trust, let alone who to attack. His instincts told him to keep his cool, even though his brain was telling him he shouldn't trust anyone and this could be another trap. He decided to commit to his instincts. They'd never failed him before. The fog cleared and finally he acted. "You and your men go inside until this plays out." There was still a small chance this was some kind of ambush, and men could be waiting in the surrounding buildings, so he headed to the cockpit of the nearest aircraft and signaled to the men to spread out, take cover, and expect a fight.

At the cockpit, he reached in the back seat and pulled out his M74. "Fire up the motors and be ready to dust off and provide some air cover." He closed the door and stayed close to the aircraft, scanning the skies and the surrounding buildings, waiting for whatever was about to happen. He may not be good at all this diplomatic stuff, but when it came to a fight, he knew exactly what to do.

His PDP squawked again. "They're slowing down and coming in for a landing. If this is an attack they aren't doing it very well. I've got a lock on them and will take them out if they try anything."

"Thanks, Chuck."

Less than a minute later a flyer appeared out of the clouds. It looked no different than any other medium flyer. He brought his weapon to bear, waiting to see who was crashing their party.

The flyer landed gracefully, kicking up a little dust. The door opened and four men climbed out and cautiously made their way toward Thomas and the other flyers. None of them were armed although two of them were wearing armor. One of the unarmored men came from the pilot's seat, the other, dressed more like Thomas but looking like he had been living in his clothes for several days, approached confidently. "Looks like I'm late for the meeting. I'm Andrew. I would say it's a pleasure to meet you but judging by the number of armed men with you, I'd hazard to guess you have intruded on my humble home. As you can see, we're unarmed, so I would appreciate it if you would lower your weapons."

The clarity of a potential fight disappeared and once again Thomas was dumbfounded. He had no idea what the hell was going on. "Your wife just told us you disappeared. I'd suggest you explain, and quickly. I'm a bit fed up with lies and deception and as you can see, we came prepared for answers, whether they are offered freely or not."

Andrew nodded in deference, holding his hands up in a calming motion. "I understand completely. I'll tell you anything you need to know, but please, I have not seen my wife for a week and I am quite sure she is worried sick about me. Can I please have a moment? I'll have her bring us out some refreshments and chairs and we can sit and have a proper meeting."

Suppressing a laugh at the carnival this mission had turned into, Thomas shrugged and shook his head. "Why not." He signaled to his men to form up and stand at rest, but be ready. "Wait, your men stay here. You go in alone." Andrew nodded, looked at his men, and headed to the door. Again Thomas opened the door and tossed the rifle in the back seat. Looking at the pilot, he said, "Tell Chuck to patrol the area and see if he can spot anything out of the ordinary."

"What's going on?"

"Hell if I know," he replied.

Several minutes later, Andrew emerged once again from the nondescript door, this time trailed by the two younger men carrying an assortment of goods. The three original guards followed, carrying tables and chairs and in moments had a regular picnic set up. It seemed Andrew wasn't kidding about that part. "Please, come and have a seat. I'm afraid we don't have enough seating for everyone, but we certainly have enough food. If your men are hungry, they are welcome to come and get a plate."

Thomas shrugged and went along with it. He didn't signal the men to relax and eat, however. The last thing he needed was to be caught off guard, his men holding food and not their weapons if there was an attack. He took a seat opposite Andrew. The woman from earlier emerged from the door to sit next to her husband, fresh tears in her eyes, practically clinging to him as if letting go would mean him drifting away again.

"Now," Thomas sighed heavily, "tell me what the hell is going on."

Andrew took two cups and poured some liquid into each, placing one in front of Thomas. "I'm sorry, I didn't catch your name."

"Thomas. Where are Jack and my men."

Andrew nodded. "Let me start by saying your leader is alive and in good health, at least as far as I know. I realize you must be quite furious with us by now, and you have every right. My wife briefly informed me of the events of the past week and I want to apologize for the deception."

Thomas was losing patience. He sighed again and said, "Listen, just tell me where Jack is or things will start to get ugly."

Andrew grimaced, "I'm trying but it isn't as simple as it might seem. I'm not entirely sure where he is; only that he is a long way off, somewhere on the East Coast, and most certainly in the custody of a very unpleasant man who recently double crossed me and held me captive for the past week."

Slamming down his fist, he said, "Details! I want to know everything that happened from the time Jack and his crew landed to meet with you, until the moment you landed here."

Andrew took his cup and drank deeply. "Mmm, that's good. I missed our tea. Please, indulge all you want. We have the best iced tea left on the planet, and plenty of it."

"For a man in your position you sure seem aloof. Do you understand the gravity of the situation, or do I need to remind you how anxious my men are to get the answers we came here to get?"

Andrew set the cup down and leaned forward. "I have been alive for nearly two hundred years, Thomas, and in that time I have learned that rushing things leads to mistakes. Also, I was raised to believe that manners were of the utmost importance when hosting a guest, particularly when the guest is mad at you. I understand your impatience here, and I can assure you that you will leave here with everything you came for and probably a lot more. However, I would like to keep this civil, so please, drop your threats. You clearly have the advantage here and if what I have learned is true you could have brought twice this force and laid waste to everything we hold dear. I have little left to give, so if you would be so kind as to accept what I can offer, I would greatly appreciate it."

Thomas had to take a long slow breath to ease his impatience. Again he referred to his instincts, ignoring his mind telling him to reach across the table and throttle this smug sonofabitch until he started to talk. His instinct told him the area was secure and he was in control. They had all the time in the world and what he really needed was someone to make sense of everything. Andrew was the man who could do that, and he was being a polite and gracious host. He let the breath out slowly and clarity once again flooded in. Feeling more relaxed, he took the cup in front of him. He cautiously took a sip. Andrew wasn't kidding, this was good, and it had been a lot longer since he had a cup of iced tea. He drank half the cup, smiled, and set it down in front of him. "Thank you. Now, you were about to explain what happened?"

Andrew smiled. "Yes. So about six years ago a group of men showed up, not in a manner unlike the way you arrived. They had about a dozen armed men and a few flyers. At the time we had enough people to match a force like that, but when a bunch of men with guns show up to your door uninvited, you don't shoot first unless you are completely sure you will walk away unscathed. As you probably know, we had been talking with Theodore about the idea of a merging of several communities to aid in our effort to rebuild our population. Where is Theodore anyway? I would have expected him to be here speaking for New Hope."

"He's indisposed. I'm aware of the history." It appeared Theodore had been honest with the Board so far. He filed it away for later.

"Right. Send him my regards. The last time we met wasn't entirely pleasant, and I feel bad about it in retrospect. So these men showed up and they had some interesting things to say about New Hope. We were already cautious about an alliance, although Marcus had been helpful to us in the past, even providing us with some supplies when we first got started. I guess you could say the arrival of these strangers muddied the waters a bit."

"What sorts of things did they say about us?"

Andrew pursed his lips and said, "Oh, just some old history, stuff I am sure you wouldn't understand, but for those of us who lived back then it certainly widened the rift between us and New Hope."

"Why don't you think I would understand?"

"Well, correct me if I'm wrong, but you're one of them, right? The 'Reborn' as you call yourselves?" The words took the wind out of Thomas' lungs but he tried hard to not let it show on his face. "You weren't around back then so little tidbits of information about what really happened over a century and a half ago probably wouldn't mean much to you. It's not really relevant right now, however, and frankly at this point I wouldn't be surprised if it was all misinforma-"

Finding his words, Thomas interrupted with, "What exactly do you know about the Reborn?"

Andrew took another sip of his iced tea and leaned back in his chair. "Far more than I knew a week ago, that's for sure."

Chapter 26

A dozen questions were burning inside her head, but with the other Mutes here Wendy didn't want to say anything. Max and Jason looked about how she felt right now – a bit pale, very nervous, but fully trusting that Bart knew what he was doing. "How far is the camp?" she asked. They'd been walking for about an hour already.

Thran chuckled, "You smoothies are deaf. Our clan is large, perhaps one of the largest in history, and even over the noise of your clumsy footsteps I can hear the bustle of my people. For someone so small you sure make a lot of noise."

"I could say the same about you, Thran," Bart rumbled. "My friends here may lack many of our physical abilities, but never forget that they were smart enough to create the Evolved in the first place. I can promise you if you had attacked them, even without me around, at least six of your men would be growing cold by now, if not all of you. Underestimating humans based on their size is one of the Evolved's greatest weaknesses."

"Bartholomew, I never underestimate their weapons. But take those away and no smoothie can defeat an evolved warrior. In unarmed combat, most of them couldn't even defeat one of our women!" Laughter could be heard from a few dozen feet away. It was a chilling reminder that several more of them were just out of sight.

"How many times have you come across a lone unarmed human? I could say that if you sent a warrior into a nest of pinch ants without a torch he wouldn't stand a chance, even though a pinch ant alone could be squashed without a single bit of effort. You have to judge every threat as a whole, not just look at the individual parts."

Wendy had never heard of a pinch ant before and she certainly never wanted to find out what they were. Listening to the conversations between Bart and Thran was enlightening to say the least. For a race with such propensity toward violence, they didn't react the way she would expect to insults. Granted, most of her encounters with Mutes had been violent, so she just assumed that as a race they were somewhat unstable, quick to anger and even quicker to resort to violence. The fact of the matter is her only real experience with their culture was with Bart, and she just assumed he despised his people so much he chose to live an entirely different lifestyle. Perhaps there was more to them than just their lust to kill every regular human they encounter.

The scent of a campfire crossed Wendy's nose. A few dozen more steps and she could see a clearing ahead. A knot of anxiety tightened just above her belly. She would feel more relaxed assaulting Cali with nothing but a sidearm. It took every ounce of courage to keep her rifle on her back and not turn and run. Bart seemed to sense this and turned to her and the two men. "Listen, I'm sure you are all nervous, but right now you are safe. Just walk tall and don't let them intimidate you. If anyone harasses you, insult them and don't flinch. You will gain more respect with your wits than anything else. Keep your weapons hanging on your shoulders and in their holsters. Above all, don't openly question what I say or do. That doesn't mean you can't ask questions, just don't challenge any of my actions."

Quietly, Wendy asked, "Do you really think your brother is the clan leader?"

"Undoubtedly. It makes sense too. I had been listening in on his activities for months, but a few weeks after I met you, the devices I left behind stopped working. Either they discovered them or moved the clan out of range. This area would certainly be out of range."

"But your clan wasn't very large, and Thran is boasting of being one of the biggest in history."

Bart shrugged, "In our culture the clan leader is the Alpha Male. All it takes to lead is to challenge the leader to a fight to the death. Farnak is a great warrior, very skilled in combat. If he met another clan and wanted to merge them together, I could see him being successful."

"So what's your plan? He threw you out of his clan. Won't that cause problems for us here?"

Bart winced a little at the comment. "Let me worry about that. Whatever happens to me, I will make sure you are released, unharmed."

Wendy didn't like the sound of that. "What exactly is that supposed to mean? I won't let them do anything to you. We're all prepared to fight our way out of here."

Bart smiled. "Don't worry, Little Red, I'll be fine. Trust me. You won't have to fight your way out of here, and if anything happens and they escort you out of here, don't put up a fight, just go. I promise I will catch up to you later. Now let's go see what they're up to."

Every instinct she had was screaming to do anything other than walk into this frying pan. She had to push it all aside and trust her friend. He had never led her astray and had risked his life to save hers on more than one occasion.

The outskirts of the camp looked as she would expect. Several portable shelters were erected in groups of three and four, a small campfire sat in the middle of each group, with supplies stacked up here and there in an orderly fashion. There was a haze of smoke through the trees here, and she caught the smell of meat cooking. Mutes didn't normally wear much clothing, but some laundry was spotted hanging on lines tied between the large cedars, and the first people Wendy saw were a group of women busying themselves with domestic chores.

She'd never seen a female Mute, but they looked exactly like she suspected. They shared the same rough skin as the men, were smaller than the males but about the size of an average human man, and only wore what looked like a dress or apron around their waists. Their breasts were exposed, and she was surprised to see they mostly appeared smooth, at least around the front. This shouldn't really surprise her, the primary function of a breast was to feed an infant, and if the skin were rough and harsh a newborn wouldn't want to grasp at it and suckle it. The last surprise was they all had a long ponytail coming off the back of their head. They wore them braided and draped over their shoulder, dropping between their breasts. The hair only grew from the back of their heads, the rest of their heads and faces were covered in the same rough skin as most of the rest of their body. Their facial features were somewhat masculine in her opinion, although their cheek structure was more female and overall their bodies were more slender than the male Mutes.

As they passed the group of women, all of them turned to watch Bart. He seemed to notice this and pretended to not see them. Although his skin was dark and leathery, she was pretty sure he was blushing. He even stumbled on a rock he didn't seem to notice, and the women giggled and went back to their work, chatting away quietly. One of the women stole a few more glances in their direction before they were out of sight.

As the trees thinned out and the clearing opened, Wendy had to hold her breath to keep from gasping. There were hundreds of tents and other portable shelters here, and they had already passed over a dozen as they neared the clearing. If the camp extended in every direction from the clearing, there were easily more than five hundred of them. They were all large – most looked capable of housing several people. Thran wasn't boasting at the size of the clan.

Children darted through the camp, chasing after each other. Some men sat around relaxing, talking, or even just whittling on a piece of wood. Laughter could be heard here and there. In fact, if it weren't for their size and hairless bodies, this could be any nomadic community. It all seemed so normal.

Some of the Mute men stopped what they were doing as the group passed, watching with curiosity as the giant and his three small friends made their way toward the middle of the camp. Thran led the way, and once they cleared the tree line, three more of the Mutes from the forest got in line behind them. As they neared the central hub of the clearing, more of warriors joined the entourage, looks of curiosity and sometimes even anger on their faces. Max looked over his shoulder at Wendy, his face pale and clammy. She smiled in assurance but didn't say anything. It was far too late for words.

They finally reached the main part of the camp. Three large structures were erected in the center; one was easily fifty feet on a side and the other two looked like large tents flanking the main one. They appeared to be timber frames with animal hides stretched over them. That made sense for a nomadic people – lightweight and could be broken down and moved easily. The area in front of the large structures was clear of any living quarters but a hive of activity. Some tables were set up to one side and several men sat eating or just talking. Along another side was a row of cooking fires with several men and women attending to the food cooking on them. They even had several stone ovens set up and Wendy caught the scent of some kind of bread baking. Rows of makeshift weapons – spears, clubs, rifles, and even some heavier rocket launchers and other evil looking apparatuses stood in an orderly line opposite the cooking fires. The front of the main structure was open, and inside were tables, chairs, and desks sitting in orderly fashion. Most of the chairs were occupied.

As the group entered the area, things got quiet. Conversations stopped, the clatter of the cooks paused, and everyone slowly stopped what they were doing to see who the visitors were. "Well, I never thought I would see *you* again!" Wendy turned to the loud and angry sounding voice. The Mute walking toward them looked like a smaller version of Bart, meaning he was still impressive in size, almost as wide as the gentle giant but still nearly a foot shorter. He didn't look too happy, but at the same time he didn't look all that surprised either.

"I'd be lying if I said I never expected to see you again, brother. This day had to come sooner or later."

"What, have you come to take retribution? Or are you still a coward."

The statement made Wendy's blood boil, but this wasn't her fight and she knew saying anything now would only make matters worse.

"A coward would pillage helpless humans and kill his father while he sleeps. I think maybe you need to re-evaluate who you're labeling. Tell me, did you assassinate this clan's leader in his sleep as well, or did you have the balls to actually kill him in fair combat?"

Several of the brutes watching this exchange looked surprised at Bart's statement. An insult had been thrown, and an accusation that made their leader out to be underhanded. Suddenly this conversation was of interest to them. Farnak spit angrily and said, "The pacifist second son returns to spread more lies and deception. There's a reason you were pushed out of your own clan, Bartholomew, and it had nothing to do with our father's untimely death. Besides, he was a coward like you, wanting to hole up underground like the last few smoothies. If he'd had his way we'd be sitting around waiting for death just like they do. I took charge of this Clan because their leader was a coward like our father and I faced him in unarmed combat as a true leader should. Unless you came here to challenge me, I'd suggest you just keep walking. Take your smoothskins with you before I decide to dine on their bones!"

Bart shook his head and smiled, but the smile didn't reach his eyes. "When I left you the first time, I did so out of respect for our father. He saw how misguided and cruel you had become and made me promise that if anything happened to him I would do my best to protect you and try to sway you back to reason. I failed to help you learn reason and look beyond your nose but I honored our father's last wishes by letting you live, even at the cost of losing my family, friends, and my honor. Now that my debt to him is paid, you won't get rid of me so easily again. Tell me now what you are doing all the way over here, so close to the human community that has used you like a puppet."

"I don't owe you any explanation; you aren't a part of my Clan! Don't think for a moment your empty threats hold any weight with me. Our father may have passed on his size and prowess to you, but you chose to throw those natural abilities away and let them atrophy as you wasted your life trying to befriend the humans." A few of the warriors sized up Bart and then looked back at their leader with trepidation, seeming to doubt his judgement of Bart's physical condition. "Oh, don't think for a moment I haven't been keeping an eye on you. I knew about your cabin with all your science experiments and gadgets and how you spent so much time trying to keep tabs on your *former* clan." He turned to his people and said, "That's right, this... *man*..." he sneered while using the term to describe Bart, as if it was an insult to be just a man, "hid in his cabin like the coward he is, wearing clothing like a human and stealing pieces of their technology so he could watch us from afar, probably crying every night at what he had lost with his cowardice!" Some of the warriors in the group laughed at this, but most didn't seem to be buying it.

Bart looked around at the crowd and joined the laughter, keeping it going long after everyone else had stopped, mocking his brother's weak insults. Finally he stopped and said, "It's true. I kept an eye on you, and when I knew you were about to slaughter some helpless people who did nothing but offer you tribute to leave them alone, I stepped in and helped. How many of your warriors did I take down? Oh, wait, did you think they just happened to slip and fall and break their necks? That's a lot of accidents, Farnak, but I don't expect you to be able to keep count. After all, it was more than ten, and I'm not sure you could count that high without having to sit down and use your toes."

This got more chuckles than Farnak's insult, and it seemed to really infuriate him. He didn't skip a beat in his retort, however. "Ah, the people you murdered. Your own people, the friends and family you were so sad to let go so you could go hide in your cabin... I'm not surprised you stalked and killed them. I'm sure you approached them as friends, waited for their guard to be down, and then snapped their necks when they were turning to help you by giving you their breakfast scraps so you wouldn't starve to death. Yes, I found them, and after you murdered each you took their food stores, another sign of your inability to fend for yourself alone."

The group of Mute warriors had grown, and now some of the women had joined to watch the verbal battle unwind. As one, a hundred heads turned to see what Bart would say in response.

Bart shook his head, "You always find a way to twist the truth, brother. The greatest asset of a weak leader is the ability to take any truth, no matter how damning, and twist it to appear to be in his favor. How could I have used cowardly tactics to trick your warriors the day you sent Ungo and Gratch to ambush that group of scavengers? You remember the day, right? When Joshua, Cali's leader, called on his whipping boy to go and ambush four men?

You sent what, thirty soldiers to take them out? With advanced weapons like that rocket launcher over there." He pointed to the stack of weapons lined up next to the main tents. "Your general sent seven trackers to find all four of them, who'd already escaped your first trap, and none of them returned. They were all together, yet somehow four of them were left with broken necks, all in a group. Do you really think I was able to distract all four of your best hunters at the same time and break all their necks before they realized I was an enemy? I got great amusement watching those four smoothies take down your soldiers and trackers one by one, setting easy to spot traps that they blundered into blindly. They must have been trained by their Clan Leader. Matter of fact, one of the smoothskins they were chasing is here today." He pointed at Wendy, the one hundred and twenty pound pregnant woman who looked like a frail child among hundreds of brute warriors. Wendy was surprised at the sudden attention, and scared out of her mind that he would admit to a large group of Mutes that she had been partly responsible for the dozens who were killed that day. "This small woman was able to evade Farnak's best trackers while injured. I sincerely hope he has done a better job of seeing that you men are all trained properly. My brother never did learn why it was just as important to exercise his mind as it was to exercise his body. Perhaps it's time someone with a little more brains takes over as your leader. With him as your general, it seems all the enemy would have to do is send their women out and wipe out the lot of you!"

Wendy watched Farnak closely as Bart went on and on, insulting him in front of his people. He was clearly losing his temper, but she could also tell he knew he was outwitted. His eyes shifted back and forth as he tried to come up with a response. Locking eyes with Wendy, he seemed to hit on an idea. She almost flinched at his evil smile.

"So, you not only show up to confess your treachery against your former clan, but you go so far as to bring one of the human's responsible for so many deaths? It seems you have proven how little respect you have for your own people. It's no wonder you walked away from your clan so easily, not even pretending to defend your honor before you tucked your tail between your legs and ran." Farnak leaned back, looking smug and satisfied. Wendy had to admit, if the tables had been turned and one of her own race had admitted to killing her fellow humans, she would be ready for some retribution.

Bart hesitated and she feared he'd made an error bringing her into this. She tried to sit a little taller and not look guilty of doing anything wrong, wanting desperately to tell these men how brave Bart always was in the face of danger, but she sensed it would only hurt. For all she knew, her defending him would be seen as a sign of weakness. The crowd seemed to sense this too. Some of the men who laughed along with Farnak sent more hostile looks toward Bart, and even a few of the women shook their heads and turned to walk away. Bart lowered his head, as if defeat was right around the corner and he was about to leave, cast out once again by his brother.

Quietly, he said, "I'm disappointed in you, brother. See, you just made a crucial error. You told me you knew I was watching you, listening in on your conversations. The day I overheard your conversation with Cali where you planned to ambush those four humans from New Hope, you made sure I was listening. I always thought it was good fortune that I happened to be listening in at the exact moment you spoke with Joshua over an open radio."

Bart stood up, his size causing some of the crowd to lean back just a little. Pointing to a pile of gear next to the tent, he said, "Over there is the laser transmitter that Joshua provided you with so you could have secure communications with Cali. I never should have been able to intercept that transmission, yet I did. And when your men failed to capture a single person in that ambush, you sent seven of the best trackers to get them. But not just any trackers, every one of them were men who were loyal to our father, and every one of them had the loudest voices when you assumed leadership after our father died. I told you when I left that any warrior in your clan who I found trying to hurt innocent humans would be dealt with swiftly. See, I had a short conversation with Teba before I broke his neck. He told me you'd given him specific instructions that I would be watching and he was to flush me out. You told him I would be an easy kill though, soft and weak. His last words were a curse against you, Farnak, for misleading him to believe I was easy prey. You sent your own people after me and either you did so to kill them off, knowing full well I could easily take them down, or you did so with the ignorance you have proven to be so full of time and again. If anyone here should be accused of treachery, it's you. Those were no longer my clanmates, they were the ones who stood behind you and cast me out, even if they didn't agree with the direction you wanted to take the clan. I had every right to kill them in battle. But you, their Alpha, their *Leader*, sent them to their death, either on purpose or unwittingly, and either way that makes you a sorry excuse for a leader."

Wendy was stunned. Bart had set a trap for his brother and unleashed it in front of hundreds of his own people. The silent crowd was no longer silent, a lot of chatter, mumbling amongst the men, some anger from the women. One voice said, "Someone challenge him! We need a new leader!"

Bart scanned the crowd, seeming to watch closely looking for who would step up to the challenge. When several men motioned for him to come forth, he shook his head and said, "I have no desire to lead your clan. I have other responsibilities. Surely one of you is brave enough to strike down your cowardly leader! After all, if he sees you as a threat he could be giving you the most dangerous detail tomorrow, trying to get rid of you. Perhaps he would even send one of you to assassinate me in my sleep."

A few of the now angry crowd looked like they had already experienced what Bart was saying might happen, but still none stepped forward. "Did you really think you could turn my loyal clan against me, brother? I'm the clan leader because every warrior here knows I would defeat him in battle. You might have outwitted me tonight but make no mistake, my prowess in battle is unmatched, and everyone knows it!

"Sure, I sent those fools to kill you, and I should have known they'd fail. They were planning to unseat me anyway, and I wasn't about to let that happen. They deserved the death they received, just as our cowardly father deserved to die drowning in his own blood after I stuck him in the lung with a dagger while he was laying on his bed, passed out from too much ale. I took charge of our clan and would have brought them glory if Joshua hadn't broken our agreement to provide weapons in exchange for captured humans. Now I have an army and I intend to show Joshua just how big of a mistake it is to double cross the Evolved! While you cower with your friends we will wipe this planet of one of the reasons it is so broken. When that's done we will turn and finish off the rest of these communities, your friends included, one by one until only the Evolved are left on this planet. Then we will nurse our glorious world back to life and live in harmony with nature, and I will be the one who didn't just lead our people to glory, but the one who saved our planet from a scourge!"

Wendy was holding her breath, at once both scared to death of this crazy Mute leader and feeling bad for all these people who would be slaughtered if this lunatic led them against Cali. Some of the warriors shouted war cries when their leader finished his speech. Most didn't look as convinced. Bart was among them.

"You fool," he said when the crowd died down, "just like my former clan, you will lead these folks to their death. If you don't, you will only end up bringing more destruction down on this planet. The humans seemed to have learned that war is not the answer, but our own people haven't had the same lessons. If nobody here is brave enough to challenge your idiocracy, I will leave you to your fate."

Farnak grinned, knowing he had ultimately won. It was a win by default, but nevertheless he had won. "Since you are too cowardly to challenge my authority, here is my decree: You may stay the night, get a taste for what you once had before you lose it, this time forever. But with the rising sun you will be on your way. At noon you become an enemy of this clan, and as such every scout and warrior will be instructed to kill you on sight or suffer expulsion. So run away, go and hide, and when we are finished with Cali we will come your way to destroy your friends. If you choose to defend them, you will die beside them."

With that he turned and went inside the large structure, his aides closing the heavy hides behind him. The people in the clearing started to disperse, many looking worn out and beat down. Some threw angry glances toward Bart and Wendy and the men, some sent looks of desperation, silent pleas to help end this madness before it destroyed them all. Bart shook his head and said, "Let's go find a place to rest. Nobody will bother us tonight and in the morning we will put many miles between us and these fools."

Jason nodded and stood up to follow, but Max said, "Why not challenge him? I mean, I know he's your brother, Bart, but he admitted he murdered your father and sent his own people to be slaughtered at your hand. You were right, you know. These people will also be slaughtered if they attack Cali. I mean, if outfitted properly and led by someone competent I'd be deathly afraid of them, but a dozen men with the right weapons could cut them to pieces before getting within a hundred feet of Cali."

Bart looked weary, as if the verbal sparring took more of a toll on him than any physical struggle. "I understand what you're saying, Max, but you don't understand my people. To kill my brother would put me in charge. I told them I have no desire to be a clan leader and I meant it. Right now my responsibility is getting you home before Little Red's pregnancy makes it too hard to travel."

Wendy chimed in, "Don't use us as an excuse here. I know you better than you think, and I know you miss being a part of a clan. You have a chance to not only get back what you lost, but to do the right thing for your people. Besides, if you don't want to be leader, can't you just pass on your leadership to someone else?"

The big man shook his head. "No, to do so would weaken the clan. They need a leader who is strong, not one who is incapable of defeating the former leader. If the successor is a relative and the leader is injured or getting too old to lead, out of respect he can pass on the role but if the new leader is not seen by the entire clan as the strongest, he will be shunned and the clan will break apart. I won't disassemble this clan just because I think their leader is a fool. They will die but they will die by choice. Nobody stepped up today because they knew it wouldn't matter. Farnak might be cruel and shortsighted but he isn't boasting about being their best warrior. I would be hard pressed to beat him in fair combat, and knowing my brother he would find a way to stack the odds in his favor."

Wendy understood, even if she didn't like it. She put her hand on the man's arm and said, "Okay. As long as you don't use us as an excuse, I'll respect your decision. I know you aren't a coward and I believe you could defeat your brother even if he cheated. Now let's go find a place to rest and get some sleep so we can get an early start. The miles aren't going to pass by themselves."

Chapter 27

The door closed behind Jack. Anton rushed over to meet him. "What happened? You look like you were rode hard and put away wet."

He just nodded, which took effort. Drawing on what little reserves he had left, he still barely made it to his cubicle where he practically collapsed onto his bed. He'd never felt so drained, so devoid of energy. Even the death of his wife and daughter hadn't hit him this hard.

Anton hovered close, looking concerned. "Is there anything I can do for you? Are you hungry?"

Jack shook his head grimly. According to his internal clock, maybe six hours had passed. It was past dinnertime but he had no appetite. "Anything happen while I was gone?" His words came out slow and slurred, but Anton didn't seem to notice.

"Well, actually I met a very interesting woman. Learned a little about where we are too." He said it proudly, like he had accomplished his mission.

"I can tell you exactly where we are – about a hundred miles north of Washington D.C. Or rather what used to be Washington D.C. It'll be a thousand years before anything other than cockroaches lives there again."

Anton stared at him, seeming to deflate. He cursed under his breath. "Sorry. Please, tell me about this woman."

"No, it's okay. If you need some sleep, Jack, I can just tell you later."

"Just tell me what you learned. What's her name?"

Anton smiled shyly. "Andrial. She's... unusual." He related the entire encounter, which included details about the way she smiled, the way she talked, and the way she dressed. Clearly the man was smitten, something Jack didn't really expect, particularly given the fact that his wife was pregnant with another child back home.

As he talked, Jack's eyelids grew heavy. It wasn't the story, which was filled with a lot of interesting information. He just desperately needed to recharge his mind, and only sleep would do that. He zoned out for a moment then snapped back to the conversation. "...so they call themselves Bastards, and I suppose it fits. The most interesting thing is what she said about her father."

This caught his attention and was probably what brought him out of the near comatose state. "What's that?"

"She doesn't have one. Sebastian created her in a lab and implanted her in her mother. She said most of the population here was conceived that way. They only have three virile men in their city, two of whom are being held in this room, so Sebastian creates the babies. How the hell is he able to do that do you suppose?"

Normally hearing something that twisted would give him a burst of adrenaline and at least generate some kind of adverse emotion – anger, disgust, or even just surprise. Instead he just felt hollow, as if the chemicals that cause the emotions were spent. He did feel something, but it wasn't an emotion. He felt determination, a hardening of his morals and ideals. There was no question in his mind – Sebastian has to be stopped.

~~~~

Chuck slowly circled the area, watching and waiting. The pilot he had contacted earlier had relayed Thomas' orders, and every time Chuck called him to check in all he said was they were still talking.

It hadn't been hard to spot the medium flyer a few miles out, parked next to a tree with some camouflage netting trying to hide it. A scan showed there were warm bodies in the hold, but if he had to guess they were women and children, not soldiers. He'd kept an eye on them, but they never got out and never fired up their motors.

The community was sparse but seemed defensible. Outside the main wall, a series of sturdy looking fences would slow any ground assault. The trees had been cleared for a mile in every direction, so anyone approaching would be easy to pick off as they slowed to get past the fences.

Outside the perimeter he came across several miniature versions of the main compound. They appeared to be farms or ranches with housing, utility buildings, and barns, all enclosed behind the heavy walls. Grazing land for livestock and large plots of land for farming were located outside the walls. It was a smart layout. At night they could herd the livestock indoors behind the walls and not have to worry about predators, and during the day the open landscape meant they could spot potential issues long before they became a real threat. Simple but it would work.

Although the communities mostly got along, it would be stupid not to include some kind of air defense system. They weren't easy to spot, but Chuck's keen eyes were used to looking for small details from above. He managed to locate a half dozen small camouflaged structures placed evenly around the perimeter of the main camp. Those would house sensors and probably some kind of anti-aircraft weapons. Either they'd turned them off in anticipation of the visitors or they simply no longer functioned. He doubted they had ever had need of them as anything other than a deterrent.

Overall the defenses of Camp Wisner were impressive. If they hadn't been invited, he wasn't sure how they would have gotten in to interrogate Andrew without casualties.

He kept up his patrol for a few hours before his radio finally came to life. "Hey Chuck, come on in and get some food before we head home. Thomas says he's ready to go after you eat."

"Roger that." In minutes he was setting the aircraft down in the same place he had landed before. It wasn't a complicated move. These flyers were pretty easy to maneuver. Whether they found Wendy or not, his next order of business would be to train some new pilots.

The soldiers sat around the clearing having what could only be called a picnic. The atmosphere looked relaxed and even casual. Thomas sat at a table near the heavy door that Chuck figured led down into their converted missile silo. He jumped out and scanned the area, wondering why nobody seemed to be on their guard.

"Hey, Chuck," Thomas said, not getting up, "thanks for watching our six while we talked. Please, sit and have some dinner before we head back. Try the iced tea, it's quite good."

Not sure how such a tense situation had turned into a damned picnic, Chuck suppressed the urge to express his feelings toward their nonchalant attitudes. Instead he held his anger and merely asked, "Did we get any answers, Thomas?"

"We'll talk about that later. Please, just sit and enjoy the food these folks were kind enough to offer up."

The evasive answer only frustrated him more. He stood at parade rest, hands behind his back, staring holes through Thomas, who had turned back to the other people sitting at the table. It took effort to contain his anger.

The other man at the table stood up and said, "I am Andrew, pleasure to make your acquaintance. Please, I would be honored if you would have a seat and eat some of our food." The man gestured toward the spread on the table.

The anger bubbled over: "Did everyone lose their fucking minds while I was up there? A couple hours ago these people were the enemy, responsible for Jerry's death and the disappearance of five of our people, one of whom is our leader and a close friend of mine, and now you're having brunch with them?"

Thomas stood up quickly and said, "You're out of line, soldier!"

Andrew frowned and said, "Given the late hour, it's more like a dinner than a brunch."

He reached for his sidearm but felt a hand already on it. "Chuck! Listen to me carefully!" Thomas said loudly, now mere inches from his face. "The situation has changed and you will NOT do something impetuous or I will have your ass thrown in a cell next to Theodore! Now either sit your ass down and have some dinner or go wait in the flyer while we wrap this up!"

He held his superior officer's gaze for a full minute before taking a step back, turning around, and marching toward the flyer. Behind him he heard Andrew say, "Wait, Theodore's in the brink? You need to tell me that story, Thomas."

As he walked he glanced at the soldiers sitting around, making eye contact with some of them. Every one of them was looking at him and most had a look of guilt on their face. Before he made it halfway back to the flyer, they all stood up and followed, leaving half eaten plates of food lying on the ground.

Climbing back into the seat he had spent so many hundreds of hours flying patrols in defense of New Hope, he had to grip the controls hard to calm down. He wasn't sure what was going on with Thomas but they would have some words on the way back to New Hope. This was the sort of thing he had feared since the moment he found out Jack was missing. New Hope was falling apart rapidly. Thomas seemed to be a good officer, at least up until now, but he's not a real leader. His resolve was already flapping before they arrived here and only God knows what they talked about to make him presume it was okay to sit and have a casual dinner with people who had created this whole shit storm to begin with.

Through the windshield of the flyer he watched Thomas shaking hands with that smug sonofabitch Andrew. He powered up the motors and was tempted to take off and leave the man with his newfound friends. If he wasn't burning to know what information they shared, he wouldn't have hesitated.

The door opened and Thomas threw a bundle into his lap then climbed in and closed the door. "There's some food for later. I know you're hungry and there's no sense in letting it go to waste. It's pork ribs. Real pork ribs."

Chuck set it aside and pulled back on the controls, swinging the aircraft toward home. They sat in silence for at least a half hour. Finally Thomas said, "Look, I know why you were pissed back there but it doesn't excuse your behavior. Like it or not, New Hope isn't strong enough to stand up to the threats facing us, and we'll need every community on our side. As much as it stings, that includes Camp Wisner."

His anger had mostly faded but he wasn't about to let this go. "My behavior? You had no right to sit there with the man who murdered one of our soldiers like you were old friends who had just worked out a minor misunderstanding. We were supposed to be showing unwavering strength and instead you had the men sitting around having a picnic! What if the surrounding buildings were full of soldiers just waiting for you to drop your guard? What if the flyer I spotted just a few miles out was loaded with a dozen armed and angry farmers ready to finish us off once and for all? Jack trusted Andrew the way you were trusting him back there and it cost one man his life and several more their freedom!"

"I considered the situation carefully and after hearing what Andrew had to say I decided I believed his story. Besides, I had a couple men search the buildings, at Andrew's urging, just to make sure this wasn't another trap. I knew about the flyer sitting outside the community and it wasn't filled with angry farmers it was filled with women and children. Plus, I had you up there in the air, watching all our backs, and I knew I could count on you if something happened. So don't second guess my decisions. You had a chance to step up and take leadership, but you declined because you feel you are of better service to New Hope as a soldier, so be a soldier and next time listen to my orders and don't get out of line like that again!"

The response took a lot of wind out of his sails, but he wasn't quite finished. "You could have briefed me about the situation and what you'd done to secure the area. Don't forget that your last order was to be alert and keep everyone safe. Imagine my surprise when I return from that mission to find you lounging around with the enemy, acting as if you were long lost buddies looking for another drinking partner."

Thomas didn't respond right away. Finally he said, "Look, I get your anger, but next time I say you need to relax and sit down, just do it. You made me look like I can't control my soldiers and that certainly didn't help show unwavering strength in the face of the enemy. Like I said, with what we're facing next we need all the help we can get. If Andrew thinks we are weak he will just cut and run to someone else. He may only have a few men and limited resources, but we're going to need him."

His anger spent, now he felt concerned. "So, what exactly is the danger we face?"

"It's not good, Chuck. As we suspected, the Yanks captured Jack and our men. Right now he's somewhere on the East Coast, probably having every secret about New Hope's defenses being extracted from him in an unpleasant manner."

Shit. "And how did this all come about?"

Thomas took a deep breath, signifying this was going to be a long story. That was okay though because they had a few hours of flight left. "It started years ago, before the Freezer was found. The way I understand it, back then the communities were all aware they'd never be able to perpetuate the growth of the human population on their own. They knew they needed to join their resources if they were going to make it work. However, each one of them is led by people like Marcus or Andrew. After surviving the fall of the cities and creating a stable community, each of them feels like they are the best choice for an overall leader. Nobody could agree on one plan, and Cali of course had the muscle and the resources to push everyone else around. The Yanks, or actually the Bastards, as they refer to themselves, had been slowly infiltrating each community. They had more people and more resources than all the rest of us combined, but since nobody ever talked with them I guess nobody really considered them either a threat or a potential ally."

"So they have spies in each community?"

"It seems that way, although Andrew couldn't say for certain. He never even learned who was spying on him, but when they showed themselves for the first time they knew everything about his community already. Sebastian, the leader of the Bastards, knows about the Reborn too, so I would bet whoever took the missing head has been feeding them information as well."

The thought made him shiver. "So how did they get Camp Wisner to betray us?"

"They sowed the seeds of discontent while we were holed up bringing back the Reborn. See, when the negotiations started falling apart, the Bastards sent envoys to visit places like Camp Wisner. They showed up, much like we did today with a show of force, just enough to make sure they were taken seriously without showing exactly how strong they are. They left peacefully after bringing gifts of resources and a lot of information about the other communities. The only catch was they asked that Andrew held off on an alliance until they could paint a more accurate picture of how things would go if they formed an alliance. Since he was already resistant to the proposals on the table, specifically the idea that they all join New Hope under one roof, he listened."

"And what did they tell him?"

"There was something about Marcus from before the fall of the EoS, but Andrew didn't go into detail about it. He said it was irrelevant now and that I wouldn't understand since I wasn't around back then. I pressed him about it later, just before you arrived actually, and he was right, it doesn't mean anything to me. It had something to do with another super computer, whatever that means. My best guess is he was talking about... well, never mind. Anyway, the information meant something more to them and it was enough to keep him from trusting Marcus. From there they fed bits of information about other communities, bits that turned out to be true. Mostly little things but they all turned out to be true. They even warned of a pending trade with Cali, saying Joshua intended to force their breeder to stay longer than agreed. Andrew didn't think even Joshua would be so bold as to break an agreement involving breeders, since that was the only way they were keeping the gene pool from becoming too inbred as it was. But sure enough, Joshua did exactly as the Bastards had predicted, and that convinced Andrew that not only did they have spies in each community, but that the other communities would screw him out of his power the moment they moved in with us."

"But Jack wasn't trying to get them to move in with us."

"True, but we'd been silent for so long everyone just assumed we still wanted the same thing we'd talked about years ago. When we started trading embryos that always grew into breeders, they thought for sure we had a cure for the virus. With the seeds of distrust the Bastards had been sowing, everyone assumed we were already being deceitful. It wasn't much of a leap to assume we would use what we had to integrate other communities under our power. The Bastards came to Andrew with an alternative. Help them capture Jack and they would use him as leverage to get the cure and then share it with everyone."

"And of course Andrew went along with it."

"Do you blame him? Think of it this way, Chuck, if Cali had discovered the Freezer before us and we found out about it, would it be better for New Hope to join Cali to help rebuild humankind with Joshua as the leader or to double cross them and steal enough of the treasure to be able to make it on our own?"

"But that's different, Joshua isn't like Marcus, he doesn't care as much about human survival as he cares about making sure he's the one ruling whoever's left. Joshua would never have looked at someone like Jack and decided he was a better fit for leadership and then willingly hand over control."

"You and I know that now, but Andrew didn't see Marcus as any different as his brother. You've known Marcus longer than all of us. A year ago would you think he would suddenly turn all his power over to a Reborn and walk away?"

He was right; until Jack came along he was convinced Marcus was no different than any of the founders. He shook his head.

Thomas continued, "Look, you can blame Andrew for what he did, but I see the bigger picture now, and while I'm pissed that it came to this, I understand why it did and I can't blame him. He was a pawn in a game he didn't even know he was playing. He was just trying to protect his people."

Again, this was true: Andrew was just a pawn, but still a pawn for the enemy. He wasn't going to be as quick to forgive or trust as Thomas. "So what exactly happened at that meeting last week?"

"Well, Jack showed up and they started talking. He intended to chat for a bit and get everyone to relax, and then the Bastards would strike. Just before that went down, Jack told Andrew his plan to form a central government and how if he agreed they would share all the knowledge that had led to the embryos producing breeders, all without costing Andrew any of his power. Before Andrew realized he'd been manipulated by the Bastards, they attacked. When everyone was secure, Andrew demanded to talk to Sebastian. He'd expected to get the man on his radio and have some words, but the soldiers instead disarmed him and his men and took them too."

"But he conveniently showed up today to talk us into trusting him. That doesn't seem fishy to you?"

"It does, but his radio was disabled and he had no way of calling Camp Wisner to tell them to turn off their air defenses. Since yesterday he's been parked about ten miles out, waiting for one of the patrols to spot them. But then today the patrols didn't go out because they were preparing for the confrontation with us. When his radar picked up our three flyers entering their airspace unchallenged, he figured the defenses were either disabled or turned off, so he took the opportunity to fly home."

This actually made sense, but it still didn't explain everything. "How did he get away from the Bastards?"

"He says he was held for a few days and finally met Sebastian face to face. The community is called Bastion, hence the term Bastards."

Chuck grinned, "Hmm, I figured they called themselves bastards because the fathers usually don't marry the mothers."

"Yeah, it's a fitting nickname either way, isn't it," Thomas chuckled, "Anyway, Sebastian told him all about the Freezer, about how New Hope was bringing back the Reborn, and how we had the resources to bring back over a thousand virile men. Then he just let him go home."

"I don't understand, why let him go home?"

Thomas shrugged, "If I had to guess, I'd say so he could tell the other communities what we have. Think about it, if everyone knew what we found at the Freezer before we had some kind of alliance in place, things could get ugly. At the least they won't trust us any more than they trust Cali. At the worst, they'll decide it's worth the risk to try to take what we have. We're well defended, but nothing is impregnable. And if Joshua finds out exactly what kind of wealth we have in our basement, there's no telling what could happen."

Chuck already felt a little shaky after the adrenaline from the earlier confrontation wore off. This revelation sent a chill down his spine and left him feeling positively weak.

"Oh and there's one more thing, something I learned before Andrew showed up. It's not good."

"How could it be worse?"

"Well, it seems Wendy has already been to Camp Wisner. She showed up about four days ago, broke into their silo, and questioned Andrew's wife at gunpoint. She was told the men who were responsible for Jack's disappearance wore orange markings on their armor."

Shit. "So that's why she thinks Cali's responsible. And if she withheld that bit of information it's because she wanted to do something she knew she would never get permission to do."

Chapter 28

Wendy woke to the sound of laughter, not something she expected to hear much of this night. It felt late. The light from the campfire danced through the fabric of her tent. She unzipped the door and peeked out.

Bart sat at the fire, a woman sitting next to him. She looked like the woman Wendy had spotted when they first made it into the camp, but she couldn't be sure. Not just because of the dim light, but because she couldn't tell one Mute woman from another. Until now it hadn't occurred to her that Bart was the only Mute she saw as a person. The rest had always just been dangerous animals. She might feel bad about that if the history of violence between Human and Mute wasn't so absolute.

She couldn't make out their conversation but the way they kept their gazes locked on each other told Wendy there was a lot of chemistry happening. It warmed her heart to see her friend enjoying an intimate conversation with one of his own kind.

Feeling a little too much like a mom spying on her teenaged kids, she zipped up the door and settled back into her bed. It had been a crazy week.

At first, being cut off from any potential news was enough to induce a panic attack, but ever since her meltdown this morning, she felt oddly at ease. She missed Jack, but whatever he was going through, surely he was alive at the least. There wasn't a scenario that made any sense to her that would involve the death of a virile man, at least not at the hands of another human being. Holding him captive to gain knowledge of what his community was hiding made sense. Taking him hostage to use as leverage to gain some of the wealth New Hope had also made sense. Capturing him simply because he could father more children was enough of a reason in itself. But going through the trouble of capturing him and then killing him later did not make sense. Sure, there was always the possibility that he would die trying to escape or simply be tortured beyond his limits, but she felt like she would know if he were dead. As long as he was alive, there was hope. It was that simple.

If he'd somehow escaped or for some oddball reason been let go, he could be out with Chuck on a patrol looking for her right now. No, actually that wasn't true, he would be back in New Hope where he belonged, watching the screens with Chin but not putting himself in danger. He'd agreed not to run off impetuously and put himself at risk if she went missing. She had agreed to never go charging into danger again after the situation at Saber Cusp, but obviously she broke that agreement. If there were a realistic chance Jack was back home right now, pacing nervously while praying she was still alive, she might feel guilty for her actions, but that was unlikely and even so, what guilt she felt this morning was now very detached.

Perhaps it was just acceptance of the situation. Perhaps she was just in denial that this could end in any way other than seeing her lover again. Whatever it was, she didn't feel the pressure that drove her to impetuously fly her and her companions straight into the face of danger. It was a peaceful feeling she hadn't felt since the night before Jack left.

Another laugh made its way to her ears, sending another burst of warmth through her heart. Tomorrow would be tough on Bart, having to leave his people behind once again, in all likelihood forever this time. Tonight he could enjoy being around his kind. Wendy settled into her pillow and drifted off to sleep with visions of Bart stealing away a woman with a long flowing ponytail and large supple breasts to have babies and grow old in his little cabin.

~~~~

Jack woke with a start, feeling like something was wrong. Immediately he felt the presence of a person close by. It was dark, pitch black in fact. With no windows to the outside world, when the lights went off in their room his eyes never adjusted enough to see anything. Holding his breath, he listened closely. He heard it – a quiet breath, the soft rustle of clothing shifting ever so slightly. Tensing his body, he prepared to spring out of bed and turn the tables on his would be attacker.

"Shhh. It's me, Trystana."

"Trys?" he said weakly, "What the hell are you doing here?" He wasn't sure he wanted the answer.

She sat down on the bed and leaned close. "I… I'm not sure really. I just wanted to talk I guess."

Trying to clear away the cobwebs of sleep, he drew a long steady breath. Her scent filled his nostrils and sent a tingle down his body, all the way to his toes. The desperation in her whisper combined with the heat coming off her body instantly aroused every inch of his body. Even his skin seemed to harden.

This wasn't what he wanted though, and he shifted uncomfortably, trying to put distance between their bodies. She rolled into him as he rolled back toward the wall. "What are you doing?" he whispered, trying to add an inflection of disapproval, which was about impossible to do when whispering.

"I just need to be close to someone right now. I know you don't want me, but please, just allow me to lay here with you. You don't even have to hold me."

Breathing grew short and blood pumped in his ears. This felt wrong. Yet his body told him it was oh so right. So maybe not *wrong*, but certainly improper. At the same time, her request sounded innocent, and if she truly was a friend, he couldn't kick her out of bed. *Besides*, he thought, *I'm under a blanket and she's lying on top. Perfectly innocent.* It still took effort to suppress the reflex to roll into her and hold her. "So… what now?" he whispered.

When she spoke, her warm breath tickled his week old beard, telling him she was lying on her side facing him. "Now I use every ounce of willpower to honor your desire to remain monogamous to your woman."

He almost laughed. "Thank you for that, I guess. But what I mean is what did you come here to tell me that couldn't wait until morning."

"I suppose I just wanted to apologize for what my father did today. I saw you when you returned and you looked pretty beat up."

"He didn't lay a finger on me."

"I know, I mean you looked like he'd beat you down emotionally. I have a pretty good idea what kinds of conversations you two had."

"It wasn't pleasant. Enlightening maybe, but not pleasant." He was thankful for the serious conversation. It instantly switched his mind from dangerous flirtation to troublesome speculation. "You realize your father thinks he's a god, right?"

She shrugged, or at least it felt like she shrugged. "I suppose so. I mean, maybe not a god, but certainly something more than a regular human being. I know he feels like he's the father of all the people in this community. In a way he's right. Most of us were not created naturally."

"And you don't see the danger in that?"

"My father lived through the last fall of humanity and he spent the past hundred and fifty years trying his best to ensure the survival of our species. If he has to use powers reserved for the gods to do so, I stand behind him."

Engaged in the conversation, the sexual tension eased and his mind cleared. That brought back all the troublesome feelings and emotions his meeting with Sebastian had stirred up. He pressed the subject. "You know, there's a terrible irony in the sort of things he showed me today."

"I'm not sure I follow."

"The tour he took me on, showing me the result of the wars that nearly extinguished this entire planet… he had a good point but it was completely lost on him."

Her whisper took on a defensive tone. "My father is a lot of things, and I certainly don't agree with many of them, but I can assure you, Jack, he would never do anything that could cause that kind of devastation. He's lived through and overcome too much of it."

Feeling he was on the right path, he pressed on. "Let me ask you a question. Do you believe people like me caused the wars that led to the wastelands I toured today?"

She didn't answer right away. "No," she said finally, "but I think the people of your time didn't understand how easily they could destroy everything they cared about. We have an insight that your era didn't."

"I won't argue that, but stay with me on this point. Even knowing the people of my generation built the atomic weapons and pointed them at centers of population, do you really think anyone from my time thought their actions would actually lead to systematically wiping humanity off the face of the planet?"

"No, I can't believe that any sane human would want that, and no, I don't think you are insane either."

"So why do you think it happened? Billions of people with the core instinct to see the next generation thrive, yet somehow they allowed a war to escalate until it nearly wiped out their entire species. How could they willingly launch nuclear weapons knowing it would kill their own families?"

"I can't answer that, Jack. I don't understand it, but I do know that it happened."

"Yes, it did happen. It happened because egotistical scientists tapped into the very forces that gave birth to our universe with the idea that they could control them. Then they turned those forces over to men who believed they could defeat their enemy with a nuclear bomb or an engineered biological disease and bring about peace. In the end the folly and arrogance of a few men nearly destroyed our entire species."

"So you're saying my father's use of science to save humankind will eventually lead to another wave of war and destruction?"

"No," he said, "not just another wave of destruction. Eventually his meddling will lead to the total extinction of mankind and quite possibly the destruction of this entire planet."

She didn't reply, and he figured he had gotten his point across: It wasn't people like the Reborn who brought on this apocalypse. For some reason it felt important for him to convince her of this; to convince her that her father was no different than the people who *had* caused it.

They lay there in silence for what might have been hours. At some point, he drifted off, caught somewhere between wake and sleep. Visions of a dark wasteland mixed with the memory of mortars exploding all around him. In his half dreams he was huddled in his foxhole with another soldier, pressed up against the raw earth as the barrage exploded all around them. The soldier turned to him in the chaos and whispered, "Save me." It was Wendy, and he embraced her protectively, trying to shield her from the chaos all around them. The assault eased and now the embrace turned emotional. She held him tight, pressing her body into his. They kissed, almost frantically, as if it could be their last. The kiss turned passionate, and he felt his body react to hers. He tried to touch every part of her body at once, wanting to be one with her. She wrapped her legs around him and pulled on his clothing. His desire to be inside her overwhelmed his senses. She writhed in passion. "Oh, Jack, make love to me." He kissed her shoulder, her neck, and moved his lips across her face. Lining up to enter her, he looked into her eyes... but it was no longer Wendy. Trystana smiled seductively.

He woke with a start and a gasp. It was still pitch black, and he was still under the covers, pressed up against the wall with Trystana's body lying mere inches away. Heart pounding in his chest, he could still feel her lips on his, her body pressed against his. But that wasn't real. It was just a dream. His body's reaction was real, however, and his loins ached for release. He took another sharp breath and shifted his body, trying to move further from the woman lying next to him.

She stirred then slowly sat up. "I should go."

He didn't respond, perhaps afraid if he opened his mouth he would ask her to stay.

"Thank you, Jack."

"For what?"

"For letting me be close to you. I needed it."

He nodded, although she wouldn't be able to see it.

Her scent filled his nose again as she leaned close. "And thank you for the conversation, it was enlightening. Before I go, I have one question."

Cautiously, he asked, "What's that?"

"How come you can use the same technology to bring people back people from your era and call it saving mankind? What makes you any different than my father?"

Chapter 29

Jack stared at his breakfast. Anton had already finished and was sitting on his bunk flipping his spoon in the air and trying to catch the handle. When you spent most of your days locked in a room, you learned to entertain yourself with whatever you had at hand.

The food looked more appetizing than the gelatin they normally ate in New Hope, but his mind just wasn't on food. He felt a lot of emotions when he woke up, guilt being the foremost. It was just a dream, but when he woke it could have been real. Sure, he could have had the real thing, and he hadn't, so it wasn't like he cheated on Wendy. In fact, he could come up with a hundred reasons why the vivid dream had shifted like that, and every one of them would be perfectly legitimate. Yesterday had been a traumatic day for him. That kind of trauma would surely lead to weird dreams.

No matter how he rationalized it though, he felt horrible. Wendy was probably holed up in their apartment, climbing the walls and crying her eyes out wondering if she would ever see him again, and here he was having erotic dreams about a woman he barely knew – the same woman, consequently, who had made it clear she would gladly have sex with him. What did that say about his character?

"You should eat. You missed dinner last night and ended up sleeping for nearly fifteen hours. Your body needs the nourishment." He wasn't about to correct the man about how many hours of sleep he got. Thankfully nobody noticed the woman paying a late night visit.

One of Anton's men appeared in the cubicle entrance. "Hey, boss, you gonna eat that?"

He almost shook his head, but Anton was right, he needed to keep his strength up. His body was still healing. Without looking up to respond, he picked up a spoon and started shoveling the food into his mouth.

"Fair enough," the man said. "Hey Tony, those guys at the other end of the room asked if we wanted in on their game today. You wanna join them? Looks like some kind of poker, although they made their own deck of cards so I'm not too sure how fair it is. I'm just thrilled that we finally met some natives who know what card games are."

Tony shrugged, "Maybe later." Then he said, "Hell, I ain't got nothing going on, tell them we'll be over in a few minutes."

Jack finished the food and leaned back. He did feel better.

"You want to talk about it?"

He looked up at Anton, wondering if he *had* heard the woman in his bed last night. "What?"

"Your time with Sebastian. You want to talk about what happened?"

He sighed, feeling relieved. "Not much to talk about really. He took me on a tour over what used to be Washington D.C. It's just a wasteland now, all dark dirt and rocks with craters the size of a city."

"Why'd he do that? Was he trying to make you feel like we aren't worth saving?"

"No, he was trying to show me what will happen if the Reborn try to lead humanity back from extinction. He blames it all on us and feels that our ideals lead us to what happened."

"That's nonsense. I became a soldier so I could protect my country, not so I could go to war."

He shrugged, "That's what I tried to tell him, but he's got a bit of a God complex. He feels like he is the only one suitable to lead and intends to keep cloning himself forever so he can keep his position of power."

Anton shivered visibly. "Guy sounds like a psycho. Did he tell you why he's holding us captive then? He doesn't think we all need to die, does he?"

"He didn't exactly tell me what he had in mind, but I think he wants me to turn over control of New Hope to him and then spread the Reborn across all the different communities."

"And if you don't?"

Jack didn't respond, which was answer enough.

"Do you think he could take New Hope by force?"

"Eventually, although it would be costly. He has the resources, but I'm not sure he has the manpower. Either way, I'm not going to let that happen."

They sat in silence for a few minutes. Finally, Anton said, "Whatever you decide to do, Jack, my loyalty is to you. I care about my wife, my baby, my men, and some of the people I've been around in New Hope, like Chin. As long as those people are safe and can live their lives pursuing the things that make them happy, I don't really care about who's in charge. If you want to try to take this guy out, I'm in. If you decide New Hope is better off joining him than fighting him, I'll stand behind you on that as well."

"Thanks, Tony." It felt good to know his men would back up any decision he made, even if it meant putting their lives at risk. He still wasn't sure what to do. He needed to find out more about what Sebastian had in mind. Trystana's final words last night resonated in his mind, muddying the waters quite a bit.

"Hey, Tony! You guys gonna come join us or what?" The shout came from across the room.

"Whattya say, Jack? You bored enough to go meet our roommates and play some poker?"

He stood up and said, "I could care less about playing poker, but maybe we can learn a little more about them. If they're enemies of Sebastian they might be useful."

They sauntered across the room. Anton's men were already seated around a big table, five of the other prisoners sitting with them. Anton took a seat, leaving a spot for Jack between him and his other men. *Always the protector.*

Jack looked across the table at the first of the five men, taking in the details and making snap judgments about each. The first man looked like a refugee. His facial hair hadn't been trimmed in months and he looked like someone who was only recently recovering from starvation. The second was the exact opposite. Clean shaven and chubby, a rare sight these days. Neither man looked like any kind of threat, and discouragingly neither looked like they could be an asset in a fight.

The next two men were more promising. They looked like they were used to hard work, their hands were calloused and looked strong. Both were also very typical native born men – they had dark hair, skin that looked perpetually tan, and brown eyes. Their facial features were similar to every other native born as well with a mix of Latino, African, American Indian, European, and Asian. Seldom did you see a native born with features specific to any one descent. It made sense, particularly when you considered how the gene pool had been cut down to just a handful of people. After dozens of generations of being in a closed environment, Americans were finally one single distinctive race. Unfortunately, Jack and his men weren't really a part of that race. They were all Caucasian of European descent and looked pale in comparison. Anton looked like the typical Italian New Yorker, and one of his men could have been in Hitler's army – six foot tall, blond hair and blue eyes. It wasn't terribly rare to meet a native born with lighter skin, and not all native born had dark hair, but five men of distinctively different origin in one room would stand out a bit. Jack only hoped it wouldn't lead to questions he couldn't answer.

"Welcome. We were wondering how long before you guys would come over and socialize. We had a pool going. I said a week, so I think that makes me the winner." This came from the last man, the one sitting next to Anton opposite Jack. He could tell right away that this was the alpha in the group. He was young, easily the same age as Jack. In fact, he looked more like a Reborn than any native. Flawless light skin, light brown hair, and an air of familiarity that Jack couldn't quite put his finger on.

"Thanks for having us. We would've joined you sooner but I was in pretty rough shape when we arrived and my men were being rather protective of me. Plus we weren't sure what this place was or who you were at first, and we got the impression you weren't very receptive." As he studied the man, he couldn't shake the sense of familiarity.

"Totally understandable. So let me explain this game. It's called five card poker."

"We're familiar," Anton said, "What are we playing for though?"

The man looked taken aback. "Oh. You've heard of the game? I… Um… Well, we play for fun mostly. None of us really have anything of value, so it's just for fun. Sometimes we'll bet some of our meal if things get really out of hand, but mostly we just keep in gentlemanly. So where did you learn to play poker?"

Anton squirmed in his seat a little. "Uh… I don't know, I guess the other guys taught me when I was younger. You look surprised."

The man shrugged, "I've just never run into anyone who even knew what playing cards were, let alone someone who knew how to play poker. The only game of chance any of these fine gentlemen have ever known involved dice. Maybe I should go over the rules, just so we all know how it's played."

The man directly in front of Jack rolled his eyes and said, "Oh just deal already, Phil! The man said he knew the game. It isn't like you invented it or something."

Jack's blood ran cold and the room shrank. He studied the young man holding the deck of makeshift cards. The details that looked so familiar coalesced into a younger version of a man he knew very well. "Phil?"

The man met his eyes and smiled. "Oh, sorry, I suppose some introductions are in order. I'm Phil, to my left are Jace, Rand, Stefan, and that guy on the end never had a name, so we call him Bob. And you?"

"Phil Norland."

The man went pale. He looked at Jack, then at the men around him. His eyes narrowed. "Funny, I never thought I would meet another man with my name."

"No... I mean... You don't recognize me?"

"Um... No? Were you one of the... uh... guards in my last room or something? I apologize, I didn't pay that close of attention to everyone I met."

Jack looked at Anton, who looked back with about the same confused expression Phil was wearing. *Why didn't he recognize me? Did he lose that much of his memory?* Then it hit him. He reached up and rubbed his week old beard. If the youth and lack of facial scars didn't disguise him, surely the beard and the remaining bruises on his face would alter his features enough that even his own mother wouldn't have recognized him. At least he hoped this was the reason Phil didn't recognize him. "Does the name Jack Taggart mean anything to you?"

~~~~

Wendy sat cross-legged in front of the fire, waiting for the water to heat up. She was already dressed and ready to move on. Max was up and getting his stuff together, but Jason was still sleeping, as usual. The oddity was Bart, lying across from the fire spooning the woman from the night before. She had never seen him sleep so soundly and comfortably. Max took a seat next to her and checked the coffee. "Warms your heart, doesn't it?"

"The coffee? Yeah, it does. Warms my fingers too."

She giggled. "I mean Bart. Lying there looking so happy."

He shrugged, "Yeah. It's sad though, the way he will have to leave soon and never look back."

She didn't want to think about it.

"Well, isn't this a lovely sight."

Wendy jumped and Max stood up, taking several steps toward his gear… and his gun. Farnak stood no less than ten feet away, two tough looking warriors flanking him

Without even opening his eyes, Bart said, "To what do we owe the honor of your visit, brother?"

Wendy colored, wondering how long her friend had been awake.

"I just came to see you off. And I wanted to remind you that at noon it becomes open hunting season on you and your friends. Is that Laran? How fitting!" He laughed.

The woman lying with Bart opened her eyes at the sound of her name. She looked around at all the people watching them, settling for a moment on her Clan leader laughing at her expense. With an expression of horror on her face, she quickly got to her feet and shuffled off to the side to get out of the limelight.

Bart opened his eyes and rolled to his back. Without looking at his brother, he said, "Don't you have more important things to do with your morning?" He stood up gracefully and brushed the leaves and needles from his clothing. Ignoring his brother and the two warriors, he casually sauntered over to Laran. "Looks like I'll be heading out soon. My offer still stands."

Farnak laughed again. "Don't tell me he asked you to join him in exile. How pathetic!" He laughed some more and the two behemoths joined in. "I'm not sure which is more amusing, that you asked her to choose you over her own Clan or that you somehow picked out the only woman of age who can't seem to attract a mate. I hate to say it, Laran, but you would be better off alone than with cowardly scum like this."

Wendy's blood boiled. She was fed up with the way Farnak talked about her friend. "Enough! You already won, Farnak. You banished your brother and we will leave. Why can't you just leave him in peace to say his goodbyes?"

Farnak strolled up to her, looking down from his superior height. If she wasn't so angry she might feel terror. He grinned, and then looked at Bart and said, "You might want to put your pet human on a leash before she says something that gets you killed."

Rage flooded her mind and she stepped closer. "I don't care if every one of your Clan is too afraid to challenge you, to me you're still just a fool who can't accept that his brother is superior in every way! You probably believe what you're saying too, which makes you even dumber than the average Mute!" Before she registered the motion, she was flying through the air. His blow had struck her just below the shoulder on her left side, lifting her body off the ground and hurling her a dozen feet. In midair she heard Bart roar, "Noooo!" Her body crashed through Jason's tent, the pain of the blow hit her brain simultaneously with the pain of landing and the realization that she'd made a horrible mistake.

The tent, which Jason had exited just before she lost her temper, cushioned the fall enough to keep her alive and conscious. As she landed, several thoughts went through her head. First and foremost was about her baby. She curled up around her belly just before skidding past the tent and impacting a tree.

Time seemed to slow. The world spun and pain clouded her vision. Later she pieced together those first few moments: Max cried her name, "Wendy!" She heard a roar, one that would have sent a shiver down her spine if she could feel anything but pain. She heard the unmistakable snarl Silver makes when there's a threat. She heard the distinct sound of an M74 bolt sliding home.

Then she opened her eyes. Somehow she had landed in such a way that she had a clear view of the entire situation. To her far left Jason raised his assault rifle. Max rushed toward her. Bart had his arms spread wide and charged at Farnak, who also assumed a position for combat. The two bodies clashed with a thunderous impact.

Jason searched for a target, waiting for the two warriors who were with Farnak to attack. Both Mutes didn't seem to pay attention to Jason. One was holding Silver by the collar, keeping him from joining the fight. The other was simply intent on watching it unfold. Laran looked thrilled. Max kneeled next to Wendy asking, "Are you okay?"

She tried to respond but the impact had knocked the wind out of her lungs and she was struggling to take a breath. Through the pain, she watched the fight unfold in front of her. Bart slammed Farnak to the ground, driving his shoulder into the smaller man. A move like that would have instantly killed any regular man, but Farnak seemed to absorb the hit like it was nothing. He drove his elbow into Bart's shoulder.

Bart rolled away and was on his feet in an instant, sprinting toward his brother who was just a fraction of a second behind in rising. Again they collided, this time Bart's massive fist slammed into the side of Farnak's head, and again Wendy watched the warrior shrug off a blow that would have killed a lesser man. However, the blow caught him off balance and he stumbled back to the ground.

Finally her solar plexus relaxed and she was able to take in a gasp of air. The relief new oxygen brought was overshadowed by a new wave of pain as she took air into her lungs. She glanced at Max. "Kill him!"

Max looked back and the fight and said, "No! You heard what Bart said last night, this is a challenge and if we shoot Farnak it will just be a fight that we will end up losing. Let him finish. He can win this. Is anything broken?" She frowned and shoved him away weakly, pain coursing through her body with the movement.

Bart jumped on his brother, throwing blow after blow, but only landing a few solid hits. Farnak's leg came up and hooked Bart's torso, pushing the larger man off and giving him a chance to regain his feet. The two fighters squared off, circling each other. Farnak grinned, revealing blood on his teeth and said, "This reminds me so much of our childhood, wrestling for the attention of our father. Do I need to remind you who always won?"

Bart replied, "I had enough attention from our father, and I knew you needed it so I always let you win."

Farnak roared and charged in. The two men clashed but this time they didn't go down. Muscles bulged as the two grappled with each other trying to gain the upper hand. Bart's knee came up and delivered a blow to Farnak's rib cage. This elicited a grunt of agony, but the experienced warrior took the blow because it left his opponent off balance. He shifted and swept at the other leg, giving Bart the option of taking the fight to the ground with his brother on top or losing his leverage to keep his feet. He chose to stay upright and Farnak struck, driving a fist hard into Bart's kidney and forcing the giant to hop away, off balance. Farnak could have charged in and taken him down, but instead he circled the larger man, taking his flank. Already off balance, Bart tried to turn so he could defend against an attack, but the smaller Mute was fast. Farnak dove in, and Wendy caught a flash of metal.

"Bart, watch out!" she shouted, way too late to make any kind of difference. Her friend had been correct the night before: in a fair fight, Farnak would find a way to turn the odds in his favor. If he connected with that blade it could be all over.

Somehow Bart managed to evade the thrust. He spun to his left, rolling out of it then pushing off a tree to regain his balance. Reaching behind his back, he pulled out his own blade. Wendy had seen the knife several times but never seen him use it for anything other than cleaning and skinning a kill. It was a wicked tool, close to two feet in length and probably weighing forty pounds. Farnak didn't look impressed. His own blade, now brandished openly, was smaller but somehow looked more lethal. The two hulks squared off again, this time taking up a position with the weapons leading.

Wendy put a knee under her and with a grunt pushed herself to a kneeling position. Her left arm was just a mass of pain; probably broken along with several ribs and perhaps even her collarbone. It took effort to move at all, and getting to one knee nearly blacked her out. With her good hand she drew her sidearm. Movement to her right interrupted her aim and she missed an opportunity to put a bullet in Farnak. Before she could see who it was, the pistol was gone and she was back on the ground. Laran stood above her, holding the weapon. "Leave them to fight this out. If you try to interfere again it will be the last thing you do." Helpless against the far larger woman, she turned back to the fight.

Bart feinted and then shifted his weight and closed the gap again. The blades met and Bart scored a blow with his left fist. He followed through and spun past Farnak, coming around his left flank and slashing out. The blade drew blood, but it didn't look mortal. Farnak didn't even flinch.

"Give it up, brother, you can't match me in combat. Your size and strength are impressive but you lack speed."

"I've drawn first blood, Farnak, and before I am done I will bathe in it!"

"Hah! This is but a scratch. I've had women do more during sex!" He lunged again, this time getting past Bart's defense and scoring and equally bloody wound.

By now dozens more had heard the commotion and were watching. A few of the warriors cheered when Farnak drew blood. Over the next few minutes the crowd grew to hundreds. Bart and his brother traded blows, but neither could seem to get the upper hand. Bart's chest was heaving and blood marked at least a half dozen spots on his shirt and pants.

Farnak was equally bloodied but didn't look winded at all. He grinned and said, "See, your size is going to be the death of you, brother. Already you are exhausted from trying to defend against my attacks, and I'm just getting started."

"You know why I'll win, Farnak? Because a bad leader is a sign of terrible weakness, and you are the worst in our short history." He paused and lowered his guard slightly while taking a breath. Farnak saw it and dove in, causing Bart to sloppily raise his guard. The smaller warrior dropped to his knees and slid in, driving the knife deep in the bigger man's thigh. Wendy cried out.

Bart went down to one knee as Farnak slid past him. The smaller brother gracefully hopped to his feet, spun around, and lunged. The blade leading, Farnak drove his entire weight toward the base of his brother's neck. Wendy's breath left her body again, watching what was clearly going to kill her friend.

At the last possible second, Bart did the impossible. Dipping down so the attack would overshoot its target, he grabbed ahold of the arm that was now centered over his left shoulder. Then he shot to his feet, not letting go. The arm bent, but in the opposite direction it was meant to. Bart didn't stop there, however. Belying his massive size, he continued his upward lunge, leaving the ground and executing a back flip. Twisting as he leapt, he didn't let go of the arm. As if the snapping of tendons and bones wasn't horrifying enough, his momentum carried him over Farnak's body, twisting the now rubbery appendage around the warrior's own neck. When he landed, he swept his brother's foot with his leg, putting the man on the ground face first. Still holding the arm, he drove a knee down into his opponent's spine, eliciting another disgustingly wet crunch of bone. Now with his right hand, he grabbed his brother's right leg and pulled. The former leader didn't even have a chance to cry out before his body folded backwards, breaking every bone in his spine and killing him instantly.

Part 4

Chapter 30

Matthew couldn't sleep. In just four short days he would be doing what he had only dreamt would happen in his lifetime. It scared the hell out of him. There were too many 'what-ifs'. *What if the world was a radioactive wasteland? What if there were some kind of biological contaminate in the air or the soil and he died a horrible death, or worse, brought it back into Sanct with him to kill off his friends and family? What if he found a thriving world that had survived the wars and moved on without knowing an entire community was living in the ground beneath their feet? What if some other species of animal had thrived and taken over the world?*

Sure, some of it felt more like something Carter would program into the Net, but anything was possible. Before the wars, mankind had aspirations of travelling to other worlds and even sent robots to explore some of them. Nobody really knew what they would find on those foreign planets, but one thing was mostly certain: there wouldn't be life of any kind. People fantasized about it, but when it came down to it, the science suggested it was highly unlikely, perhaps even impossible. The outside world was every bit as alien to the thousands of people living in Sanct, but there was one very distinct difference: when the doors to Sanct were closed over three hundred years ago, life thrived on the planet. That made just about every fantastical and horrific idea a very real possibility.

His empty bed usually felt normal. There had only been a few times in his adult life where he had shared his bed with another person. Tonight, however, it felt as cold and foreign as he envisioned the outside to be. He desperately wished Angela was lying next to him, even if she only slept. Perhaps if another person could be close to him right now, he wouldn't feel so alone and scared.

Things were going well with Angela, but unfortunately they hadn't progressed to the point where she would be staying the night. Hell, as strong as their feelings for each other seemed to be, they still hadn't consummated their relationship. There had been some intimate moments, and his body was more than ready to explore the few remaining parts of her he was not already intimately familiar with. Something kept holding him back. He wanted to believe it had to do with wanting to savor every part of their new relationship before adding sex to the equation. Lying here in bed with a knot of anxiety preventing any hope of sleep suggested perhaps his hesitance to take that final step had more to do with his uncertainty in the future of Sanct.

She was unaware of the momentous decision the council made two days ago. Despite their relationship, it was his duty to keep the decisions of the leadership from the citizens. It wouldn't just be irresponsible, it would actually be illegal. If he shared what he knew and she slipped up and told anyone else, it could spread like wildfire, creating unrest. The only loophole in the laws involved marriage. The spouse of a department head eventually learns about all the secrets. Even if the person they're married to doesn't share the details, eventually they will overhear something. For this reason, spouses are sworn to secrecy the same way as the council members and hence held to the same standards. There is even precedent of spouses being imprisoned for gossiping about the meetings. Unrest is taken seriously in Sanct.

As much as he would like to share his burdens with Angela, he would have to wait until they were married to do so, and that wasn't going to happen in the next few days. If his fears came to fruition, it may never happen at all. He wasn't sure what was worse: the thought of dying some horrific death on the surface or not even being able to tell Angela he was going in the first place. At least his parents were a part of the leadership and knew exactly what was going on. He couldn't imagine going on such a potentially dangerous mission without being able to tell *someone*.

Frustrated by his insomnia and not all that happy with the direction his thoughts were taking him, Matthew slipped out of bed and made his way to his office. He took a seat in front of the ancient computer and flipped the switch to bring it to life. Everything in Sanct was old. They had machine shops and tools to repair most everything, but nothing new had been manufactured since the day the doors closed. Some things lasted dozens of years without needing any kind of maintenance, but others required regular repairs to keep working. Vernon, the head of maintenance, had one of the most difficult jobs. He was in charge of making sure everything stayed working, and these days that encompassed nearly every item in the city.

Computer parts aged every time you ran power through them. Electronic devices had a lifespan that was usually measured in years, maybe decades. Yet all the electronics in Sanct had to survive centuries. Thankfully the designers had the foresight to plan for that and stock their vast warehouses with replacement parts. Unfortunately they didn't have the technology to build equipment that could stand the test of time. Computer displays seemed to be the most vulnerable to time. Seldom did you get the opportunity to look at a display that wasn't slightly malformed, missing pixels, or showing colors that weren't even close to what they should be. Matthew's monitor was no different even though he was Head of Supplies and could tell you exactly how many pristine and unused monitors sat on the shelves. Nobody would ever know if he waltzed in to the warehouse and picked brand new components out for his personal use. Nobody but him, of course, and he wasn't the type who would break the rules. His screen had been repaired countless times but it still functioned well enough. The day a technician told him his screen was unrepairable was the day he would issue himself a new one. Until then, he would live with what he had.

Thankfully, the screen came to life without so much as a flicker. Rapidly working the keys, he did what he hadn't done in months – he logged into the Net. Donning a pair of well-worn headphones, he prepared to immerse himself in a world of fantasy.

An image appeared in front of him. Blue skies, green trees, brown soil. The gentle sound of the forest surrounded him. In the distance, a flock of birds fluttered out of a large Oak tree, dancing in the sky before settling back in the same tree. He could hear their songs in the distance. He manipulated the mouse, swinging his view around to take in the whole landscape. Mostly he enjoyed looking upward at the sky. It looked exactly like he envisioned, which of course made sense since it was modeled after the pictures every man, woman, and child in Sanct had seen. White fluffy clouds meandered across the wide open expanse. He maneuvered his avatar – nothing fantastical like most people chose – toward a tree and started climbing. He wanted to get a better view of the landscape. A part of him knew it was just a rendering, probably one designed by his good friend, but right now it was reality. He had escaped into this fantasy world.

A sound behind him broke him free of the illusion. He removed the headphones and looked around. Of course his apartment was empty. The sound had come from the game, although the psychoacoustics had tricked his mind into believing the sound came from behind him. Carter had explained how it worked once but he didn't really understand. All he knew was it worked well enough to trick him. Putting the headphones back on he swung his viewpoint around to look toward the new sound. He nearly jumped out of his seat when a completely naked woman came into view, hovering mere feet away from his avatar, which was fifty feet up in a tree. The woman was perfect in every detail, although her features were somewhat exaggerated. No woman Matthew had ever met had breasts that large with a waist that slender. The woman giggled.

"Jesus, Carter, you scared the crap out of me."

When the woman spoke, it wasn't the voice of a female that came out. "Do you like it? Look close, I even got the goosebumps around her areola."

Matthew laughed at the absurdity of it. Carter was a demented individual. Stealing a glance at the breasts, he admitted that his friend was a hell of an artist. If he hadn't known better, he would think he was looking at a video of a real woman. "Why are you running around as a naked woman?"

The woman shrugged, her breasts bouncing lightly. She reached up and ran a finger around a nipple seductively. "Because I like it." The combination of Carter's voice on this perverted fantasy girl was too much.

"You are one sick individual, you know that? I thought you were more mature than this."

The woman spun rapidly in the air and suddenly Carter stood there, thankfully fully clothed. "Oh come on, I'm just messing with you. I only bring her out to mess with the kids who think if they log in at two in the morning they might meet a lonely girl looking for some cybersex. I'm pretty sure when I appear and then speak in my own voice they are scarred so badly they don't think about sex for months."

"I'm not sure what's more twisted, the fact that you crafted that avatar to begin with or what you like doing with it."

Carter laughed as if Matthew was just kidding. "So what brings you here at this hour? I hope you aren't trolling for cybersex."

"Not tonight." They both chuckled. "No, I just couldn't sleep. I figured maybe I could find solace pretending I was outdoors looking at the clouds and enjoying the green trees and sunlight."

"It is pretty spectacular, isn't it? This is one of my programs, and I think of every world I have created I like this one the best. Every detail I used was taken from pictures of how the world really looked."

"Ever wonder if it still looks like this?" It wasn't an uncommon question. Every kid talks about this sort of thing with his buddies at some point in their lives. The only thing odd about it would be that they weren't kids.

"I'm not sure I want to. Best case scenario it looks just like this. But odds are it's something far less, so I never really want to find out. As long as I don't question it, I will never be disappointed. To me, this is what it looks like, and that's good enough for me." The way he said it sounded like he had been telling himself that for years. Perhaps he even believed it.

Matthew spun his view back to the tree and continued climbing.

"You know, I can give you the ability to fly so you can get these views without the hassle of climbing."

"I prefer it this way," he said. "It feels more real." He reached the upper canopy and looked out over the sea of green trees and blue sky. He took in a deep breath and wished they could add the scents. As much as he feared the outside world, he desperately wanted to take it in with every sense. The warm sun on his skin, the vibrant colors, the sounds of nature all around him, the smell of clean natural air, and even taste the rain. As if on cue, rain began to fall, a rainbow forming off in the distance. He looked up at a blue sky. "Shouldn't it be cloudy if it's raining?" Clouds rolled in, darkening the sky and hiding the rainbow. "Never mind, I liked it when the sky was clear." Again, on command it cleared up.

Neither of them spoke. Carter seemed to sense that he needed some space, so they just enjoyed the scene together. After what might have been an hour, the sun started to set, brilliant colors of yellow, orange, and red stretching across the horizon. Ten minutes later it was dark and the sky filled with stars, another sight Matthew had never seen. There were billions of them, and he felt like he could reach out and touch them, swirling his fingers through the sparkling morass. Crickets chirped in the distance. His eyelids grew heavy with the tranquility of it all. The fifth time his head nodded down, he carefully removed the headphones and turned off the computer, not even saying goodnight to his friend. He barely made it to his bed before falling into a deep sleep.

Chapter 31

It was late. Thomas rubbed his eyes. "Chuck, at least wait until morning. Get a few hours of sleep and approach this with fresh eyes."

"We already wasted days."

"She's probably holed up not far from the Warehouse waiting to hear some radio chatter."

"Or she could be in trouble at this very moment."

"Hell, at this hour she's probably asleep. You aren't going to find anything in the dark."

"The sensors on the flyer are better than my eyes anyway. Besides, this way I can get to the Warehouse and look for any sign of where she might have headed and get an early start in the morning. Why are you so against me going? You still think it's better if she doesn't come home?"

"Dammit! Don't twist my words around, Chuck! You know exactly what I meant. I just think it would be best if you got some rest and in the morning we will come up with our next move."

"I'm tired of waiting around for decisions to be made."

"I could order you to stay."

Chuck stopped going through his pack and stepped up to Thomas. "You could, but then what if I go anyway? Are you going to arrest me for insubordination? With Wendy gone and me in jail, how long before the rest of the population decides the Board isn't the authority here? How would it play out with the people when I testify that all I wanted to do was go after one of our own who is in trouble?"

"We don't know if she's in trouble."

Chuck just scoffed and returned to his pack. He was right, and Thomas knew it. Even if he tried to stop him right now it would only hurt New Hope. He was a fool to rush out like this, but there were bigger concerns. "Fine. You report in every hour until you are secure for the night. You don't go further than the Warehouse without my permission, and you take two men with you."

Chuck just nodded and continued packing his supplies. Johnson was manning the control center, but he had already shut everything down for the night after they landed. "Johnson, you're going to have to pull a few more hours. Let Chin know he will need to be here bright and early too." The man froze when Thomas started addressing him. His shoulders slumped and he turned back to the screens and started turning them all on.

"The board should be assembled by now and waiting for me. Be safe, Chuck. We can't afford to lose any more people, least of all you."

Knowing he wasn't going to get a response, he turned and headed for the rail car to travel back to the main bunker.

Ten minutes later he entered the old council chambers. Caleb and Teague were already there, both looking lost in their own minds. There was one thing Thomas could say about the people like them – they were patient.

They could sit for hours without any talk. Back in his old life, people weren't like that at all. They couldn't stand even a few minutes of downtime, so they were constantly attached to their phones looking at Facebook and Twitter and texting their friends. They didn't even talk about anything; they just had a steady feed of contact with others. Thomas never quite understood the millennial generation. Perhaps, he considered, they were so disconnected from reality that they didn't understand each other either. Hell, maybe that was why the wars escalated like they did.

When he took his seat, he asked, "Is Scott going to join us?"

"Only if we need to make a decision. He was… busy… when we called and asked to sit this one out since it doesn't really seem to concern any of his authority anyway. How about we get started. I am anxious to hear what you found."

"Well, Theodore wasn't lying. Everything he said was spot on." He relayed the events, trying to remember all the details.

"So," he was saying, "Andrew decided at that moment that he'd been deceived. He asked to speak with their leader. Instead of getting the man on the radio, they hauled him all the way to their home on the East Coast."

"Did he tell you who their leader is?" Caleb asked.

"He said the guy's name is Sebastian. I guess they named the community Bastion after him. And get this – his people call themselves Bastards." That name thing wouldn't get old any time soon. Caleb didn't seem to find the humor in it, however. In fact, he seemed to pale at the mention of the name. He shot a glance at Teague who looked equally pale. "What am I missing here guys. You both look like you just saw a ghost."

Both men remained silent, looking at each other as if communicating telepathically.

"Guys?"

Finally Teague asked Caleb, "Do you think it's him?"

"No, but who else would it be?"

"But he disappeared before the fighting erupted. I assumed he just crossed the wrong person and ended up dead."

Teague shrugged. "That is what I assumed to. Perhaps he managed to renew himself and slip in to Bethlehem as a young man. We do not know much of the last few years there. Perhaps he rebuilt his empire. For all we know, he had his own church in the end."

"You think he would willingly renew himself? Surely even he understands what that means."

Teague nodded, "I do. In fact I am sure of it."

"Hey," Thomas interrupted this conversation that was taking place on a level he didn't even understand, "care to enlighten me about what you're talking about?"

Caleb looked at him like he'd forgotten he was in the room. "Sorry, Thomas. If Sebastian is who we think he is…" He seemed to get lost in his own mind again. Thomas waited it out. Finally, as if he hadn't paused at all, he said, "well, let us just say that would be problematic."

"So you know this guy?"

"Only by reputation. I believe Teague worked with him." Teague only nodded. "Marcus too. He was one of the original founders of the EoS. Sebastian Christopher Maddoxson. Most knew him as Christopher and he came up with the methods we use to transfer memories from one brain to another. It made him one of the most respected men in the EoS, but not until after the churches had begun their rise to power. By then status was not quite what it had been before the churches. He still managed to build quite an empire."

"What happened to him to make you think he was dead?"

"He made a lot of enemies on his way to the top. Then he disappeared. Nobody ever even found a body, so it is possible he got out."

"And renewed himself?" Caleb nodded. "Is that like cloning?"

Teague jumped in and said, "Renewal is the transfer of memories into a freshly cloned body. It is the same process we used to bring you back as it is the process we have used to stay alive for all this time."

"But I thought you told me you had to die before you could transfer your memories into a new body?"

"You do."

This sent a shiver down his back. "So he would have had to kill himself first."

"Exactly," Teague said, grimly.

"So you think this guy figures that by offing himself he wakes up in his new body?" It wasn't a difficult leap in logic, particularly if you had gone through the process. Thomas could easily believe he was actually the same man who lived all those years before the war, but the fact of the matter is he only shares the memories of living as that man. He isn't the man who lived before him, that man died nearly three hundred years ago.

"There is some research that could lead one to believe renewal is truly a reincarnation." Thomas realized the men sitting before him might very well believe they were the same person they were cloned from. He decided it wasn't a good idea to press the subject. As far as he knew, these men waited until they were dead before being renewed. At least he hoped that was the case. Teague seemed to be reading his mind and said, "Renewal is nothing new, but regardless of whether a person believes it is a continuation of their life or an entirely new one, it is always done after death, not before."

Thomas sighed in relief. "But you're sure Sebastian would end his life to undergo this process?"

"I am. He did it earlier in his life, so it would stand to reason that he wouldn't hesitate to do it again." He seemed lost in thought while he said this, however.

Changing the subject, Thomas said, "So until right now, you had no idea he survived?"

"No. About forty years back we found a man who claimed to have come from there. He also claimed the Yanks-"

"Bastards," Thomas corrected.

"He also claimed the Bastards had nearly two thousand citizens and dozens of cloning tanks to sustain the population."

"But he didn't tell you his leader's name? Or the name of the community? If he came from there, wouldn't it make sense he would have known these things?"

Caleb looked uncomfortable. "Well, I remember we asked about their leader but he was vague. Theodore spent some time interrogating him more thoroughly and couldn't find any holes in his story. In effort to verify what we had been told, we managed to get some images from our satellite. We got two clear pictures. One shows an airfield with several dozen aircraft, all similar to the type we have in our flight bay. The other shows a gathering of some kind with at least a thousand people. The resolution of the picture isn't clear enough to get an accurate count, but the gathering is bigger than anything we have seen since the collapse of the EoS."

"You did this in response to what you learned from the man?"

"Yes, why?"

He shrugged, "In World War Two, it was common practice to set up camouflage netting covering cardboard decoys of tanks or aircraft so the enemy aerial photographs would appear to show more forces than we had. Any chance this was all an elaborate ruse to get you to believe the Yanks had more people than they really had?"

"Bastards."

"Exactly."

"To what end?"

"I don't know, to prevent you from sending anyone to attack?"

"But we never would have done that even if they were weak and vulnerable."

"Did Sebastian know that? You said he had a lot of enemies. Perhaps he saw you as an enemy."

Caleb looked skeptical. "Every community knew exactly who was leading New Hope. Sebastian would have known he had no enemies here."

Thomas looked at Teague for confirmation but the man still seemed lost in his own world.

"Andrew couldn't say how many people they had, but in their hangar he saw enough heavy equipment to move an army across the continent. That's obviously a problem. If he has the people to man those machines, he could be much more of a threat than you ever imagined."

"I think it would be best just to assume he has enough people. That way if we are wrong he simply is not a threat. If we are right then at least we are doing what we can to prepare for it."

Teague, who was still looking pale, said, "I think he does."

"If so," Caleb said, "then it would confirm the story that they have dozens of tanks and further prove that the man was being honest."

"Not necessarily."

"Oh come on, you have done the math a dozen times, Teague."

"What math? You realize you are talking over my head here, right?" said Thomas.

"Sorry," Caleb said. "One theory on bringing back our species from the brink of extinction involved breeding as quickly as possible. Ignoring whether you have the resources for several hundred or even thousands of infertile people, you can use math to calculate your chances of it working out."

"Go on," said Thomas, intrigued.

"Okay, say you had three virile men and two dozen women. Each woman could get pregnant a dozen times in their life, maybe a little more. In the first generation you could have nearly three hundred people. With roughly one in fifty being a virile man, your next generation would be able to increase that, theoretically of course, to over two thousand."

"Theoretically?"

"Well, although there is about a one in twenty chance of a virile man's son to share his immunity and also be virile, in reality the numbers are seldom as generous. Over a million pregnancies the numbers work perfectly, but when you talk about a few hundred you could end up with zero virile men. Even if the statistics held up perfectly, the second generation might end up with six or seven virile men out of nearly three hundred. Each of those men would have to impregnate at least twenty five women a dozen times each. Given that even in the best of circumstances it would take upwards of a dozen attempts to get a woman pregnant, it is a stretch for those men to hold up over time. They would be having sex several times per day, every day for decades. Do you know any men who could keep that up?"

Thomas laughed. "I get your point. But it is possible."

"Not really. See, even if you segregate the populations by ancestry, it would be nearly impossible to avoid inbreeding. Inbreeding shows a significant drop in the rate of successfully passing on the immunity genes. So does malnutrition, illness, stress, hardship, and a dozen other factors that are a part of life in this world. By the time everything is factored in, the chances of success are measured in the fractions of a percent. And if it fails, you have a population of thousands without the means to maintain it. At some point, you run out of people to provide for those who can no longer work and you have a choice of starving or eliminating huge percentages of your population. Some communities tried this method early on and it not only failed, we lost the opportunity to use those virile men to slowly build our population. Those communities failed and set us back several decades as a species."

"So it's unlikely the Bastards are that large without cloning tanks."

"Exactly. If they have enough cloning tanks they could bring their population up and just renew people as needed."

"But," Teague interjected, "Sebastian knows a way to do it without cloning tanks."

"What are you saying?" asked Caleb.

"The project he was working on before he disappeared-"

"That was only a rumor, Teague. He disappeared before anyone could confirm what he was working on. We should not jump to any conclusions until we have all the facts."

Teague shook his head. "No, I can say without a doubt he was working on it."

"How can you be so sure?"

"Slow down, guys, you're getting ahead of me again. What project?"

"Do you know anything about cloning, Thomas?"

"Only what you've taught me and what I read about it back before the war."

"Well, to create a clone, you start with a fertilized egg. To get that you need a man's seed and a woman's egg. Once you have a fertilized egg you basically remove the DNA and replace it with the DNA of the person you want to create. Without the fertilized egg you can't do anything."

"But as long as you have one virile man you can fertilize eggs for use in cloning, right?"

"Yes. But Sebastian wanted to find the secret to creating life from chemicals. His last project involved trying to figure out how to fertilize an egg without a man's seed."

"Did he succeed?"

"He disappeared before anything came of it," Caleb said. "Surely without the aid of Marcus' computer he could not finish what he started."

"No, he did succeed, but he kept it to himself."

Caleb scoffed. "How could you possibly know this?"

"Because I was his first success. He took an egg from my mother and fertilized it without using his seed."

~~~~

Caleb was floored. This entire conversation had been filled with information that turned his insides to liquid, but this revelation went far deeper. "All these years and you never told us."

"We all have our secrets," Teague said, as if that was justification. "Do you really think I am the only one?"

He felt the remaining blood drain from his face. "With the fate of our species on the line, none of us should have kept anything from the others."

Teague shrugged. "We all have things from our past that we are not proud of. My secret was not relevant until now. Frankly I never thought it would be. Marcus knew because he worked with Sebastian. The process used to fertilize an egg without a man's seed leaves the embryo with over ninety five percent of the donor's genes. If you had ever met the man you would think I was a direct clone."

"You still should have told us. If anything it might have changed our opinion of you."

Teague laughed. "It always seems to come back to superiority with you. Did you ever stop to think I just cared more about getting the human species back on track than I ever did about who had the ultimate authority?"

"No, actually I just assumed you did not have what it took to be a leader." As soon as he said it he regretted it, even if it was the truth. He added, "Until recently I never saw it in you."

Teague looked away. "Well, when you live under a man who commanded absolute authority, I suppose the last thing you want to do is become like him."

The room went silent. A few minutes later Thomas broke it with, "Well, now that that's all out of your systems, maybe we can get back to the issues at hand?"

Caleb almost laughed, not in humor but rather from the tension. "Of course. So Andrew went to visit Sebastian. What came of it? And how did he get back home if he was double crossed?"

"Frankly it isn't all that important. What matters here is Sebastian, and now Andrew, know what we found in the Freezer. They know about the Reborn and know almost exactly how many we have recovered to date. They know way more than they could possibly know without there being a spy actively keeping tabs and relaying that information."

Caleb didn't think it could get worse, but it just did. This was his fault. Internal security was his responsibility unofficially when the council was in power, and now it was his official title. Not only did he fail to keep New Hope safe for all those years, he still hadn't found the spy even once he knew there was one. Weakly, he asked, "Is there anything else we should know? It is late and we have a lot to process, I think we need to break until morning."

Thomas didn't respond right away, seeming to mull over his response. Another twinge of anxiety went through him as he wondered what would make the man pause. "Well, I'm not sure I should say anything after the drama that unfolded between you two, but in the spirit of uncovering secrets, there was one piece of information I was given that means nothing to me but apparently played a key role in swaying other communities from allying themselves with us."

"Just say it." He almost held his breath.

"Like I said, it doesn't mean anything to me, but Sebastian told the other communities that Marcus secretly built a second supercomputer."

Caleb sighed. *Thank God it wasn't more bad news.* "Don't worry about it, we know. In fact you met it already back in Saber Cusp."

"Oh, okay. That makes sense. I guess I just didn't get what it meant because he said this one was for the Church of the Fallen Saints."

The room spun. Blood pounded through his ears. Through the noise he heard someone talking but he couldn't make out what was being said.

~~~~

Wendy woke with a start. She wasn't sure where she was, but it wasn't her tent. Her mind felt muddy. "Your human friend will be fine. A few cracked ribs, a dislocated shoulder that needs to be set, and a lot of bruises. I forced some passion flower tea down her throat. She should sleep relatively well for the rest of the day. I'm surprised at how frail these people are. Your brother barely delivered a love tap yet it looks as if she tumbled down a mountain. If it hadn't been for her body armor she would be in far worse shape."

"And the baby?"

"She seems okay. No bleeding, which is a good sign. I've never seen a pregnant human before. I thought they were all barren?"

"No, most of the men are sterile, but the women are all capable of bearing child. Thank you, Laran. Can I have some time with my friends please?"

"Bartholomew, you are the Clan Leader now, you can have anything you want, including me. If I may be so bold, I would suggest you speak with the warriors soon. They have spent the last month preparing for war and they need to know if the plans are still the same."

"Laran, if I have you it will be at your discretion, not as a prize for being Clan Leader."

"Either one would be an honor."

"Please, tell the warriors I will meet with them soon."

The room got brighter as Laran opened the heavy hides that covered the door. It was daylight outside and they were clearly in the large tent structure in the center of the camp. She tried to sit up and pain exploded in her left side.

"Little Red, please don't try to get up. You took quite a blow and have some injuries. Just rest for now."

"What the hell did she give me?"

"It's a natural sedative to keep you asleep. I suspect she underestimated how much to give you though or you would still be asleep. She believes you to be as frail as a child." The big man chuckled.

"When did I black out?"

"After the fight, Max tried to move you and you screamed and passed out. Laran carried you in here and tended to your wounds. I'm afraid you will not be traveling for a while."

"My bag. Where's my pack. Medicine." The room spun and she lay back down.

"You never replenished your med kit after you used it on me. I already checked for some of your healing medicine."

The room brightened again and Max stepped in. "Is she awake?"

"Yes, I'm awake. Help me sit up."

Max rushed to her side. "Just relax, Wendy, you need to rest."

She rolled to her right and pushed herself toward a sitting position, gritting through the pain of movement. The blanket slipped down and she realized she was completely naked underneath. She quickly pulled the blanket to cover her exposed breasts which sent another wave of pain through her body. "Dammit!" she exclaimed, "Why the hell am I naked?"

"Laran had to strip you down to examine you and check your baby."

She involuntarily closed her legs, shivering at the thought of that woman poking around down there. Through the haze of whatever they had given her, she didn't stop to think that maybe the woman knew more about child birth than even Teague.

"Max, can you please leave so I can get dressed?"

"Don't worry, I didn't see anything. Look, I found one ampule of that healing juice in my med kit. It isn't going to have you on your feet right away but in a couple days you should be feeling much better and maybe even able to walk again."

She nodded with relief. The idea of being cooped up in this tent for a few weeks while healing was too much to bear, and even through the stupor she felt anxiety. "What are you waiting for?"

Max quickly injected the medicine into her shoulder. It always seemed to work best when you could inject it near the injury. When he was finished he pulled the blanket up and tucked her in.

"What the hell are you doing?" She wasn't sure why she was being so bitchy.

"I'm just making you comfortable. Do you need some water?"

"I need to know what's been going on. How long was I out?"

"Just for a few hours."

"Where's Jason?"

"He's packing his things. He says he's going to head out, with or without me."

"Wait... what? Why is he heading out?"

"He's nervous around all these..." Max stole a glance toward Bart. "Uh... Evolved." Bart chuckled.

"That's absurd. Where does he think he's going to go?"

Max shrugged. "He says he will head north and try to get as close as he can to the Warehouse. He figures he can reach it in a week, maybe sooner if he can find a safe path through the mountains. If he gets close enough, he thinks his PDP will link up to the laser transmitter there and he can establish communications with New Hope. He said we can send a flyer to come get you once we are home. Frankly it isn't a bad plan."

Something he said nagged at her brain but through the haze she couldn't think of what it was. "I think it's a silly plan. I'll be fine in a day or two and we can head out together."

"No offense, Wendy, but Bart has responsibilities here and I would feel safer if you stayed with him. We can take care of ourselves out there. Or if you prefer, I can stick around here with you. Jason doesn't seem to care if I go along or not. He just wants to leave."

"No. If he's going you should go with, but I would prefer you stick around at least until tomorrow. Give me a little time to clear my head and then we can talk about it more. Please, just give it a day. They'll be safe here, won't they Bart?"

"Of course, Little Red. But if they leave I can send one of my trackers to aid them."

The medicine was kicking in and combined with the tea she was starting to fade fast. "Please, Max, just… stay with me… until…"

Chapter 32

"How. I mean, I know how, but how did you end up here?" Jack's head spun with questions. "Maybe the right question is why."

"I wish I had answers for you," Phil replied, "I probably only have more questions for you. This is still just some weird dream to me. How is any of this possible?"

Jack shrugged. He didn't know where to begin. The last time he had this many questions flooding through his brain he was laying on the table talking with Teague. He thought back to that time when all his questions had such urgency but none of the answers seemed to ease the anxiety. In the end it just took time to absorb it all and let his brain sort it all out. In the meantime he needed to take one question at a time. "So how long have you been here?"

"I'm not sure. I woke up for the first time around seven weeks ago. I spent about a week in that room, and then once I was capable of managing myself, I was brought here."

He ran the numbers through his head. The timeline would suggest his head had been stolen maybe a couple weeks after their big operation at the Freezer. "Have you been here the whole time? Did anyone come to talk to you? Have you been out of this room?"

"Oh yeah. Well, first there were the women. So many women and all of them just wanted one thing. That's one of the things that makes this whole thing just feel like some kind of crazy dream. Women don't just walk into your life and start begging for sex."

"They do here. And it seems to be the same wherever you go. Do you know why they're like that?"

"Sebastian told me it's because there are so few people left on the planet. Then he walked me through town and there seem to be plenty of people. He said they are all sterile though, that none of them can make their own babies. I didn't really understand because I saw several pregnant women. When I asked he just said that he had found the answer. The way he said it creeped me out so I let the subject drop."

"Where was this town? On the surface? And how many people did you see?"

"Yeah, there's a whole city up there. Not a very pretty sight though. I spent some time working in some third world countries before I... well, before, and frankly they reminded me of the villages I visited in my travels. The thing that doesn't add up here is those third world countries suffered from overpopulation in areas not exactly suitable for living. That's why those people lived the way they did. If what I've been told here is true, how could there be overpopulation?"

"I'm not entirely sure yet but the picture is getting clearer every day. I think Sebastian is using women instead of tanks to make his clones."

"I have no idea what you are talking about."

Jack wasn't so sure himself. "Look, let's start at the beginning. What's the first thing you remember since waking up?"

"You mean in that room? Well, I couldn't move, couldn't see, and everything was foreign to me. A woman was there and she talked to me. She answered questions but they didn't mean a whole lot to me. I was asking things like 'where am I', but that didn't really matter, did it."

"Not really. So did they explain how long it has been and how they brought you back?"

"Sort of, but it took a little while to sink in. They said there were wars. Great wars that lasted decades and left the world a devastated shell of what it once was. They told me about it and later they showed me. It was pretty horrific."

"Yes, it is. I guess there were nearly eight billion people on the planet when it started. Now there are maybe ten thousand." Jack still got an ill feeling when thinking about it.

"Maybe more."

"More what? More people killed?"

"No, eight billion is probably about right. I don't know for sure, I wasn't around at the very end. Last I had heard the population of the planet was around seven billion."

"What are you saying, Phil?"

Phil waved him off. "Tell me about you, Jack. I have to say, even though I'm still skeptical that any of this is genuine, it is one hell of a pleasure to see you. I buried you, old friend. I mean, I didn't bury you of course, but I bought the casket that we put in the ground. Mabel and I arranged your funeral. It was larger than…"

A chill went up Jack's spine. "Larger than the funeral for my wife and child?"

"Sorry. Ever since waking up I don't seem to think before I speak."

"It's okay. I've put my foot in my mouth on many occasions. It has to do with the hormones in our system. Going from a fertilized egg to a twenty five year old adult in eight weeks leaves behind a lot of the hormones you would have had while going through puberty. Not only are you like a horny teenager, a lot of the stuff that plagued us as young men are back. Not having very good control of emotions is one of them."

"That would explain a lot."

"Speaking of explaining, did they explain anything of how you came to be here?"

Phil nodded. "Yeah, I mean, Sebastian went on for hours about how he was able to clone my body and then use my frozen remains to transfer my memories into this body."

Jack was curious how Phil handled it so he asked. Phil shrugged and said, "It was pretty easy to accept given I always knew I would be frozen and stored away to maybe be brought back later. Mostly I didn't really expect it to work but I'm here, so…"

"I had a bit of a tougher time with that part. You never told me what the facility we were building was really for."

"Sure I did, right after your first surgery."

Jack just stared at his old friend.

"Wait. You don't remember, do you? I thought they only backed up our memory a few hours or maybe a day or two? You passed nearly a year later."

"I guess I was the first... candidate at that facility and back then they didn't really know how to preserve the bodies. Most of the people there were unrecoverable."

"You were the first, almost a year before the place was scheduled to start taking in bodies. Your tube was custom made. So then how did they bring you back?"

"I got lucky. Something to do with all the chemicals they were injecting into me trying to kill the cancer. All I know is it was something of a miracle that I'm standing here."

"Yeah, no kidding. Small world, huh."

Jack laughed. "Yeah, but I don't think it's a coincidence that we're both here. I think Sebastian brought you back for a very specific reason. Any idea what that might be?"

Suddenly Phil looked skeptical. His eyes darted around the room as if looking for something. He then focused back on Jack and after several seconds finally said, "No... Do you have any ideas?"

"Nope, but from the way Sebastian's been talking lately..." It occurred to Jack that there wouldn't be a better person to pull information from his mind than a friend he never thought he would see again. Someone he trusted implicitly in his old life. He decided it might be best to hold off on talking about anything that might help Sebastian. He mimicked Phil in waving the subject off. "So tell me more about when you woke up. Did Sebastian tell you anything else about how you came to be here?"

Phil shifted uncomfortably. "Well, he blathered on about how my metaphysical self is built from a combination of my memories and my DNA. He spoke a lot of reincarnation, but I have to be honest with you, Jack, I just don't buy it. I spent a lot of my final years getting to know God, and regardless of what Sebastian told me, I think I'm a new person, created in the image of my former body, implanted with my memories, but without the sins that are associated."

This interested Jack. He didn't get into this type of discussion with other Reborn very often, simply because it's a sensitive subject with some people. "I have to agree with you there."

Nodding, Phil said, "You know, this might sound weird, but I think the thing that convinced me has to do with my wife."

Out of habit, Jack almost asked how she is doing. "Was Barb still around when you..."

"When I died? Boy I never thought I'd say something like that. No, she passed a few years before me. After she died I could still look back at our life and remember any of a thousand things about her and feel the warmth of our love. I remember that feeling vividly. But I don't feel it now. See, I never so much as looked at another woman after she was gone because that warmth was still there. I just didn't need anything more. Now I can remember loving her and my brain is trying to tell me I still feel the same way but it isn't the same. I crave that feeling, and that's what tells me I'm no longer the same man."

Jack nodded, remembering when he found the same thing about himself. He thought back to his conversation with Sebastian and how the man would kill his own daughter if she could no longer contribute to society. *Perhaps the reason he doesn't love his children has to do with the detachment that comes from being cloned.* It was a bit of a revelation, something he filed away for later. "I know this is an awkward question, but how did you…?"

Phil smiled and said, "Die? You're right, it's an awkward question and again, not the kind of conversation I ever thought I'd ever have. I guess I passed from natural causes, or at least that's what my file said. It was 2006 and I was ninety one. I led a very full life, Jack. I grew just old enough to see some wonders I never thought I would behold – computers that fit in your hand and double as phones and cameras… buildings nearly a mile high… space stations orbiting the earth. I traveled the world and saw every continent. I had children, and grandchildren, and then great grandchildren. I grew up riding on a horse as a kid and before I died I drove a car to over two hundred and twenty miles per hour. Let me tell you, that was a rush. I can honestly look back at my life with happiness, Jack, so it isn't really a bad question to ask." His eyes were welled up. Perhaps he did feel something when looking back at those memories. "The only catch, I suppose, would be how it ended after I was gone. My kids never got to finish their life like I did. The hardest thing to think about is how they died. Did their lives end in the flash of a nuclear bomb, or did they have to survive in a world after the apocalypse, wondering if they were left behind because they were unworthy." A tear rolled down his cheek. Jack even had to swallow. You didn't need latent emotions to feel sorrow for the innocents who died in war.

Phil sniffled and wiped at his eyes. "Anyway, enough of the past, let's talk about now."

"So why are you here? I mean, in this room? As far as I know, this is the analogue of a prison."

"Prison?" He looked around. "Not exactly. It's far better than how things are up top. The only thing I miss is the sky, but the room is warm and the food fills my belly. From what I've been told this is just temporary quarters while they figure out where to put me. I mean, not everyone in here wants to be here, so in some respects it's a prison. Some of these guys have been here for a few years, and I guess when they finally decide they want to be productive to Bastion, they get a place to live. The two tough looking fellas came from a place called Deering. They've been here the longest I guess. Bob, the fella who doesn't have a name, was just found living in the mountains a few hundred miles from here. I guess his parents used to live here and they took off to live on their own. They've been out there since he was a baby and he's been alone for over five years. He was picked up on a patrol and brought here. He doesn't say much, but he seems thankful for having such an easy life now. Not sure where they will put him, he doesn't even like to shower. The chubby one is from here, but from what I gather he isn't sterile like most men, so he's led a pretty easy life. He had his own place, but I guess he did something wrong so they moved him in here. The women don't really like him but they will still sleep with him because he can make them pregnant. There were two others since I have been here. I think they were like me though, new bodies, old mind. But they didn't come from our time. They said something about being renewed… I didn't quite understand. They weren't here for long."

"Why are you still here? I would think they could put you in a dozen different jobs easily. Did you turn them down or something?"

"You know, I wondered about that. I even told them some of my job skills, although they seemed to already know much of what I did in my former life. I've been whiling away my time here for weeks. It isn't all that unpleasant. The women… Ha! Well, let's just say I've been living out some of my dreams…" He paused with a smile on his face. "But it still didn't make much sense, at least not until you introduced yourself."

It seemed his old friend also realized this situation was no coincidence. Clearly he was put here in anticipation of Jack's arrival. The question of 'why' came down to whether Sebastian's spy took Phil's head knowing his connection to Jack or whether the connection was discovered later. There was a significant difference: if he knew ahead of time, it meant Sebastian was planning to capture Jack from the moment he took command of the operation at the Freezer. If he figured it out later, it could mean his decision to capture Jack was influenced by the man he already had. Unfortunately neither scenario helped to answer the important question: what is Sebastian's end game? Is he truly after Jack's influence over the other Reborn, or is he after something more? Pieces started shuffling around in Jack's head, looking for a way to fit together.

"Look, I'm not sure what all they've told you yet, and I'm not sure what they intend by putting us together here, but there are some important things you need to know-"

Right then the doors opened and several guards entered. Immediately Anton and the other men jumped to attention, quickly taking up a line of defense around the cubicle where the two men sat. "Relax, guys. They aren't going to hurt us." Anton just glanced at Jack grimly and held his ground.

The guards came straight to the cubicle. The same guard Jack had tripped held up his hand and the men stopped. Instead of pushing past Anton, he looked at Jack and said, "Sebastian sent us to get you. Is there going to be a problem?"

"No." He stood up and pushed his protector aside, throwing a look his way that told him to stand down.

"The other one too."

Jack looked back at Phil. "I guess we've got a double date."

~~~~

They were taken to an office of sorts. It was a room, sparsely decorated but luxurious in size. An imposing desk sat in the middle of the room. A large, comfortable looking chair sat on one side of the desk, and on the other sat two very uncomfortable looking chairs. Otherwise the room was empty, devoid of character and emotion. The guards directed the two men to the chairs and then took up positions on either side of the door.

About ten minutes passed before the door opened and Sebastian entered. "My apologies for keeping you waiting, gentlemen." Jack nearly scoffed at the feigned politeness.

Taking a seat in the big chair opposite them, he continued, "I was starting to wonder when you two would finally meet. I take it you were both a bit surprised?"

"Shocked was more the word I would use," said Jack. His expression was as fictitious as Sebastian's apology for being late. Sure, he was thrilled to see his old friend, but he already knew the remains had been stolen from New Hope so it wasn't much of a surprise. There was no need to admit this, however. By now Caleb should have the situation in hand, but if for some reason the spy still eluded them, not knowing he was being sought would give them a better chance. "It wasn't an altogether unpleasant surprise though."

Sebastian chuckled. "Well, I figured you would feel more at home here if you had people you cared about around you, so I arranged this ahead of our... meeting."

Jack remained skeptical. One thing he noticed about Sebastian was his propensity to brag about his own abilities. Even if this whole situation with Phil was a mere coincidence, he would take credit for it. On the other hand, if this was just chance it was one hell of a farfetched coincidence.

When neither man said anything, Sebastian continued, "I'm sure you have a lot to catch up on, so I won't keep you long. Jack, I think there is a misunderstanding between us, and I believe it has to do with the history you were taught."

No misunderstanding, I just think you are cut from the same cloth as Hitler and Stalin, he thought. Curious where this was headed, Jack held his tongue.

"I know Teague relates the basic history of the world since the wars began in 2012 to all of his Reborn, mostly as a means to help them accept where they are and how they came to be here. I have to admit, it is a solid approach, one I would have struggled to come up with in his shoes. He shares enough of my genome to be like me in many ways, but he still has some of his mother's compassion and it gives him a different perspective on life. Perhaps that is why things ended up the way they did."

"Are you saying he isn't an exact clone of you?"

"Oh, no. He wasn't conceived through natural means, but he is still my son in every sense of the word." Not wanting to derail Sebastian's recitation on history, Jack didn't press for more. "The point I am making is that I have no doubt he has spent hours giving you his version of history. Of course, his version is influenced heavily by Marcus, and for good measure."

Jack's skepticism spilled out. "I've spent a lot of hours reading about the history of this world since the wars and what Teague told me seems pretty accurate."

"It isn't difficult to alter historical documents to change history. It has been done since the first man put a chisel to stone and carved his own version of how he wanted to be remembered. During the time of the EoS we recovered several thousand computers from before and after the wars. Our records are nearly as complete as mankind had before things fell apart. Yet if you compare every single historical document in our extensive records, you will several inconsistencies. People rewrite history to suit their own purposes all the time."

Jack could accept this in part. However, painting everything with that brush would allow Sebastian to form his own version of the truth and try to sell it. He steeled his mind and prepared to start reading between the lines. This was one of the things he did best and he was ready for it. "And what would make your version of history any more accurate?"

"Because I lived through much of it."

"That doesn't mean you will be honest about it."

"Jack, unlike the people you have placed your trust in, I have no reason to distort the facts."

"What is that supposed to mean?"

Sebastian shrugged. "Let us find out. What do you think you know of the EoS?"

Phil, who hadn't spoken since leaving the cubicle, asked, "What's the EoS?"

When Sebastian didn't answer, Jack turned to his friend and said, "It stands for the Enclaves of Science. It was the last rise of human civilization before the virus that causes infertility was used to try to end our existence on this planet."

He looked at Sebastian, waiting to see if the man would correct him. "Go on," was all he said.

"Well, not much is recorded about how they originated. The prevailing theory suggests the founders came from an isolated society of scientists, scholars, and artists. They came to power quickly with the aid of pre-war technology that allowed for a lifestyle far better than any that could be found on the planet. They had modern weapons, modern amenities, and within a few years, a city that rivaled most pre-war cities. They grew fast by offering sanctuary to anyone willing to work. The only catch was that your value was completely dependent on your contribution to society. Stop contributing and you were told to leave. Work or die."

"You make it sound so dark and evil," Sebastian interrupted. "I can understand, however, why you feel this way. You do not truly understand the alternative. Most of the planet is uninhabitable, scorched with radiation or worse. Whatever can survive the hostile environment usually sees everything as food, including humans. Life outside the cities was not living, it was surviving. The cities offered peace, but like everything in life there is a price. The cost was far less than the alternative."

"But even the founders didn't like it once they grew too old to work," Jack retorted. "They'd built an empire and didn't want to be turned out from their own cities. That's when the churches started springing up. Religion gave them a way to stick around long after their value to society was used up. The churches taught people that life was precious, a gift from God, and not something to throw away once they were too frail to contribute. Ironically this gave the founders and other members of the higher society a way to retire and keep their status and their very lives. But it led to a shift in power from the scientists to the church. Like every war, it starts with a struggle for power. There isn't much more to say about it after that. The struggle resulted in the cities falling and mankind becoming nearly extinct."

The room went silent, as if the story held some kind of reverence. Finally Sebastian said, "I have to admit, your story is flavorful but it paints both the people who built the cities and the religions that came later as the evil enemies of humanity. It gives me some insight into how you feel about my own philosophies. Perhaps this is more a problem of filling in some important holes than one of misinformation."

"I'm not sure what else I need to know. The cities rose and fell and the result was the near extinction of our species."

"For a man who prides himself on understanding history and the cause of war, you do not seem to want to know much detail about what caused the last one."

There was no point in arguing this subject, the man wanted to tell his story, so Jack conceded. "Please, enlighten us."

"Thank You. The Enclave of Science *had* been a community since before the wars. When the time was right, they emerged and began rebuilding as they were tasked to do from the start."

"Tasked by whom? And where did they come from?"

Sebastian looked at Phil and seemed to grin ever so slightly. He turned back to Jack and said, "It is not relevant at the moment. They knew what needed to be done and they did not waste any time getting started. They gathered several dozen people who lived in the area and offered them a chance to be safe, to be able to rest easy and never have to fear the day. They came forth with machines and knowledge and within months the first city was built. Within a decade, three cities had been raised and you were right, they rivaled any pre-war city in every way except population, and it was only a matter of time before we grew to rival the biggest cities in all of history."

"You say this like you were there in the beginning."

"I was. I was only a teenager at the time, but I was there contributing blood and sweat with everyone else. Here, I have a picture." He tapped the desk top in front of him and behind him a screen Jack hadn't noticed before lit up. A photo of a teenager wearing a hardhat and a tool belt came up on the screen. It could have come from one of Jack's worksites – no sign of the devastated planet, just a kid, dirty from a long day of labor standing in front of a partially built building. Even the heavy equipment behind him looked like the stuff Jack used.

"So you were a common laborer?"

The jab was meant to sting and it seemed to land. "I was hardly common, even as a kid! Everyone labored so we would have a place to research and expand our own fields of science. I built my own laboratories and then used them. As a matter of fact," he tapped the desk again and the picture changed, "here is a picture of my first lab." A man in his thirties stood proudly in front of a complicated looking machine. Next to him was a much younger man. Both smiled as if the machine was some kind of accomplishment they shared. "Do you recognize the other man in the picture?"

Jack studied it more. The hairs on the back of his neck stood up. "That's Marcus!"

"Who's Marcus?" Phil asked.

"He founded New Hope, the community I… come from."

"Oh come on, Jack, you did not even tell your old friend yet that you are the leader of your own community?"

Ignoring this comment, he said, "You didn't show me this picture so we could talk about New Hope. What did you work on with Marcus?"

Sebastian shrugged. "His field was artificial intelligence and it followed that where there is intelligence, there is personality. Where there is personality, there is memory. I wanted to understand how humans stored memory. Marcus wanted to implant human memories into his artificial intelligence. We traded my memory research for time with his computer. The computers I had used up to that point were too simple. I needed something far more powerful and something that could aid in the detection of patterns and help with the more complicated algorithms. His advanced computer was the perfect platform. We worked together for several years, and became close friends."

"So why have I never heard of you, and why didn't Teague or Marcus tell me about you?"

"Oh come on, I am sure Teague told you all about me, even if he failed to mention that I was his father and worked with Marcus."

"No…" Jack searched his memory, wondering if he missed something in his early discussions with Teague. After all, at the time his mind was somewhat preoccupied trying to process everything. Nothing came to the surface. "In fact I never heard of you before you captured me. I've never read anything about you either."

"Well," Sebastian leaned back in his chair, "That is probably because I went by my middle name, Christopher, back then."

The air left Jack's lungs. Pieces started falling into place. The way Teague had glazed over the subject, talking about the technology and not the man behind it. It made sense but there were still holes. He pushed on. "It seems like everyone has their secrets, even if a world where there shouldn't be a need for them. So what happened? Why aren't you living in New Hope with your friend and your son? And why wouldn't they tell anyone about you."

"I doubt they know I am even still alive."

"Why would they believe you were dead?"

"To understand that would be to understand more about the society we lived in. Things were complicated. The more prestige you gained, the higher your standing and wealth, but also the bigger of a target you were from competing interests. Everyone had a rival, someone who studied the same field you did and wanted to beat you to a useful discovery. Most fields were open to be studied, but you still had to produce results that were useful. If you had a breakthrough that led to something major for all of science, your field could end up as a Principle Science. Medical Science, Agriculture, Engineering, all of them were Principles, but not all started out that way. Energy storage, for example, was not considered important until a breakthrough led to power units that were compact and could last months and years instead of hours. The benefit to society put Energy sciences at the top of the list. When a field becomes a Principle, a Preeminent Scientist is named. Usually this is the person who had the breakthrough that led to the contribution. That meant any rivals had a choice of either going to work for the Preeminent Scientist or to change fields. If they refused or simply could not change fields, they had no value and hence were expelled from the city."

"Conform or die. You say it with such ease."

"What is so bad about it? Look at it this way: if you failed to make the discovery yourself and then refused to work as a subordinate, there had to be a reason for it. Pride should never have entered the equation because you were there only to serve the city, not yourself. Knowing the consequences meant that anyone with even a little sense would swallow whatever pride they had and work with the P.S. If you still refused, the most likely reason was because you were a hack, a scam artist incapable of doing the work, and if you went to work for someone who did understand the field, they would find out. If you couldn't change your field of study and be productive in it, you no longer had a place in society. Plus, it was rare another city would take you under their wing, at least before the churches came to power, so usually expulsion meant death."

"Why not just let the scientist work on their own? Most of the breakthroughs in history came from the scientists everyone thought would never succeed."

"Once a field became a Principle, it was granted unlimited resources. Anyone else working in that field would be denied all resources and could never be productive."

"Sounds like a recipe for a lot of animosity."

"It was which is why I brought it up. If the Preeminent Scientist left the city or passed away, the next in line took their place. It was not uncommon for a P.S. to inadvertently find themselves on a flyer headed away from the city, usually with a mortal wound for good measure."

"I thought you said the cities were a safe haven. The picture you're painting doesn't sound all that safe."

"To a common worker, the cities were very safe, especially in comparison to life outside the cities. Crime was practically non-existent as any crime, no matter how petty, was met with swift punishment, usually expulsion from the city. As your prestige grew, so did the risk that someone would take it from you, either by being smarter than you or simply by force."

"Is that what happened to you?"

"More or less. I was… forced to leave."

"And I suppose you are now going to tell me that Marcus was behind it?"

Sebastian laughed weakly, as if the idea were preposterous on the surface but filled with uncertainty. As if in effort to reinforce the absurdity, he said, "Marcus had his own Principle Science and was the P.S. He had little to gain from my disappearance."

"So then who forced you out?"

"Perhaps you should ask my son."

"Teague was involved?"

"Everyone has their secrets."

"Was this right at the end? Is this how you ended up here instead of in the cities when they fell?"

"No. This was a few years before the cities fell. I managed to get out of Saber Cusp alive. A relatively new city, Bethlehem, had gone up about a decade before, built on the ashes of the town from which it inherited its name. I had the foresight to build a lab there years before. I renewed myself in my new lab and as a younger man was unrecognized enough to be able to start over. I went back to my given name and continued my work until the cities fell."

Jack mulled it over. "There's something that doesn't fit. The virus was released, what, about eighteen years before you left Saber Cusp?" Sebastian nodded. "So you were born long before the virus. Yet you didn't conceive Teague naturally. Why were you sterile?"

"That's a good question, Jack. I continue to be impressed by your ability to pick up on details." This sounded so much like something Teague would say it sent a chill down his spine. "The answer lies in my research. With the aid of Marcus' computers I was able to move from theory to practice in just a few years. It was a decade before my work had a practical purpose and became a

Principle Science, but I had perfected it long before then. This was fortunate for me as I was born with a minor defect. I could have overcome it with artificial limbs and extensive surgery, but at the time my status did not command that sort of luxury. As time went on my pain became a hindrance to my work. The answer was staring me in the face, and once I realized I could simply clone myself without the defects and then inject my memories into my new body, it was simply a matter of getting a few favors from people in the right places. It took me a couple years but I managed to renew myself. Younger, stronger, and free of defects, I was able to be far more productive."

Jack looked at Phil but didn't say anything. This man firmly believed that the cloning process was truly reincarnation and that was disturbing. "But by cloning yourself you shouldn't have been sterilized by the virus. You weren't missing the genes that the virus takes from your children."

"Nobody knew about the virus at that time, but it was everywhere, including in the fluids we used to create the clones. My body was infected at birth and the part of my DNA that would have led to my virility was destroyed. I was perhaps one of the first victims of the virus, but since nobody knew about it, I chalked it up to a glitch in the cloning process. In retrospect it was a good thing."

"How could it possibly be good?"

"It led to a new line of research. I had pretty much done everything I could with memories, and while Marcus was building a very high reputation with my research, I had little to work on. So I turned my focus to a new field"

"Which was?"

"The creation of life."

"But others were already working on cloning. Wouldn't a move like that drop your status?"

"Not cloning, creation. And I did not change fields, I just took this on as a hobby. I wanted to figure out how to create life without the aid of the seed or egg. Obviously I had a motive – I was sterile and wanted to father a child. It took me another year but with the aid of Marcus' computer I was successful. I was able to impregnate Teague's mother with just my genetic material and her egg. It was just a hobby back then but after the fall of the cities it became perhaps the most important discovery in the history of mankind. The irony is I never shared it because I didn't think it had any practical value."

With all the pieces in place, Jack finally had a full understanding of the history, although it didn't seem to change anything. Almost afraid to ask, he said, "This is all very enlightening, Sebastian, but where are you leading me with this?"

"You keep talking about the virus and the near extinction of our species, yet you never ask who was involved."

Another chill went down Jack's spine. "What does it matter? The lifestyle you created allowed it to happen. What else matters?"

"Why do you suppose we have never found a cure?"

"I'm no scientist, but the way I understand it, DNA is very complicated. Millions of genes and removing just one can drastically change everything about the person. Remove the wrong one and the person is born without a heart valve or something equally devastating. The only real way to figure out how to fix it is to know which gene to splice in, and exactly what is missing. Nobody wants to experiment with this because the results are inhumane."

"To say the least. I worked with the cloning team and when they made a mistake it was horrific. Finding the right gene to fix and figuring out how to fix it the right way is like finding a needle in a stack of needles. Only the needles are poisoned and touching the wrong one will kill you. And the prevailing theory regarding the sterility assumed it was more than one gene. It is a near impossible task."

"I understand this, but what's your point?"

"If this is so complicated, how did a preacher figure out how to do it?"

"I have no idea. I assumed there were plenty of scientists who could create a biological weapon. Every church has followers, and this was in a city of scientists."

"Sure, but making a virus that kills people is easy. Making a virus that alters your seed so that your offspring is missing a very specific gene or genes is something else entirely."

"Do you know for sure this was intended? Perhaps it was just an accident."

"The Church of the Fallen Saint took credit for it before it affected the first children. Nobody believed them at first."

"Why not?"

In response, Sebastian tapped the desk again. The image on the wall changed to a picture from before the war. A homeless man stood on a street corner with a sign around his neck. The sign read, 'The End is Near.' "Have you ever seen someone like this?"

Jack nodded. Even in his small town of Great Falls some acid fried hippy would be walking around telling people the world was going to end, or that aliens were among us.

"Did you ever believe them?"

Good point. "So they took credit and when what they were saying came to pass, it proved they did it on purpose. What is that supposed to mean?"

"Even the Preeminent Scientist in cloning was incapable of altering genetics on this level. It would take someone far more intelligent than even our best scientists to figure out how to do this."

When it finally sunk in, Jack felt sick. "A super computer with Artificial Intelligence. Are you implying that Marcus was involved in creating the virus that nearly wiped out humankind?"

"Marcus was the Preeminent Scientist in Artificial Intelligence. Everything related to AI went through him. The team that came up with the quantum computer worked under him. When I discovered Marcus had his team build a second quantum computer, I started digging into where it went. Turns out he donated to a church – The Church of the Fallen Saints."

This had to be a lie, but it still hit him hard. Another piece fell into place. A part of him wanted to call him out, prove he isn't being honest, but it would mean revealing where the second computer really went. Perhaps this was part of Sebastian's goal – to see if Jack knew the location of such a powerful tool. He had to play along. "I know Marcus. If he was responsible for placing a tool in the hands of fanatics like that it was unintentional."

"Of course you would think that, Jack. You have to believe everything you were told is true or your loyalty to New Hope would come into question. Nevertheless it is true. Marcus and Teague are not the people you think they are. Everyone has secrets."

"Except you, of course. You aren't hiding anything from me or being deceptive, right?"

Sebastian shrugged. "I have not been deceptive with you. I have not held back any secrets. In fact, I made my motives clear from the beginning, as well as the consequences if you decide to turn me down."

The renewed threat was another blow. "If you're being so honest, tell me the real reason Phil is here."

Leaning back, he seemed to ponder this for a moment. Then he smiled. "Earlier you spoke of the origins of the EoS. My parents were a part of the group that emerged into this world to set things straight. That group lived underground since the war began, a part of a government program to ensure the survival of humanity beyond a nuclear war. The bunker they lived in makes this one look like a simple fallout shelter. They stayed below the surface for an entire century, pure and untouched by this horrible world. I was born only months before they emerged. I never got to see where I came from. In this room are the two foremost experts on building underground bunkers. I think you can do the math."

Jack looked at Phil. The man was unreadable. Phil was a poker player and he had the best poker face Jack had ever seen. When he became unreadable it was because he was didn't want his opponent to guess his hand. Unfortunately this meant Phil was hiding something and didn't want to share it with Sebastian. "I died before finishing the project in Montana. That was the largest project I was ever involved with, and according to the records we recovered from there, Phil retired after it was complete. If you want advice on building a new underground home, we would be the ones to ask, but if you're asking if we know where your old home is located, I think maybe you're barking up the wrong tree."

Sebastian studied Phil's face. He never even looked at Jack. Obviously he still thought Phil knew something, but his old friend wasn't giving anything up. "Thank you, Jack, but I think I would like to hear from your friend directly. What do you think, Phil, any chance you consulted on any big projects after you retired?"

Phil just looked at him with that unreadable expression and said, "Like Jack said, I retired after the Montana project. I consulted on the bunker we are sitting in right now, but never ran a crew here. I was even approached to help with some projects that were supposed to be big, most likely the place you are talking about, but my wife was tired of moving. She wanted to go back to Virginia and settle down. We moved there and I started a small contracting company and built custom homes for a few years. Business was good so I sold it off and didn't work another day in my life. Wish I could help you more, Sebastian, but I have no idea where they might have built your former home."

Sebastian stared at him for another moment, perhaps trying to read deception in his face. Finally he smiled and said, "Well, it was worth a shot." He turned back to Jack. "So there you have it. I am not here to deceive you or trick you. I cannot say the same for the people who brought you back, however. You asked why I am not with my son and former friend, and even why they seem to be unaware of my existence. The truth is I see them as the enemy, Jack. When things fell apart I stayed away from them. I want nothing more than to rebuild our species and ensure its survival. I am not sure I can do that while the person who is responsible for it falling apart is still alive. I told you yesterday that your intent is not what makes you dangerous, it is your potential. I feel the same way about Marcus. He has the potential to finish what his church started, and I am not going to risk that. On the other hand, I believe if we work together you will no longer be a potential risk to my plans. I see greatness in you and I still want you as my right hand."

The man had some good points. Jack thought back to Trystana's parting words last night: what makes him any different than Sebastian? There were obvious answers, but in the end he was still a hypocrite – criticizing the man for using technology he himself would not hesitate to use. As Sebastian's right hand man he would have the influence and the power to secure the future of humankind, and once that was done he could deal with Sebastian if it became necessary. There was just one thing holding him back: his loyalty to his people. Even if what he was being told of Marcus and Teague was true, his loyalty was not just to them. He couldn't see a scenario where everyone would walk away unharmed. If he went to them and told them he had someone to answer to, there would be resistance and a lot of people would not go softly. He could just carry on without telling anyone, quietly accepting Sebastian's actions as his own and nobody would know, at least not until later and by then it would be too late for anyone to do anything about it. But that wasn't who Jack was. He couldn't be deceptive and lie to the people who put their trust in him. In his mind there was no decision to make.

Before he could answer, Sebastian added, "I know you see me as the enemy, Jack, perhaps even as some kind of lunatic with too much power to wield. I promise you after some time together you will start to see why my values are important. I love my people, Jack. They are all my sons and daughters. But like any good parent I have to do what is best for all of them, even if it means culling out the weakness so the strong can flourish. If we build our communities strong enough we will never have to turn someone out, never have to eliminate the weak so the strong can survive."

"I do see you as the enemy, Sebastian. You are my enemy because you are a threat to the sovereignty of my people. One of the tenets of my character is to live free or die. I have killed so my country and my people could keep that kind of freedom and I won't throw that away for anything. I don't think you are a lunatic, I think you are a brilliant man who is disconnected from your own emotions and was raised without any appreciable morality. But you are unquestionably a sociopath. You care about your species but not about any individuals. We aren't ants mindlessly doing the bidding of our hive; we are independent people who only want to live our lives in peace and happiness. Humankind is better off extinct than under the rule of a man who thinks himself a God. You don't just have the potential to be a threat to me and my people – you *are* a threat. You don't know me at all, Sebastian, because if you did you would know that I would never enter into an alliance with you when the terms involve eliminating two of my closest friends."

Sebastian's face darkened, probably in anger, but he didn't jump up or yell or scream. "I can understand and appreciate your loyalty to your own morality, and even to your Reborn friends. I fail to understand your loyalty to the likes of Teague, Marcus, or the others. They are not your people and certainly not your friends. They are just the ones who brought you back to do their bidding. You are a tool to them, yet you choose to keep your allegiance even in the face of losing everything you hold dear. Is your morality that important to you?"

"My morality *is* important, but more important is keeping someone like you from being in power. I could live with deceiving my friends; I couldn't live with being a part of your maniacal plans."

"I am sorry you see things that way. It is a shame. I will still achieve my goals, and true to my word I will see every Reborn killed, a bullet to the brain so that their dangerous ideals will never taint my empire. I will keep you here, reminding you that their blood is on your hands. Perhaps we should start with your friend here, he no longer holds any value to me." He signaled to one of the guards. The man stepped over and pulled his gun, pointing it at Phil's head.

"Jesus, you *are* insane!"

"Whoa, Sebastian, no need to be hasty. Give me some time, I will talk some sense into my buddy here. He's stubborn but if anyone can convince him to do something it's me. I mean, isn't this the real reason you brought me back?"

Sebastian looked at him and shook his head. "No, Jack will never change his mind about me. His foolish pride will ruin everything he stands for, but he will die feeling like he did the right thing. Shoot him."

"WAIT! New Mexico!"

Sebastian put up a hand. "What?"

Sweat rolled down Phil's forehead. The confident poker player was replaced with a man fearing for his life. "New Mexico. That's where your former home is. I didn't retire, I spent the next decade building the home your parents and grandparents lived in. I can show you exactly where it is, but you need to stop the threats and stop this madness."

Sebastian smiled. "Okay, you will live… for now." He turned to Jack. "See, I can be reasonable. There is little doubt your friend is lying here just to save his life and buy some time to talk his way out of it, but I am willing to give him the benefit of the doubt and perhaps give him a chance to talk some sense into you. However, the next time we meet I will not hesitate. And unless you come to me accepting my offer and can convince me you are sincere, I will make sure you witness every single execution personally. You will not die in peace knowing you did all you could to keep me from power, you will be forced to live an eternity with their blood on your hands. I will keep you alive forever, a constant reminder of what you could have had but chose to foolishly throw away."

He waved his hands to the guards and they escorted Jack and Phil out of the room.

Chapter 33

"Jesus Crist, Jack, what the hell are you thinking?"

Jack looked nervously at the guards, assuming they are listening to every word uttered out loud. "You know as well as I do that anything that man decides to do will end badly. You told me yourself how poorly his people live. Do you really think any human under his rule will ever be happy? He sees them the same way a farmer sees his cattle."

"Sure, but he gave you a chance to gain his trust. Why wouldn't you take that and turn him into a Caesar?"

Chances are the guards wouldn't know what Phil was talking about. "I'm not Brutus, Phil. At some point he would demand an act of loyalty, and I would be the one who would have to pull the trigger to prove I am with him and not against him."

"But you were willing to let him shoot me in there! Just so you could prove that you won't be his puppet? At least tell him yes and then figure out a better plan! I don't know about you, but I have some things to live for here. I'm not ready to die for anyone's cause."

Jack wanted to explain how he knew Sebastian wasn't going to kill him, but this wasn't the time or place. The guards led them off the elevator and around the corner, heading back to their room. At the door, Trystana was waiting. "I've got this, men." All but two guards turned without a word, leaving the floor the way they came.

"Escort this one inside, I am going to have a private word with Jack." One guard opened the door and pushed Phil in ahead of him, closing the door behind him. Trystana looked at the other guard, the same man Jack took down the day before. She said, "What part of private don't you understand?"

The guard shrugged and walked to the end of the hall.

In a low voice Trystana said, "You're an idiot, you know that?"

"You aren't the first to tell me that. Did you spy on our meeting?"

She colored a little, answering the question. "Even after everything you now know about Marcus and my brother, why are you still so loyal to your people?"

"Is this you asking or your father?"

"Me!" she whispered.

"Last night you asked me a question. What is the difference between me and your father. I have two answers for you. First, I am using the tools I have to help humanity, but I would never have allowed them to be created if it were up to me. Your father willingly experimented on his own species to perfect his tools. How many people suffered for what he did? Not only that, he would do it again if it meant bringing back his version of the human species. Sometimes the means do not justify the ends."

"But you kill people to accomplish your goals."

"Only those who would do the same to me or put the people I care about at risk. The people your father has killed had nothing to do with threatening his way of life. You may not see a difference but I do."

She nodded. "And the second?"

"I just want to live my life. If that means being a leader and helping my people, I will do what needs to be done. But I was given just one life and when it is over, it is over. If I do my job well, the next generation will be better than me. People were never meant to live forever. If your father gets what he wants, thousands, maybe millions will end up being the example of why immortality is such a bad idea."

Again she nodded, not saying anything this time.

"So now it's my turn. Why do you care so much that I agree to stand beside your father?"

Again she colored, but she met his eyes, "I've never met anyone like you, Jack. I… I don't want to see you suffer, and I don't want to see the people you care about suffer. My father will follow through with his threats."

"They will suffer either way. The only difference is whether I am a part of it or not."

She looked conflicted and nervous, glancing down the hall in the direction of the guard.

"Listen, I enjoy our talks and would like for you to visit me again, but right now I need to go talk to my men. I expect your father will not waste much time using them against me, if not to sway my mind then to punish me. They won't go down without a fight and I…" His voice caught.

"What do you intend to do, Jack?" He didn't answer, not because he didn't trust her but because he didn't know. "What do you intend to do?" she repeated, not accepting his silence.

With steel in his voice, he finally said, "Whatever it takes."

She smiled. "I'm glad you said that." She turned and put her finger to the panel. The door opened and Phil, Anton, and the rest of his men stood there. Anton was holding the guard's sidearm. "Come on, we don't have much time."

Confused, Jack looked at Anton. "Don't ask me," he said, "it was his idea." He gestured toward Phil.

Turning back around, he saw Trystana walking toward the guard. By now he has to know something is up so he grabbed the sidearm from Anton and followed. When they reached the end of the hall, the guard pulled out his gun. Before Jack could raise his, the man flipped it over and handed it to Trystana. "Nobody would believe one guard is escorting all these people, so if someone sees us, shoot and run."

"He's with you?"

She smiled, "Actually, he's with you. You have a way of gaining people's respect, Jack. I saw how he deferred to you last night when bringing you back to your room so I approached him this morning with my plan. A lot of people are tired of how they are treated around here and want to see a change. I told him he could join us, I hope that's okay with you."

They loaded on the elevator. It would take a couple minutes to get to the top. "So you and Phil arranged this ahead of time? How?"

"What does it matter? You almost let Sebastian blow my head off!"

"He was never going to shoot you."

"What makes you so sure?"

"Because the guard was standing directly behind you. If he had pulled the trigger the bullet would have hit Sebastian after passing through you. It was a bluff. He was testing my resolve. If I changed my mind just to save you he would know I could be manipulated easily, molded into what he wants me to become."

"And if the guard had moved to the side?"

"Then I would have tackled him and done my best to kill Sebastian before the other guard could do anything."

"He's right," Trystana said, "but if he'd jumped on the guard to save you a dozen more would have rushed into the room and issued a first class beating. It was all a test to see how strong Jack's willpower is."

"Wait, did you know this would happen too?"

"No, but I was watching and I know my father. I've seen him perform similar tests with other men. I think he was surprised Jack didn't spring up before the guard had his gun out."

"Look, we can analyze this later. What's the plan?"

"The doors will open and we will casually make our way to your flyer. It's parked near the door. I will get the door open and we will get the hell out of here."

"Is it going to be that simple? What if the door doesn't open for you? What if your father knows you're doing this and an entire army is waiting for us?"

"Then we do what we need to do."

Anton asked, "Shouldn't we just grab the first flyer we get to?"

Jack shook his head. "If we take one of their flyers they'll be able to track us and maybe even take control remotely. We want to take our own flyer."

"And if he already has it reconfigured like the rest of his fleet?"

"Then it'll be a short ride."

"One more question."

"What."

"Who's going to fly it?"

"I will," Trystana said.

"Well alright then. Let's do this."

The elevator stopped. Seven men and one woman held their breath. The door slid open... and the path was clear. The guard led the way, walking at a normal pace, looking back and forth scanning the cavernous room watching for potential problems. So far they didn't see anyone, not even a mechanic. Jack's heart pounded in his chest.

Halfway to the end of the room the massive door started to open, a faint whine could be heard through the gap in the door. He looked at Trystana questioningly. The look she returned said she didn't open it. The group upped their pace, shuffling toward the door.

The whine grew louder and dust started swirling around the door. As it swung open, Jack saw a large flyer hovering just outside. "Run!" the guard shouted and took off at a sprint. Everyone followed. It was still over a hundred feet away and would take time to fire up the motors and get it in the air, not to mention getting it out of the room past that large flyer in the entrance. The door was big but only about twice the width and half again as tall as the aircraft blocking their way.

They made it to their flyer and Anton led the men to the back ramp. Jack waited for Trystana, Phil, and the guard to get in. The large flyer slowly made its way inside. There was no way to know if they had spotted Jack and his group or if they were even aware something was wrong. He stood there nervously, waiting to see what would happen.

A claxon sounded, echoing through the huge flight bay. It seemed their time was up. He looked at Trys to see if she was ready. The propellers in each wing were turning but they hadn't even started to hum. She shouted, "I need twenty more seconds!"

The large flyer shifted course, turning toward them. It was still hovering but now it looked like it was going to maneuver to block their exit. Jack knew if that pilot centered the flyer at the entrance they would never get their own aircraft past, at least not without some damage, and escaping in a damaged flyer when you are several thousand miles from safety was probably a bad idea.

The blades were humming now, signifying the aircraft was ready to lift off. Jack turned to Trystana and shouted, "GO! I'll meet you outside!" Without waiting for a response he turned and sprinted back the way they came, toward the elevator at the other end of the room.

Behind him he heard the change in pitch of the electric motors, she was taking off. The elevator was still several hundred feet away when it opened. Guards flooded out, running toward him. He raised the pistol and fired off several rounds. The guards spread out, taking cover or just diving to the floor to avoid being shot. They returned fire but it was erratic. Still, Jack had no armor, not even his under suit, so even one lucky round would make this a very short escape attempt. He dodged to his right and skidded to a stop in front of the armored transport. This vehicle was large with six big wheels and armor plating. It would do. He yanked on the door, praying it wasn't locked.

It opened with a squeal, a sign it hadn't been used in a while. He jumped in headfirst, wriggling into the driver seat. When the door closed behind him the noise stopped. It was eerie and for a moment he paused, feeling like something was wrong. Through the front windshield he saw the guards getting back to their feet and running toward him. The controls were a morass of switches and buttons. With no idea how to operate this beast, he started flipping everything. Lights came on, doors locked with a click and even music started blaring. He recognized it as something from the Doors. Nothing else seemed to happen and he just about shouted in frustration over the loud music.

A quick glance showed the men were almost on him. The gauges didn't tell him anything, but then he remembered this wasn't a regular vehicle. It was electric. He mashed the gas pedal and the vehicle surged forward. Desperately trying to steer the vehicle toward the entrance, he managed to maneuver it right across the walkway into the vehicles parked on the opposite side. With no idea how to go in reverse, he jammed his foot on the pedal again and turned the wheel, hoping it had enough power to push through the parked vehicles. Metal squealed over Jim Morrison's voice. "Break on through to the other side," he howled through unseen speakers. Loud pops echoed through the cab, counter to the beat of the music. Jack looked back to see several guards shooting in his direction. "Shit!"

Finally the vehicle broke free, rocketing ahead. He turned the wheel to straighten it out but was still drifting toward the other line of vehicles. Letting off the gas, he finally regained control. The concrete floor in here was smooth and slick and this thing had enough power that he would have to finesse it out of here if he wanted to keep from spinning out of control. Unfortunately he needed speed more than finesse.

Easing into the accelerator pedal, he finally got the vehicle pointed in the right direction. The large flyer hovered squarely in the middle of the entrance, leaving no room for the medium aircraft to get around, under, or over and make its escape. To make matters worse, now the door was beginning to make its slow journey from all the way open to closed. They only had a handful of seconds to clear the way and get out. Risking another spinout, he hammered the accelerator. The vehicle shot forward, music blaring as he rocketed straight toward hell. "Break on through. Break on through!" He reached behind for some kind of seatbelt and felt a harness just over his shoulder. He pulled on it and struggled to get it latched. This was going to hurt.

The pilot of the large flyer must have seen him barreling toward him. The aircraft gracelessly dropped a half dozen feet, slamming into the ground. The cockpit door flew open and the pilot fell to the concrete. He lay there a moment, probably injured from the fall before scrambling to the side on all fours. Jack fumbled with the latch, sparing a fraction of a second to look down. It clicked home just as he impacted the aircraft.

The momentum carried both vehicles all the way through the door and out onto the concrete pad. He never let off the accelerator. The motors whined and smoke obscured all the windows. An airbag had deployed in front of him probably saving him from more broken bones, but his half healed wounds from a week ago still screamed in agony. He let off the accelerator and struggled through the pain to unlatch the harness.

The smoke around his windows cleared off almost instantly as the medium flyer passed next to him and landed. The cockpit door opened and Phil jumped out, followed closely by the guard. They pulled on his door but it was locked. Trying to focus on the controls, he just started flipping all the switches. The windshield wipers came on and then the radio turned off, throwing the cab into silence once more. The two men banged on the window as if they might be able to break the armored glass. Finally he heard a click and the door flew open. Four hands reached in and pulled him from the vehicle, dragging him unceremoniously toward the flyer. "Easy, EASY!" he shouted as he tried to scramble to his feet. They let him go and he nearly went back down but caught his balance. The world spun but he managed to point his body toward the aircraft and with the aid of his two friends, got in. Trystana pushed hard on the stick and the aircraft shot into the sky.

Pumped full of adrenaline, the guard said, "Holy shit that was cool!"

Phil asked, "Was that the Doors I heard playing?" Jack just laughed.

Chapter 34

Caleb's door chimed and he picked up his datapad. Seeing no missed calls he almost set it back down. He wasn't sure he wanted visitors right now, and if there was any kind of emergency someone would have called first. The door chimed again. He pressed the button to open his door and threw the tablet on the table, leaning back in his chair and closing his eyes.

"Is this any way to greet a guest?"

He sprung out of his chair. "Marcus?"

"Hello, old friend. I understand things have been a little chaotic around here?"

"For the love of God, where the hell have you been?"

"You know where I've been. I was only gone for two weeks. I needed to come back to gather some more personal belongings and when I arrive I am bombarded with all the news."

"Yeah, well… we will persevere, we always do. I do have some questions for you, however."

"I figured as much. I have already been to see Teague. I think he is the only one more surprised than me to find Sebastian is still alive. I suppose now that he is alive some things that were irrelevant from our past are now fairly significant. I would like to clear the air and share some of that with you. It will aid you in the decisions you will be making in the coming days and months."

"You say that like you will not be here to aid in those decisions."

"I stepped down, Caleb. I gave Jack everything he needed to know, or at least as I knew it, and left this place in capable hands."

"Well Jack's gone and…"

"And what? Is New Hope not still in capable hands? I would say between you, Teague, and Thomas it is in better shape than it could have been."

"Except Jack did not have a chance to fully flesh out his new government and we may be holding a new election very soon. It would be wise of you to stick around, at least for a few more weeks until things settle down."

"Let us talk about it and see where it goes from there. No promises."

"Have a seat." He settled back into his chair. It was a shame it was so early, otherwise he would pour himself a stiff drink.

"What would you like to know?"

"Everything. How about we start with how this affects New Hope. Why would Sebastian have any animosity toward us?"

"Probably because Teague was the one who killed him."

"Excuse me?"

"He shot him. We thought he was dead. I guess he somehow got away and renewed himself. There is little chance he survived the wound. I paid a man to load him on a flyer and haul him out of the city and leave his body to rot."

"This is quite disturbing."

"That is because you did not know Sebastian. Teague did the world a favor. He did me a favor, one I was never able to repay."

"Can I ask why?"

Marcus hesitated. "Because he was going to pin the virus on me. He was going to release damning evidence that would place the engineering of the virus squarely on my shoulders. It was not the whole truth but it wouldn't matter. You know what would have happened had that kind of information gotten out."

"What is the whole truth?"

"The truth is I was in love with Teague's mother."

"This was before he was born?"

"Yes. Sebastian and I were the closest of friends, and when we met Mika, it was something of a friendly competition vying for her heart. Sebastian saw it as a challenge, but I was smitten."

"How did this lead to the virus?"

"She was seeking what many were at the time. It led to her involvement in a church-"

"The Church of the Fallen Saints?"

Marcus nodded. "They were a cult, plain and simple. She was seeking spiritual guidance and redemption for her soul. They exploited her relationship with me. They convinced her that the only path to heaven lay in helping them achieve a greater congregation. If they could get a Preeminent Scientist in their congregation it would draw thousands to their cause. So she talked me into helping but I had no desire to join their church. Instead I built them a quantum computer and loaded it with my latest Artificial Intelligence. At the time it seemed harmless. After all, my goal was to put one in every house. Being the first to have one would give them an edge – if not for the novelty of it the at least they could rent it out to other science divisions. Perhaps it could even help them come up with better ways to attract followers. It was a priceless gift. I had no idea they were planning anything nefarious."

Feeling mortified, Caleb looked his old friend in the eye. "So in a way you are responsible for the fall of the EoS and the near extinction of our entire species?"

"That is one hell of a leap, Caleb. You know me and know I would never intentionally do anything of the sort. I had been a Preeminent Scientist since before the churches even started popping up. I had no desire to see all I had built be destroyed by some psychopathic nut cases. Be that as it may, unwittingly, I was a contributor. I was as responsible for the virus as Einstein was for the nuclear wars that devastated the planet. I created a computer. Hell, I did not even create a computer – I simply created the operating system. Men with evil intentions used it to create the virus."

"You are right, Marcus, you are more like the father who gives his two year old a loaded gun. I am not so sure it excuses you."

"Like a gun, there were several safety measures on the computer. I had no idea they would be able to bypass them. When the Church released their statement years later claiming what they had done and taking credit for it, I was devastated. Mika..." He paused. "She took her own life."

"I am sorry, Marcus." He was. This was a very dark part of their past and to know one of his oldest friends played such an intimate role was not easy to hear at all. He couldn't even imagine the guilt he felt.

Marcus just nodded. "It was a long time ago. It never should have happened. The safety mechanisms should have prevented anything like this from happening."

"So then how were they able to create the virus?"

"It turned out Sebastian had bypassed several of the safety measures when doing his research. He had unfettered access to development on the AI platform and I trusted him implicitly. Of course he would re-enable them after he was done but the computer was smart and figured out how to get around them as a result. The memory in a supercomputer is nothing simple. The computer learns like a person and the memory can't simply be looked at to see what it contains. When I created the second computer, I uploaded the latest version of my AI, which happened to contain not only the knowledge of how to bypass security measures, but also a detailed database of genetics that Sebastian had been using in his research."

"So Sebastian holds even more blame? Then how could he threaten you?"

"My evidence was circumstantial and hard to prove. Nobody other than me understood the AI, so I couldn't just show them the code and prove my innocence. After Mika passed, I spent the next year researching the cause. When I figured it out I was angry and I confronted Sebastian. He is no idiot though, he knew if word got out he could easily avoid any blame, so he turned the tables on me. By this time we were both Preeminent Scientists and we both had a lot of power. We could all see the writing on the wall. Things were going to boil over soon and the entire system could easily collapse. Teague and I had discovered New Hope and Teague had already been working on retrofitting it with modern amenities, just in case we needed a place to hole up. I spent my time working on MOM, trying to ensure that if a cure could not be found in time, humankind would still survive. Sebastian wanted both. He demanded the supercomputer be moved to New Hope and to be given control of it. If not he would release evidence that would cause the city to riot and destroy everything I had ever created. I agreed. What I did not know was that Teague was there, in my lab when I confronted his father. He hid in the shadows listening to our conversation. Then he followed his father back to his lab and shot him. When he told me what he did, I paid one of Sebastian's subordinates to get his body out of the city. The subordinate was next in line and he would take over as the P.S. for the Renewal Sciences. It all seemed to work out. Things quieted down for three more years before the cities fell."

"And you never felt it was relevant to share this?"

"Be honest, if back in the early days when the horror of what had happened was still fresh I had shared how I had provided the very tool used to create the virus, how would you have reacted?"

Caleb thought this through. It was a long time ago and he no longer felt the same way about it as he had back then. "I cannot answer that. Perhaps I would have accepted it, given all we had been through together. After all, there was never any intent. From what you have told me here I think it was an honest mistake and I imagine it has haunted you. It also explains your desire to finish your research."

"I am glad you understand. I should have shared it with you at some point. In the end people blamed me anyway and destroyed my lab but not before I secured my legacy. Now I just need to finish it."

"At least stick around for a few days. In fact you could aid me right now in a problem that has been plaguing me. I need you to write a program…"

~~~~

Jack woke with a start. Despite a million questions rattling around in his skull, the quiet cabin of the flyer combined with the post-adrenaline drowsiness must have caused him to fall asleep. It was still daylight but the sun was low enough to signify he'd been out for at least a few hours. He blinked a few times to clear away the cobwebs. Trystana was sitting sideways in the pilot seat, chatting quietly with Phil. The aircraft was obviously on autopilot. The guard – Jack didn't even know the man's name – was staring out the window watching the clouds roll under them.

"Good afternoon," Trystana said, "have a nice nap?"

"How long was I out?"

"About four hours."

"Jesus. Why didn't you wake me up?"

"You've been through a lot today. We all figured you needed the rest."

"Is everyone okay? Nobody was shot?"

"Thanks to you, everyone is fine. How are you feeling?"

Jack stretched as best he could in the cramped cockpit. Muscles groaned in agony but otherwise nothing seemed to be injured. "I'm fine." It was time for answers. "How the hell did you arrange this? And Why? How do you know Phil? And why didn't you tell me you were planning something like this?"

Phil smiled. "Slow down, Mad Dawg. You aren't the only one here with questions."

"Please don't call me that. The man who earned that name is dead."

"Not after what I just saw. I mean, I heard stories about you over the years, Jack, but that was pretty amazing back there."

He turned back to Trystana without responding and waited for some answers.

"We didn't really have a chance to plan this out. In fact I only decided to help you after our talk last night."

"But I only recognized Phil this morning. I was with him the entire time."

"She came to see me before the lights were on."

A twinge of anxiety roiled through his stomach. "Wait, you mean after you left my bunk?" *Is this jealousy I'm feeling?* He pushed the feeling aside. Surely it was something else. He barely trusted Trystana, let alone had feelings for her. Besides, he loved Wendy. That didn't leave room for anyone else.

"Yes, Jack. I didn't leave the room after our talk. I went to see Phil. I realized there were two men in that room I didn't want to see hurt by my father. I knew he was planning to sit down with both of you once you two finally realized you were living in the same room, and after our talk I knew you would never agree to work with him."

"So you two..."

"Are lovers? Is that a problem, Jack?" She seemed to be enjoying this.

"Wait," Phil said, "you two aren't..."

Jack quickly said, "No."

"Oh, good. For a moment it looked like you were jealous or something." He turned to Trystana. "And we only had sex a few times; I wouldn't say we were lovers. I mean, not that I don't like you Trys... But uh... you realize I was with other women too, right? You didn't think we were exclusive..."

She just laughed. Jack rolled his eyes.

"Look, I was there when Phil first woke up. I talked him through his first awakening, which I know can be pretty disorienting. I was attracted and, well, you know how it is when you first wake up. You men would screw anything that moves if you had a chance."

"Hey!" Phil and Jack said simultaneously. Trystana just laughed again.

"I'm just making fun." She reached over the seat and took Phil's hand. "Phillip, I enjoy being with you, but no, I would never stop you from being with other women, even if things between us got more serious. I'm even open to joining you in bed with other women, if that turns you on."

"Jesus Christ, can we get back on topic here?" Jack was uncomfortable enough with the subject – he certainly didn't want to listen to Trystana talk about it with his oldest friend. He turned to Phil and said, "So you knew about me before our poker game?"

"No. I mean, Trys told me I needed to befriend the new guys and that we would end up in a meeting with Sebastian. That's why I invited you all to play cards. I had no idea it would be you, Jack. After the meeting, and she told me if things didn't go well that she would intercept us at the door and whoever escorted me in was to be subdued and tied up. I was never much of a fighter, but when I turned and jumped on that guard your men jumped right in to help."

"And if things had gone well in the meeting?"

"Jack," Trystana said, "I'd be lying if I told you I didn't want you to agree with my father. It would have been far safer and far more preferable to my treason. I'm still a little unsure if I made the right choice, particularly considering how he has the means to make you and your people suffer greatly for this." She looked out the window. "Now we could all end up dead. Or worse."

"My people would suffer either way – the only difference is joining him would make it easier for him to go forth with his plans."

She turned back to him. "I figured you would feel that way. It's a shame we didn't find the facility in Montana first. If you had been reborn in Bastion first, perhaps you would feel a sense of loyalty to my father and not to Marcus."

"Perhaps at first, but I would've seen through him sooner or later. My loyalty to Marcus and the people of New Hope has little to do with the fact that they brought me back. The moment I met Marcus I was skeptical and as time went on I was certain I would end up rebelling against him or leaving New Hope. By the time I had a grasp on the full weight of the situation Marcus had already won my loyalty by doing something I would never have expected."

"What's that?"

"He stepped down and offered all the control to me. Your father would never have done something like that."

"Why would he step down?"

"Because he recognized that his own history, and his immortality, did not grant him the ability to evolve as his people did. He recognized that he came from a time where the needs of the many altered his perception of the value of human life. He saw us as numbers, as a mathematical equation that needed to be solved. Sometimes in math you need to subtract to come up with the answer you're looking for. With the discovery of the Freezer, there would now be enough diversity in our DNA pool to perpetuate the species so subtraction should never enter into the equation. The next leader needed to see human beings as the most precious thing on the planet. Marcus couldn't be that leader, so he stepped down."

"I've never met Marcus but the picture you paint is far different than I was taught. Marcus was a smart and ruthless man who never let someone get in his way. He was the youngest Preeminent Scientist in the EoS and you don't get to that position without stepping on others. His involvement in the Church of the Fallen Saints is enough for me to pass judgment on the man. I'm not sure I would trust his benevolence in stepping down. Surely there is an ulterior motive involved."

"Even if your father was being honest, I would like to hear Marcus' side of the story before I pass judgment." At least this was his first inclination, but in light of all he had learned he couldn't help but doubt his own certainty.

"Well, that brings up sort of an important question. Where are we headed? I haven't turned the radios on yet, and I flew the first hundred miles close enough to ground where Bastion's radar systems would never pick us up. Right now we are over what was once Tennessee but on our current heading we will be over the Gulf of Mexico in a couple hours. I'm pretty sure nobody knows where we are, so it's time to decide our destination."

"I need to get home. I didn't exactly leave things the way I should have, and of course I want to see Wendy. I can't even imagine the hell she is going through."

"About that…"

Another knot of anxiety formed in Jack's gut. "What."

"Our sources indicated your girlfriend is missing."

"What! What do you mean? How…? And how do you know this?" His mind was going a million miles per hour.

"Well, all I know is she took off about a week ago and never returned. I don't have much detail. I do know that the people in charge decided not to go looking for her yet."

Near panic, Jack said, "Tell me everything you know."

"That's it. I mean, there was something about a friend she was with and there was some debate as to whether or not she was safe and just laying low somewhere."

Bart. Knowing Wendy, she's out looking for Jack. If she hasn't checked in for a week it could be bad news. However, Bart would lay down his life for her, and there isn't much on this planet he can't handle. It eased some of the anxiety and fear and allowed him to compartmentalize his emotions. It wouldn't hold for long, he could already feel it clawing at his heart.

"There's more."

He wasn't sure he could take more. He sighed.

"This isn't bad news, but I think it's important. Phil and I were talking while you slept. Phil?"

His old friend hadn't seemed to be paying attention to the conversation since the detour about sex. "Sorry, what?"

"Tell Jack what we were talking about earlier."

"He already said he didn't want to talk about that."

"Not the sex stuff, silly, the Ark Project."

"Ark Project?"

"Ah, yes, the Ark project. It actually came up for the first time at your wife and daughter's funeral…" He explained how the General arranged a series of secret meetings between a few key military leaders, top NSA men, and of course himself. The NSA wanted reassurance that the human species, particularly American humans, would survive even a worst case nuclear war. Together, they came up with the requirements for what would perhaps be one of the largest single projects mankind had ever endeavored to tackle. Bigger than the Hoover Dam, larger in scale than even the Golden Gate Bridge or the Empire State Building.

"They had already located several potential sites."

"What kind of sites?"

"Natural caverns and cave systems. They needed massive amounts of room underground where not only a bunker could be built, but a way to sustain life could be constructed as well. Room to grow crops, a plant to generate energy, storage for dozens of years of supplies, and room for hundreds or even thousands of people."

"So you chose New Mexico?"

"Yes. We built a facility that rivaled anything you could imagine. You would have loved tackling the logistics. I had a crew twenty times the size of the one in Montana, and it was made up of contractors from all over the world. Only a handful of people were aware of the entire project. We spent millions just constructing natural looking walls to block off entire sections and cover up the scale of the project whenever we brought a new crew in to work on one section. If you asked any of the hundreds of people who were involved, none would ever tell you it was more than a few thousand square feet of underground bunker."

"How big was it?"

"In total, over three hundred acres of space."

"Acres??" He did a quick calculation in his head. "That's over ten million square feet! That isn't a bunker, it's an underground city!"

"Exactly. It was built to sustain a minimum of five hundred people for up to three hundred years. It had a maximum capacity of over a thousand."

"And that's where the Enclaves of Science originated."

"Yes. From what Sebastian told us, they stayed in there for about a century, not bad for a practice run."

"Practice run? In case you didn't notice, the world ended so it wasn't exactly a practice run."

"That was just phase one, Jack. The real project started when we completed that facility."

Chapter 35

Matthew paced in his small apartment. He was about to fulfill one of his lifelong dreams and it was almost too much to bear. In fact, it took everything he had not to hole up down in the bowels of Sanct and spend a few weeks hiding from everyone. The door chimed.

He took a final breath to steel his shaky nerves and answered the door. "Hello, handsome." Angela probably didn't look any different than she usually did, but to him she was more beautiful than ever. The dress she wore was simple as most clothes were but to Matthew it looked special, as if he were seeing her in a different light. Perhaps it was because she dressed up specifically for him.

"Hello, beautiful. Please, come in." She stepped into his home and they embraced and kissed. It was meant to be a greeting, the start of their date, but he held on tighter than usual and she sunk into the embrace. The passion exploded and their kiss went from something pleasant but awkward to something more wantonly lustful.

She broke away, flushed and breathing heavily. "Let's... Let's save that for later."

He took a deep breath and let it out slowly, not wanting the moment to end. "Promise?"

She moved closer and leaned in for another kiss, this one softer and more formal but somehow more erotic. "Promise."

They took a seat on the couch and made small talk, but the passion sat heavy in the air, a sexual tension that was hard for either to ignore. "So how's your new job working out?"

"It's a job. It suits me. How are things on your level?"

He wanted to explode, not just from the tension but from the news of what he would be doing later. He held back. "Stressful."

"I've sensed that lately. I hope our relationship hasn't been the root of that stress. Do we need to slow down? I can give you more space if it helps."

"No! The last thing I want is space." He thought back to just before she arrived and his introverted desire to flee and hide. He decided he couldn't let the half-truth stand. "What I mean to say is I do feel like I want to run from my duties, but wherever I went I would want you to be with me."

She smiled. Angela understood him, she had grown up around him and knew he was introverted and how difficult dealing of a time he had when being forced to deal with people. To include her in his desire to close himself off from others for a while spoke volumes about how he really felt toward her. "Is this why you are feeling so passionate tonight?"

"Well," he said, "perhaps but I think that dress has a little to do with it too." He put a hand on her leg and stroked gently.

She seemed to melt. Moments later all sense of propriety was gone and they were back in that frantic embrace. It moved quickly to the bedroom.

An hour later they lay on his bed, sheets twisted up around them, their naked bodies entwined chaotically. "I have to be honest, Matthew," she said breathlessly, "if you had shown even an ounce of that kind of passion for me when we were younger you would have had me. I've never seen this side of you."

The passion stemmed from over a decade of pent up feelings toward her but would never have overflowed like this if it weren't for what he was about to do. "Angela, I can't express how I feel right now. I only wish…"

"That you had made a move earlier?"

"Well, that. And… well, I guess you nailed it."

She rolled into him, her flesh both hot from the exertion of their marathon lovemaking and cool from the sweat evaporating slowly. They embraced and again he held her tight.

"I like this. A lot. The way you're holding me like you may never see me again if you let go."

His heart ached at the comment. *If only she knew. She needs to know. I can't not tell her.* "I need to ask you something."

He felt her stiffen slightly. "Okay, as long as you aren't going to get all gooey and jump the gun and ask me to marry you."

His heart fell into his stomach. He knew he was rushing this but it was the only way. And clearly she didn't want him to ask.

When he didn't say anything, she said, "Shit. You weren't really going to ask that?" She pulled back to look at his face. He frantically tried to come up with the right words.

When he still didn't say anything she pulled back even further, allowing the sheets to fall between their bodies. It was like being unplugged and he felt lonely already. "Matthew, I really like you. Hell, I love you. I always have. I just don't want to rush this."

"Look," he said, finally finding his voice, "I love you too, and normally I wouldn't even consider rushing this. I've been very happy since we started dating. But there're things with my job…"

"That you can't talk about unless we are married," she finished for him. "I understand that, Matt, but you are going to need to hold that back a little longer. I DO want you to ask me, just not quite yet. I hope you understand."

He sighed. "I get it. I really do. If you knew what's going on though…"

"Stop. You can't tell me anything more, even to sway me into speeding things up. I moved to a different job so we could be together but it doesn't change the fact that you are leadership and I am working class. I don't want you breaking the law or breaking the vows you took when you accepted the position. I respect you too much for that. So let's just change the subject. Or we can just lie here and hold each other. Hell, we can do what we were just doing all night long. I'm yours Matthew; you just have to accept that as enough for now."

He didn't have more to say but he was happy she was still here with him. He pulled her close and held back his tears. He had waited most of his life for this and it would have to wait until after he came back. If he ever came back.

~~~~

Wendy opened her eyes. The room was dark but she could still see light filtering in. It was enough to tell that nobody else was in the room with her. She pushed herself to a sitting position and pain exploded through her body. She still had a lot of healing left to do but upon waking she had a revelation and needed to get up. A fur beside her stirred and Silver's muzzle poked out. She froze. The beast stood up and stepped toward Wendy, sniffed her bruised left side, and whined softly. She tentatively reached out and rubbed the animal behind his ear. He sat back down, content to allow her to move around but still vigilant, as if he was there only to protect her.

It took several minutes to make it to her feet and even then she was unsteady. Through the drowsiness and pain she spotted her clothing. After a few steps she started sagging and stopped. Taking to her knees she shuffled the rest of the way.

Every motion caused a spike of pain. The worst was when she tried to slip the left side of her tight fitting under suit over her left shoulder. Finally she gave up and left it tucked under her arm. At least it covered her breasts. After pulling the armored pants on, she gave up and grabbed her blanket and wrapped it over her shoulders.

Pushing through the heavy hide, the sunlight caused her to close her eyes. The smells and sounds of the bustling camp hit her just as hard as the sunlight only she couldn't close her nose and ears.

"Little Red!" She opened her eyes to see Bart walking toward her protectively. She held out a hand to stop him in his tracks.

"I'm fine. We need to talk." She shuffled toward him.

"You could have called for me."

"And have you come running to help your weak human friend in front of all your warriors? No, I needed to get up anyway. Where's Max?"

"Your friends left a couple hours ago. Max told me to tell you he would be back in a week or two with a flyer. He wanted to stay but was torn between leaving Jason to make the trek alone and figured you were safe here."

"Dammit! Those fools. I only asked them to stay until I was a little better."

"You won't be in any condition to travel for several days if not longer, Little Red. I understand your frustration though, it is unsafe out there. A lot of predators that gave us wide berth when we travelled together will not hesitate to stalk them now. They are competent soldiers but their skills in the wild leave a lot to be desired. I took the liberty of sending two trackers to ghost them on their journey, to keep them safe but not show themselves."

"It isn't that, Bart. I mean, thank you for watching out for them like that, but that isn't why I wanted them to stay. Something was bugging me earlier but the drugs had me too addled. I'm thinking more clearly now. The laser transmitter. Where is it?"

"The one my brother was using to communicate with Cali?" He pointed to a stack of equipment next to the main tent. "It's over there but it won't be of much use to you. It is dialed in to Cali's satellite and unless you have the passcodes and coordinates to reprogram it for New Hope's satellite, you aren't going to be able to use it."

"Didn't you get the passcodes and stuff from New Hope when we gave you one of these transmitters?"

"It was preprogrammed with encrypted passcodes. These are old military units, and they're designed to give mobile units access to secure communications, the kind that cannot be spied on. I have no way of even hacking my way into that system. Don't fear, Little Red, your men will make it to the Warehouse and help will arrive before you know it. In fact, I'm counting on it. I need to speak with all the leaders of the communities so we can start negotiating peace between us."

An idea popped into her hazy mind. "So you need to contact Joshua anyway, right?"

"Well he is a community leader and considering our distance from him I would think it would be prudent to at least talk. Why?"

"Let's call him. Right now. I want him to discuss terms of surrendering Jack back to us."

"Surrendering? Wendy, we are in no position to demand anything of Cali."

"Bart, you are the leader of the largest assembly of your kind in the world, fierce warriors who only lack in technology and resources. If led properly you are a threat to all the communities."

"But I have no desire to wage war against Cali."

"Do they know that?"

"Well, no. I… I suppose it wouldn't hurt to flex our muscles a little. Do you think Joshua will meet with us?"

"If not then we will go to him."

Bart shook his head. "Jack has someone special in you, Little Red. You don't give up. I think any one of our women would be proud to have your fire."

~~~~

Bart flipped the switch. "This should do it." The device came to life. His brother was given the transmitter and just a simple radio set to communicate with Cali. Bart wanted to take it a step further so he figured out how to interface it with his datapad. When he tried to explain it, several of the large brutes watching just looked at each other in confusion, not even sure if their leader was speaking in the right language. Their species had a lower capacity for intelligence, which didn't necessarily mean they were all stupid, but the average Mute was usually fairly one track minded, and usually that track involved fighting, hunting, or tracking. Advanced electronics was not one of the things passed down from father to son in this culture, and there were no formal schools.

He connected his data pad and tapped the communication program. It didn't do anything for perhaps thirty seconds, and finally it read, "Connection Established."

He opened a utility he had programmed himself several months ago, one designed to look at all the hidden layers beneath the communication protocols in any connection. Working rapidly, he 'hm'd and ha'd' as he figured things out. Finally he announced, "I think I cracked their network. Wow, the things I could do in their system."

"Can you call Joshua's personal data pad?"

"Yup, I have the directory up now. Let's see if he answers." He tapped the sequence needed to make a call.

A moment later, an image came on the screen. If Wendy didn't know better, he would have thought she was looking at Marcus. It took a moment of studying the face to see that while the man bore a resemblance, it was certainly not Marcus on the screen. "Who the hell... Farnak? How...?" He seemed to pale a little.

"No, my name is Bartholomew. Farnak was my brother. I apologize for hacking into your system but I felt it necessary to have some words. Is this a good time?"

The politeness was almost comical and Wendy stifled a laugh. Of course she was still a bit loopy from the medication and the adrenaline rush from what they were about to do added to the tension and excitement that was hard to contain.

He recovered his composure quickly. "Well, it seems I do not have much of a choice here. What can I do for you, Bartholomew?"

"You have something I want. A few things, actually. I would like to discuss them, preferably in person."

Joshua didn't even blink. "I think this is as close to 'in person' as you and I will get. What exactly would you like to discuss?"

"I recently defeated my brother and took over this clan. Before I dispatched my brother he did quite a lovely job growing our numbers. It seems he had a chip on his shoulder and wanted to exact some justice on a man he believed reneged on a deal."

"Interesting. Your brother was smarter than the average Mute, but I have to be honest, I get the impression you are quite a bit more intelligent. In fact, I would have expected your brother to just make threats and gestures. So with that in mind, I do not think it will be difficult for you to understand that my deal with him was not fulfilled because he did not meet his end of the agreement."

"Frankly, Joshua, I don't really care about your deal. The point I was making was how my brother was rather focused on razing your little community and making sure that nothing larger than a pebble was left of you, your people, or your city. Now I am in charge of a clan a half dozen times larger than your population and my relationship with other communities gives me access to the weaponry that would make it easy to accomplish his goals. As you said, I am no idiot and I am actually quite well versed in military strategy. If I have an inclination, I can assure you I would wipe Cali off the face of this planet."

"So you went through all this trouble to warn me that you will be coming to destroy me and my community? Perhaps my earlier impression of your intellect was wrong."

"Not to split hairs, Joshua, but if I wanted to destroy you, I would just do it. Frankly you aren't significant enough to warrant the effort. I just want to make sure you understand exactly who and what you are dealing with. Like I said, you have some things I want. I would also like to discuss our future. I know a little about you, Joshua, mostly from what your brother told me, and I am fairly certain that until you see the threat for yourself you will not be willing to accept it. So I invite you to peacefully come and speak with me. I would guarantee your safety and the safety of anyone you bring with you. You are allowed to bring all the firepower you would like to ensure your safety, but unlike my brother I am a man of my word."

"And what would we be discussing?"

"Peace between the Mutes and the Humans for starters. I already have a good relationship with New Hope, and I know there is animosity between the two of you. I believe if we can strike up a treaty of peace, other communities will view this as a sign that I am not looking to fight."

Joshua practically scoffed, "A clan of Mutes not looking for a fight? That is something I would be hard pressed to believe. But I understand the merits of your proposal, even if I am skeptical you have the ability to enforce it. How about I send an emissary to speak with you on my behalf?"

"Joshua, I figured you for a man who understood the people he deals with. Surely you realize that sending an emissary is insulting."

The man showed just a hint of nervousness. "I apologize if it is insulting but surely you can understand that there is no basis for trust between us."

"Nevertheless, you have insulted me. Perhaps there is something you can do to make up for it."

"Well, I can surely try. What do you ask of me?"

"I have a friend here who has some requests. Perhaps if you can satisfy her needs I can forgive this insult."

"I would be pleased to at least hear what she has to say."

Bart handed the data pad to Wendy. Joshua's reaction showed he clearly did not expect to see a regular woman. "Hello Joshua," she said. It took everything she had to hold back what she really wanted to say.

"Hello there. Who do I have the pleasure of speaking with?"

"I'm Wendy, I'm a pilot from New Hope."

"Hello, Wendy, I did not realize they had someone so attractive living in New Hope."

Is this guy hitting on me? She shuddered. "Let's skip the pleasantries."

"Of course. What can I do for you?"

"Well you can start by returning Jack."

The confusion was clear. "Excuse me?"

"Jack, the man you captured a week ago in the mountains of Colorado? Please don't play dumb with me, Joshua. I spoke with the people of Camp Wisner and I know it was you who orchestrated this attack. I'm giving you a chance to make this right."

For the first time in the conversation he seemed rattled. "I... I am sorry, I do not know what you are talking about. I do not even know who Jack is, let alone who captured him. You say Andrew told you I was involved? I thought you were from New Hope?"

"Andrew didn't because you captured him too. Like I said, don't play dumb here. You know who Jack is and you set up an ambush with Andrew to capture him in retaliation for what happened in Saber Cusp. The way I see it you set a trap, expecting New Hope to retaliate in some way, maybe in hopes of recouping some of your losses. Only I was the only one dumb enough to fall into it."

Again he looked to be at a loss for words. His mouth opened then closed. "Wait... you said you are a pilot. Are you the one who flew into our airspace? Ah, that actually makes sense, I was told you were killed by Mutes, but here you seem to be friends with them."

"Dammit! Stop pretending! It's simple, I just want my... I just want you to return Jack, unharmed. And my flyer, for that matter. You don't want to challenge me on this, Joshua, I have an army of Mutes behind me who want nothing more than to lay waste to your community."

"Well, I am not sure what I can do to appease you here, ma'am. I do have your flyer and I suppose I would be willing to give that back. You have to understand, you flew into my airspace unannounced and then refused to land for an inspection. It is standard practice to intercept all incoming trading vessels and ask them to land before letting them near Cali. Surely you can understand that. I am surprised you nearly crashed your vessel to avoid this inspection. It is a mystery we thought we would never solve. As for this man you claim I took, I can assure you I have done nothing of the sort. In fact I am of the mind to contact Andrew myself and have some not so pleasant words. Last I checked he was in no position to threaten me, even indirectly."

Why was he being so stubborn? "Listen, everyone knows you are the only community with orange markings on your armor. Your people visited Camp Wisner and threatened them into helping you capture Jack. Drop the feigned ignorance or you will suffer for it. This is your last chance."

"Perhaps I could help you if I just knew who this man is?"

"Jack Taggart, elected leader of New Hope! Now stop playing games!"

The look on his face could best be described as shock mixed with fascination. "Elected leader? You mean my br… Marcus is no longer the leader of New Hope? Was he deposed? How did this happen?"

This wasn't going well and her frustration was at an end. "Little Red, can I have a word with you?" She punched the mute button and turned to him.

"I think he is telling the truth. Let's allow him to send an emissary to prove my clan is a threat and if he still keeps up the ruse knowing the consequences, we can be sure."

With doubt in her mind that she refused to let override the conviction in her heart, she said, "He has to be lying. There's no other explanation."

"Well, let's get your flyer back and you can return to New Hope and see if anything new has come up. Perhaps they have an explanation that makes more sense. I'm not going anywhere and if in the end you want me to force the issue, I will. But in the meantime, let us get what we can from this."

She didn't want to agree but she was rapidly running out of energy. "Fine." She punched the mute button with her finger and handed the data pad to Bart.

He faced it toward him and said, "Listen, here is how this is going to go: You are going to send an emissary to meet with me and he will bring my friend's flyer with him. Consider it a gesture of good will. I will discuss my terms with him and to prove I am to be taken seriously I will allow him to inspect the size of my camp. When he returns to you with proof we will have this discussion again and I will expect a lot more transparency in our discussions."

"I will have your flyer in the air within the hour. I can assure you, Bartholomew; I take your threats seriously and do not wish to engage in any kind of warfare with you. However, I do want to point out that my defenses are strong and my offensive capabilities even stronger. You may very well have the numbers you claim, but you will not find me an easy enemy if it comes to that. That being said, I do not know what your friend is talking about and that will not change. Our armor was standard issue law enforcement armor for all EoS cities and it is entirely possible that other communities possess some. I sincerely hope she finds out who committed this crime against her community but she is pointing her finger in the wrong direction."

Bart signed off without another word and sent the coordinates of a clearing a mile to the south.

Chapter 36

"What was phase two?"

"Phase two is my life's work. You think the first was a city? This place makes the first phase look like the bunker we built in Montana. It has room for over ten thousand people with the capability of sustaining them indefinitely. Not just for a century or two, but forever if need be."

"How is that possible?"

"A massive void was discovered deep beneath a mountain. Not inside it, but beneath it, as in below sea level, ten thousand feet below the highest peak of the mountain. We bored into this void at the edge where it was only several thousand feet of solid granite. Inside we found everything we needed. There's a massive aquifer running directly under it through what must be old lava tubes. With over a thousand acres of open space inside it was perfect for agriculture. The network of caves around the cavern allowed us to build housing very similar to what we built in our bunkers but we really had little digging to do. The biggest challenge was utilizing all the space we had and making sure it would hold indefinitely. Mostly we could do that because we used what was already there. Much of the stone we removed to make room for housing was used to construct that housing. It was a whole new approach to building underground and I spent most of the rest of my life working on it. They were picking the first generation of candidates to live there when I passed."

"I imagine it was quite an accomplishment. But there is still one big question: Where is it?"

Phil hesitated. Not for a moment, but for much longer. He glanced at Trystana. Jack knew what he was thinking. The guard spoke for the first time since Jack woke up. "They don't trust us."

Trystana locked eyes with Phil. He said, "I don't know who to trust. This information sure seems to be valuable these days, but right now there's only one person on this planet who I have any reason to truly trust, and that's Jack. I hate to be that guy who sees conspiracy in everything, but frankly I was the one involved in the conspiracy for most of my life. We spent billions of the government's money on projects that even the President of the United States was unaware of. Some of our hoax's to misdirect anyone who started asking questions were so elaborate it would make the idea of this escape being a ploy to get information out of us look like child's play. In fact, this whole situation could be viewed in a very simple light: What better way to find out what Sebastian wanted to know than by having his own very attractive daughter seduce the man then pretend to rebel against her own father by route of a daring escape? You have to admit, it seems a bit fishy."

"I'll concede that it looks bad. But how do I prove I'm being genuine."

"Frankly, Phil, if this is a setup, they're already tracking us and probably listening in. We're screwed either way."

He shrugged. "Still, I'm not sure I want to divulge the location quite yet. If you are truly on our side, Trys, I hope you understand."

"I can't say it doesn't hurt, but if the roles were reversed, I would probably draw the same conclusions. The question remains, where are we headed?"

Jack mulled this over. As much as he needed to get home, perhaps it wasn't the right time. If he went home, his first order of business would be to start looking for Wendy, assuming nobody is already looking. The second order would be to get to the bottom of the secrets Teague and Marcus have been carrying. However, with the discovery of treason within the old council, things in New Hope were already tenuous enough between the Native born and Reborn populations. If he started asking questions about Teague and Marcus, his two closest friends and members of the original council, it could break whatever trust is left within the community. And there is still the matter of the spy. Perhaps Trystana will point him out, or maybe she will point her finger at someone who is innocent and cause even greater harm. Perhaps it would be better to stay away until he could sort some things out.

But where will he go? He could try Bart's place, but surely if Wendy were there she would have checked in by now. Plus if Sebastian is tracking them, he'd be leading him straight to one of their biggest assets and quite possibly his best chance at a safe place to go if things go sideways back home.

During his capture he got the impression that Andrew was misled into helping Sebastian with the ambush. However, he couldn't be completely sure and while he had enough fighting men to ensure he wasn't led into another trap, they lacked the weapons and armor to do much of anything. At best, even if Andrew welcomed him, there could be a spy in his community. In fact, Sebastian could have spies in all the communities and perhaps even have a presence at some, so anywhere he went would only be safe for a day at best. The only other places he knew of that could provide any kind of safety were the Freezer and the Warehouse. The Freezer was set up with strong defenses but Jack didn't have the codes or even the remote to disable it right now. That really left only one option.

Something Wendy told him a couple weeks ago popped into his head. He rattled off some rough coordinates. "I'll guide you to our destination from there."

She punched in the directions and said, "It'll be dark by then."

"Yes, but it's safe."

~~~~

Matthew said his goodbyes to Angela. Under any other circumstance he would have insisted she spend the night. Unfortunately he had plans.

To say his mind reeled with emotions would be an understatement. Right now his body was moving on autopilot. Ahead was a task that could determine the future of his entire world and all the people living in Sanct. He should have focused on that but instead he made a move that could jeopardize it all. He wasn't thinking about what he had to do in a few hours, he was thinking about a girl. Instead of steeling his mind for what lay ahead, he was contemplating her words.

This added to the tumultuous thoughts roiling through his skull and it only served to frustrate him further. "Dammit!" he shouted to nobody. He picked up the phone and rang his father.

"Matthew, I expected this call sooner. It's late, you should be in bed."

"Sorry, dad, I…" his voice broke. He wasn't sure what he even wanted to say. *I'm not the right man for this job. I'm not in the right place right now. Send someone else.* Even in his own head it sounded pathetic. He was the only man for the job. It was his responsibility because he brought it to the table. He wasn't in the right place because he let his relationship get in front of his responsibility. Sure, they could send someone else but to what end? Whoever went would have decisions to make that would affect the lives of everyone in Sanct. That is not a responsibility that could be given to a subordinate. And no other department head was as qualified.

He had made the arguments himself. This was the smartest decision, and the entire council agreed. There was no backing out now.

"You…?"

"Sorry, I just, I'm having second thoughts. But I know I don't have that luxury."

"Like I said, son, I expected this call. I'd like to think I know you fairly well and I suspect you don't feel prepared. How do you prepare for something like this? And I would bet a week of food allotment that you are scared out of your mind. Who wouldn't be?"

Matthew smiled. Sometimes his father seemed cold but he always seemed to know the right things to say. "It isn't just that. I made a mistake."

"You don't make mistakes, Matthew. That's why you are the youngest head of your department in history. If your numbers show that we have no other choice, then we have no choice. You have to get to the root of this problem and your proposed solution is the best chance of that."

"No, I mean, I didn't make a mistake with that, I made a mistake with…" He didn't know how to put this. "With Angela."

Silence. Then, "Nobody would blame you for telling her you what you were about to do. She's a smart woman, Matthew, she won't say anything and even if she does we should be able to manage it. I would rather nobody hears until after you get back but…"

"I didn't tell her."

"Oh. Well then trust me, the way she looks at you there isn't much you could do that would be a mistake." He chuckled, "It'll be years before she sees anything you do as bad. Whatever you did or said you need to just put it behind you for now. When you get back you can make it up to her."

"I was going to ask her to marry me. She caught on and stopped me. Now I can't think about anything else. I sent her home. I had to because how else would I explain having to get up so early? But I can't sleep not being able to tell her I'm leaving. My mind is a mess and I need to focus on what's ahead. I don't know what to do!"

"Relax. Did she tell you she didn't want to get married or something?"

"No, she said it just was too soon, that I needed to take my time."

"Well then there's nothing to worry about. She just wants you to wait until the time is right. All women do. She needs you to chase her for a bit, show her that even if you can't have everything you want from her right now you will still pursue her tomorrow."

"But I might not be back tomorrow. Or ever."

"See, now we're back to being nervous about it. Perfectly normal. You'll be back, son. It's a simple trip to the surface to collect some samples. The quarantine afterward is just a precaution. In a week you will be back in Angela's arms and she'll see you as a hero."

"But she won't know what I did, or where I was. At least not until after we're married. That's the law."

"Yeah, well, I'm sort of the authority there, and I see her as family, even if you aren't married. I'll invite her over tomorrow evening, swear her in under spousal rules and then let her in on your little secret. By the time we are done you should be back anyway and her mind will be at ease."

A burden lifted from his shoulders and the churning in his head eased. "Thanks, dad. Look, if anything bad happens…"

"It won't."

"But if it does, tell mom I love her. And tell Angela…"

"I will son. Good luck tomorrow. Now get some sleep."

~~~~

Marcus finished the last line of code. "This will use facial recognition and play us every clip of video from the cold room entrance that doesn't include the guards, Teague, or his assistant."

Caleb nodded. "How long will it take to run?"

"A few hours. Maybe longer. There are several months of video footage for it to go through."

"How about outgoing communications? Any luck there?"

"No anomalies. All the traffic that went through our system was legitimate and I even scanned the recordings for voice patterns looking for anything talking about stolen goods. I used hundreds of key phrases and none of the hits I got were your man. If he is communicating with Sebastian, he isn't using our network."

"That would mean he has to get out of New Hope to send messages."

"Or he is working with someone else, maybe several people, to get messages and items smuggled out of the facility. For all we know, he could just be using people unwittingly. The problem is we have over two dozen regular patrol, several traders, and even the long list of people who helped with the Warehouse. If there is more than one person involved it could be impossible to figure it out."

"But someone had to take the head out of the cold room, so if we can find that on the video, we will have at least one man. From there we should be able to get what we need."

"And what then?"

It was a good question. *Would leaving him alone and watching him be more beneficial than capturing him and putting an end to the spying? What if there are others? On the other hand, what if he is able to cause destruction that they could have stopped by simply apprehending him?* "We need to identify the guy first. We can figure out what to do with him later."

"Okay, this is your show, Caleb. I am just here to help. So are you planning to contact Sebastian?"

"How? And even if we had a way, what would we say?"

"Good points, but I think it would be wise to come up with a means. If he captured Jack and did not kill him, he has plans for New Hope. I think Jack will be back sooner than you think. The question will be whether he will be looking out for our interests or for Sebastian's. Either way, it might be prudent to open up communications with them now. Surely by now he is assuming we know he is behind this. If we keep quiet it will make us look weak and unsure of ourselves."

"I do not even know where to start; this was Theodore's area of expertise."

"Then perhaps you should ask him."

"You know, Theodore has been very cooperative in this situation. We even gained some insight into his motives and I have to be honest, Marcus, he had some very strong points. I am not sure I would have done much different if I had been in his shoes."

"Would you have conspired with my brother to set me up and kill me?"

"Point taken. Although you know how our time on this earth can affect our way of thinking. Theodore latched on to the idea that he needed to save us all, and the biggest obstacle in the path he saw was you. By the time things came to a head he could not see any of the myriad of alternatives ahead of him. When the same problem consumed me, you recognized it and helped me understand and avoid that pattern of thought."

"You did not follow through with your ideas."

"Only because you intervened. We all saw Theodore's lust for your position. Why did we not recognize it for what it was?"

"Are you saying I should just forgive and forget?"

"I am just saying that you and I have insight into his behavior that nobody else has. His actions deserve punishment, but I believe he still has value to this community. Whether you forgive him or not is between you and him."

Chapter 37

It took some scrambling but Bart managed to gather several hundred of his warriors and march them to the clearing. It only represented about a third of his warriors and not even a fifth of his entire clan. If it came down to an all-out war, the women and older children would join the fight and bring the fighting force up to nearly fifteen hundred. Even knowing Bart would never allow this army to march on a human settlement, the sheer size alone made Wendy sick to her stomach.

Despite her protests, Bart arranged for a stretcher to be assembled to carry Wendy to the clearing. She still needed several hours of rest before she would be capable of making a walk like that, so her protests were more a matter of pride than anything else.

A runner charged into the clearing and shouted "Flyers approaching!"

Bart sat in a chair, flanked by two fierce looking warriors. Silver sat obediently by his side, unconcerned with the chaos around him. Bart waved a hand in the air and the warriors milling around all faded into the surrounding woods. The clearing went eerily silent.

Wendy shifted nervously. She was fully dressed this time, and every inch of her body ached. She just wanted to climb into the pilot's seat and get in the air. The apartment back at New Hope that sounded like a prison a week ago was calling her like a siren trying to attract a lonely fisherman.

Four aircraft came into sight – two medium flyers and two of the smaller four seater craft. As the medium flyers positioned to land in the clearing she could feel the tension in the warriors standing next to her. All their lives they would have attacked or scattered in a situation like this. For them to remain still was a testament of their loyalty to Bart.

One of the two flyers was in rough shape. This was clearly the aircraft Wendy had crashed into the trees. It would take her days to get it repaired. At least it was operational.

The two smaller flyers stayed in the air. If a fight broke out they could provide air support. She didn't blame them. In fact she would be surprised if there weren't another half dozen aircraft waiting nearby, just in case.

Both flyers shut down and the cockpit doors opened. The lone pilot of Wendy's aircraft climbed down and walked to the other. He was dressed in armor with the familiar orange markings. The ramp on the second flyer opened and a dozen soldiers filed out, taking up a position between the aircraft and the few Mute warriors standing beside Bart. The pilot of Wendy's craft approached, trailed by another man. This one was unarmed.

The two men stopped a dozen feet in front of them. To her surprise, the pilot stepped forward first, walking right up to Wendy. "I just wanted to say that I'm happy you're alive. When I followed you into the woods and saw these… uh… friends of yours, I thought for sure you had run into a grisly death. I felt responsible and it has been a heavy burden." A tear rolled down his cheek. "When I got word that you were alive and we were returning your craft, I insisted that I be the one to bring it back."

This was perhaps the oddest thing Wendy had ever witnessed. She was at a loss for words. Bart came to her rescue. "What's your name, soldier?"

The man paled at the deep rumbling of his voice but stood his ground. "Carlos, uh, sir, but I'm no soldier, just a pilot who realized he doesn't have a taste for violence."

Bart chuckled. "Tell me, Carlos, were you involved in the ambush in Colorado a couple weeks ago?"

The man looked confused. "Ambush?"

"In the mountains. Where several men were captured while having a peaceful meeting."

"Sir, I've been flying patrols for two decades and I know every pilot we have. If there was an ambush recently it didn't involve Cali."

"Did Joshua tell you to say that?"

"Joshua doesn't talk to people like me."

"Thank you Carlos."

The man nodded, then nodded toward Wendy and turned to head back to the aircraft.

The emissary stepped forward. "I assume you are Bartholomew?"

Bart stood, his nearly eight foot tall frame casting a shadow over the emissary. Silver stood up next to him, as if that could make his master even more intimidating. The man looked like he was about to lose control of his bodily functions and he actually took a step back. "I am. And you?"

"I... I'm Henry. Joshua sends his, uh... warmest regards. He hopes we can start our relationship peacefully. As a show of respect he has returned your friend's aircraft. We haven't had the chance to start any repairs, but she'll fly."

"Thank you, Henry. I'm sure my friend here appreciates you returning the craft you stole."

"Well, she was flying in..." Bart raised his hand again and over three hundred Mute Warriors appeared from the woods. They moved into formation, neatly lined up and standing at attention. Wendy imagined it was perhaps one of the most terrifying sights a man of this era could witness; it certainly sent a chill down her spine. Mute clans were never organized, so to present not only a large contingent of soldiers to the emissary but also a well-trained one would send a clear message: We are a force to be reckoned with.

It was a farce of course. This army was neither organized nor well trained. In fact it had taken every bit of effort Bart could manage just to get them to line up this way. Hopefully the meeting wouldn't last too long or the warriors would begin to get restless and the illusion would quickly dissolve into chaos.

"You were saying?" Bart rumbled.

"Uh… nothing. Is there, um, any message you would like to send back to Joshua?" Sweat poured off the man's face and Wendy was impressed that he had not turned to run.

"I think the message is clear, don't you Henry?"

He nodded frantically, sweat flying off his forehead. "Crystal clear."

"And, of course, you will deny that Cali had anything to do with Jack's abduction?"

"Of course. I mean, only because it's true." He seemed to regain a small amount of his composure. "Joshua made a few calls before we left. We were able to confirm that several communities have had visitors in recent years. Whoever these men are, they aren't from Cali. From what we could gather, they seem to be trying to influence the relationships between the communities." He turned to Wendy. "Ma'am, Joshua gave me a message specifically for you. He said 'Our skirmishes and animosity toward each other are both unwarranted and counter to our common goal. It is high time we put our pasts behind us and look toward the future, hopefully a future filled with peace and cooperation.' He said he would be ready to meet with whoever is in charge at New Hope and he would be willing to make amends for past behavior."

Wendy nodded but didn't reply.

"Unless you have anything further, Bartholomew…?"

"You may leave now. Just be sure Joshua gets my message. I look forward to speaking with him again."

The man nodded and hastily made his way back to the flyer. His soldiers shuffled back into the hold and in minutes they were gone. When they were finally out of sight, Bart waved his hand again and the warriors broke formation and headed back toward camp.

"Well, Little Red. It seems you have your flyer back. What's your next move?"

"I guess I'll see if I can track down Max and Jason, pick them up, and head home. I wish you were coming with me though."

"Me too, but my place is here with my clan."

This made her sad. "I have no words to thank you enough, Bart. You're one of the few people who have made this world bearable. You've saved my life countless times in the few months we've been friends. I enjoy your companionship more than I can express and I will miss it."

Bart took a knee in front of her, bringing them eye to eye. "Little Red, it has been my pleasure to be considered your friend. You are welcome to visit any time you desire. I promise you, one day we will travel together again, exploring new places and having adventures like this one. Perhaps we will even have our own children in tow."

A tear rolled down her cheek. "I would love that, although this adventure has been a little more than I ever wanted. And it isn't over yet."

"You will find your man – I will do everything in my power to help if I can. There is little doubt Cali is not involved, but I will make certain of it before I start talking about peace between Mute and Human."

"Thank you Bart. Would you like me to stop by your place and gather your belongings?"

"I was hoping you would do that. I'd go myself but if I left right now my clan would start falling apart. Farnak pieced this clan together with his lust for glory in battle, but I will not follow in those footsteps. I need to give them reason to remain together and that's going to take some effort. Nobody will challenge my authority but that doesn't mean the clan won't break up into smaller groups."

"I couldn't think of a better man to do this. I'll be back in a few days, maybe a week with your stuff. I need a couple days to recover properly."

"Take all the time you need Little Red, there is no rush. Be safe."

He held out the arms he had used to protect her so many times and she fell into his embrace.

Bart stuck around until she'd inspected the aircraft from top to bottom. Everything was in order and she didn't find any sign of tampering. After she recovered she would go over it more thoroughly to make sure Joshua hadn't sabotaged it in some way.

Once settled into the pilot seat, she powered up the motors. Through the windshield she watched her closest friend wave goodbye then turn to head into the forest, Silver following solemnly. In moments he was gone as if he had never been there. She lifted off and set a heading toward New Hope. With the craft pointed in the right direction she set the autopilot, put her face in her hands, and cried.

~~~~

The computer beeped. Anxious to finally learn who was behind the disappearance of the Unborn asset, Caleb looked at Marcus and nodded. The screen flashed three lonely words: "No results found."

Frustrated, Caleb said, "What the hell does that mean?"

Marcus shrugged. "It means nobody has entered or left that cold room other than the men who guard it, Teague, or his assistant."

"So we didn't capture video of the spy?"

"The first thing I did was make sure the video logs were complete. This scan made sure every person who entered the cold rooms was identifiable. If they disguised themselves I would have had a result. Only one of two possibilities exists: Either the head was never in the room or the thief who took it is one of the guards."

This was bad. "Okay, how about we look at each one again."

Marcus punched some keys and a picture came up on the screen. "Gregory, head of security for the cold room."

"The man is loyal and not all that bright. Plus he is Reborn. How could Sebastian possibly turn one of our own Reborn on us?"

Marcus punched the keys again. "Heather."

"Another Reborn. She was the female soldier with Jack when he went after Wendy."

"The one who almost died from blunt force trauma?"

"Yeah. She was thrown against a tree and suffered over a hundred broken bones. It took days to set all the bones and she was incapacitated for over a week." A week was a long time when you could accelerate healing. "When she recovered she had no desire to go back out, so she was assigned to Gregory's crew."

More key tapping, another picture. "Mitchel. I remember this one. I was interested in his past so I had Teague bring him back. He has never left New Hope. He was a chaplain in the Army and spent his later years as a minister at a small church in Dutton, Montana. Nice guy but very meek and certainly not cut out for this world. He runs a small prayer group with some of the Reborn."

"So who the hell could it be? That covers all the guards and anyone who would have access."

Marcus punched another button. "No, there's one more. Johnson. Native born. Fills in when someone is sick. I recognize him, is he the one we found with that family east of here?"

"Yes," Caleb said, "I only remember because his father was virile. The family was made up mostly of girls. Some of them were pregnant with their father's child."

"That guy? We traded him to Cali, right?"

Caleb thought it over for a moment. "Yes, for Franco Senior, Chin's grandfather."

"I remember. So this guy was his son. Not virile, right? Ended up sort of being a handyman?"

"Yes, he jumps around from job to job, seldom sticks with one for long. Lately he has been filling in for Chin in the flight bay."

"So he has access to flyers."

"And he has done some scavenging in the past."

"I would say we probably have your man. Now what?"

"Where is he now?"

"Give me ten minutes. If he is in any public area I will find him." He rattled his fingers across the keyboard.

~~~~

"New Hope, this is Wendy, do you copy?"

"Wendy? Uh... a lot of people are looking for you. Where are you? What happened?"

"Who's this?"

"Johnson, ma'am."

"Where's Chin?"

"He called an early day. Aside from one flyer out looking for you, not much else is going on here and he hasn't had much of a break for quite some time."

"Why isn't anyone out looking for Jack? Is he back home?" Adrenaline surged through her tired body.

"No, ma'am."

She deflated. "Well what the hell is going on then? What's the latest news?"

"I'm sorry, I'm not at liberty to say. You would need clearance for that kind of information."

"Excuse me?"

"I'm not allowed to discuss things with anyone who calls in unless I have express permission. New rule."

"Are you being serious? I'm…" *What are you?* she asked herself. She wasn't the First Lady, if that was even the title you would give the elected leader's wife. She was just a girlfriend, and that's if they still recognized Jack as their leader. "Just get Chin or Chuck on the line."

"Sorry, ma'am, Chuck is out looking for you and Chin is not available."

"Then patch me through to Chuck!" There was a pause. "Dammit, just do it!"

"Okay, hold on."

A minute later Chuck came over the radio. "Wendy?"

"Hello, Chuck."

"Where in the hell are you!? I've been looking for you since last night."

"Last night? I haven't called in for nearly a week and you've only been looking since last night? And why they hell is nobody out looking for Jack? For that matter, what in the hell has been going on while I was gone?"

"Jack was taken by the Yanks. I mean the Bastards. I just learned yesterday that you were missing."

Oh shit. "Bastards? So Cali didn't take him? Where did you get your information?"

"We can catch you up later. Where the hell have you been and where are you now?"

"It's a long story. I'm over Northern California now, looking for Max and Jason. As soon as I find them I'm going to head home."

"Are you okay? What happened? Why aren't Max and Jason with you?"

"I'm a little banged up but I'll be okay. Like I said, it's a long story. Does anyone know if Jack's alive? Has anyone talked with the Yanks?"

"Bastards. No. I mean yes, Jack's alive, or at least we're pretty sure. Nobody's talked with them directly but Andrew is confident he was captured for a reason. If they wanted him dead they wouldn't have gone through so much trouble."

"Andrew? How did you talk to Andrew?"

"I suppose he wasn't there when you took it upon yourself to assault Camp Wisner?"

She felt her face flush. She knew they'd find out sooner or later. In fact she would have a lot to answer for when she returned home. "Yes, I was there, and Andrew wasn't. His wife told me Cali was responsible. So what changed?"

"Andrew returned while we were having a sit down with his wife. Thomas had a picnic with them and they kissed and made up."

"What!?"

"Look, the information you got was legitimate but it wasn't the whole story. Cali wasn't involved, at least as far as we can tell."

"That makes sense. Joshua was pretty adamant that he didn't have Jack. I guess he *was* being honest."

"Wait, you spoke with Joshua? You've been in Cali this whole time? How did you get out?"

Again she flushed. "Like I said, long story. I'll tell you all about it after I get back. Well, maybe after I get another dose of meds and a few hours of sleep. What was that about the bastards who took Jack?"

"That's what they call themselves. Their community is led by a guy named Sebastian, and they call the town Bastion."

"Well the name fits. Why hasn't anyone tried to contact them, find out what they want?"

"I can't answer that, I left to come find you right after we returned from visiting Camp Wisner."

"Well, at least someone decided to come looking for me."

"I told you, I just heard about your disappearance yesterday. Listen, I'm just about an hour out from the Warehouse. Why don't you meet me there? I've got a full medpack and I want to hear your story before we get back home. I'm not entirely happy with the way the Board is doing things and if you show up with this story it might just make it worse. Let's talk it over first and maybe we'll edit things just a bit."

"Soon as I find Max and Jason I'll be there."

"Need any help?"

"Nah, they couldn't have gone far so I should be in range of their PDP's by now."

"Okay, see you soon. And Wendy?"

"Yeah?"

"It's good to hear your voice. I was worried about you."

Choking back tears, she clicked off.

~~~~

Johnson looked around the flight bay. A lone mechanic worked on one of the flyers but otherwise it was empty. He made his way toward the exterior entrance, a wide door tucked into the side of a rocky slope. Looking around to make sure he hadn't attracted the mechanic's attention, he walked over to a wall of storage shelves. Right on the top shelf hiding in plain sight was a crate. He reached up and carefully pulled it down, trying to keep quiet. The crate contained a laser communicator and headset. He pulled the unit out, set it to point toward the east, and flipped the switch.

When the light turned green, he slipped the headset on. He waited.

After a moment, a voice said, "Go." No hello, no questions.

"Jack's woman just checked in. She's heading to the Warehouse site to meet the soldier out looking for her."

"Hold." A pause. "Your cover could be blown. Jack escaped and might have one of our own with him. She knows your identity."

"What are my orders?"

"Your primary objective is to bail out. Steal a flyer and head to the Warehouse site, try to capture Wendy. If you think you have time, we want you to take something first."

~~~~

Marcus sighed. "I cannot seem to locate him. About ten minutes ago the cameras saw him at the control center but since then I can't get anything from facial recognition."

"Can you track him from there?"

"I can, but I will be at least ten minutes behind him." His fingers flew over the keys again and video feeds came up on the monitor. "Okay, here he is leaving the flight bay. This was about ten minutes ago."

Caleb picked up his data pad and punched in a call. A moment later the call was answered but without video. "Yeah?"

"Chin?"

"Yeah, what's up?"

"Where are you right now?"

"I'm in… I'm at my apartment. Why?"

"I can't get anyone at the command center. I need you there right now."

A pause. "Give me a few minutes." He closed the call.

"Here he is getting off the rail car. I know it is him because I timed it out but he is doing a good job of avoiding looking at any camera. He knows exactly where they all are."

"Do you think he knows we figured him out?"

"How could he?"

"Maybe he knows you were looking in the computer?"

Marcus shrugged. "Possible. If you want me to stop tracing his movement I can check to see if he detected my video scans."

Caleb thought it over for a moment. There is only one way out of New Hope and Chin was on his way to watch that. This spy isn't going anywhere, eventually they would pin him down. "Do it."

Marcus paused the video and opened a command line. He worked his magic and after a few minutes he said, "Nothing I can detect. Unless this guy is some kind of computer genius, there's no way he was alerted to our poking around."

"Okay, go back to tracking him manually."

~~~~

Chin stepped off the elevator. Pissed off about the call, he tried contacting Johnson again. No answer. All he asked for was one day off to spend some quality time with his woman. Nothing was going on outside the community, other than Chuck looking for Wendy, and he didn't need babysitting.

The rail car was just starting to pull away and he jumped to the button to stop it. The door opened back up and he slid in, not all that surprised to see Johnson sitting there. "Where the hell have you been?"

"I needed some food. Why?" The door closed and the rail car started making its way to the flight bay.

"Caleb called me and told me to get my ass up to the command center because nobody was manning it. You can't just leave your post like that! You know, if it weren't for Margie vouching for you, you'd still be stuck changing light bulbs and cleaning hair out of the drains up on the family level. Maybe you need to go back?"

Johnson smiled. "You know why Margie insisted you give me that job? It's because you were spending all your time working and not paying attention to her. She was lonely, so she was fucking anyone she could get her hands on, including me. Half the time she was still juicy from the last guy. I have to admit, you got yourself a good one there, Frances. A first class lay if not a little loose. From the smell in here I would say you were just with her. She has a particularly unique scent, doesn't she?"

Chin's blood ran cold. Regardless of the open nature of their culture, there was a line you simply didn't cross. This man had just sprinted across it. "Where the hell do you get the nerve talking about her that way?"

He just laughed. "What are you going to do about it?"

Adrenaline surged. This guy needed to be taught a lesson in manners. He launched from the seat toward the smug son of a bitch. A light flashed and the room got very quiet. Somehow his legs buckled and he dipped to the left on his way toward the man, barreling into the empty seat next to him. Another flash. Confusion. *Why is there so much smoke in here?*

Johnson took his arm. Chin looked at him, unsure of what had just happened. The man's lips were moving but he couldn't hear any words. The silence turned to ringing. Now a muffled sound penetrated the confusion.

"...and the irony of it all is you don't even know how good you have it. Trust me, Margie will know soon enough. When we finally come back, and mark my words we will be back, I will see to it that she gets raped a hundred times over. Too bad you won't be here to share her pain."

He lifted his hand and Chin saw a gun and suddenly it all made sense. "No!" The lights went out.

~~~~

The blood drained from Caleb's face when he watched the scene unfold. Johnson entered the room and approached the desk. Mitchel was on duty and he looked to be reading something on his datapad. He set it down and looked up just in time to see the gun go off. His body sagged and Johnson strode past him, firing two more times into the still corpse.

The man pushed on the airlock door but it didn't open. The keypad they installed just days before blocked his way. He looked at it then back at the corpse of the man he had just executed. For a moment it looked like he was going to leave, but instead he turned to the airlock door and started shooting. It took nearly a minute before he was able to force his way past the electronic lock. When he entered the cold room, fog rolled out from the damaged door. Less than a minute passed before Johnson reappeared carrying an object. He stripped off the cold suit and left it lying in the room.

Without a word, Caleb grabbed the datapad and called Chin. No answer.

Marcus yelled, "Get men to the flight bay, now!" He then turned and his fingers flew across the keys. The video quickly shifted as he tried to manually locate the spy. The scene they watched was at least twelve minutes old, and by now Johnson could be back in the flight bay.

Caleb punched up Tiny. When the big man answered, he shouted, "Grab some weapons and get to the flight bay! Do NOT let anyone leave! Call me when you get to the rail car!" Tiny didn't even answer, just hung up. "Is anyone in that flight bay?"

Marcus brought up the cameras there. Two legs stuck out from under a flyer. "There! Who is that?"

"I can't tell. Let me see if he has a datapad with him." A moment later he said, "Got it, the man's name is Gordon. Gordon Riggs."

Caleb punched up the man's datapad. The legs in the video didn't move. "Can you override the pad and force it to answer?"

"Done."

The video came on and at first Caleb couldn't tell what he was seeing. It looked like the underside of a flyer. He turned the datapad sideways. "Shit." The corner of the screen showed part of the man's bloody hand. "Gordon! Can you hear me? Help is on the way!" The hand never moved.

Caleb looked at Marcus and shook his head. "Get Teague on his way. Tiny should be ahead of him but if the man is still alive he will need medical attention immediately. And have him send a medic down to the cold room, just in case there is anything that can be done."

Caleb nodded and worked the datapad as quick as he could. He called Teague and got him heading toward the flight bay and had him send one of his doctors down to the cold room. His next call was to Scott. "Get down to the cold room immediately! The door is damaged and the guard is shot. Someone from medical will meet you there. Make sure the cold room is functioning, the last thing we need here is to lose all those heads." He hung up without waiting for a response.

The datapad dinged and he punched the answer button. "Sir," the big man rumbled, "I'm at the rail line waiting for the car to come back. What's going on?"

"We located our spy and somehow he figured out we were on to him. His name is Johnson. He killed the guard in the cold room and took something, probably another head. That was about fifteen minutes ago. Surely he is heading to the flight bay and I am pretty sure he's already there. A mechanic is injured, maybe dead. Get there as quick as you can and secure the area. This man is dangerous so use caution. Is anyone with you?"

"One of my trainees, Clayton."

"I'll send more men your way, and Teague should be there any moment. If the car arrives before he's there, go."

"Here it comes now, sir. Hold on."

The video went wild as Tiny shifted the datapad around.

"Oh shit!"

More chaos.

"Tiny, what is it?"

"It's Chin. And it's bad! Where's Teague?"

Dread filled Caleb's heart. He was afraid of this. If Chin had intercepted Johnson on the way back...

More shouting could be heard through the datapad. "Tiny, talk to me."

A face came on the screen, a native born man Caleb recognized as one of Red's militia. "Sir, Tiny is treating Chin right now, but it doesn't look good. I think he was shot in the head. Here comes Teague right now."

"Listen to me, Clayton, you stick with Teague, help him get Chin down to the medical level. Tell Tiny to get to that flight bay and do what he can to secure it!"

He listened to the chaos for a moment longer, then knowing there was nothing more he could do to help, closed the call.

Chapter 38

Matthew stood staring at the door. It had not been opened in three centuries. Dozens of sensors lined the mile long tunnel that led to the surface and all of them signified that the main entrance to Sanct remained unchanged from the day it was sealed up. In fact the tunnel was kept sealed and the air pumped out. A perfect vacuum, devoid of any moisture or contaminates that could cause the tunnel walls or the mechanism beyond to decay.

The people who built this place were thinking ahead, not just a few dozen years, but hundreds or even thousands of years in the future. They knew the biggest danger to anything manmade was water, followed by oxygen, followed by biological life forms. The tunnel walls were sealed with progressive layers of concrete and bentonite, making it air and water tight. The stainless steel doors were heavily armored airlocks.

A keypad lit up next to the door. He looked back at the two men who would accompany him. They were the closest thing Sanct had to military – police who had gone through hundreds of hours of simulators to learn combat techniques. They had grown up practicing martial arts, learning every form of hand to hand combat known to man. The only thing they lacked was real life experience. Hopefully they wouldn't gain any today.

Both men nodded, signifying they were ready. He punched in the code. More lights came on and a gauge inset in the door began to climb. The chamber ahead would be a perfect cylinder, eight feet in diameter with only the floor being flat. It would be a thousand feet long before the next door. That was a lot of air, and Sanct was a closed system. If they didn't fill the chambers with air first, everyone in the city would feel the air pressure drop. Aside from Matt and his team, only about a dozen people even knew they were opening these doors and they wanted to keep it that way. The air had to come from somewhere, so several rows of liquefied air lined the walls of the chamber. Frost began to form on the first tanks, a sign the air was being rapidly released into the chamber.

The gauge needle moved into the green. Hydraulic rams came to life, moving as if they had been built yesterday. A loud hiss signified the seal being broken. The door swung open and lights came on, in sequence, each with a loud snap as the breaker closed. From the entrance Matthew could barely see the end of the first section.

He checked his gear one last time, took a deep breath, and stepped ahead.

It took an hour to get through all five airlocks. The tunnel progressively sloped upward and he estimated they climbed at least a few hundred feet. With all the gear and protective suits, he was winded by the time they reached the last door.

He turned to the men. "Chances are, the most dangerous thing we will encounter will be wildlife. If there are people still living on the surface, it's unlikely any would be living anywhere near this exit. Just use your best judgment if we do encounter a threat, and remember that any noise we make could attract attention." The men nodded again. They knew the drill and Matthew felt like he was stalling.

Before he could think about it further, he punched in the last code. The door seemed to hesitate then started pushing outward.

~~~~

Wendy pushed the stick and the aircraft lifted off. Max and Jason waited patiently as she piloted the aircraft to cruising speed.

Max was the first to explode. "How the hell did you get this back?"

"If you had waited for me to get some rest like I asked you would know."

"The sooner we got back on the trail, the sooner we would make it home." This came from Jason.

"And you had no way of knowing I would end up getting the flyer back. I get it and I told you, I'm not mad that you left me behind."

"So how did you get the flyer back?"

She smiled. "I asked."

"You talked to Cali?"

"Yes."

"How?"

She explained the laser transmitter and then went over the details of the conversation with Joshua and the meeting soon afterward.

Jason said, "So this was all just a wild goose chase?"

"Oh for Christs sake, Jason," Max said, "You were there when we got our intelligence. We all thought Cali had Jack, and I'm not convinced Joshua is being completely honest about his involvement. No way those assholes would just fess up about it."

"It isn't Cali," said Wendy. "As much as I hate to admit it, it turns out it isn't them."

"How do you know that?"

"Chuck told me. Turns out they've been doing their own investigating and it turned up a little more than we got. Yes, Jason, it was a wild goose chase and I apologize."

"No need to apologize, Wendy. Max is right. We all thought for sure Cali was behind it. And I'm sorry I just took off. I should have at least waited until you woke up. How long before we get home?"

"Well, we're not going there quite yet."

"What?" the two men said at the same time.

"Chuck wants to meet at the Warehouse first. He should be there by now waiting. We can all compare notes and then I'm going to get some more sleep. I feel like I was run over by a truck."

~~~~

Phil leaned over the seat and whispered to Jack, "How did you know?"

The guard was snoring softly in the back seat, and Trystana looked to be out as well. He leaned close and said, "I didn't but I was guessing. Wendy, my… girlfriend… found your records by mistake. She recognized your name from the Warehouse. Then she put it together with my diary and figured out we knew each other. When I was deciding where we should go, it all clicked into place."

"So you discovered the quonset hut with all the equipment?"

"Yeah, Wendy did a few months ago. She's searched the area a hundred times though and never found any sign of a bunker."

"You wouldn't. It is completely camouflaged."

"Yeah, but at least you would think we would find some vents or something. We have some pretty sensitive equipment that can pick up the faintest electromagnetic frequencies and any kind of thermal anomaly. We found nothing."

"The facility is a sealed environment. There are no vents and with nearly two miles of granite on top of it there's no way electrical or thermal signals are getting out."

"Look, I know it's premature, but when it comes time, are you going to help us gain access?"

"Let's cross that bridge when we come to it. The Ark is designed as a failsafe for the human species for after the wars are over. After what I saw back on the East Coast, I don't think the war is quite finished."

Jack nodded. He understood, and while the prospect of a place like this existed, he had to agree that it might be best to remain undiscovered for a while longer, maybe even a few hundred more years.

A light started flashing on the control panel. Jack nudged Trystana and she started. She saw Jack and smiled. There was something in that smile that hit him right in the chest. "Looks like we're almost to our destination. Any clues as to what we can expect?"

"It's an old warehouse high in the mountains. It'll be safe for a few days before we can decide the next step. Shouldn't be anyone up here and if there is they will be friends."

She examined the controls again and said, "Well, it looks like your friends are already here."

"What?"

Pointing at the display, she said, "One small flyer is parked about four hundred feet from here. Are you still sure you want to land?"

Jack studied the display and then looked out the windows. The night was clear but he saw nothing below them but darkness. "Yes. But be prepared for anything. Phil, wake up sleeping beauty and let the men know we're about to land. Tell Anton to be ready for anything."

Trystana gracefully piloted the flyer to the ground next to the smaller aircraft.

~~~~

Matthew pushed the brush aside and stepped out into the world. It was night. This didn't particularly surprise him. Nobody in Sanct had synchronized their clock with the sun in several centuries, so even the smallest of deviations in the computer's clock could have set it off by hours by now.

He looked up. Stars twinkled above him and he got dizzy. He quickly looked back at the ground. He hadn't expected that. Years of studying the science and looking at pictures and videos didn't prepare him for the depth. In his wildest imagination he could never have imagined what it truly looked like to be staring at stars that were millions of light years away.

The two men were scanning the area with their lights. Matthew knew they had him covered so he immediately went to work scanning the area for radiation.

His devices all read zero, confirming what he suspected the moment he saw dark green shrubbery and evergreen trees. "No radiation, guys, you can lose the rad suits."

He shed the first layer of protective clothing. Underneath was another suit, this one a biohazard suit. He would leave this one on until he returned with samples. In quarantine the doctors would study both the men and the samples, looking for signs of any kind of biological contaminate that could infect Sanct. With forty less pounds to carry, he felt almost fleet of foot.

He risked looking up at the sky again. This time he was prepared and the wave of dizziness didn't affect him as bad. It was beautiful, at least what he could see through the clear plastic of the suit. If he turned around and went back in now he would be content for the rest of his life.

He caught movement out of the corner of his eye – an object that didn't belong. Adrenaline pumped through his body and his breathing grew short as he watched the craft move across the sky then slow down and descend not far from their current location.

"Sir, did you see that?"

"Yes. I guess the odds of running into other people just changed significantly."

"Would you like to investigate?"

This was a good question, one he was trying desperately to come to terms with. "Well, I suppose we should at least assess the situation. This close to the entrance they could be a threat even once we go back inside.

The men didn't wait for more postulating. Matthew followed, taking in everything. To the left he spotted a pair of eyes glowing in the beam of his flashlight. As he passed a large cedar he paused to touch the bark and run his hands along it. He yearned to shed his protective gear and climb as high as he could, but this was no video game and right now was hardly the time.

Ahead he could see light. The men froze and turned off their own lights. Matthew followed suit. They crept closer and closer, trying to get a glimpse of who just landed an aircraft next to what should be a building housing all the equipment they would need to start over on the surface.

~~~~

Wendy blinked. She was tired but not so tired that she should be hallucinating. She could swear she saw lights flickering in the forest below. When she looked again they were gone.

Ahead she spotted a flyer. Chuck had already arrived. Then she saw the second. "What the hell?"

"What's up?" Max asked.

"There're two flyers here. I only expected one."

Jason said, "I hate to be the conspiracy theorist here, but do you suppose Cali put a tracking device in this flyer?"

"I checked everything over and didn't spot anything but they could have reprogrammed the radios and GPS to send info to Cali instead of New Hope."

"So do you think they listened in on us and found out where we were going and sent people ahead?"

"I don't know, but we'll find out soon enough."

Jason set to work readying his gear. Max said, "Are you sure we should land? Maybe it would be best just to hightail it back home."

"If Cali is in there, then Chuck is in trouble. He came out here looking for me, so I'm not about to leave him to fend for himself."

"That's what I admire about you, Wendy." He slipped his helmet on.

~~~~

Anton dove through the door into the Warehouse, rolling through the dive and coming up with his sidearm at the ready. His three men, unarmed and lacking any protection, followed quickly behind.

Chuck spit out his coffee and threw the cup down, choking as he drew his sidearm.

Anton smiled. "Chuck? What the hell are you doing here?"

"I was just about to ask the same of you," he coughed, "right after I went and cleaned my drawers. How the... and where were... is Jack with you!?"

"It's clear!" the man shouted.

Jack strolled through the door. "Chuck? I didn't expect to see you up here, especially at this hour."

"Oh my God!" He rushed over and embraced the man. "Where the hell have you been? And what in God's name are you doing up here? Did you already stop at home? Why didn't you just call?"

"Slow down, buddy. We just escaped earlier today and… well, I wasn't sure heading home right away was the best choice. I figured this was safe, at least for the night. I thought it would be empty though. Why are you here?"

"I was up here looking for Wendy. I just spoke to her a couple hours ago and she is supposed to meet me here."

"You found her? Oh thank God! I just found out today that she was missing."

His eyes narrowed. "If you haven't been home, how did you find out?"

Three more people walked in, a woman and two men. The woman was strikingly good looking, very out of place given their location and the situation.

"She told me."

"And she is…?"

"Trystana, meet Chuck. Trystana is Teague's sister."

"What!?"

"It's a long story, but if Wendy's coming we should probably try to reach her and tell her to expect company."

"Shit, good idea." He started tapping away on his PDP.

Jack turned to the guard. "Why don't you keep an eye out for another flyer." The man nodded and went back out.

"I sent Wendy a message, as soon as she's in range she will get it. Who's that?"

"Uh… I don't actually know his name. He helped us escape."

Trystana said, "His name is Royce. I can't believe you never asked. The man gave up his life to help you."

"Well, it got a little chaotic, and when things settled down he was already asleep."

Chuck looked Trystana up and down, unsure he liked her. The way she and Jack were talking was a little too familiar. He wanted to ask what went on for the past ten days but held his tongue. "And who is your other friend?"

The man was looking around the building in awe. "Oh yeah, this is Phil. He's an old friend from… well from way back."

"Wait, is this the guy whose head was stolen from New Hope?"

Jack laughed. "Yup."

"So Sebastian is also responsible for that, huh."

"You know about Sebastian?"

"Pretty much, at least as much as Andrew was able to fill us in."

"What the hell went on while I was gone?"

"Like you said, buddy, long story." His PDP beeped. "Is that all your people?"

"Yeah, why?"

"Because the motion sensors just went off again."

Jack looked at Anton. "Go check it out. Probably just an animal." He looked back at Chuck and asked, "Any word from Wendy yet?"

"Nope. Should be any time."

Voices shouted outside. Everyone rushed toward the door.

"Move!" he told the men in front of him. They were unarmed and in his way.

~~~~

Wendy landed on the far side of the Warehouse, hoping the trees and vegetation would cover up the hum of the flyer. To keep it even quieter, she went in low and dropped her prop speed as low as she could without stalling. The landing was hard and she was reminded just how tender her body still was. Max and Jason jumped out of the flyer, rifles up. They had their night vision turned on and didn't need light. Wendy lost her helmet back when they crashed the flyer into the trees and sadly it wasn't here when she got the flyer back. She crept ahead, trying hard not to trip.

A path had been worn along one side of the building and once they found it, they moved fast. It still took several minutes to make to the other end of the huge building.

When they reached the end, Wendy caught up. "Max, you go ahead. Get close to the door and see if you can tell whose inside. Jason, you cover him. I'm going to slip over to the flyers and see if I can identify them."

Max nodded and crept ahead.

She tried to stay low as she made her way to the two parked aircraft. The small one was most likely what Chuck flew in on, the larger one looked like any medium flyer. She popped the door and climbed up inside. Nothing told her who it might belong to. She flipped the controls on and checked the flight log. When she saw where it came from her heart sank.

She lifted her PDP and clicked the button to talk to Max. Nothing happened. At the top it said "no signal." *What the hell is going on?*

Shouting drew her eyes back to the building. Max was shouting at someone with a gun. The man had no armor and wore plain clothing. She saw movement around the corner of the building, behind the man but out of Max's sight. She threw the door open and jumped out. Arms wrapped around her and a hand covered her mouth. Pain exploded and she blacked out.

~~~~

Chuck peeked around the corner and dropped back again. *Was that Max?* Anton was on one knee, pointing the sidearm and everyone was yelling to drop their weapons.

Chuck peeked around the corner again to confirm. *Yup.* "Max! Stand down!" he bellowed. "Anton, drop the gun, it's Max!"

Anton lowered the gun. Chuck cautiously stepped outside. "Max, it's me, Chuck. What the hell are you doing?"

Max lowered his rifle. "Chuck? Anton? Oh shit, you guys freaked us out! We saw the second flyer and figured the worst."

"Didn't you get my message? Where's Wendy?"

Royce burst from the side of the building, sprinting toward the flyers.

Everyone looked to where the man was running. A figure could be seen by the flyers. "Wait! Wendy's over there! Where's that guy going?"

Max ran after Royce. Confusion erupted. Chuck cursed and started running toward whatever everyone was chasing when Jack shot past him.

"There's someone dragging her into the flyer!" Max shouted. With his helmet he had night vision, so whatever he was seeing, nobody else could see it. Chuck cursed again.

The flyer began to power up and he got a sinking feeling in his gut.

~~~~

Wendy came to. She was back in the cockpit and someone was next to her flipping switches. Pain radiated from her left side, particularly her shoulder which felt dislocated again. Her hands were bound behind her back, probably the reason she was in so much pain. Whoever was trying to power up the aircraft must have lifted her in by her arms, which would explain the re-dislocated shoulder.

She took a moment to get her bearings and assess the situation. It was difficult not to panic. There was no way she could get the door open in this position. She bit her tongue to keep from crying out in pain as she tested the strength of the bonds. They weren't tight but in her condition she would be hard pressed to break free. If her assailant was able to lift her into the cockpit, it was unlikely she could overpower him, and without a clear escape route and no use of her hands, there was nothing she could do.

"Come on, come on!" the man said, probably trying to coax the flyers motors to spin up faster. If he was in a hurry it probably meant someone had spotted him. She needed to give them more time. Twisting into position, she lined up a kick that would force him to defend himself. Just then the pilot's door flew open and hands reached up. She saw her abductor lift a gun and she summoned all her strength, kicking out with a scream. The man grunted in pain and the hands got a firm grip, pulling the abductor out of the cockpit.

She struggled to sit up so she could open the opposite door. The pain intensified and she felt herself starting to black out again.

~~~~

Jack heard Wendy's name and he pushed his way to the door. He saw Royce rocket across the clearing disappearing into the darkness. When another man, this one in full armor, turned to chase, he heard Wendy's name again.

He followed. Everyone around him started running toward the flyers. It was nothing but blackness ahead of him – his eyes were still attuned to the light inside the building. He heard the whine of the flyer motors. His vision improved and he started to piece together the situation ahead. Someone sat in the pilot seat of his flyer. Another form raced toward it.

His first inclination was the guard, Royce, had a change of heart and was stealing their flyer, but what did that have to do with Wendy? He only saw two flyers ahead, so she hadn't even arrived. The shadow ahead of him reached the aircraft and opened the door. Jack heard a grunt and a scream. He knew that scream. Adrenaline surged and he doubled his speed.

A shot rang out and he heard another grunt. He could now see the armored man in front of him, running toward the fight. If Wendy was in the flyer then perhaps this was one of her companions. Instinct told him to go to the other side of the aircraft. He was unarmed and would be of no use in a firefight.

Chaos and shouting erupted and more shots were fired. He reached the passenger side door and threw it open. A body lay in the seat. Without wasting time identifying it, he grabbed and pulled. If it was a man, he wasn't very big. As it slid out of the cockpit he fell backwards, dragging it with him. He let the body fall on top of him, taking the brunt. Air rushed from his lungs and he saw stars.

The motors ramped up, kicking up dust and debris. It intensified into a hurricane. He rolled over onto the body, covering it with his own to protect it from the onslaught of rocks, twigs, and dust. The aircraft's thrust pounded his body and he held on tight, struggling for breath.

~~~~

Silence, or at least compared to the chaos a moment before, it felt like silence. Wendy tried to take in a breath but something was on top of her. A body? She remembered falling, but was in and out of consciousness.

She pushed at the body, but pain exploded again. She lacked the leverage and strength and panic set in.

Hands surrounded her and she heard voices all around. The weight lifted and she took a shallow and painful breath. The bonds came free, causing more pain as her shoulder was now free to move. She screamed.

"Get them to the building!" she heard. More hands pulled and tugged, and she lifted off the ground.

The pain was too much. Her world spun.

"I think he's dead."

"Just get them inside."

"Who was that?"

"I don't know!"

"Jason, stand guard out here, if anything moves out there, shoot it!"

The light grew and she tried to make sense of the chaos. "Chuck? Max?" she croaked.

"Just relax, you'll be okay, just let us get you inside."

She recognized the voice but through the pain and dizziness she couldn't place it. The world darkened once more.

~~~~

Jack sat kneeling next to Wendy. She was unconscious again but breathing. Her shoulder was obviously in the wrong place and he was afraid to touch her. The chaos of the last few minutes started sorting itself out.

Royce lay dead a few feet away. He must have spotted whoever the assailant was trying to abduct Wendy. He gave his life to protect her, something Jack would never forget.

Max was explaining what happened from his perspective. "When we saw the extra aircraft, we slipped around back so we could get an idea of what was going on.

Chuck said, "But I sent a message to her PDP, when you were a couple miles out you should have gotten it."

"I told you, we didn't get any damned message!"

"Dammit Chuck," Anton said, "just let him finish his story!"

"Sorry, I just... Go on."

"I headed for the door with Jason covering me and Wendy went to see if she could find out who the flyers belonged to."

"You didn't see Royce at the door?"

"Nope. Nobody was there, so I approached. Then Anton comes barreling out with his gun on me. I shouted for him to drop it and he shouted at me. Next thing I knew Chuck was outside yelling at us both and then I saw Royce fly out from behind the building."

Jason poked his head through the door. "He was taking a piss."

"What?" said Anton.

"Around the corner, I could smell the urine. He was taking a piss when all this happened. From around the corner you can see the flyers more clearly because the light from the door isn't glaring in your eyes. He must have seen Wendy get grabbed and he took off to help."

"Well his quick thinking probably saved her life, but from who?"

"Hey, is your PDP working Max?"

"What?"

"Your PDP, there are several in this room and they should all be linked. Hell, at the least I should be connected to the flyer but mine says there's no signal."

"Sonofabitch, mine too. How's that possible?"

"Some kind of jammer?" asked Anton.

Trystana said, "I think you guys are missing something here."

"What?"

"This man who tried to abduct Wendy... how did he get here? Chuck flew in alone, we came in a flyer with eight people, all accounted for even if poor Royce here is no longer with us, and Wendy landed out back with only two other passengers. How did this guy get here?"

"Had to be another flyer, there isn't even roads up here."

"And since he left in our flyer…"

"His is still around here," Chuck finished for her. "And there is probably some kind of radio jammer on board, keeping us from being able to communicate."

"So let's find the flyer," she concluded.

"Um, if I might be so bold?" Phil interjected.

All eyes turned toward him. "Do you think he showed up alone?"

"Shit," Chuck said, "If he had friends and the signal is still jammed, that means they might still be here."

"So let's go find out."

"No," Jack said. Everyone turned to him.

"Look, we only have a few armed men. I'm not sending anyone out in the dark alone and I'm not leaving the rest of the people here, Wendy included, without some protection. We're safe in here and we have perimeter sensors in case anyone decides to try to sneak up, right?"

"Yup."

"So we hole up for the night. Go out at first light and see what we can see. In the meantime, I need a med kit and someone to set her shoulder."

A hand rested on his back and he looked up to see Trystana. "Let me do it." He hesitated. "Jack, I won't hurt her. I know how special she is to you." He moved aside.

Trystana probed the shoulder and then positioned Wendy's arm. Placing a knee against her chest, she twisted. A grotesque grinding pop could be heard. Anton put a hand to his mouth, looking like he was swallowing back some vomit.

Chuck handed her the med kit. "You familiar with the drugs in here?"

"Yes." She administered some more medicine to accelerate healing, then checked her vitals and probed around her body. "It would be wise to get her home, Jack. Who knows what kind of trauma all this has caused to the baby."

Jack's heart pounded. After all they've survived, to lose the baby would be horrible.

The perimeter alarm sounded.

Chuck cursed, "Well, so much for holing up."

Jason shouted, "I've got movement out here." Max grabbed his rifle and ran out the door, followed closely by Chuck. Anton moved to the door to stand guard.

~~~~

Matthew watched the scene unfold from a few hundred feet to the side. Whatever was going on, it wasn't peaceful. A part of him wanted to just head back inside but he still had a mission and he needed time to collect the proper samples. With these people right at his back, he wasn't about to start unpacking all his gear. Besides, he was hoping to set up his equipment in that building.

There was a bigger issue at hand. If people were living this close to the entrance to Sanct, sooner or later they would have to make contact. Sure, he could head back inside and close the door for another century or two and they would probably never be discovered. Someday, however, whether it be him or his kids, the people of Sanct would have to emerge. Man was not meant to live underground forever. That day might be forced on them sooner rather than later if what they were searching for out here couldn't be found.

The flying machines they had were well ahead of any technology that existed when his ancestors first locked the doors. That meant the human species hadn't just survived the wars, they rebuilt and prospered. The implications were huge.

When things calmed down and everyone was back in the building, Matthew decided he wanted a closer look. It was dark and there were plenty of trees and shrubs to hide behind, so there was little risk. If these people planned to leave in the morning then perhaps he could wait them out and complete his mission. It was worth a shot. He signaled to the men to follow and slowly crept his way closer.

Now he could hear voices. He couldn't make out words but there was some argument. A man stood outside the door but seemed to be paying more attention to what was inside than what was outside.

He started to creep closer and one of his men put their hand on his shoulder. The message was clear, it was a bad idea. He looked at the door only a couple hundred feet away and considered the risk. If he went just a little to their right his angle on the door would change enough so he could see inside without getting closer. He pointed and the guard nodded. He crept toward the new vantage point.

He located the perfect spot to sit and watch. As long as he didn't make much noise, there was no way they could be spotted, at least not until the sun came up.

The man at the door shouted and pointed right at Matthew. Two more men shot out of the building running toward him. Dumbfounded, he hesitated. *How...?* One of his men grabbed his arm and pulled. They all took off, running back toward the entrance.

He felt shame as he ran. He didn't see any night vision goggles on these men so he assumed they would never see him. However, if technology had continued to grow, it made perfect sense that they would have the means to watch their perimeter even in the dark of night.

It was a long way to the entrance and although he had a long lead, he was sporting about fifty pounds of gear. He shed the backpack. Perhaps he could come back for it later. He glanced back over his shoulder to see them twice as close as before. One of his men stopped and turned. "Keep going!"

"No! Don't kill anyone."

"Go!"

Matt looked up and saw the three men closing fast. He had a decision to make. If his men attacked, even in defense, it could blow any chance of making peaceful contact in the future. Without soil samples this entire mission was a bust anyway and they would need to come back out. He turned back. Something told him it would work out better this way.

~~~~

Jason was closing. With his night vision he could see the shapes but they didn't look quite right. One of the men stopped and turned, waving the others to keep going. Clearly this man was going to try to slow them down to allow the others to escape. Jason wasn't about to let that happen. Everyone back at the Warehouse wanted answers.

A second man turned back, hesitating. Jason got closer. The third man finally stopped too. Now the second was coming back toward them, but he didn't appear to have a weapon. The other two appeared to be armed but those weren't standard issue M74's. Jason slowed down but continued to close. Max and Chuck caught up.

The unarmed man seemed to be arguing with the others. They were only fifty feet away now. He shouted, "Drop your weapons and get on the ground or we will fire!"

"We won't fight!" the man shouted. "Drop the weapons, men, that's an order!"

They hesitated and Jason prepared to fight it out. He closed the gap to twenty five feet and stopped. "I won't tell you again. Drop the weapons and lay down!"

He switched on the flashlight and turned off his night vision. "What the fuck!" The three men in front of him were wearing what looked like hazmat suits. The two he pegged as guards were clearly holding Army issue M16's, nearly identical to the M4 model he had been issued back before he died.

"Please, we aren't looking for a fight. We just want to talk."

"Who are you?"

"My name is Matthew. I'm not with that fellow you were fighting with earlier."

"Drop those weapons and lay down, we won't hurt you if you don't put up a fight. Trust me, Matthew, those old guns wouldn't even scratch me but what I'm holding will cut you in half before you can blink. Where did you even find those?"

The men dropped the guns and put their hands in the air.

"Down guys, all the way."

They all complied.

~~~~

Anton said, "They're coming back. Looks like they caught whoever was out there."

Jack breathed a sigh of relief. He didn't want any more dead bodies or fighting tonight.

Jason pushed the first man into the building then entered, turned and led the other two inside. All three were wearing some kind of hazmat suit. Jason threw down two rifles. "This is what they were armed with."

Phil put his hand on Jack's shoulder and quietly said, "Jack, I think we need to talk to them, alone."

He instantly understood. "Bring them back to one of the offices. Phil and I will have a word with them, you guys all stay out here and keep an eye out for more trouble."

He walked up to Chuck and said, "Give me your rifle."

"No. Not before you tell me what the hell is going on here."

"I'll explain later, but this is important, Chuck."

"Fine, but dammit, I want answers after this."

"You'll get them. Just keep an eye out."

Chapter 39

"You know, this is my old office," Phil said, "Talk about a trip."

Jack stood by the door, the rifle at the ready. All three men sat on the floor on the opposite side of the room, cross legged.

He examined their faces through the cloudy clear plastic visors. Two traits stood out that would set these men apart from anyone Jack had met since being reborn. First, their skin was pale. More so than even the women in New Hope who only got 'sunshine' from the sun lamps in the park level. Second, their eyes looked wrong. It took him a moment to figure out what it was that seemed so out of place. Their pupils were huge, making them look like someone who was jacked up on drugs. What little Jack knew of biology told him these men spent all their lives living in a darker environment.

"Who's Matthew?"

"Me." The one in the middle raised his hand.

"Matthew, I'm Jack. This is Phil. We know where you came from but those people in the other room don't. For now I want to keep it that way."

"I don't know what you're talking about, Jack. We live in a small community a few miles from here. We were just out taking some samples of the soil, looking for places to plant crops."

"Matthew, I'm going to be completely honest with you and I would appreciate the same in return. I'm not here to hurt you and when we're done here you might even get to head back home, although I'm not sure you will want to. The world might not be ready for you to come out yet. On the other hand, you may be just what we need to make it through the next few years."

Matthew didn't respond but all three men seemed to pale further, turning their already light skin nearly translucent.

"Phil, why don't you convince them that we know what we're talking about."

"This will be interesting," he said under his breath. "Correct me if I'm wrong, the place you came from has an entrance just a few thousand feet from here. It starts with a tunnel nearly a mile long. Five airlocks before you enter the main chamber that houses your home. Your city has the capacity for ten thousand people and is a sealed environment, a closed ecosystem that perpetuates itself. The crops and other plants produce oxygen, your waste feeds the crops, and you get water from an aquifer. Your power comes from a modified hydrogen energy cell bank that sustains a radium core and is fed with simple water from the aquifer. I can go on if you want me to."

"How did you know? And who else knows?"

"Coincidence," Jack said, "The mother of all coincidence, really. You picked a bad day to come out looking for samples. There isn't a living community of people for four hundred miles in any direction. On just about any other day you would have never even run into anyone. Up until a few months ago you would have found this building exactly as you left it three centuries ago."

"So you found our warehouse and learned all this about us? I wouldn't have thought the builders would have left that much information behind"

"They didn't. In fact the only thing that would suggest an underground facility nearby would be the existence of a building like this with so much heavy equipment so far from any towns or cities. We scoured this area with very sensitive equipment looking for signs of your home but came up empty handed. In fact, up until a few hours ago, I had no idea you even existed. Phil, on the other hand, well… you probably wouldn't believe us and I'm not sure I should take the time to explain it."

"Try me."

Jack laughed. Phil said, "Okay, I built your home. I put the whole thing together before the war. I was perhaps one of the only people alive who knew everything about it."

"You're right," Matthew said, "I don't believe you."

"It's irrelevant, but now you have one very big problem."

"What's that?"

"First tell me why you came out? How often do you come out? Is this a regular thing?"

Matthew seemed to hesitate, perhaps thinking it over. Finally he said, "This is the first time. We have a problem and we needed soil samples to aid in fixing it. This was a huge risk for us but it needed to be done."

Phil said, "Soil samples? Is there something wrong with your crops?"

Matthew nodded. "Production is down. We can't explain it, so we decided to come out here and get some samples of healthy soil. We had no idea if the area around here would be irradiated or not, but being so far from any kind of population or military base we figured it would be clean. The site was picked partly for that reason."

"Actually," said Phil, "the location of the entrance was picked for that, the site was created by Mother Nature."

As interesting as it all was, it wasn't relevant right now. "Production is down, but are your people in immediate danger?"

"No, but if we don't act now it could cascade into a major problem. It was a choice between dropping the birth rates and making one last effort to find a way to return crop production to normal."

"So if you don't return right now, your people aren't going to starve."

"Not for a decade or two, no."

"If you don't mind me asking, what is your current population?"

Matthew hesitated again. "I'm not sure I should share that with you just yet."

Jack understood, even though it was important to know. Phil told him the place could hold nearly ten thousand, but if they only had food enough for a few thousand then the space was irrelevant. He filed it away for later. "So when you spotted us, why didn't you just run back into your hole?"

"Personally I was curious. But my decision stemmed from a number of factors. If there were people living right outside our entrance, I needed to know more. I could have just gone back in and holed up but then what happens if the people living near here found our entrance?"

"Well, I think you made the right choice. I'm not a doctor but you might have put your entire population at risk if you went back inside."

If the man could get any paler, he just did. "How's that?"

"A virus was engineered about two hundred years ago that makes your male babies sterile. Sure, you have those suits on but if even one single virus made it through your filters you could already be a carrier. You would never know it. You won't have the equipment capable of detecting it because that equipment wasn't even created until long after you closed up your hole. You wouldn't know until the next generation of children grew up and started trying to have children of their own. By then, of course, it would be way too late and you would suffer the same fate that most of the rest of the world suffered."

"So how are you here?"

Jack looked at Phil and chuckled. Both of them had gone through this conversation in the not too distant past and it felt odd to be on the other side. "We're special cases, but the rest of the world didn't fare too well. There are maybe ten thousand people left on the entire planet, possibly less."

"So even if we had waited it out for another century or two, let the rest of the humans die out, the moment we emerged we would be doomed?"

"As far as I know, but like I said, I'm no doctor. So it's actually fortunate you came out when you did."

"Why's that?"

"Because my doctor has a way to immunize you and future generations from the virus. If you get immunized before you have been infected, you will become a carrier but your offspring will not be born sterile. As long as you keep up the immunization, life can go on."

"So what are you suggesting we do?"

"Come with us. Back at our home we have the means to keep you from getting infected. You keep quiet about your real origins and when the time is right you go back home and bring the immunization with you. We might even decide to join you – things could get really ugly up here for a while."

"And if we say no?"

"Then I will let you go and you can collect your samples and head back home. Perhaps your suits have kept you from getting it. Perhaps you can close up your doors and spend the next century waiting things out. If I knew for sure I would tell you but I don't, so it has to be your decision."

~~~~

The rest of the night was relatively uneventful. Relatively because while it was incredibly exciting to hear everyone's stories from the past week and a half, there were no new intruders, no more fighting or violence, and nothing to interrupt them as they filled each other in on their adventures. It was nearly dawn before they all finished sharing. The only thing Jack had left out of his story was the discovery of the Ark project. That would remain between him, Phil, and Trystana, at least for now.

Jack was amazed at what Wendy had gone through, and disheartened to realize dire of a situation he had left his community in. When the talking was over, he lay down next to her. Her breathing sounded normal and if he didn't know better he wouldn't even know she was injured. Despite everything, he felt at peace.

There were still several unanswered questions and more than one problem with going home, but before falling asleep for a couple hours he decided it was time to face the music. And confront the issues head on.

Chapter 40

They found the thief's flyer the next morning. With no other word to describe the man, they settled on 'thief' because he stole their aircraft and tried to steal Wendy.

The flyer was parked about a half mile south of the Warehouse in a small clearing. Chuck brought it back to the building and then moved Wendy's flyer to the landing pad outside the door.

Despite the late night, everyone was up fairly early. Wendy was still asleep and probably would be for a while longer. Jack didn't want to wake her, preferring to let the medicine do its job for as long as possible.

While he waited, he went around back and dug a grave. He, Phil, and Trystana said a few words and laid Royce to rest. As much as he hated funerals, this man deserved a proper burial. He died because of his loyalty to Jack, a man he barely knew. Jack's biggest fear was that this was only the beginning. How many more of his people would die for him?

When the funeral was over, Jack let Matthew and his men out of the office. They kept it locked overnight, only as a precaution.

Jack lied to everyone, using Matthew's back story to explain where they came from. He explained how their small community was very germaphobic, so whenever they traveled far from their home they wore the old hazmat suits. Nobody asked questions.

The men stood by the door of the Warehouse, looking out into the sunshiny day. After several minutes, Matthew stepped through the door. Jack watched him closely as he took in the surroundings. He kept looking up at the sky and quickly looked away.

"Is there a problem?"

"It's so bright. Far brighter than the sunlamps we use over our crops. Is this a normal day?"

"It's Fall, and we are high up in the mountains, so the sun is a bit intense up here, but not too unusual."

"I want so badly to look at the sky."

"Your eyes are probably not used to this, give them time to adjust. Look, we're heading out soon. What is your decision?"

"You didn't make this easy, Jack. My biggest fear in leaving was that I might not ever return. I have family in there that will be devastated if I don't come back. I didn't even get to say proper goodbyes to everyone. Hell, most of my friends don't even know I'm out here. To walk away by choice is perhaps the most difficult thing I would ever do."

"I know this isn't easy."

"But I can't risk my people. I knew the risks coming out here and while I might be perfectly safe, I would rather err on the side of caution. I would, however, like to go close up the entrance and leave a note."

"You've got an hour. If you aren't back I will assume you changed your mind."

Matthew nodded and he and his men left.

~~~~

He sat down on a rock next to the door, pulled out his notebook, and started writing. In big bold letters he wrote "SANITIZE THOROUGHLY BEFORE TOUCHING!" The paper should be just fine once the air was evacuated out of the tunnel.

Below that he wrote, "Bio-contaminate outside, do NOT leave, even with suits. I will return with immunization when I can – Matthew."

On the next page he composed a letter to Angela. He told her he loved her and would return in not so few words. He then did the same for his parents, for the council, and for his friend Carter. He explained, in detail, everything he knew, which wasn't much. Mostly he assured them that he would return and for now he was safe. He let each of his men compose similar notes with less detail for their families. The council would know what parts of the message they could deliver and what they had to hold back.

He walked to a tree and dug up several samples of soil, sealing them in the sample jars. He placed the notebook and samples just inside the door. Perhaps the soil samples would yield some kind of answers.

He looked at the men once more and said, "I know my decision affects you both and I would like to give you a final chance to argue against it." They both agreed that he was doing the right thing. He punched in the code and stepped outside. He had a way back in but he wouldn't use it unless he knew it was absolutely safe. The door swung shut and when it sealed he could no longer tell it was a door. They brushed dirt and rocks into the path to cover where it swung open. With a heavy heart, he turned to leave.

~~~~

Wendy woke up slowly. It took a few moments to realize where she was. It took longer to remember what had happened the night before. "Chuck? Max?"

"Oh, you're awake? How are you feeling?"

She turned to the voice. Max walked toward her and sat down. "What happened? I remember gunshots. Who tried to grab me?"

"We aren't sure. Chuck is out looking at his aircraft right now." He asked again, "How are you feeling?"

She stretched, feeling stiff and sore but otherwise not too bad. "I'm okay. How long was I asleep?"

"Not long, maybe ten hours."

"I thought the man who attacked me flew off in his flyer? Did you stop him?"

"No, he got away."

"So what is Chuck looking at?"

"Oh, I suppose you didn't pick up on all that before you passed out. I think I need to go grab someone, I shouldn't be the one to tell you what's happened since we got here."

She was still a little hazy from the drugs but not so much that she should be this confused. "Just tell me what's going on, Max."

"I… No, sorry, I'll be right back." He got up and walked toward the door.

She cursed under her breath and sat up. Thankfully she was dressed this time. A few more hours of sleep would be nice but curiosity started burning in her gut. She got up and headed toward the door.

~~~~

Jack turned to head back inside to check on Wendy. Trystana stood there, giving him a start. "They aren't a bunch of germaphobes from a community a few miles away, are they." It wasn't a question.

"Nope."

"You don't really trust me much, do you."

He turned to her and stepped close. Intimately close. He took her hand. "Look, Trys, I like you. If I weren't already involved… well, you understand. Plus, you helped me escape, and even if there is an ulterior motive I can't ignore that. The point is my heart trusts you, but I'd be lying if I didn't say my brain was still a little unsure. I'm willing to give you the benefit of the doubt. All I ask is that you don't abuse that trust. I don't know how the next few weeks and months will go, how your father will react or what kind of dangers we face, but I can almost guarantee you it will not be easy. You'll have plenty of time to ease any of my doubts. Until then, you have to accept that there are things I will keep from you."

She hugged him. "Thank you, Jack, I understand and I won't disappoint you." She planted a kiss on his cheek and gave his hand one final squeeze before walking away.

His eyes lingered as she walked away, but only for a moment. When he turned back to the Warehouse, his heart jumped. Wendy stood in the doorway looking like she had seen a ghost. He smiled.

~~~~

Wendy made it to the door, winded but otherwise not in too bad of shape. She certainly needed a few days of bedrest but compared to yesterday she was feeling spectacular.

Outside the sun was shining and it took a moment for her eyes to adjust. The first thing she saw was three men wearing what looked like some kind of bio hazard suits walking away. Then she spotted a woman, well dressed and looking very out of place out here. She approached one of the men, but Wendy couldn't tell who it was. He stepped close and took her hand. Out of habit she looked away, not interested in some public display of affection. There were three flyers parked on the landing pad just past the couple. Chuck must have moved hers over here because she recognized it immediately. She figured the couple arrived in the third flyer, but she had no idea who they were or what connection they had to the man who tried to kidnap her last night. Max was nowhere to be seen and she wanted some answers.

The woman turned away and headed toward the flyers. The man watched her for a moment then turned to walk toward Wendy. When she saw who it was her knees nearly gave way and she felt her face go numb as the blood drained away.

The man smiled and ran toward her.

"Jack!?" She felt herself sagging to the floor, the world spinning. He reached her just in time to support her and keep her from ending up a puddle on the floor. Tears flowed down her cheeks and she found it hard to breath. "How?"

He embraced her gently, trying to support her as she collapsed into his arms but acting like if he held too tight he would break her. "I arrived last night, just before you. I guess you don't remember?"

She couldn't respond. Emotions overwhelmed her. She slapped him, hard across the face.

He pulled back, confusion written all over his face. "What the hell?"

She jumped onto him, embracing him as hard as she could, not wanting to let go. He staggered at the sudden shift in weight but recovered, returning the embrace, this time not worried about her condition. She pulled her head back and looked him in the face, just to make sure this wasn't some kind of hallucination from the medicine. She kissed him, long and hard. There was no question it was him.

When she finally let go several minutes later, the first thing he said was, "Why'd you slap me?"

Emotions swirled again and anger boiled to the surface. *Or was it jealousy?* "Who was that woman you were so intimate with right before you saw me?"

His face turned red. "Oh. That's Trystana. She uh... helped us escape."

Yup, it was jealousy. "So this is your new squeeze? My replacement?"

"What? Of course not, Wendy. You know I would never... don't you?" He looked hurt.

Now she felt bad. Somehow he just showed up out of the blue, and her first thought was that he was cheating on her. "No, I just... when I saw you embrace her like that... I know it's been rough since I became pregnant... we don't get the intimate time I know you want, and that woman is beautiful."

"Wendy, Trystana is the reason I'm here with you right now. I made it clear from the start that there is only one woman in my life, and that's you."

The warmth of her love mixed with all the other emotions and she hugged him again. "I'm not letting you go again, so get used to me being this close, Jack."

~~~~

Reluctantly, Wendy let him go, at least long enough to join Chuck in looking over the flyers.

It didn't take her long to find the radio jammer, and when she turned it off, Chuck's PDP lit up like a Christmas tree. There were dozens of messages from New Hope.

Jack climbed in the cockpit with Chuck and Wendy and grabbed the radio headset. "New Hope, this is Jack Taggart, are you there?"

"Jack?" It was Tiny's unmistakable voice.

"Tiny?"

"Yeah, I wasn't expecting to hear from you. Three of our flyers just came back online. I've been trying to reach Chuck all night."

"Yes, we're all here together. What's so urgent?"

"I'm not sure where to begin, Jack. My map shows you are at the Warehouse site. How did you get there? Last we heard you were on the East Coast in the custody of some bastard."

"Well, it's a long story Tiny. We'll be home in a few hours, but I need to know what is so urgent. Tell it to me straight, Gunny"

"It's Chin, and a couple others. I'm afraid the news isn't good."

"Oh no," said Wendy. Jack's heart sunk once again. How many times in his life would he have to get news like this?

"Last night Marcus and Caleb discovered our spy. Somehow he got word of it and went on a rampage. He shot and killed Mitchel, who was manning the front desk of the cold room. Then he ran into Chin on his way back to the flight bay and killed him. Then he shot Gordon, one of our mechanics who was working late, before escaping in the flyer you are sitting in. The spy's name is Johnson."

The previous night's events finally made sense. Wendy held on to Jack and cried. He had to choke back his own tears. "Listen, tell everyone we will be back soon. We can talk about it then. We have a lot to discuss and some hard decisions to make."

Twenty minutes later they were in the air. Jack, Phil, Wendy, and Anton flew in the smaller four seat flyer. Jack spent the majority of the flight thinking about Sebastian. The man sent his spy to capture or kill Wendy, and he almost had her. At some point Jack would be forced to face him again, and whether it could even possibly end in peace was a big question. The man insisted he didn't have a taste for war, but then out of the other side of his mouth he made threats of genocide that could only lead to war.

Oddly, this situation was not what Jack was contemplating. His discussions with the man made him question if bringing back the dead was such a good idea. For the men from the Freezer, it made sense. Right now humankind needed them. Not just for their DNA, but for their skills, philosophies, beliefs, and ideals. However, the line needs to be drawn there. Each time a person is brought back they seem to lose a little more of their humanity, their morality, and their sanity.

Marcus seems to understand this, but when it comes time to move on to the next world will he want another life to live first? Most of the existing communities are led by people like Marcus who probably believe they are truly immortal. How long before they all think like Sebastian? Is Jack going to have to fight them all?

Chin was a good friend and even if they could bring back his body with memories and personality intact, he wouldn't be the same man. It wouldn't be easy to lay his friend to rest, but perhaps it would be the right thing to do. It was only one of the myriad of difficult decisions that lay ahead.

Once again he wondered if life was a balance. The events of the past couple weeks had been devastating. He lost a good friend, learned of threats that could very well destroy everything he held dear, and quite possibly started a war that could end human life once and for all. But he gained a lot too. Now he understood what needed to be fixed at home. He knew the threats that existed and had a good idea for how to begin to address them. New people had entered his life, including his old friend Phil. And he now knew of a pocket of humankind that could change everything. Was it an equal balance? That was tough to say, but it was the hand he was dealt, so he would make the most of it.

"Jack," Phil said, interrupting his reverie. "I can't help but wonder something. This spy. If he knew his cover was blown, why risk going all the way back to the cold rooms? What was so important there?"

Curious where Phil was going with this, he grabbed the headset and called New Hope. "Tiny, you there?"

"Yeah, Jack, just setting up a homecoming party."

"Well, we should be home soon. I have a question: any idea what Johnson stole from the cold room?"

"Yeah, Tara told me it was another head. This time some kind of General. Uh... Edward I believe. Edward Romeijn?"

Phil paled. "Oh shit."

DRAMATIS PERSONAE

Jack Taggart	New Hope Leader, Reborn, Main Character
Jenn Taggart	Jack's Wife (Died, Jan 1964)
Ally Taggart	Jack's Daughter (Died, Jan 1964)
Mabel	Jack's mother-in-law
Phil Norland	Jack's boss (in his former life)

New Hope

Wendy	Jack's Girlfriend, Reborn, Pilot and Mechanic
Chuck	Soldier, Reborn, Friend of Jack
Teague	Doctor, former member of Council, native born
Marcus	Former Leader of New Hope, native born
Theodore	Former Council member (imprisoned), native born
Caleb	Former Council member, native born
William	Former Council member, native born
Thomas	Officer, Reborn
Emmet	Soldier, Reborn (twice)
Ezekial "Tiny"	Soldier, Reborn, Jack's friend
Francis "Chin"	Soldier, Jack's friend, native born
Cathy "Cat"	Citizen, Chin's grandmother, native born
Anton	Soldier, Reborn
Jason	Soldier, Reborn
Max	Soldier, Reborn
George	Salvager, native born
Nicholas "Nick"	Maintenance, native born
Scott	Engineer, Reborn
Red	Former Officer (imprisoned)
Clayton	Soldier under Red (imprisoned)
Tara	Medical Assistant to Teague, Reborn
Johnson	Citizen, native born
Heather	Soldier, Reborn
Mitchel	Soldier, Chaplain, Reborn
Wayne	Soldier, Reborn
Gregory	Soldier, Reborn
Gordon	Maintenance, native born

Sanct

Matthew Miller	Head of Supplies
Tobias	Jr. Head of Supplies
Angela	Sanct worker, Supplies
Carter	Jr. Head of Systems
Jonathon Miller	Head of Laws and Justice, Elder division head
Monty Phillips	Head of Systems
Alden Karls	Head of Medical

DRAMATIS PERSONAE (Continued)

Margaret Johnson	Head of Education
Vernon Daniels	Head of Housing and Maintenance
James Gilmore	Head of Security

Other

Joshua	Cali Leader
Farnak	Mute Clan Leader (Northeast Idaho)
Bartholomew "Bart"	Farnak's brother, Mute, outcast
Tanner	Mute General
Sebastian Christopher Maddoxson	Bastion, Leader
Trystana	Sebastian's daughter
Laran	Mute woman
Mika	Teague's mother
Henry	Cali emissary
Carlos	Cali pilot
Edward Romeijn	General, U.S. Army (pre-war)

ABOUT THE AUTHOR

David Kersten was born in Minnesota but spent most of his life in Montana. An IT Manager for his family's business, David enjoys just about anything having to do with technology. He also enjoys creating things, whether it involves writing fiction, writing software, woodworking, carpentry, or electronics. As an avid reader since the age of 11, one of his long term goals was to try his hand at writing, and as with everything, when he dove into it, he submerged himself for many months. Although he enjoys many different fiction genres, his first series, "Genesis Endeavor", is set in his favorite genre, Post-Apocalyptic Fiction, and is a proud accomplishment for him.

When David isn't writing or working in his shop, he can be found spending time with his 3 children, sitting at a computer playing games, enjoying a good television show or movie, or out with friends at the bowling alley or favorite bar.

He intends to continue writing novels and is currently working on a more of the Genesis Endeavor Series. If you have any questions or comments for David or would like to see a list of his other books, you can visit his website at www.davidakersten.com

A PERSONAL NOTE FROM THE AUTHOR

I want to extend my gratitude to my readers. Just knowing people are reading my books makes them worth writing, and if you enjoy them it makes it even better. As a new "Indie" author it is easy to get lost amongst the thousands of new aspiring authors who self-publish their works each month. Independent authors don't get the marketing power of a big name publisher, so we are left to our own devices to market and promote our work. As a reader, there are two things you can do to help.

First, you can leave a review on Amazon.com to tell other readers what you thought of this book. Reviews make a major difference to an independent author because it tells other potential readers that this isn't just another poorly written self-published work that will be a waste of their money. It also tells readers that someone other than my mother has read my book.

Second, you can give me feedback. If you found errors in the formatting or story, I would love to know so I can correct them. I spent hundreds of hours editing this book, but even after so much effort mistakes can be missed. If you didn't like part of the story, or conversely if you loved something about it, I would love to know! Criticism, both positive and negative, helps me to stay connected to the readers and become a better writer. You can visit my website at www.davidakersten.com and leave me a message, or just email me at thefreezer@davidakersten.com. I get those messages directly and will respond to any reader interested in hearing from me. Again, thank you for reading, I hope you enjoyed it as much as I enjoyed writing it.

Sincerely, David Kersten

50901328R00175

Made in the USA
Charleston, SC
10 January 2016